SECRETS AND LIES

SECRETS AND LIES

A Truth or Dare Novel

JACQUELINE GREEN

poppy

LITTLE, BROWN AND COMPANY
NEW YORK BOSTON

Poppy

Hachette Book Group
1290 Avenue of the Americas, New York, NY 10104
Visit us at lb-teens.com

Poppy is an imprint of Little, Brown and Company.
The Poppy name and logo are trademarks of Hachette Book Group, Inc.

The publisher is not responsible for websites
(or their content) that are not owned by the publisher.

First Paperback Edition: December 2014
First published in hardcover in May 2014 by Little, Brown and Company

Library of Congress Cataloging-in-Publication Data

Green, Jacqueline, 1983–
    Secrets and lies / Jacqueline Green.—First edition.
        pages cm
    Summary: "In Echo Bay, Massachusetts, a beach town haunted by misfortune, Tenley Reed, Sydney Morgan, and Emerson Cunningham come together to investigate a murder, while old mysteries resurface and new dares appear"—Provided by publisher.
    ISBN 978-0-316-22031-6 (hc)—ISBN 978-0-316-22029-3 (electronic book)—ISBN 978-0-316-22030-9 (pb) [1. Murder—Fiction.   2. Conduct of life—Fiction.   3. Massachusetts—Fiction.   4. Mystery and detective stories.]   I. Title.
    PZ7.G8228Sec 2014
    [Fic]—dc23
                                                                2013018521

10 9 8 7 6 5 4 3 2 1

RRD-C

Printed in the United States of America

For Mom and Dad—for everything

PROLOGUE

FOOTSTEPS.

They thrummed behind her—relentless, insidious. Her legs pumped harder. Sweat coated her face, mingling with her tears. Around her, the woods were a kaleidoscope of shadows, shapes twisting and flickering. Her homecoming crown tumbled off her head. Glitter speckled the mud, trailing flecks of gold in her wake. And still she heard them. Pounding. Closing the gap.

If she got caught, it would be over. *She* would be over.

Just like Caitlin.

She had to hide. She threw herself into a clump of bushes. Branches tore at her dress, but she ignored them, crouching low. She couldn't move. She couldn't breathe. She squeezed her eyes shut, willing the darkness to erase her, turn her invisible. The note crumpled in her grip. She could almost feel its typewriter letters against her skin. They were poison, seeping into her blood. *I'm invisible*, she chanted silently. *I'm nothing.*

And then she heard it: rustling.

Fear surged through her. She wanted to sob, to scream, but instead she felt her heart slow down, as if it were already giving up.

A flashlight jabbed roughly through the bushes. Her eyes shot open against her command. The beam was bright, blinding. Spots danced in her vision as a cruel wisp of laughter floated down to her. "There you are," a voice said.

Then the blinding light went out.

CHAPTER ONE
Monday, 8 PM

THE OCEAN WAS A BEAST. IT WAS WHAT EMERSON'S mom always said, as she carefully steered clear of the water's edge. As Emerson walked across the beach, her bare feet sinking into the cold, damp sand, she could see it: how the waves roared as they rose mercilessly into the air, jaws snapping and teeth flashing.

Soon the beach would be filled with revelers for the party that Abby Wilkins had planned in honor of Tricia Sutton's birthday. But for now, Emerson was all alone. She sank down onto the sand with heavy limbs. In the distance, moonlight glinted off the tip of the Phantom Rock, a rock visible only during low tide. The silvery light made it look bright and glossy, like something out of a postcard. It had been a whole month since Caitlin and Tricia had died out there, a whole month since her best friend—and her best friend's murderer—had been minted the town's newest Lost Girls. That meant there were five Lost Girls in Echo Bay over the last ten years—five beautiful, young women all lost to the ocean in tragic accidents.

But of course, Emerson knew the truth: Caitlin Thomas's death was no accident.

It all started with a party Tenley Reed, Caitlin's childhood best friend, threw to celebrate her move back to Echo Bay, Massachusetts. She got everyone to play truth or dare that night, and the very next day the notes began. Caitlin, Tenley, and Sydney Morgan, Winslow Academy's resident artsy loner, all started receiving them. They were anonymous, and they dared the girls to do terrible things. Each dare grew more disturbing—and dangerous—than the last. And if Caitlin, Tenley, and Sydney didn't do exactly as the notes commanded, the darer promised to reveal each of their darkest secrets.

All along, the darer had been Tricia Sutton, a girl they'd gone to school with forever, a girl who'd been Caitlin and Emerson's *friend*. Tricia lured Caitlin, Sydney, and Tenley onto the *Justice*, Tenley's stepfather's yacht, so she could take them to the Phantom Rock and kill them—turn them into Lost Girls.

After setting a fire in the cabin that forced everyone onto the deck, Tricia attacked Tenley. Caitlin threw herself at Tricia just in time, pushing her overboard. She saved Tenley's life, but in doing so, she lost her balance and tumbled into the ocean. The darer was dead—but so was Caitlin.

Days later, at Caitlin's memorial service, Tenley received another note while she was with Emerson, warning her that the game wasn't over. It made no sense; Tricia was buried six feet underground! Still, Tenley, Sydney, and Emerson had been on edge ever since, waiting for a new message. But a month had passed now, and nothing. Tenley was convinced the whole thing had been a fluke—a note Tricia had set up before she died—and Emerson was starting to believe her. Still, she had to admit: She'd never been so happy to be left out of something in her life.

"Emerson?" The voice sliced through the air like a knife. Emerson shrieked, jumping to her feet. She whirled around to find Tenley walking toward her, her long chestnut waves lifting on the breeze. She had on a dark cashmere sweater over jeans, and her flat boots, which made her appear even tinier than usual. As always, Emerson towered over her.

"Tenley," Emerson said, relieved. "I didn't hear you drive up." She and Tenley had planned to meet early so they could show up for Abby's sham of a party together. A month ago Emerson would have chosen a *math* test over spending time alone with bitchy Tenley Reed. She might not have become a friend, exactly, in the Tricia aftermath, but she'd definitely become less of an enemy.

"I didn't," Tenley replied. "I decided to walk here on the beach."

Emerson's breathing returned to normal. "I am so not looking forward to tonight," she said, slipping into the beach-proof rain boots she'd brought with her. She'd considered skipping the party altogether. She had zero desire to celebrate the birth of a murderer. But she and Tenley had agreed: They had to keep up appearances when it came to Tricia. *They* knew the truth about her, but to everyone else, she was just an innocent Lost Girl.

Sometimes Emerson wished that Tenley and Sydney had just gone to the police after the tragedy on the *Justice*. But she understood why they hadn't. Tricia had taunted them with notes about their deepest secrets. If they exposed her, they exposed her notes—and all of their secrets. And not just theirs, but Caitlin's, too: that she'd been abusing antianxiety medicine. The last thing any of them wanted was to smear Caitlin's dirt around town postmortem. So they'd agreed: no cops. Besides, what was the point, anyway? Tricia was dead. It was over.

Now, if only this night were over, too.

"I tried to talk Sydney into coming tonight," Tenley said. "But, apparently, she's never been to a Winslow party before, and she's not about to start now. I think it's possible that girl has an allergy to human interaction."

Emerson managed a weak laugh. Sydney Morgan wasn't exactly her favorite topic of conversation. A pair of headlights swung into the parking lot, drawing Emerson's attention away from Tenley. For a second everything turned daytime-bright, making the asphalt shimmer. Then the driver turned off the car and darkness settled back in. Abby Wilkins, Winslow's Purity Club cofounder and newly appointed student-body president, climbed out. She was wearing a total mom outfit: a white blouse tucked into khakis, with her beloved blue Hermès scarf wound through the belt loops. Her stick-straight brown hair fell loose over her shoulders, and there was a thin smile on her long face. Immediately Emerson began to edit Abby's outfit in her mind, a habit she'd had for as long as she could remember. *Swap the khakis for skinny jeans, the scarf for a wide leather belt, and those blindingly white sneakers for slouchy boots. Then she might look somewhere close to eighteen, rather than eighty.*

Abby gave them a wide smile as they approached the parking lot, making Emerson tense. She'd never been a fan of Puritan Abby, but watching her seamlessly take over Cait's role as student-body president had brought her hatred to a whole new level.

"I'm so glad you girls could make it tonight," Abby chirped.

Tenley narrowed her eyes at her. "I still don't understand why we're bringing our whole grade out, at night, to the beach where Tricia died—where *all* the Lost Girls died."

"I never pegged you for a wimp, Tenley," Abby said lightly. She was obviously joking, but Tenley didn't break a smile. Tenley Reed had a killer poker face when she wanted to. Emerson should know; she'd been on the receiving end of it many times. Abby cleared her throat, fiddling with her scarf belt. "I just wanted to bring things full circle," she explained. "Honor Tricia's birth instead of staying focused on her death."

They were interrupted by two more cars whipping into the lot. Delancey Crane, Abby's best friend and Purity Club cofounder, climbed out of one. She looked like the kid to Abby's soccer mom: wildly curly hair barely tamed by a hair tie, a heart-shaped face with big, wide-set blue eyes, and a sweater whose color would best be described as *bubble gum*. She always reminded Emerson of the porcelain dolls displayed in the window of the antiques store downtown.

Several other girls from their grade spilled out of the car alongside her. Emerson blew out a sigh of relief when she saw Marta Lazarus's familiar head of red hair emerge from the second car. She was wearing a short, flowy green dress that showed off her curves, with a cropped jean jacket. Marta's style was exactly like her personality: effervescent and fun.

"Em!" Marta exclaimed. "Tenley! You guys came." She wrapped her arms around Emerson, hugging her tightly. "Everyone's going to be so happy to see you."

Emerson felt a wave of guilt wash over her. She knew she'd been a little M.I.A. lately when it came to social events. No one could blame her; Caitlin had been her best friend. But she could tell Marta missed her. "I decided it was time for a night out," she said, forcing a smile.

"Hallelujah," Marta cheered. As she launched into a story about a cute boy she'd met that afternoon, the parking lot began to fill up with people. Soon half their grade was piling out of the cars that kept pulling into the lot.

7

Emerson adjusted the chunky black sweaterdress she was wearing over tights, watching as Delancey and Abby pulled several tiki torches out of Abby's car. Abby caught Emerson's eye as she sauntered past with the torches. She gave her a sharp wave, gesturing for her to join them on the beach. Emerson sighed, pushing a strand of her carefully straightened black hair out of her face. "Guess we should see what the purity princesses want."

She tried to go to her happy place as she followed Tenley and Marta to the beach. It was a calming technique Caitlin had taught her once, gleaned from her years of therapy. *Her first day modeling in New York City: walking down Fifth Avenue as if she belonged there, each window showcasing an outfit more beautiful than the last.* By the time she stopped in front of Abby and Delancey, she was breathing a little easier.

"I'm planning to give a speech about Tricia and Cait tonight," Abby informed them. The gold promise ring she and Delancey both wore flashed in the moonlight. "Kind of like a Lost Girl tribute. Is there anything you want me to include? I know how close you all were with both of them." Her voice was oozing sympathy, and immediately Emerson tensed back up. "I can imagine this day is especially hard for you," Abby added.

Emerson clasped her hands together tightly. She wanted so badly to reach out and smack Abby right in her pale face. She was acting as if she knew them, as though she *understood*, but she knew nothing at all.

"It is," Marta said, saving Emerson and Tenley from responding. Tears sprang to her eyes and she quickly reached up to swipe at them. "Which is why we really need to celebrate tonight. The way Tricia would have wanted it. Make this the party of the year!"

"Did I just hear 'party of the year'?"

Emerson started at the sound of Hunter Bailey's voice. Spinning around, she found herself facing their group of guy friends: Hunter, Tyler Cole, Sean Hale, and Nate Roberts.

"That's exactly what you heard," Tenley said, winking at Hunter. Tenley and Hunter weren't dating, exactly, but they didn't hide their flirtations, either.

"Good thing I've got a case of beer, then," Hunter said. His chiseled features relaxed into a smirk.

Abby exchanged a disapproving look with Delancey before taking off to set up tiki torches along the beach. "For the record, I do not like our new student-body president," Tenley said, watching the two of them go.

"Join the club," Emerson replied. "And I don't mean the purity one." She took a can of beer from Hunter gratefully. She wasn't in the mood to drink, but just holding it made this feel more like a party than an over-the-top memorial. Sean clearly felt the same way, because he immediately began chugging his down, his eyes glazing over as he watched the flame of a nearby tiki torch dance on the breeze. Emerson hurt for him. Tricia had been Sean's girlfriend. The Ken to her Barbie, their friends used to joke. Like everyone else in town, he'd never known what a monster she was. Emerson reached out and squeezed his shoulder. She wished there were something she could say, but sometimes there just weren't any words.

"Purity Club, student-body president, *and* running the homecoming committee," Marta said, shaking her head. "That girl must never sleep."

Emerson glanced over at where Abby was carefully straightening a tiki torch, Delancey at her side. "At least she can't *vote* for everyone. Not that I want to be queen anyway," she added, rolling her eyes at Marta.

"I know, I know," Marta groaned. "You're *soooo* over high school."

Emerson laughed. It had been her mantra before everything

happened with Caitlin. She was done with high school classes and high school drama and, most especially, high school boys.

"Abby will find some way to fix the contest," Tyler said. His amber skin and glossy black hair seemed to glow under the light of the torches. Tyler was Vietnamese—he'd been adopted by the Cole family as a baby—and Emerson was always admiring his shiny, *never* unruly hair, which he wore long for a guy. "Or so Jessie says," he added.

"Where is Jessie?" Emerson asked carefully. Jessie Morrow, the captain of the cheerleading squad that Emerson—and, at one point, Caitlin—cheered on, had started dating Tyler recently, which meant she was suddenly around Emerson and her friends all the time.

"Her parents locked her in to study." Tyler made a face. "Lame."

Relief rushed through her. At the beginning of the school year, Emerson had done something she wanted desperately to forget. Mistaking the dare Caitlin had received from Tricia as some kind of best-friend-abduction ploy by Tenley, she sent Tenley a fake dare, challenging her to slip an antianxiety pill into Jessie's water bottle before a pep rally. She never thought Tenley would actually *do* it, just that she'd learn her lesson and stop trying to steal Emerson's best friend. But, believing the dare was from the real darer—the one sending her mysterious threats—Tenley went through with it. Neither of them could ever have known that it would trigger the seizures Jessie used to have, that it would make her fall from the very top of the cheerleaders' pyramid.

Jessie had healed completely since her fall; it was almost as if the whole terrible accident hadn't happened. But Emerson still felt uneasy around her. "Too bad she can't come," she managed to croak out.

"Since she's missing the party of the year," Marta said, holding her beer up in the air, "I say we toast!" she declared.

"To senior year!" Hunter offered.

"To beach parties every single Monday!" Nate chimed in, making a goofy face.

"To Caitlin," Emerson said softly.

"And"—Tenley added, coughing lightly—"Tricia."

"To Tricia," Sean repeated. His grip tightened on his half-empty can, making it collapse in on itself.

"To the Lost Girls," Nate added as they all clinked beers.

Emerson could feel herself relaxing a little as Hunter rallied everyone to play "would you rather," his favorite drinking game.

"I'll go first," Tenley declared. "Would you rather make out with Miss Hilbrook or…Mr. Dickson?" Miss Hilbrook was Winslow's token hot teacher, while Mr. Dickson was the creepy gym teacher who'd been around for about a hundred years.

"Hilbrook," all the guys yelled. Emerson looked over at Marta. But before either of them could answer, an unfamiliar voice cut in.

"I surmise you're playing more games?"

Emerson looked over to see Calum Bauer walking toward them. At first glance, he was almost cute, with broad shoulders and a lopsided grin. But when she looked closer, he was unmistakably *Calum*, his wild white-blond curls swaying like a treetop in the breeze, and his skin paler than ever in the dim light of the tiki torches.

"Abby really did invite *everyone*," Marta muttered.

"Let me guess." Calum pretended to stroke a nonexistent beard. "Truth or dare? I remember it was quite the salacious game the last time we played."

Emerson glared at Calum. That game was the last thing she wanted to think about right now. It was what had started everything, what had changed everything. "We're not really into that anymore," she said coolly.

"Too bad," he said, eyeing Emerson thoughtfully. "Your dare was to Tenley's party as ice cream is to my stomach."

"Someone stop him!" Nate made a show of covering his ears with his hands. "There's no SAT prep allowed at parties."

"Though he does have a point." Tenley put her hands on her hips and glowered up at Emerson. "It *was* your dare."

Emerson smiled sheepishly. When they'd played truth or dare at Tenley's housewarming party, she'd dared Tenley to kiss Calum. She was so intimidated by Tenley that night, afraid she was going to swoop in and steal Caitlin away from her. She'd just wanted a dare that would embarrass her. But Tenley, being Tenley, made it seem like no big deal. And then soon after, they'd both lost Caitlin anyway. Emerson swallowed hard, shoving the memory to the back of her mind. "Sorry," she said with a shrug. "He seemed like your type at the time."

"First impressions usually are accurate," Calum offered.

A few feet away, Abby lifted onto her toes, waving frantically at Calum. "Looks like duty calls," he sighed. "Abby has apparently confused 'class treasurer' with 'personal assistant.' But if any of you are in the mood to play some more later, you know where to find me." He fluttered his eye in what might have been a wink before jogging over to Abby.

"Such potential squandered," Marta said as she watched him go. "With a dad that rich, it's a mystery how he became such a loser."

Abby blew loudly on a whistle, drowning out Hunter's response. "Time to commemorate Tricia and Caitlin!" she announced.

Emerson squared her shoulders, bracing herself. More like time to pretend that just the sound of Tricia's name didn't make her want to barf.

Abby had just launched into an infuriating speech about celebrating "those we've lost" when Tenley's phone beeped loudly. "Oh my god," Emerson heard her sputter. Immediately Tenley grabbed Emerson's arm and pulled her roughly away from the group.

"Ow! What the—?" But she, too, fell silent as Tenley shoved her phone at her.

On the screen was a text, sent by a blocked number. Emerson's heart seized as she read it.

Time for a new game, girls: show and tell. The only rule? Don't tell. Or I'll show your secrets to the world.

Emerson looked wildly around, but the beach was dark, the shoreline crowded with classmates. It could have been sent from anyone—here or elsewhere. "Maybe it's a joke," she said nervously. "Maybe someone found one of Tricia's notes and thought it was just some game."

Tenley nodded, but her expression told Emerson she wasn't buying it. "I'm going to try responding," she said tightly. Tenley typed out a quick text, but a second later, she held up an error message for Emerson to see. *Invalid Number.*

Emerson's head started to pound. "I guess it's one-way communication," she muttered.

"We should go see if anyone we know has their phones out," Tenley said.

Emerson reached up to massage her forehead. She felt hot and stuffy all of a sudden, as if she were standing inside a sauna instead of on a wide, cold beach.

"Are you okay?" Tenley asked.

"I actually don't feel so good." Emerson wiped a bead of sweat off her brow. "I—I think I need to go home."

"Go. Please." Tenley sounded tense, but her forehead was

scrunched up in concern. "You look like you're about to faint. I can look into the phone thing myself."

Emerson nodded. "Text if you find anything. But I bet it really is just a terrible joke." She gave Tenley a weak smile before hurrying toward the street. Her mom had dropped her off earlier, which meant she'd have to call for a ride home, but right now it just felt good to be moving. The farther away she got from the beach, the less her head pounded and the more her body cooled down. She decided to walk a few blocks before calling.

Tenley's text circled through her mind as she turned onto Maple Avenue. Joke or not, she felt a stab of guilt at how relieved she was that it had nothing to do with her. She wasn't part of Tricia's horrible game, never had been. Her secrets were safe.

"Hey, Lion!" A car rolled to a stop in the street behind her. Before she even turned around, she knew who it was. Matt Morgan, Echo Bay's resident fire chief. And Sydney Morgan's father. He was the only one who called her by that nickname—coined because she was a Winslow Lions cheerleader. His voice made her stomach lurch. It had been weeks since she'd seen or heard from him, and she'd hoped to keep it that way.

She turned to face him. He was in his blue pickup truck, his arm propped up on the rolled-down window. He was as good-looking as ever, his thick brown hair just starting to turn salt-and-pepper. "Let me give you a ride," he offered.

"No thanks," she said coldly. "I'm fine."

"Come on, Em." He leaned out the window. He was in his gym clothes, his muscles toned underneath his thin T-shirt. She quickly averted her eyes. "This is a good coincidence. I've been wanting to talk to you, actually. You know, get some closure on everything."

Emerson snorted. Forget closure; she wanted to erase the whole terrible Matt Morgan Mistake from her mind.

"Please," Matt said. There was a pleading note in his voice that surprised her. "You look like you could use a ride, anyway."

Emerson sighed. It *would* save her parents the trip. "Fine." She climbed into the truck, keeping her eyes on the road as he pulled into the street. "Go ahead," she said woodenly. "Talk."

"What happened between us this summer..." Matt paused. It was clear he was choosing his words carefully. "I'm not saying I regret it, because, of course, I don't. It was great, but...it still shouldn't have happened. You might be eighteen, but in the eyes of this town, you're still a kid. I'm the adult; I shouldn't have let it go on."

A laugh escaped Emerson. "You probably should have thought of that before giving me your number." He'd done it slyly at the cheerleaders' end-of-year car wash, smiling that knowing, little smile of his, with his eyes glued to her wet, sudsy sundress. She knew it would be wrong in about a thousand different ways if she called him. He wasn't just older, he was *Sydney Morgan's dad*. A girl in her grade. But that's what made her do it in the end: the *wrongness* of it. She wanted it to consume her, to help her do the one thing nothing else had been able to: make her forget Josh.

She'd tried everything that past year, dating the senior quarterback, throwing herself into cheerleading, dragging Caitlin to party after party. But still the memory of Josh clung to her, like a cold she couldn't quite kick. So when Matt gave her his number, she wanted to believe that *this* would work—let her box up that part of her life and ship it far away at last.

It had, for a little while. But then Matt had ended it, and all she'd been left with was a new batch of memories she wished she could erase.

"I know I was the one who started things," Matt continued, "but I was at a different point in my life then. Now I have a real chance of working things out with my ex-wife. And if she found out…"

Emerson nodded. She kept waiting for the emotions to hit—anger or sorrow, maybe even a pang of lingering desire—but all she felt was regret. Hot, snaking regret. It made her feel itchy inside her own skin. "Believe me," she said. "I'd like to forget about this as much as you would."

"Good." Matt blew out a relieved breath as he turned onto her block. "Because it's not just me I'm worried about; it's Sydney. If this got out, I could lose my job—and Sydney's Winslow scholarship is contingent on my being a fireman." He braked the car at the bottom of her driveway. "I couldn't live with myself if she lost her scholarship her senior year." He put a hand on Emerson's shoulder, but she shrugged it off.

"Like I said, I don't want people to know about this, either." She slid down from the truck. But as she started toward her house, she glanced back. Matt was slumped behind the wheel, a defeated look on his face. "I won't tell anyone," she called to him. "Okay? You have nothing to worry about, Matt."

She took off toward her house without waiting for a reply. All she wanted to do right now was curl up in bed and pretend Matt Morgan didn't exist. But as she climbed onto her porch, she saw something propped against the front door. It was a small package, wrapped up prettily with a sticker of the letter *E* on the front. Emerson crouched down and picked it up. The wrapping paper tore off easily, fluttering to her feet.

It was a pink rabbit's foot key chain. *Her* pink rabbit's foot key chain. The one she'd named Big Foot and taken to every game and pep rally she'd ever cheered at—until she lost it over a month ago. There was a folded piece of stationery with it, and she quickly smoothed it open. A message was printed across it in boxy, faded letters, as if it had been typed up on an old typewriter.

"No," Emerson whispered. She knew that font. She'd seen it before, on one of Caitlin's dares. Light-headed, she sank into a porch chair to read.

```
You're already a naughty girl, Em. Follow
  my rules, or you'll become a Lost Girl,
      too. Welcome to the game.
```

CHAPTER TWO
Monday, 11:02 PM

TENLEY WAS BOOKING IT DOWN THE BEACH. THE
party was over, and she wanted to get far away from it as fast as possible. The more distance she put between herself and the scene of that
text message the better. Still, she couldn't resist pulling her phone out
as she walked. She swiped at the screen, making a thin beam of light
cut through the darkness.

Time for a new game, girls. The words made the hairs on her arms
stand on end. After Emerson left, she walked up and down the beach,
looking for anyone acting suspicious. But it was a party: People were
drinking and laughing and running into the waves fully clothed. No
one's behavior screamed, *I just sent a creepy stalker text!* She tried to
forget about it after that and have fun, but the same question looped
through her mind all night: Could this text be related to the last one?

At Caitlin's memorial, only seconds after finding the note in her
purse, she'd received a text. No words, just a photo: Tenley fast asleep
and curled up against her stepbrother, Guinness, Photoshopped to

look as if they were sleeping in a coffin. She deleted it before Sydney or Emerson could see. She didn't need Sydney—or *anyone*—seeing her with Guinness like that. She knew exactly when the photo had been taken, and it wasn't her proudest moment.

It had been just a few nights after the *Justice* crash. She'd been lonely, missing Caitlin like crazy, and desperate for some comfort. So she crawled into Guinness's bed. He'd been passed out drunk, and she left before he woke up. He never even knew she was there. But someone did. She wasn't sure which part scared her more: that someone had been inside her house, *photographing* her... or that whoever it was would rather see her in a coffin than a bed.

It was almost a good thing that Sydney hadn't shown up tonight, or she might have slipped and finally told her about the photo. She'd thought about telling her many times, of course, but what would be the point? Sydney and Guinness had practically been dating; she would hate Tenley for that photo. Besides, there had been no more notes, no more threats. Until now.

Tenley quickened her pace. When she was little, she used to take this walk with her dad all the time, oohing and aahing over Dune Way's grand, majestic beachfront houses. Her dad would always admire Caitlin's house: one of the smallest ones on the strip, but the closest to the water. "I'll take that one," he loved to joke.

Now Tenley lived on the strip, and not in one of the smaller houses like the Thomases', but in her stepdad's house at the very end, the largest and grandest of them all. When she took this walk home, retracing the steps she and her dad had taken so many times, she could almost hear him talking to her.

But tonight she heard no traces of her dad's voice as she walked along the beach. Instead, all she could hear was the ocean, its waves clapping against the sand like a taunt. *I took Caitlin, I took Caitlin.* She'd never noticed just how dark this section of the beach was. Beads of sweat gathered on the back of her neck as she walked even faster.

Out of nowhere, her toe hit something hard. She lurched forward, losing her balance.

"Whoa!" someone yelled. She didn't have time to wonder who it was. She was too busy wheeling her arms through the air, trying desperately to right herself. But it was a lost cause. She toppled over, landing in the sand with a muffled thud.

"Oh, crap," the voice said. *"Tenley?"*

Tenley pulled herself up to sitting, pain reverberating down her spine. A guy was sitting a few feet away, looking up at her through strands of shaggy blond hair. Tenley recognized him instantly. Tim Holland, the boy Caitlin had just started seeing before the crash.

"Are you all right?" Tim asked. "You tripped over my board. I didn't even hear you coming." He nodded toward a surfboard lying in the sand by her feet.

"I'm fine." Tenley wiped some sand off her arms. "Though, in the future, you might want to think about getting warning cones for your surfboard." She frowned. "Wait, you were surfing *now*? In the dark?"

Tim laughed. "Even I'm not that nuts. No, I was surfing earlier and then I sat down and..." He looked around, as if noticing for the first time that night had fallen. "I must have lost track of time."

Tenley shifted a little, ignoring the bruise she could already feel blooming on her hip. "So Abby's party tonight wasn't your thing?"

"Nah." Tim dug his hand into the sand, letting it fall through his fingers. "I knew everyone would be talking about Caitlin, and I just don't need all that pity, people acting like they understand what it feels like when they obviously don't, you know?"

"Oh, do I. I was ready to clock Abby Wilkins right in her long horse face by the end of the night."

Tim burst out laughing. "That's part of the reason I've been skipping school so much. You probably have more self-control than I do when it comes to clocking people."

"I wouldn't count on it," Tenley said with a small grin. "So what have you been doing with all your newfound free time?"

Tim shrugged. "Surfing mostly. And thinking."

"About her." It slipped out before Tenley could yank it back. The pain on Tim's face was unmistakable. It gave Tenley a surprising pang in the pit of her stomach. She'd dated plenty of guys over the years, and she was pretty sure not a single one had ever looked so...*raw* over her. "I understand," she added softly. "I think about her, too. All the time."

Tim gave her a half smile. She'd forgotten how good-looking he was, when you got past the whole board-shorts-and-hemp-necklace thing. "I just keep waiting for it to get better," he said.

Tenley looked down, rubbing at a faint ink stain on her jeans. She wanted to say something—anything—but her mouth felt as if it were filled with wet sand.

"The worst part," Tim continued, "is how I never know when it will hit. Like I'll actually be doing something seminormal, feeling okay, and then *bam*: Something makes me think of her and I just lose it. The other day I had to sprint out of English class because Miss Harbor was reading a passage aloud from *Romeo and Juliet* and it reminded me of how Caitlin had said she was excited to read it." He let out a thin laugh. "Such a stupid, meaningless memory, but there I was, bolting out of the room."

"Physics class," Tenley found herself responding. "Newton's laws of motion. It hit me how Caitlin would have helped me understand it and... suddenly I just had to get out of there. I went home sick for the first time in like ten years." She blinked. She hadn't told anyone that until now. Her mom still believed she'd come down with a twenty-four-hour bug.

Tim was quiet for a moment. "Sometimes I feel like I have no right to miss her this much. I barely spent any time with her until this summer."

"What does that matter?" Tenley blurted out. Until she moved back to Echo Bay, she'd barely spent any time with Caitlin in the last four years. But it didn't make it hurt any less. She put a hand on Tim's arm. "You're allowed to miss her."

Tim met her gaze. She could smell the salty scent of the ocean on him, mixed with something soft and citrusy. For a second they just looked at each other. Tenley's hand was still on his arm, and it struck her how little space there was between them. She pulled away with a cough.

"I should probably get going," she said. "Unless I want my mom to send out a search team." As if on cue, her phone rang, Madonna's "Like a Virgin" blasting through the night air.

Tim gave her an amused look. "Madonna?"

"It's in honor of Cait," Tenley informed him. "It was our favorite song when we were kids." She looked down to see her mom's name flashing across the screen. "She is too predictable," she groaned.

"At least you know she cares, right?" Tim offered.

Tenley made a sour face. "Personally, I prefer the noncaring Trudy Reed." Ever since Caitlin's funeral, Tenley's usually hands-off mom suddenly had both hands on her—insisting they go on long walks and eat family dinners and discuss every minute of Tenley's day in torturous detail. The last time Tenley had seen Trudy in this kind of full-on

Alpha Mom mode was after her dad died. "At least *that* mom let me breathe without asking permission."

Her phone continued to ring, and she pressed the ignore button, silencing it. She'd be home soon enough; her mom could launch her tell-me-every-second-of-your-night offensive then. She dropped her phone back into her purse and stood up.

"You sure you can't stick around for a bit?" Tim asked. "I mean, I love the seagulls and all, but they're not exactly the best conversation-alists."

"You think I'm better company than a seagull?" Tenley put a hand to her chest, pretending to swoon. "I'm honored. But if you don't want a SWAT team surrounding us in approximately four and a half minutes, I should get home."

Tim laughed. "Your mom can't be *that* crazy."

"You would think.... Okay, I'm off. See you at school. The next time you deign to show up, that is."

"Who knows when that will be," Tim said. "But hey... if you ever need to talk to someone, hunt me down, okay?"

"Ditto," Tenley replied. She gave him a quick wave before taking off down the beach. As she walked, she kept replaying their conversation in her head. It surprised her how nice it had been to talk to some-one who really *got* it. It was different with Emerson and Marta; they'd had years with Caitlin, all of high school. Tenley was the one who'd only just gotten her back. Sometimes it made the loss feel even more unfair.

She was practically jogging by the time she reached Dune Way. As she hurried along the pavement, she kept her eyes on the rocky shoreline to her left, ignoring the houses to her right. It was still hard for her to see Caitlin's house. She wondered if it would ever get easier. It never had with her old house. Sometimes she drove ten minutes out of her way just to avoid passing the yellow house they'd lived in when her dad was alive.

She'd just cleared Caitlin's house when she heard a car rev in the distance behind her. Her pulse sped up as she glanced over her shoulder. The street was dark and empty, no cars in sight. The noise must have carried in on the wind. Still, she picked up her speed, the text from earlier seared in her mind. *New game, girls.*

She'd thought this was all behind her now: the running, the fear, the jumping at every noise. She was supposed to be safe again.

No sooner had the thought crossed her mind than a car zoomed loudly onto the street behind her. Tenley spun around, her heart leaping into her throat. She was instantly blinded, a wall of white shimmering across her vision. She could hear the screech of tire against pavement as the car sped toward her, but she couldn't see a thing.

"Turn off your brights!" she yelled. She shielded her eyes as the car continued to drive toward her, but it was useless. Through the haze of white, she couldn't make out a thing, not even the size of the car.

"Asshole," she muttered under her breath. She hated people who acted as if they owned the streets. The car swerved a little, making Tenley jump. Spinning on her heels, she marched toward her house, the car at her back. This had been a long, crappy night, and she still had the Trudy Inquisition to face. Mr. I-Can't-Drive-For-Crap could blast his lights all he wanted; she was going home.

She'd made it a few steps when something slammed down on the sidewalk beside her. Whatever it was shattered instantly, pieces flying left and right. Tenley shrieked and spun around. "What the hell?" she gasped.

In the street, the car idled only feet away. Its lights bore into her, blinding her. Her hands clenched into fists at her side. *"Turn off your—"*

She never got to finish. Something cracked next to her against the ground. Then something else. They were *bottles*. Another one came flying at her, sending bits of glass swirling around her like hail as it shattered to pieces. They were coming from the car. The driver was throwing bottles at her!

"Stop it!" she screamed as another bottle flew at her—then another. Suddenly they were coming fast and furious, the noise ringing in her ears as they shattered around her.

A bottle crashed into her knee, sending pain thrumming down her leg. Her heart pounded wildly. Why hadn't she answered when her mom called? Asked her to come get her? What was she *thinking* walking home alone?

She turned and broke into a run. "I'm calling the police!" she yelled over her shoulder. But before she could reach for her phone, a bottle smashed into her back. Knives of pain radiated through her. She could barely breathe as she ran even faster, her feet kicking up fragments of glass as bottles crashed and crackled around her. She could hear the car tailing her, could feel its lights boring into her back, a spotlight.

A bottle landed against her ankle and another smacked against her shoulder blade. "Stop it!" she shrieked.

In response, another bottle sped toward her, missing her head by only a centimeter. She heard the car inching closer. She turned to look back, but at that moment a bottle slammed against her temple. Her head swam, her vision going fuzzy. As the bottle tumbled to the ground, splintering loudly, Tenley stumbled forward. "No!" she wailed. She tried to right herself, but she was too dizzy. Suddenly she was tipping over for the second time that night.

She landed hard on the pavement, a shard of glass stabbing at her palm. Tears filled her eyes as a thin line of blood sprouted on her hand.

She was struggling to pull herself up when she heard a noise coming from up ahead. Another car.

"Help! Someone!" Tenley yelled as she dragged herself to her feet. Immediately the mystery car cut all its lights and sped off—so fast, Tenley was left spinning. In its wake the night grew inky black. Then, seconds later, another set of headlights swept over her, lighting up the street once again.

"Ten Ten?" Her mom's voice reached Tenley as if from a great distance. Her car screeched to a stop next to her.

"Mom?" Tenley choked back a sob as she threw herself into her mom's car. "What are you doing here?"

"I got worried your phone died when you didn't answer. I thought you might need a ride." Her mom studied Tenley appraisingly. "What's wrong, honey?"

"I—I was walking home and someone started following me, and...and..." Tenley trailed off, trembling all over. Her palm stung and a dull ache was spreading through her head, but all she could think about was that car. Whoever was in it had been following her, *chasing* her. The photo from Caitlin's memorial flashed through her mind: her and Guinness, ensconced in a coffin. If her mom hadn't shown up, how far would the driver have gone?

"Following you?" Her mom wrinkled her usually Botox-smoothed forehead at Tenley. "Ten, the street was completely empty when I got here."

"No." Tenley shook her head adamantly. "There was a car, I swear. It left when it heard you coming. The driver was throwing bottles at me!" Tenley could hear the whiny tone creeping into her voice, but she couldn't seem to do anything about it.

"Bottles?" her mom exclaimed. "Are you sure?"

When Tenley nodded, her mom set her mouth in a grim line. "Do you want me to call the police? Echo Bay shouldn't have riffraff like that running loose on the streets!"

Tenley leaned back against the seat of the car, breathing hard. That was exactly what she wanted. Her mom was right; people like that needed to be taken care of. She opened her mouth to say just that when her phone let out a sharp beep, like an animal waking from a deep slumber.

Tenley glanced at it. *1 new text*, the screen flashed. The number was blocked.

All the air seemed to leak out of Tenley's body. A drop of blood from her palm smeared against her phone, but she barely noticed as, slowly, she opened the text.

Mommy dearest won't save you next time. This game is just beginning.

CHAPTER THREE
Monday, 11:40 PM

SYDNEY MORGAN PACED THROUGH THE TINY, two-bedroom apartment she shared with her mom. The text message she'd gotten earlier had left her nerves completely frayed. The words were plastered across her mind like a billboard. *Time for a new game, girls: Show and Tell. The only rule? Don't tell. Or I'll show your secrets to the world.*

She'd spoken to Tenley earlier, and apparently she'd gotten the same one, too. Who could have sent it? Tricia was *dead*. But if not Tricia…who? And whoever it was, could they really know her secrets?

Tricia had known everything, all the worst things about her: her treatment for pyromania at the Sunrise Center, the fire she'd started years ago that no one had *ever* known about, and, of course, her dad's dalliance with Emerson. In the wrong hands, that information could ruin her—not just destroy her family and kill her chances at getting a scholarship to the Rhode Island School of Design, but, thanks to that fire, maybe even send her to jail.

Sydney eyed her phone, silently debating calling her mom, who was working a late nursing shift at the hospital. But what would she even say? *Guess what, Mom? The murderous, stalking darer I never told you about seems to have risen from her grave!*

Right.

Brring! Brring!

The sound of her phone ringing made her jump. It was just Tenley. She sucked in a long, deep breath. She needed to pull herself together. "Hey," she said, pressing the phone to her ear.

"Emerson got one," Tenley announced, wasting no time with niceties.

Sydney's hand tightened around her phone. "A message?" she asked cautiously.

"No, a pony," Tenley snapped. "Yes, a message!"

Sydney fiddled nervously with the ring she always wore on her pointer finger. It was bad enough to hear from the darer again, but now to have to deal with *Emerson* on top of it? The thought made her sick to her stomach. Emerson had no idea that Sydney knew about her relationship with her dad—had no idea that the knowledge of it constantly haunted Sydney's thoughts, like a ghost with a vengeance.

"It wasn't a text this time, either," Tenley continued. "It was a printed note. Waiting for her on her porch. And Sydney..." She paused. Sydney could hear her swallowing nervously. "It was written on a typewriter like the rest of them."

Sydney inhaled sharply. "It's really happening," she whispered.

"All over again," Tenley said tightly.

"I don't understand. *How?* Tricia's gone."

"I have no idea. But whoever it is, they're not kidding around. They attacked me on my walk home tonight."

"*What?*" Sydney cried.

"Someone was throwing bottles at me from a car. I thought…" Tenley's voice faltered. "Whoever it was definitely wanted to hurt me."

Sydney stormed over to her window and snapped the shade up. It was a velvety black night, the kind that melted your vision around the edges. But the parking lot's ancient lamp cast a dim glow over the rows of cars. She took a quick scan of the lot, relieved to find nothing out of the ordinary. She let the shade drop back. "How do you know it was the same person who sent the text?"

"Because I got another text after. The message made it pretty clear." Tenley swallowed hard. "I think—I think we have to go to the cops. My mom wanted to call them after she picked me up. I stopped her after I got that text, but…I think she's right. It's time we involve the police."

"Are you serious?" Sydney balked. "You're really suggesting that after an entire month of giving us no-cop lectures?"

"No one was attacking me then," Tenley shot back.

"No way," Sydney said adamantly. "Not happening."

"But—" Tenley began.

"No!" Sydney barked. She sat down at her desk and pressed her forehead against its cool, wood surface. Of course Tenley was fine with going to the cops. With Caitlin gone, the only secret she had left didn't even count as one. Who cared about *implants*? No matter how much Tenley bemoaned its coming out, Sydney knew the truth would barely cause a ripple in her life. Sydney, meanwhile, could end up in jail for burning down three houses. She glanced at the RISD scholarship application she'd been slaving over for the past month. In jail there would be no darkrooms, and no prestigious photography degrees.

"The text made it clear: Tell anyone and our secrets come out," Sydney said. "I'm pretty sure *cops* count in that."

Tenley let out a frustrated grunt. "Listen, I've got to go. My mom's in psycho-mother mode right now. But we're talking more about this in school tomorrow."

Sydney hung up and threw her phone angrily onto her bed. Her heart was hammering so loudly she felt like a one-woman marching band. This wasn't a fluke. There was really a new darer out there. And if Tenley got her way, their secrets could end up as front-page news.

She started pacing again, faster and faster. She felt all jittery, as if she'd just downed three coffees. She tried to shake it off, recognizing the signs. In the past, feeling like this used to drive her to the one thing that could always calm her: matches. An image of flames flickered through her mind: hot and glowing and candy orange. She shoved it away. Fire didn't have a hold on her anymore—not after Tricia almost killed her with it in the cabin of the *Justice*.

She grabbed one of her cameras off her dresser. If she stayed in this apartment alone for one minute longer, she was going to explode.

Soon she was steering her car along the winding curves that lead to Great Harbor Beach. She'd avoided the beach earlier tonight, having no desire to set foot near Abby's party. Winslow parties—any parties, really—were not her scene. She'd choose shooting pictures over hearing the latest hookup gossip any day of the week. But, according to Tenley, the party had ended. Which meant the beach should be empty again.

She knew there were plenty of other beaches she could photograph. Massachusetts's North Shore was filled with inlets and bays, fingers of sand reaching from town to town. But none of them drew her to them the way Great Harbor Beach did, with an almost magnetic power. Because none of them had the rock.

At one time, the Phantom Rock had been nothing more than a fun Echo Bay landmark: a rock visible only during low tide. But after the deaths of the first three Lost Girls, people swore they saw three ghostly lights flickering over the rock, as if the spirits of the girls had never left. For a long time, Sydney had been dying to catch those ghost lights on film, seal them to paper in a way that no one else had been able to. But then Caitlin Thomas had died in a horrific collision with the Phantom Rock—while Sydney was on the boat with her—and Sydney had learned the hard way that there was no such thing as myth, or spirits, or fate, or, least of all, ghost lights. It was all just a fancy way of refusing to face reality: that people died, and nothing you did or wished for could stop that.

Still, she kept being drawn to Great Harbor Beach. Her RISD scholarship application required her to submit a "unique and awe-inspiring hometown image," and all she could seem to shoot was that rock. She photographed it during low tide and half tide, during sunlight and moonlight, before school and after school. Again and again and again, until the frames all bled together, worthless and futile, a graveyard of images. She kept hoping for unique and awe-inspiring, but, so far, all she had was dull and duller. With the application due in exactly one week, she was running out of time.

Sydney pulled into the empty beach parking lot and ditched her shoes in the car. The sand was damp against her feet as she walked down to the surf, her camera clutched in her hands. She couldn't help but glance nervously over her shoulder. But the beach was completely empty, dark sand stretching out for miles. The only remnants of people were a few tiki torches, probably left over from Abby's joke of a party.

Sydney lifted her camera, training it on the Phantom Rock. Soon she was caught up in the rhythm of taking photos, the click of the shutter a sound track to her thoughts.

She couldn't stop thinking about the new notes. Who could have sent them? And why drag Emerson into it now? Was it just to torture Sydney by throwing the two of them together?

High above the Phantom Rock, a burst of light suddenly shattered the darkness. For a split second everything was painted in light: the jagged tip of the rock and the soaring crests of the waves and the wide expanse of sand, yawning golden around her.

Sydney's finger automatically pressed the shutter release. *Snap.*

Then just like that, it was dark again.

For several long minutes Sydney kept her eyes trained on the rock, but the darkness never broke again. Her hands started to shake. Those lights...they'd been exactly like what everyone described. Had she finally done the impossible: caught the ghost lights on camera? She couldn't imagine a better photograph for her application.

Suddenly it hit her. There hadn't been three lights; there had been *five.* Two new lights for two new Lost Girls.

Her hands shook harder at the thought, and as she jabbed clumsily at the display button to see the photo, the camera slipped right out of her grip. She gasped as it tumbled to the ground.

The camera landed with a muffled thud, making the memory card pop out of its slot. "Noooo," Sydney moaned as the memory card skidded into a wet pile of sand. She grabbed for it desperately, but it was too late. It was coated with sand. She brushed it off, but when she put it back in her camera, the screen stayed black. Sydney blew out a frustrated sigh. Even if she had caught the lights on camera, the photo was gone now.

She extracted the memory card and dropped it into her purse. She'd try to dry it out later, but she knew it was probably a lost cause. This wasn't her first camera casualty at the beach. Wet sand usually meant a one-way ticket to the trash.

Disappointment trickled through her, but she shook her head. She was being ridiculous. The ghost lights weren't real. Just like the Lost Girls superstition wasn't real. What she'd seen must have been some kind of reflection off the water. That was all.

Several yards down the beach, something caught her attention. It was a guy walking slowly along, his head turned toward the waves. Sydney broke into a smile. After a summer working together at the Echo Bay Golf & Country Club, she would know that awkward gait and mass of curls anywhere. "Calum!" She lifted her hand and waved.

Calum's head jerked in her direction. "Well, if it isn't my favorite photographer," he called.

It was too dark to make out his expression as he jogged toward her, but Sydney could imagine his trademark lopsided grin. It made her own smile widen. It had been over a month now since she'd ended things with Guinness, and, still, she felt such a hole inside her. So many times she'd reached for the phone, excited about a new photographer or a funny conversation she'd overheard at Bean Encounters, just to realize she had no one to call. Over the summer Calum's dorky jokes had often cheered her up, but ever since school started, she'd barely seen him.

"What are you doing out here?" she asked when he reached her. He was wearing a Calum-tastic sweatshirt: stained at the cuffs and stamped with the phrase: I BEFORE E EXCEPT AFTER C: WEIRD. Sydney stifled a laugh. She had never met a guy with more shirts featuring superheroes and corny mottos.

"You know me. I can never resist a good party. Especially when Abby Wilkins decrees I have to be there," he added with a smirk. "I swear that girl is more slave driver than president. But she does know how to throw a shindig; I'll give her that. Unfortunately, you're a little late to partake in the festivities. I just stayed to do some cleaning up."

"One, did you really just channel my grandmother and say *shindig*? And two, I'm definitely not here for the party. You know I don't do Winslow social events." Sydney pretended to gag. "I just came to shoot some photos. I need the perfect 'hometown image' by next Monday. And I actually just saw the weirdest thing." She twisted her ring. "Five lights, flashing over the ocean... They almost looked like ghost lights." She let out a sheepish laugh. "Probably just a reflection or something," she added quickly. "You didn't see it, did you?"

Calum shook his head. "I was preoccupied with my trash hunt. But"—he gave her a sly look—"I'll have you know that you are statistically more likely to see the nearly extinct Daggernose shark than any ghost lights." His voice was light, but his expression clouded over a little. *Of course* it did. Sydney looked down, feeling terrible. First a Lost Girls party and now talk of ghost lights. Calum probably couldn't help but think about his sister, Meryl.

Meryl Bauer, Calum's older sister, was the town's original Lost Girl. She'd died in a boating accident off Great Harbor Beach ten years ago—just as Nicole Mayor had four years later, and Kyla Kern a year after that. Sydney could only imagine what kind of memories all the recent Lost Girls talk must be bringing back for Calum. She considered asking him about it, but their messed-up families was the one topic she and Calum never broached. "I'm glad I ran into you," she said instead, changing the subject. "I've seen you so little at school lately that I'd started to worry you'd been abducted into some mystical genius land."

"Well, I have been busy programming a new computer game I designed," Calum said excitedly. "But you're right; it's been much too long since I've witnessed you consuming inhuman levels of sugar and caffeine."

"Ha, ha." Sydney jabbed Calum playfully in the side with her elbow. He'd spent all summer teasing her about her sugar addiction, baffled that someone as obsessed with dessert as she was could be so skinny. Genetics, she always told him. Her mom was the same way.

"I had tofu lasagna for dinner tonight, thank you very much," she sniffed.

"I'll believe that when I see it." A blond curl flopped into Calum's eyes, and he absently pushed it away. "I think I have a remedy to our problem," he announced. "Isn't there a new gallery on Art Walk? Galileo Gallery? Let's go check it out this week."

Sydney raised her eyebrows at him. Art Walk was a long line of galleries in Echo Bay's downtown area, owned by and featuring mostly local artists. It was one of her favorite things about her hometown: the abundance of artists who lived there. But whereas Sydney was all right brain, Calum was all left—the top science and math student in Winslow Academy, with a practically guaranteed acceptance into MIT in the fall. No surprise, really, considering who his dad was. Sam Bauer was a self-made tech billionaire who was supposedly now working on a high-profile project for government security. Not exactly the type to frequent Art Walk. "You want to go to a *gallery*?"

Calum shrugged. "I figure if I'm ever going to like a gallery, it will be that one. Galileo is my people, after all."

Sydney burst out laughing. "Does that make Ansel Adams my people?"

"We should set up a double date sometime," Calum quipped.

"Sure, I'll just give Ansel a call." Sydney rolled her eyes dramatically.

"You jest," Calum said, pointing a finger at her, "but I think you are a lot like Mr. Adams, Syd. There are all these imitators and wannabes out there. Just copycats, you know? But you're the real thing." He smiled at her, looking almost shy. "A real artist."

Sydney froze. She barely heard the compliment; she was too stuck on what he'd said before that.

Imitators and wannabes. *Copycats.*

Her palms began to sweat.

Of course.

"The gallery sounds great," she told Calum hastily. "But I should probably get going. My mom will be home from her hospital shift soon." She said a quick good-bye before hurrying to her car.

What Calum had said had given her an idea. Whoever was doing this was *imitating* Tricia. A copycat. Which meant it had to be someone who knew her... probably well.

Maybe this could help them! It gave her a shot of hope as she sped toward her apartment. More than anything, she missed her old life. A life where she didn't have Tenley Reed breathing down her neck about parties—or cops. A life where RISD actually seemed within reach. A life where she never had to interact with Emerson Cunningham, the girl who'd once spilled an entire grape soda on her freshman year and never bothered to apologize. It didn't surprise her that her dad had chosen the most shallow girl in her grade to have an affair with, but Sydney should at least have the luxury of being able to *ignore* her. If Emerson was getting dares now, too, though, that would be impossible.

They had to figure out who this copycat darer was before this went any further. And she had the perfect first step. She swung her car into her apartment's lot and slammed to a stop. Grabbing her phone, she opened up a text to Tenley. *New mission: Start looking into Tricia's inner circle at school tomorrow. We HAVE to find this darer.*

Inside her apartment building, she stopped by the mailboxes, knowing there was probably several days' worth of mail piled up inside. On a good day her mom tended to forget such minutiae as getting the mail or going to the grocery store, or where exactly she'd left her keys. And thanks to her budding reconciliation with Sydney's dad, she'd been more distracted than ever lately. Just the thought made Sydney's blood boil.

So many times this past month Sydney had wanted to tell her mom about Emerson. Tracey Morgan had this stubborn blindness when it came to her ex-husband, and sometimes Sydney thought a cold, hard dose of the truth was the only cure. But at the last minute she always stopped herself. She'd seen the pain that settled into the lines of her mom's face whenever Sydney's dad let her down in the past. She couldn't be the one to do that to her again. So, instead, she'd stood idly by while her mom spiraled deeper and deeper into the black hole of Matt Morgan.

Sydney turned her focus back to the mailbox. It was packed, just as she'd predicted. She reached in to gather up the envelopes when she noticed a small velvet jewelry box perched on top of the pile. The jewelry box wasn't in a package, and it had no postage on it. Someone had hand-delivered it. A card sat underneath.

Sydney went icy cold all over. The darer had already targeted Tenley and Emerson tonight. This had to be her turn. Slowly, she reached for the card. Her fingers were stiff as she flipped it open.

Her whole body relaxed. The card had been printed off a regular computer. There wasn't a typewriter letter in sight.

S: Something blue to cure your blues.

She frowned. What did *that* mean?

Curious, she popped open the jewelry box. Inside, nestled on a bed of white silk, was a stunning ring. It was simple—a round sapphire set on a thin, gold band—but the stone itself was incredible: a deep, midnight blue and filled with facets. She couldn't resist slipping it on. It fit perfectly.

"Guinness," she murmured. It had to be from him. He was the only person she knew who could afford a ring this nice. He'd been calling her nonstop lately, and she hadn't picked up once. This must be his attempt at making her listen. She bit down on her lip. After her mom had given her the gold band she always wore on her pointer finger as a symbol of better times ahead, Guinness had joked that one day he'd give her his own "symbol," and he promised it wouldn't be a plain band. Of course, he would choose a blue stone—a reminder of his nickname for her. *Blue*, in honor of the turquoise-blue eyes he claimed made her so photogenic. Guinness knew where she and her mom kept their extra mail key; he could have easily found a way to sneak this into their mailbox sometime in the past few days.

Sydney touched a finger to the ring, a thousand emotions charging through her at once. She was touched and a little thrilled and, at the same time, so, so sad. Because as beautiful as the ring was, and as sweet as the gesture was, it wouldn't change a thing. It couldn't. She'd ended things with Guinness for a reason. He'd treated her poorly, taken her for granted. No matter how much she missed him, she had to stick to that decision. She'd watched her mom become a living doormat. She had no plans for a repeat performance of her own.

The sound of a door slamming jolted her back to the present. She started, bumping her shoulder into the mailboxes. A minute later old Mr. Lehman limped by, giving her a toothless smile as he passed.

Sydney sagged against the wall. It was just a neighbor; no darer in sight. But that didn't mean there wouldn't be soon. She slid the ring off her finger, placing it gently back in its box. She had bigger things to think about than Guinness.

The copycat darer was out there... maybe even watching her. And until she figured out who it was, she had to be on the lookout, too.

CHAPTER FOUR
Tuesday, 6:25 AM

EMERSON STARED DOWN AT HER MAKEUP BOX. SHE'D woken up before her alarm, and she knew the early morning would show on her face. But her thoughts had been too frenzied to give sleep another go. She couldn't stop rehashing the events of last night. The text, the package, and, of course, Tenley's late-night call. She'd told Emerson about Sydney's theory: This new darer was acting too much like Tricia not to have known her... maybe even well.

Emerson grabbed absently at several tubes of makeup. She hated having anything to do with Sydney. Just hearing her name sent waves of shame rolling through her. It didn't matter that Sydney was completely in the dark about the affair. She was still a walking, talking reminder of Emerson's mistake. If Sydney had bothered her before—was it really normal for anyone to wear plaid flannel *that* often?—it had gotten ten times worse these past few months. Being around Sydney Morgan was like hearing nails scrape down a chalkboard. Again and again and again.

Still, she had to admit Sydney made a good point. Whoever was doing this clearly knew Tricia's moves. Plus, the rabbit's foot that had been returned to her had been missing for over a month—since before Tricia's death. Either this darer had been around all along, or he or she had known Tricia well enough to be able to pilfer her spoils. All night long Emerson had tossed and turned, trying to think of who had been closest to Tricia. Every time, she came back to the same person: Sean. They'd been dating before she died. If anyone knew what Tricia was up to, it was Sean Hale.

Emerson hated the idea that one of her own friends could be doing this, but when she'd texted Tenley a few minutes ago, they'd both agreed: They couldn't overlook it. They were going to poke around at lunch today, see if Sean seemed at all suspicious. Tenley had brought up going to the cops, too, but she'd agreed to hold off until they looked into Sean. If they could just find this darer and put an end to this…it would be best for everyone.

Makeup in hand, she walked over to the mirror and faced it head-on. "Okay," she said out loud. "Time to beautify." She stared grimly at the circles under her eyes. "Status: ER." Emerson had been talking herself through getting ready for as long as she could remember. She knew it was silly, but when your mom was not just a model but one of the first African American models to rise to supermodel stardom, sometimes you needed a pep talk to get through primping.

"Emmy?" Her dad's voice floated up from downstairs. "You coming to breakfast?"

Emerson tensed at the sound of her old nickname. When she and her family had lived in Sarasota, Florida, everyone called her Emmy. Emmy, the too-tall, frizzy-haired, acne-faced daughter of a supermodel. When she moved to Echo Bay in ninth grade, having finally

42

grown into her looks and out of her acne, she decided she was done with Emmy. She would be *Em* now, a new name for a new start. The modeling contract she scored with Neutrogena the summer after her sophomore year helped. The only part *Emmy* could have played in a Neutrogena commercial was the "before." It was proof she was really, truly a new girl.

"Be down in a few!" she yelled back to her dad. He was probably already in the kitchen, waiting for her as he did every morning. Their *us* time, he called it. It used to be her favorite part of the day. No matter what else was going on in her life, she knew she could always count on those fifteen minutes with her dad each morning. But lately her dad's concern had been almost suffocating, especially after her fling with Matt ended. If her dad ever found out who the "mystery boy" she'd been dating really was...her stomach flip-flopped. It wouldn't be just Sydney's family in ruins.

A good scrub with Neutrogena and half a dozen tubes of makeup later, Emerson looked more like herself. It helped that she'd straightened her hair yesterday. Otherwise, she'd be spending the next hour trying to tame it. Going into her closet, she quickly pulled together an outfit: a pair of stretchy black jeans with a black-and-white printed shirt and red flats lined with tiny gold studs. At the last minute she added a chunky gold necklace before returning to the mirror. Clothes, at least, were one thing she never had to think twice about. She might not have been born with a math or science gene, but there was no doubt she'd inherited the fashion gene.

Sometimes she found it hard to believe that this model-girl with glossy black hair and smooth, toffee-colored skin was really her. With her makeup on and all dressed up, Emmy was just a thing of the past. All except her eyes, of course. Emerson looked at the hazel eyes reflecting back at her from the mirror, eyes she'd inherited from her blond-haired, pale-skinned dad. They were the one thing about her that had never changed. Her mom claimed they gave her the "exotic look" the modeling scouts had pounced on.

Satisfied with her appearance, Emerson grabbed Big Foot off her dresser. She'd been so creeped out when she'd found it on her porch last night with the note. But she hadn't been able to make herself throw it out. The pink rabbit's foot had been her lucky charm for years. There wasn't much in Emerson's life she was sure about; she had no idea where she wanted to go to college, and she certainly couldn't picture where she'd be five years from now. But she *was* sure about one thing: It was never good to tempt fate. Throwing out your rabbit's foot was up there with black cats and walking under a ladder. She dropped Big Foot into her backpack. Maybe it would give her and Tenley the luck they needed to stop this new darer.

Emerson's dad was waiting for her at the kitchen table, just as she knew he'd be. His light blond hair was long and uncombed, and he had a few days' worth of blond stubble on his chin. It was his go-to look when he was in the middle of revisions for his latest novel. Emerson could hear her mom in the other room pounding away on the treadmill, running her daily five miles.

"Well, if it isn't my nocturnal daughter," her dad teased. "Back to her old ways. Mom and I tried to wait up for you last night, but it was a futile effort."

"I was home before ten, Dad," Emerson said, rolling her eyes as she grabbed a yogurt out of the fridge.

Her dad sighed dramatically. "I guess that means your mom and I have finally become old-timers. Or is the new terminology 'parental dweebs'? I never can keep up."

"I think both are accurate," Emerson said, unable to keep from smiling.

"Victory!" Her dad pumped his fist into the air. "Guess what, Grace!" he shouted in the direction of the den, where her mom was working out. "Theodore Aurelius Cunningham has succeeded in making his daughter smile!"

Emerson's smile widened. "You're such a parental dweeb, Dad."

"A parental what, now?" Emerson's mom wiped a line of sweat off her brow as she jogged into the kitchen to fill up her water bottle.

"Dweeb," her dad replied. "It's our new classification, honey. Better get used to it."

Her mom arched a perfectly plucked eyebrow. She was puffing and sweat-drenched, her curly hair pulled back by a scarf, and, still, she looked beautiful. That was Grace Cunningham for you. She didn't have a bad side, or a bad morning. Sometimes it made Emerson hate her—which then, of course, made her feel awful. "I suppose it's better than 'geek,'" her mom mused. She took a swig of water as she turned to Emerson. "Did you have fun last night, honey?"

Emerson tried not to flinch. *Fun* was the last thing she'd call it. She spooned up some yogurt. "It was a nice party," she said, choosing her words carefully.

The doorbell rang, making her mom tense. "If that's another reporter, I might need to be restrained," her mom said with a snarl. In the weeks after Caitlin's and Tricia's deaths, reporter after reporter had come knocking on the Cunninghams' door, angling for an interview with the girls' heartbroken best friend. A best friend who just so happened to have famous parents.

"Now, honey, remember what we said about strangling reporters with your bare hands," Emerson's dad joked. He scraped his chair back, but Emerson waved him back down.

"I can handle this one," she told him. "I've got my 'no comment' down pat."

She squared her shoulders as she threw open the front door. "No comm—" she began. But when she saw who was standing on the porch, the rest of the word tangled in her throat.

Josh.

She opened her mouth again, but no sound came out. He looked exactly the same as he had her summer in New York, taller than her by a good four inches, with broad shoulders and wiry muscles from all the pickup games of basketball he played. He was wearing a beat-up, army-green jacket, and he had the same half Mohawk he used to have, which he'd always claimed was *completely* different from a fauxhawk.

He gave her a tentative smile. He had a tiny gap between his teeth and a crook in his nose, but instead of looking bad, they just made him look more *him*. "I take it you were expecting someone else." It was his voice: low and teasing, edged in gravel. She had hoped a year and two new relationships would have desensitized her to it, toughened her skin into a protective hide, but instantly it set her pulse racing.

"You could say that," Emerson managed. She shifted nervously. He was watching her with his green-brown eyes, which were like a mood ring, changing colors so fast it was hard to look away. The sight of him still gave her that fizzy feeling: electricity running through her veins. "I—I'm sorry I didn't respond to your texts."

A month ago Josh had texted her out of nowhere, asking if they could talk. The very next night, Caitlin died, and talking with anyone became the last thing Em wanted to do. He texted her a few more times after that, all variations on the same question. Instead of responding, she'd deleted them one by one.

"I didn't know you were in Echo Bay," she added.

"That was what I wanted to talk to you about...." He topped off the sentence with a shrug. "But since you never responded, I figured it was time for more drastic measures. So I brought you something." His hands had been clasped behind his back, but now he slowly stretched one out in front of him.

Sitting atop his palm was a fuzzy yellow duckling. It had orange webbed paws; a tiny, pale beak; and round black eyes, which locked onto Emerson. *Chirp*, it went.

"Meet my bribe," Josh said with a grin. "Holden."

The name brought on a hot rush of memories. Emerson took a deep breath, barring their entrance. "You brought me a *duckling*?" she asked dumbly.

"I brought you a duckling," Josh confirmed. He was wearing his you-amuse-me smirk, the one Emerson used to love to elicit. "You might be able to ignore me, but how can you say no to this face?" He lifted his palm so Emerson was nose to beak with the duck. Its wide black eyes blinked sleepily. Emerson stretched out a finger and stroked its fuzzy yellow back. The duckling twisted around and nipped at her finger with a cheerful *chirp*. A laugh slipped out of her.

"Just as I thought," Josh said smugly.

Before Emerson could muster up a response, her mom called out from the kitchen. "Everything okay, Em? You're going to be late for school!"

"Just say the word if you need reinforcements!" her dad chimed in.

"I'm fine!" Emerson called back. "It's just a, uh...friend stopping by." She turned to Josh. "My mom's right, I've got to get to school."

"You could always use the ever-popular my-duckling-ate-my-late-note excuse," Josh offered.

Emerson shook her head. "I don't think that will fly. Or, ahem, *swim*."

47

Josh laughed. "Ah, there's the Emerson Cunningham humor I missed."

Emerson looked down, her cheeks flushing. After she'd bolted from New York the summer before last, Josh left her so many messages like that, telling her again and again how much he missed her. She ached to call him back after every one, to tell him she missed him just as much. But she couldn't, because then she'd have to answer his questions, the ones that were piling up in her e-mails, her texts, her voice mails. *Why did you leave? What went wrong?* There were answers, of course; just not ones she wanted him to hear.

She coughed, clearing her throat. "I really do have to run," she mumbled.

"Wait." Josh grabbed her arm with his duckling-free hand, and that fizzy feeling shot through her again. "I just want a chance for us to talk, Em. An hour, that's all I'm asking. If not for me, then for Holden." Josh gave her an exaggeratedly pleading look, pressing the duckling against his cheek. "You do remember that day, right? With the ducks?"

"Of course I remember," Emerson said quietly. It was one of those memories that had become part of her artillery, a weapon to draw when the world came at her from all sides. "All right," she gave in. "An hour. I'll call you later, okay?"

Josh nodded, looking satisfied. "Here." He passed Holden to Emerson. The duckling was warm and cashmere-soft. She could feel his tiny heart beating against her palm. "Just wait one second and I'll get his stuff."

"He has *stuff*?" Emerson repeated. "Please don't tell me you packed him a suitcase."

Emerson looked down at the tiny animal in her hands as Josh jogged off the porch. Holden was wiggling a little, and his webbed feet tickled her skin. "Hi there, little guy," she whispered. He pecked at her wrist in response.

"No suitcase, but I did come prepared," Josh announced. He returned holding a bag of food and a small cage. The floor of the cage was covered in newspaper. A water bowl sat in the corner, and there was a small lightbulb affixed to the top. "Home and sustenance," he explained, placing it all on the ground.

"So you still don't half-ass things," Emerson said. She bit down on her lip, trying not to be amused.

Josh ran a hand through his half Mohawk. "You can thank me later," he replied breezily. "When you call me."

The second he was gone, she collapsed in a porch chair, cradling Holden gingerly in her hands. Her head was suddenly a minefield of thoughts.

Josh was *here*, in Echo Bay. He wanted to spend time with her.

He was going to want answers.

Emerson's chest tightened. The summer she'd spent modeling in New York, she and Josh had been inseparable. She was drawn to him right away; he was nothing like Echo Bay boys, or Sarasota boys, for that matter. He did things like go to the theater and read novels in Central Park and eat food like *bibimbap* and *shawarma*, things Emerson had never even heard of. He wore tighter jeans and used bigger words, and he had once spent an entire summer building houses in Africa. Being around him was like discovering an amazing new flavor of ice cream every day.

Emerson was different around him, too—freer somehow. She told him things she'd told no one else, not even Caitlin. Like how she used to be *Emmy*, the ugly duckling—and how sometimes, when she was having a crappy day, she still felt like that girl, the duckling that no one wanted.

49

The day after she admitted that, Josh took her to the Pond in Central Park. He sat her down on the edge of the water, handed her a full loaf of bread, and ordered her to start feeding the ducks. They stayed there for over two hours, laughing as the ducks swished their way through the water, fighting over crusts and squawking with joy. A few minutes before they left, he turned to her, smiling thoughtfully. "You know," he said, "if I had to choose, I'd pick the duckling."

"Oh, come on," she teased, poking him in the side. "Over a swan?"

Josh leaned in, kissing the tip of her nose. "Over a swan," he said. And even though it was a cloudy day and she'd barely slept the night before and Josh kept making Holden Caulfield *Catcher in the Rye* comments that went completely over her head, it became one of her favorite days of the whole summer.

"Em?" Her mom's voice jolted Emerson back to the present. Her mom stepped onto the porch, letting the door slam shut behind her. "What are you—oh my god, is that a *duck*?"

"Yeah...my friend brought it over. As kind of a, uh, prank gift. He's cute, though, isn't he?" She gave her mom a hopeful smile, and Holden snapped his beak, as if to agree.

Her mom wrinkled her nose. "Sure, as long as he's not peeing on you. Aren't ducks supposed to be bathroom machines?"

"I guess you'll find out." Emerson held Holden out to her mom. "Unless, of course, you'll let me skip school to take care of him..."

"Fat chance." With a grimace, her mom took Holden from Emerson. Immediately the duckling stretched out his neck and pecked at her cheek. "Go ahead," she said, waving Emerson away with a sigh. "I'll take care of him. But"—she pointed a warning finger at Emerson—"starting tonight, you take over, or he goes back to whatever pond he came from."

Emerson gave her mom a quick kiss on the cheek before hurrying to her car. The same thought circled endlessly around in her head. *Josh is in Echo Bay.* It made her feel as if she were being thrown up in a basket toss: One way or another, she had to come down.

There was some kind of promotional postcard tucked under her car's windshield wiper, and she reached for it absently, still thinking about Josh. But the moment she saw the front of the postcard, all other thoughts vanished instantly.

It was for the Seagull Inn. Also known as the place where she and Matt had spent the night together this summer. She blinked, feeling light-headed. Why was this on her car?

Her breath came out in fast spurts as she flipped the card over. On one side, the text boasted about seaside rooms and reasonable rates, but it barely registered. Because on the other side was a message. In a typewriter font.

Once a slut, always a slut. Go enjoy
some old-fashioned fun aboard Echo Bay's
Haunted Boat Ride...unless you want
everyone to know how you fanned the fire
chief's flames. The ship sails at 9!

Warning sirens blasted in Emerson's head. Who was *doing* this? And whoever it was...how could he or she know? She hadn't told anyone the identity of her mystery guy, not even Caitlin. And she and Matt had been so careful not to be seen! It was why they'd gone to the Seagull Inn; only out-of-towners stayed there.

Matt's words flashed through her mind. *It's not just me I'm worried about; it's Sydney.* If this got out, if Matt lost his job and Sydney lost her scholarship . . . it would be all her fault.

Once a slut, always a slut.

Emerson squeezed her eyes shut. She always did this: made the wrong choices, took the wrong path. With Matt, with Josh . . .

The memory slammed into her so hard she could feel it in her bones. *New York. The kind of hot August day that smothered you in its breath.* Emerson shuddered, using every ounce of her strength to shut out the image. She couldn't think about that now. Not with this new darer to contend with. Her hands shook with anger as she shoved the postcard into the trash can in the driveway and climbed into her car.

The darer wanted her on some stupid haunted boat ride?

Fine, she'd be there. And hopefully the darer—whoever it was— would be, too.

CHAPTER FIVE
Tuesday, 12:08 PM

TENLEY PAUSED IN THE DOORWAY OF THE CAFETERIA, the din of voices and clattering trays rising around her. Those first few steps into the lunchroom had become her least favorite moment of each day. So many bodies, her eyes flying from one to another until it was all just a blur: hands and arms and mouths, opening, closing, opening, closing. And then, like clockwork, it would happen: a flash of blond hair. Her breath would catch, and she'd think, *Caitlin*.

But then her eyes would focus, and she'd see it was just some freshman, or sophomore, or even a teacher—her hair stringy or bleached, as far from Caitlin as you could get. Now, as Tenley stood in the doorway of the cafeteria, her eyes locked on a bottle-blond girl, she could feel a flood of memories threatening to break through their dam. "Gabby Douglas, London," she chanted under her breath. "Nastia Liukin, Beijing. Carly Patterson, Athens." It was her new method for battling back her memories: reciting the Olympic all-around gymnastic gold medalists. Usually, by the time she reached Carly, she'd gotten herself under control. But sometimes it took going all the way back to Mary Lou Retton of 1984.

When she looked up again, she saw Marta waving at her from the table where she and Emerson always sat. Reserved for the most popular seniors, the table was set on a raised platform from the days when the cafeteria used to be a theater. Marta tossed her wavy red hair as she signaled for Tenley to join them.

Tenley squared her shoulders, smoothing down the zipper that ran up the front of her red dress. She wouldn't let them see her weakness. She'd lived by that rule her whole life: after her dad's death, after Caitlin's kidnapping, after her move to Nevada. She wasn't about to fail it now. Plastering on a smile, she marched over to the table. She'd gotten stuck talking to her English teacher after class, so most of her friends were already there. Hunter, Tyler, Nate, Marta, Emerson, and, in Tricia's old seat, Jessie. Sean wasn't there yet, but she caught sight of him in the hot-food line, waiting to fill his tray.

"Hey, Tenley, hold up!"

Tenley looked over her shoulder to see Tim crossing the cafeteria, a brown-bag lunch in his hand. He was wearing beat-up jeans and a white T-shirt, and his messy bed-head hair looked especially blond against his dark tan. He stopped in front of her, and in the bright lights of the cafeteria, she could see all the different shades of blue in his eyes. It reminded her of the ocean at dusk, the way the surface was always changing. "You're gracing the school with your presence?" she asked, feigning shock.

"I had to come make sure my surfboard didn't cause any permanent damage." His eyes ran over her, and she found herself wondering if he was checking her out. She quickly straightened up to her full five foot two. In her gymnastics days, she'd had a figure that was more boyish than boy magnet. But ever since she got her implants, her shape had drawn a lot more attention. Most of the time she loved it, but sometimes it made her feel like an impostor in her own body. "I don't believe I detect a limp," he said.

"Nope." She silently chided herself for being ridiculous. Of course he wasn't checking her out. "Just a bruise the size of Texas on my hip. But I'm sure it will heal." She shuddered dramatically. *"Eventually."*

Tim laughed. "Poor baby. Well, tell your bruise I owe it an apology coffee."

"I'm sure it will be pleased," Tenley said solemnly.

"Hey...in all seriousness." Tim lowered his eyes, suddenly very focused on his flip-flops. "It was great talking last night. About Cait. I haven't really had anyone to do that with. Just saying it out loud kind of helped, you know?"

"I do." Tim's voice had grown almost reverential when he'd mentioned Cait, and Tenley was surprised to feel a tiny twinge of jealousy. Her face flushed, and she quickly cleared her throat, willing the feeling away. "Well, you know where to find me if you're ever looking for a repeat performance. A little-known place called 'school.'"

Tim laughed. "Hey, want to come eat with us?" He pointed toward a table a ways down, where his joined-at-the-hip surfer friends, Tray Macintyre and Sam Spencer, were laughing as they watched a freshman attempt to spoon up the hot-food line's chili using a broken ladle. "I could probably cough up a pudding cup for your bruise...."

"It would have to be tapioca," Tenley replied. She tossed her hair over her shoulder. "That's all my bruise eats."

Tim pulled a tapioca pudding cup out of his lunch bag. "You ask, I deliver."

Tenley considered saying yes, ditching her friends, and spending forty-two minutes listening to surfing talk. But she couldn't back out on the plan she'd hatched with Emerson. They were going to feel out Sean during lunch today. As Tricia's boyfriend, he'd been the person closest to her before she died. He was their best bet at finding this darer. "I think my friends already saved me a seat," she told Tim.

Tim nodded understandingly. "I wouldn't want to deprive them."

"They would be devastated," Tenley agreed. "But...maybe we can talk more sometime. About Caitlin," she added quickly.

She felt a strange pang of disappointment as she carried her own bagged lunch over to her friends' table. She'd never been into surfing, but the idea of listening to a debate over wave size sounded almost blissful right now. It didn't matter, though; she had a job to do.

"How could this *happen*?" Marta was saying as Tenley took a seat at the table. Emerson was sitting on the other side, twisting a strand of thick black hair around her finger. She exchanged a tense glance with Tenley. "Have you seen this, Ten?" Marta asked. She pushed a pink sheet of paper over to her. "Abby's official Homecoming Nomination Memo. She just stuck them in everyone's locker."

Tenley studied the memo. There were four girls nominated: Delancey Crane, Emerson Cunningham, Sydney Morgan, and Tenley Reed. So it was official. She was on the ballot. She'd thought she'd be thrilled to see her name there, proof that she was truly part of Winslow again. But she felt strangely empty inside.

"*Sydney Morgan?*" Marta continued. "Is this some kind of joke?"

"Seriously," Jessie chimed in. "Marta was robbed. Hunter, Sean, Tyler, and Nate are all nominated; you should definitely be on there, too, Mart."

"So should you!" Marta exclaimed. "You're captain of the freaking cheer squad. How did Sydney get nominated over you?"

"Maybe she got the artsy vote," Nate offered.

"All eight of them?" Tenley joked as she dug into her sandwich.

It *was* surprising that Sydney had been nominated. She'd grown on Tenley this past month—being hounded by Tricia had made them unlikely allies—but she wasn't exactly popular at Winslow. She spent most lunch periods in the darkroom, and her only real friend seemed to be super-nerd Calum Bauer.

"You've got to see this, too, Ten," Tyler said. He grabbed a second sheet of paper out of Hunter's hand. "I saw Abby hanging them up."

"Please tell me it's not about that stupid statewide Purity Club contest," Tenley groaned. Abby had been publicly obsessing over the contest for weeks now. Something about winning an all-expenses-paid spa trip.

"For once, no." Tyler slid the paper across the table. "Apparently, Abby's already started campaigning for Delancey."

Marta rolled her eyes. "As if advertising the Purity Club is going to get anyone elected homecoming queen."

Tenley looked down at the flyer. It showed a photo of Delancey working with the Red Cross in the aftermath of Hurricane Sandy. PURE HEART, PURE MOTIVES, PURE REIGN, it read.

"I think Abby wants to turn homecoming queen into purity queen," Hunter said.

"I bet she puts a big gold *P* on the crown this year," Tenley grumbled.

As she said it, she glanced over at Emerson. Em's expression told her she was thinking the same thing Tenley was: This was as good an opening as any, especially since Sean was on his way over. "I wonder what Tricia would have thought of this," Tenley said. She struggled to use her saddest voice. Bringing up Tricia at lunch made her feel like Cruella De Vil. She might as well have been shoving a storm cloud directly over their table. But she didn't have a choice. She took a deep breath, channeling her beauty-pageant persona: the girl who could perform a flawless rhythmic gymnastics routine in the middle of a burning building. "Tricia was also in Purity Club for a while, right?"

"Freshman and sophomore year," Marta answered. "Before she was friends with us."

"Before she lost all that weight," Jessie added.

"Do any of you know what she was like back then?" Tenley asked. She gave Hunter her best wide-eyed, heartbroken gaze. If she could get Hunter to open up about Tricia, then Sean would be forced to join in when he sat down. She could practically feel the neon BITCH sign stamped across her forehead, but she clenched her jaw, refusing to back down. If there was one thing she'd learned about life, it was that sometimes you had to be a bitch to get what you wanted.

"Don't look at me," Hunter said with a shrug. "I thought she was a new student last year. It took me a whole week to realize the girl I kept hitting on was Fatty Patty."

"And then only another week to get her in bed," Tenley joked. She leaned across the table, flashing Hunter her flirtiest smile. "I can only imagine what other hookup secrets you're hiding, Hunter Bailey."

She expected Hunter to laugh, or even preen—she knew how much he loved his playboy rep—but, instead, he flinched. Tenley bit down on her lip, worried she'd taken it too far. "I'm kidding," she said quickly. "I know you really cared about her." Out of the corner of her eye, she watched Sean climb the steps up to their table. "You and Sean both did."

"Both did what?" Sean asked.

"We were just talking about Tricia," Emerson told Sean as he took a seat.

Sean dipped a french fry into a pile of ketchup. "Everyone's favorite topic these days."

"It's just sad to think how much we didn't know about her," Tenley said. A distraught look crossed Sean's face, making Tenley falter. *Pageant persona*, she reminded herself. Somewhere, lying in wait, was a psychotic stalker who wanted her hurt—maybe even dead. That was bigger than anything, even Sean's feelings. "I mean, there was this whole part of her that changed when she became friends with you guys, right?" she continued. "Did she ever open up about that time?"

Hunter snorted. "Only to make fun of it."

"What about with you, Sean?" Tenley popped a chip into her mouth, doing her best to act casual. "You guys dated for a while. Did she talk to you about that kind of stuff?"

"Of course she did," Sean said. He gave Tenley a strange look. "Why the sudden interest? Was there another Lost Girl tell-all on TV last night?"

"No," Tenley assured him. It's just..." She paused, summoning up her best lie. "I was only getting to know this new her. That's all."

"We all were, really," Marta said softly.

Next to her, Emerson sighed, clearly putting on an act of her own. "We had more time with her than Tenley did, though."

"Not enough time," Sean said sharply. He stood up, grabbing his backpack. His sandwich sat untouched on his tray. "I just remembered I have some homework to finish up," he mumbled. Keeping his head down, he stalked across the cafeteria and disappeared into the hallway.

Tenley watched him go. The guilt she'd managed to stomp flat suddenly twisted to life. She knew what it felt like to have Cait's memory dismembered and dissected like some rat on a lab table. It was a knife directly to the chest, every single time. And here she was doing exactly that to Sean, putting on a *performance*. Her turkey sandwich rose in her throat. What had she done? He was obviously in pain.

Wasn't he?

She cocked her head, thinking about how he'd snapped at her, the way his voice had taken on a sharp edge. It definitely could have been pain.

Or it could have been anger.

Had Sean just pulled off as believable a performance as she had? Maybe it was more than grief that drove him from the table. Maybe it was anger—anger at the very people Tricia had targeted.

Marta's wide blue eyes flitted disapprovingly over to Tenley. "I think we all need to be a little more sensitive in front of Sean."

Emerson jumped to her feet. "You're right. I'll go check on him." She hurried out of the cafeteria, shooting Tenley a pointed look on her way out.

"Sean's had a rough go of it lately," Nate said, shaking his head. "On top of everything, Coach has been riding him pretty hard. Told him he'd bench him if he missed another practice."

Tenley leaned forward in her seat, suddenly on high alert. "Sean's been missing practices?"

"More than he's been coming to them," Hunter said.

"Of course he has, guys," Jessie chided. "Marta's right; we all need to be more sensitive. He just lost his *girlfriend*."

"Believe me, we've all been saying that, too." Tyler draped his arm around Jessie's shoulders. A strand of black hair fell into his eyes. "And Coach did let it slide for a while. But, like it or not, we have a game to win."

"A big one," Hunter added. He pounded his fists against the table. "Kick Anaswan's ass, and our season will get a serious boost."

As the boys launched into a detailed analysis of their chances against Anaswan, Tenley's thoughts drifted. Either Sean was putting on a really good show, or he was truly a grieving boyfriend. Either way, he could be their darer. Tenley knew firsthand how grief could do that—tear you down and knot you up until you were just a twisted shell, someone else altogether. It made her think of her dad; when she'd lost him, she'd felt as if she'd never be whole again.

She spent the rest of the day obsessing over the possibility. If Sean was the darer, then he was the one who'd thrown bottles at her head—tried to hurt her. But why? Could he be angry about the things she had done before she left Echo Bay, like Tricia had been?

In middle school, Tenley and her friends had tortured Tricia—Fatty Patty at the time—taunting her tirelessly with fat jokes and forcing her to take an awful dare during one of their games of truth or dare. It was why Tricia had targeted Tenley and Caitlin in the first place: to get back at them for how they'd treated her. But Sean hadn't even gone to their school back then. Besides, that was a long time ago. Whenever she thought of the way she used to torment Tricia and Joey Bakersfield and even Sydney, it made her feel itchy inside, as if a thousand spiders had taken up residence under her skin. She was a different person now.

But maybe Sean didn't know that. Or maybe he didn't care. Once a sinner, always a sinner. If he loved Tricia enough, he might want to finish her dirty work for her no matter what it meant.

Between periods, Tenley dragged Emerson into the bathroom, hoping to get more answers. But Emerson hadn't learned anything new. Apparently, Sean was nowhere to be found after he left the cafeteria, and he wasn't answering his phone. Emerson had called his house, and his mom had said he'd come home sick and couldn't talk.

"Enough," Tenley declared. "I say we drop the witch hunt and take this to the cops instead."

"We might as well transfer schools now if we do that," Emerson snapped. "Because soon everyone here will know our secrets."

Tenley's curiosity flared, but before she could discover what the darer had over Miss Neutrogena Model herself, Emerson stalked to the bathroom door.

"Leave Sean to me," she insisted. "I know him best. I'll find a way to get him to talk. Until then, no cops."

The door swung shut as Tenley slumped against the sink. Sydney was on the no-cop bandwagon, too, which meant it was two against one. She'd have to give in. For now.

By the time the final bell of the day rang, Tenley felt as if her brain had been stuffed with cotton balls and then put through the blender. To make it worse, her old shoulder injury from gymnastics had stiffened up, thanks to a volleyball game in gym class. All she wanted was to go home and take a nice, long soak in the hot tub—try to wipe the darer from her mind and the pain from her shoulder. But in between classes she had gotten a call from Caitlin's mom. Mrs. Thomas had asked her to stop by after school to pick up some of Caitlin's things she'd put aside for her. The idea of going to Caitlin's house made Tenley more tense than ever, but she couldn't find it in her to say no to Mrs. Thomas. One pit stop, then she was making a beeline to the hot tub.

When Tenley arrived at Caitlin's house, she was surprised to find a note tacked to the door.

Tenley—

I had to run out, but the box is in Cait's room. You know where the key is.

Jaynie

Curt and to the point, just like Jaynie Thomas. Caitlin couldn't have been more different from her mom. The only time Tenley ever saw a soft side to Mrs. Thomas was in the sea-glass window hangings she made for her gallery. Tenley glanced at the bay window that overlooked the Thomases' porch. Mrs. Thomas always used it as a display for her latest creation.

The piece that hung there today was different from her usual creations: darker, filled with deep, saturated hues of blues and blacks. When a cloud passed, the collage looked dull and opaque, almost impenetrable. But in the sun it brightened instantly, as if there were a light shining deep inside it.

Tenley tore her eyes away and walked over to the row of galvanized metal flowerpots that lined the porch. For as long as she could remember, the Thomases had kept their spare key in the middle one. At least one thing hadn't changed.

As soon as she opened the door, the Thomases' dog, Sailor, threw himself at her, yapping at her heels as she traipsed slowly upstairs. She scooped him up and buried her face in his fur as she paused outside Caitlin's bedroom. She hadn't been inside since before the crash.

Taking a deep breath, she flung the door open. The smell hit her first. Caitlin's flowery perfume lingered on every surface. It made her feel so present, as if all Tenley had to do was pull back an invisible veil, and there Cait would be, lounging on her bed and laughing at Sailor. Tenley took one step inside, then another, squeezing Sailor tight in her arms. There was Caitlin's old beanbag chair and Caitlin's line of framed photos and Caitlin's Harvard flag taped up above her desk. Memories rushed at her one after another, an onslaught. "Gabby Douglas, London," she chanted under her breath. "Nastia Liukin, Beijing. Carly Patterson, Athens." But it was useless.

Suddenly she was eight years old and playing dolls on Caitlin's bed. She was ten years old and waking up in a sleeping bag on Caitlin's floor. She was twelve years old and daring Caitlin to call her crush and claim to be Ivana Kissyu.

Tenley made a choked noise. Sailor twisted around in her arms and nudged her cheek with his small, wet nose. She squeezed her eyes shut. A sob welled inside her, and it took all her energy to stave it off. Slowly, she opened her eyes again. When she noticed the small box on the dresser labeled TENLEY, she blew out a sigh of relief. She put Sailor down and grabbed it. She'd look through it later. Right now, she had to get out of there.

She was almost out of the room when something on Caitlin's desk caught her eye. A small, leather-bound journal with the word DREAMS embroidered across the cover. Caitlin's dream journal. Cait had mentioned that she was keeping one, but Tenley had never seen it. She hesitated. The doorway beckoned to her, fresh air and no memories. But she couldn't look away from that journal. It was a piece of Cait: her voice, her thoughts.

She couldn't resist. Putting the box down, she picked up the journal. The pages inside were lined with Caitlin's perfect, rounded handwriting. Her eyes started to burn, but she kept flipping. Midway through the book, Caitlin had penned a detailed drawing, and Tenley paused on it. It was of a toy: a circus train. Curious, she skimmed over the entry that accompanied it.

In it Caitlin had written about one of her hypnosis sessions with her therapist, Dr. Filstone, during which she'd seen the basement where she'd been held when she was kidnapped in sixth grade. It was exactly as it was in her nightmares: red walls, red curtains, red carpet.

The color of blood. But for the first time, she'd seen something new: a beautiful, steel circus train.

Tenley turned back to the drawing. Caitlin must have spent a lot of time on it, because it was impressively detailed, from the etchings along the side to the animals peeking out through the barred windows of the caravans to the number stamped onto its back wheel: 111.

She traced a finger along its inky lines. She had the strangest feeling that she'd seen that train before somewhere. But for the life of her she couldn't remember where.

She was filled with a sudden urge to pick up her phone and call Cait, talk it over with her like she used to whenever she had a problem. But, of course, if she could do that, she wouldn't have this problem in the first place. She clamped her jaw shut, refusing to go any further down that line of thinking. Instead, she grabbed her phone and opened a new text to Marta, who'd also been close to Cait when they were younger. *Do you recognize this? From elementary school maybe?* She snapped a photo of Caitlin's drawing and attached it. *I found an old drawing and it's driving me crazy that I can't remember!!*

Marta responded quickly. *Hmmm, def familiar but not sure. Will keep thinking! XO*

Tenley took a final look at the train. She'd definitely seen it before. But *where?*

With a sigh, she flipped to the last entry in the journal. Her eyes widened when she saw the date. It had been written the day Caitlin died. She sank onto Caitlin's desk chair and pulled Sailor onto her lap. Bracing herself, she began to read.

When I woke up in the hospital this morning, I wished so badly I had this diary with me. Because the dream I had last night...it was different from all the others. It was more real, for one, the sounds louder, the colors more vivid, the images crisper. And where all the other dreams had stopped—locked the door and shut the blinds, refusing me entrance— this one kept going. I made myself picture the whole thing over and over as I lay there in my hospital bed, so I wouldn't forget a single detail. So here goes. Let's see if it worked.

I was in the same red basement. But like I said, things were clearer than they'd ever been, as if a fog had been lifted. The hooded figure came in, face concealed of course. But this time, as the figure moved closer, the hood slid off. And there was my kidnapper, in full, living color. And it wasn't Jack Hudson.

It was a woman. Tears were streaming down her face, making her mascara run. Clutched in her hands was a one-eared teddy bear. As she held it out, it hit me. I knew her. I'd seen her before. Then just like that, the dream ended. I woke up after that feeling so unsure. Had that really been a memory? Or was it just my imagination working overtime? But the more I think about it, the more convinced I become . . . It was real.

Tenley gaped down at the journal. A *woman?* On the *Justice,* Caitlin had told her that she'd figured out who her kidnapper was, that it wasn't Jack Hudson, as the cops had claimed. She'd been half unconscious at the time, coughing from smoke inhalation, so Tenley hadn't taken it very seriously. But maybe she should have.

Tenley paused, debating. Before she could change her mind, she tossed the journal into the box Mrs. Thomas had left for her. She'd return it later in the week, she promised herself. She just wanted a chance to read the rest of it first. "Our secret, okay, Sailor?" She gave Sailor a pat on the head before hurrying out of Caitlin's room, shutting the door firmly behind her.

A half hour later Tenley was in a bathing suit heading into her backyard. The stop at Caitlin's house had tightened up her shoulder even more, and she couldn't wait to get in the hot tub. She shivered a little under her towel as the cool fall air brushed against her bare shoulders. Her arms were full of provisions: Diet Coke, a bag of pretzels, and her backpack with Caitlin's journal in it. She clutched it all to her chest as she made her way to the other side of the grounds.

The woods yawned off to her right, a tangle of branches and sky. Trees sent leaves pinwheeling to the ground, flashing burgundy and gold. In the distance she could hear the faint crash of waves punctuating her footsteps. Tenley breathed in deeply, inhaling the familiar scent of dried leaves and salty ocean air. This was exactly what she needed right now: peace, quiet, and hot, foamy bubbles.

The air was crisp, but the hot water enveloped her like a blanket as she climbed into the tub. She sank back, resting her head on the rim. The water level was a little higher than usual, and a few drops spilled over the edge as the bubbles skated across her shoulders, warming her skin and unknotting her muscles. She closed her eyes. She'd read Caitlin's journal in a bit; first she needed some time to relax.

The hum of the jets was lulling, and for the first time all week she could feel her worries falling away, sinking down the drain. She was the old Tenley again, the one whose biggest concern was winning a pageant, the one whose best friend was just a few yards away, alive and well and in her bedroom. . . .

She was so relaxed, it took her a full second to register the feeling of a hand on top of her head.

What?

Her eyes flew open, but it was too late. With a hard shove, the hand pushed her underwater.

Beneath the water the bubbles distorted everything, turning the world into a twisting, fun-house mirror. Her eyes burned and her muscles screamed as she flailed desperately, struggling against the hand. Water fought its way into her mouth, setting her insides on fire as chlorine rushed down her throat and up her nose. Still, the person held on tight.

She heard the crack before she felt it. *Bam!* The hot tub lid slammed down on top of her, reverberating through her bones. Instantly, all light and air were snuffed out.

She tried to shove her head above water, but there was no gap; the water level was too high. Someone had planned this! She wanted to scream, to cough, to *breathe*, but all she could do was pound helplessly against the lid. Again and again and again. It didn't budge.

Her lungs ached. Her chest constricted. She was going to drown.

Panic lashed through her. It was a living thing, crawling down her throat and squeezing her from the inside out. Her limbs grew weighted. The world flickered in and out, like a bad connection. From deep inside the blackness, a single thought crystallized.

The darer has won.

"Tenley? You out here?"

The voice was muffled, distant. She had no idea whom it belonged to, but she didn't care. She flung herself at the lid, kicking and pounding.

"What the hell...?" The voice danced above her, drawing closer.

Her chest ached and she was spinning, spinning, but she pounded even harder. Her mind darkened, fragmenting into pieces.

The lid flew open. Sunlight and salty air rushed in.

"Oh my god, Tenley!" Hunter's face floated above her. "What happened?"

Tenley choked down big gulps of fresh air as Hunter pulled her out of the hot tub. She was coughing violently as she collapsed against the side of it, soaking wet and shivering.

"Your maid said you were in the hot tub, so I came back here to look for you...." Hunter's ice-blue eyes were bulging. "What *happened?*"

Tenley sucked in more air, waiting for the world to right itself. Her throat burned and her chest ached, but she was free. She was alive. "Tenley?" Hunter pressed. "The cover was locked! With you in the tub! What's going on?"

Tenley opened her mouth. "I—" She began.

A shrill beep cut her off. Her eyes flew to the ground, where her provisions lay in the grass. Her phone's gold case glinted from inside her backpack. As if in a trance, she squatted down, her hands reaching for the phone.

She had one new text, from a blocked number.

Lucky girl. But tell the cops—or anyone—about me like you keep threatening to, and you'll make it to your grave once and for all.

Tenley whirled around, frantically scanning the yard. Was the darer here now? Had he or she watched Hunter save her? And when had the darer heard her talking about *cops?* She caught a flash of movement in the woods, but before she could scream, a bunny emerged, hopping lazily along.

"Tenley!" Hunter grabbed her arm. His fingers were cold against her skin. "Tell me what's going on."

She coughed again as her gaze landed on Hunter. What was he even doing here? Sure he'd saved her, but how did she know he hadn't shoved her underwater, too? He could easily have set the text up earlier to send automatically. She shivered even harder. The darer could be anyone.

Tenley grabbed her towel, buying time as she dried off. She had to pull herself together; she had to hide her fear. "I knocked the hot tub cover over while I was climbing in," she lied, wrapping her towel tightly around her. Her voice shook a little, but she ignored it, giving him her best silly-me expression. "Can you believe I did that? The cover locks really easily, and I guess it got stuck. There's a trick to getting it unlocked from the inside, so I would have gotten out eventually, but it's so much better having a white knight save me!" It wasn't her best lie ever, but Hunter didn't contradict her. Either he bought it, or he wanted to pretend he did. "What made you come by?" she added, trying to keep her voice casual.

"I came to talk to you." Hunter tugged at the Winslow T-shirt he was wearing. "I—I don't know what kind of game you're playing, Tenley, but it has to stop."

"*Game?*" The word made her blanch. "What are you talking about?"

"Don't play dumb, Tenley." Hunter shifted from foot to foot, looking uneasy. "I don't think I can take another minute of your flirty-girl act. I heard you loud and clear at lunch today." He lifted his voice into a terrible imitation of her. *"I can only imagine what other hookup secrets you're hiding, Hunter Bailey."* He crossed his arms against his chest. "Were you sending the notes with Caitlin the whole time?"

"*Notes?*" Tenley spit out. "What are you talking about?"

"Last month." Hunter glared at her. "The notes threatening to tell my dad I'm gay?"

Tenley's eyes popped at that. Flirtatious, playboy Hunter was *gay*?

"I already figured out that Caitlin was sending them," Hunter continued. "It had to be her; she was the only one who knew my secret. I just didn't realize until today that you were in on it, too. Were you also the ones who set me up for the Flagpole of Shame last month? Was it all just some funny joke to you guys?"

Tenley blinked, feeling woozy. Water dripped into her eyes, but she barely noticed. One after another, pieces clicked together, like a jigsaw puzzle snapping into place. She hadn't sent Hunter any notes, and neither had Caitlin. But she had a feeling she knew who had. She looked up, meeting Hunter's gaze. "These notes," she whispered. "Did they look like they were written with an old typewriter?"

Hunter gave her an exasperated look. "You know they did."

"And when did you get the last one?" she pressed.

"About a month ago, a day or two before the *Justice* crash." He gave her a pointed look. "A day or two before Caitlin died." He grabbed Tenley's arm again. "They ended then, and I don't want them to start again."

"Neither do I," she said fiercely. She shoved his hand off her. "It wasn't me, Hunter. And it wasn't Caitlin, either. It was Tricia. It was this weird kind of...revenge game she was playing."

"Tricia?" Hunter shook his head. "I don't understand. Why would she do that? And how did she even know?"

Tenley opened and closed her mouth without saying anything. If Hunter was getting notes, too, there was no way he could be the darer. She glanced down at her text. The darer had *been* here—had shoved her underwater and then watched as Hunter saved her. Whoever it was could still be lurking, listening to her every word. She couldn't risk telling Hunter the truth, not if the darer might hear her.

"She..." Her voice trembled, and she paused to steady it. If she ever needed to pull off a believable performance, it was now. "Let's see," she continued in her most flippant tone. "Tricia was practically obsessed with you, you took her v-card, and then you dumped her, like, two days later." Tenley ticked the items off on her fingers, one after another. "And you don't think maybe she got a little pissed off?" She put a hand on her hip. "Believe me, scorned girls have plenty of tricks up their sleeves. More than enough to figure out your little secret."

Hunter rocked back on his heels, looking unsure. "So this whole time you really had no idea about... me? Caitlin never told you?"

"Not a word," Tenley said. "And if you thought she would, you didn't know Caitlin very well."

"It was really Tricia?" Hunter looked stunned. "I can't believe it." He paused, kicking absently at the ground. "If it was her all along, then that means... that means it won't start again."

Tenley nodded mutely, unable to muster up a response. She could feel tears threatening to well, but she swallowed hard, fighting them. It just seemed so unfair. This new darer had left Hunter alone and had stuck to measly notes when it came to Sydney and Emerson. *She* was the one who'd had bottles thrown at her. *She* was the one who'd been nearly drowned in a hot tub. She was the one the darer wanted to see dead.

"It has to stay that way, Tenley." A note of hysteria crept into Hunter's voice. "You have to promise me you'll keep this a secret. No one else can know."

"Why not just tell? What will it change? Other than explaining why you never hit this." She waved a hand over her body, giving him a small smile. It was strange: All of Hunter's flirting had been a show, and all she felt was relief. He never had been the one she wanted. "Really," Tenley continued. "Why not just be honest? It's not like it's the eighteen hundreds anymore."

"Try telling my dad that." Hunter set his jaw in a straight line. "Especially before his Senate term is up. You don't understand. I'm supposed to be the football captain son. Not the gay son. He'd never forgive me." He took a step closer, lowering his voice. "Please. Just promise me you won't tell anyone."

The desperation on his face was raw and unmasked. It was what the darer had done to her, too—to all of them: made them feel as if they had no options, no way out. "I promise." She gave him a thin smile. "How about we go to the homecoming dance together? It will be the perfect cover."

Hunter nodded. "Thanks," he said gruffly. He glanced at his watch. "I have to get going. It's our last week of practice before the homecoming game, and Coach is already going to kill me for being this late. Think you can manage not to fall into any more hot tubs?"

Tenley forced a laugh. For a minute she'd actually managed to calm her racing heart, but at the mention of the hot tub, it kicked back into overdrive. "I'll try my best," she said weakly.

As soon as Hunter was gone, Tenley gathered up her stuff. She had no interest in being near the hot tub for even a minute longer. But as she took off for her house, her skin suddenly prickled, the tiny hairs on the back of her neck standing on end. It was a feeling she knew all too well. Someone was watching her.

She whipped around, her heart in her throat. But the yard was empty. In the woods, a breeze lifted the fallen leaves, swirling them through the air. Tenley shivered as she glimpsed behind them. There were whole acres back there, vast and rolling, enough space to mask anything—or anyone.

She was overcome by a sudden desire to sprint to her car and drive straight to the police station. But the thought left her more scared than ever. The darer had threatened her against telling anyone, especially the cops. And if this hot tub stunt had proved anything, it was that these weren't empty threats. So instead, she broke into a jog, hurrying the rest of the way to her house. She couldn't stand the idea of being alone, so when she got to the top of the stairs, she turned left instead of right. She stopped in front of Guinness's bedroom.

"You in there, Guinness?" She knocked loudly on his door. When there was no answer, she tried again. "Guinness? Come on, open up!"

She twisted the handle. The door flung open easily, and she stepped inside, half expecting to find Guinness grinning up at her from his desk. But the room was empty. She flipped on the light, wrinkling her nose as she looked around. Guinness clearly hadn't let their house-keeper, Sahara, near his room in weeks. It was a mess: clothes strewn everywhere, a graveyard of camera lenses under the window, and a whole slew of coffee mugs littering the desk, a slightly rank smell wafting out of one. A pair of boxers tangled with her feet as she took a step forward, and she quickly kicked them off.

She knew she should get out of there. Guinness would be furious if he found out she'd set foot in there without him. But her eyes had already landed on the photos scattered across his bed. There were dozens of them, and she found herself inching forward, unable to resist. Guinness had always been such a closed book, but his photos were the window to what was written on those pages.

She glanced over her shoulder, listening for footsteps. The house was quiet. She sat down gingerly on the edge of Guinness's bed and gathered up the photos. She'd expected artsy shots of Echo Bay, or lovelorn images of Sydney, but these photos were different. They were dark and a little fuzzy, and they were all candids.

They were taken at some kind of beach party. Everyone in them was around her age, but she didn't recognize anyone. She paused on one of the pictures. In it, a young-looking Guinness was standing with a group of guys, beers lifted in a toast. Most of them were wearing those ridiculous layered bracelets that had been in style for guys when Tenley was in middle school. "No. Way," Tenley murmured. These had to be Guinness's high school photos.

She shuffled eagerly through more of them. There were a lot of typical group shots—girls preening, guys brooding—but what caught Tenley's attention were a bunch of photos toward the end of the stack, all featuring the same girl. She was beautiful in a wholesome, girl-next-door way: strawberry-blond hair, full pink lips, freckles smattered over moon-pale skin. In one image, Guinness had zoomed the camera right up to her, so close that her face filled up the whole shot as she threw back her head, laughing.

Tenley bit down on her lip. Where had she seen that girl before? She flipped to another one. In this one, the girl was leaning against her friend, her gaze distant as she stared out at the ocean. Whoever she was, Guinness clearly had had a thing for her once. She paused on one of the last pictures. In it, the girl was looking straight at the camera, a half smile on her lips. She'd *definitely* seen that girl before somewhere. Was her photo up in Winslow's Hall of Fame? Or maybe she'd seen her on TV somehow? Or—

Just then, it hit her.

She *had* seen her on TV. Or at least her picture.

She was Kyla Kern. One of the Lost Girls.

"Oh my god," she whispered. The photos slipped out of her grip. As they tumbled onto Guinness's bed, something fluttered out from within the stack. It was a scrap of paper. It landed faceup on Guinness's pillow. Tenley let out a strangled scream. Staring up at her was the darer's trademark typewriter font.

Like a powerful photo, past mistakes can

haunt us until death. Good thing yours

will come soon. That's what happens when

you know too much.

CHAPTER SIX
Tuesday, 5:51 PM

SYDNEY PULLED A PHOTO OFF THE DARKROOM'S drying rack. It was from an old roll of film, since she'd ruined her digital shots when she dropped her memory card in the sand last night. The image was a close-up of the Phantom Rock during low tide, rough-edged and coated in water, like a monster slick with sweat. She'd already developed a dozen others just like it in a desperate attempt to work off the nervous energy Tenley's latest phone call had left coursing through her.

The darer had nearly killed Tenley. Another minute in that hot tub and Ten would have gone from Most Popular to Latest Dead Girl. Sydney shuddered. At least they could cross Hunter off their possible-darer list. According to Tenley, he'd been receiving some kind of threatening notes from Tricia, too. But Tenley already had a new suspect to replace him.

Guinness.

Tenley had been freaking out on the phone. Photos of Kyla Kern strewn across Guinness's bed, a death-threat note, and two attacks—both near the house she shared with Guinness? In Tenley's mind, if that didn't scream *Guinness is guilty*, nothing did.

"He was getting ready to sneak that note to me," Tenley insisted. "He was just waiting for the perfect moment. He wants us to back off. He's obviously afraid we know too much."

Sydney snorted at that. "We don't know *anything*!" She refused to believe that Guinness, *her* Guinness, could be the one doing this to them.

But Tenley wouldn't back down. "Who better to find out our secrets than someone who lives with me and dated you?" she cried. She started spouting conspiracy theories after that. The old darer was involved with Caitlin's death, and now this new darer was trying to kill Tenley. And here Guinness was, reminiscing over Kyla—*dead* Kyla—with a darer's note on his bed. "What if Guinness was involved in all of it?" Tenley burst out. "Kyla's death, Tricia's vendetta, the new dares, the Tenley manhunt."

Sydney lost her patience at that. Kyla's death was accidental. She and her friends had been out late at night on the boat float they'd made for Fall Festival when it caught on fire. The fire chief—her *dad*—determined that. Matt Morgan might have a lot of faults, but they didn't keep him from being good at his job. But nothing Sydney said could change Tenley's mind. As far as Tenley was concerned, Guinness had officially become suspect number one.

Now, as Sydney removed another photo from the drying rack, their conversation continued to torpedo through her mind. Guinness, the darer? Tenley had been so sure. But could he really do that to her?

Sydney hated the jagged pain that sliced through her chest at the thought. It wasn't like Guinness was her boyfriend; he never really had been. It was why she'd cut things off with him in the first place. She didn't want an almost-relationship; she wanted the whole thing. But still... He'd cared about her. Or at least she'd thought he did.

It was possible Tenley was just bitter, seeing what she wanted to see. Even though he was her new stepbrother, Tenley'd had a thing for Guinness when she first moved back to Echo Bay. She and Sydney were careful never to broach the subject now, but Sydney knew it was unlikely Tenley was fully over it. Guinness had gotten under her skin, and there was no magic switch to turn off your emotions. She knew that better than anyone.

A familiar ache began to tingle in her fingers. She moved more quickly through the darkroom, fighting it, but the urge only grew. *Fire.* She'd been doing so well lately, the last of the urges truly loosening their grip on her. Then the new dares started. Suddenly it was as if she were free-falling down a rabbit hole. And at the bottom was a pack of matches.

She didn't want to become that person again, the one who let fire ravage everything that mattered to her. But that didn't stop the urge from spreading through her body, hot and enticing, begging for a release.

Sydney took a deep breath, starting blindly at the drying rack. Every therapist she'd ever seen had told her the same thing. The best way to stop an urge was to kill it at the root. And this time she knew exactly what the root was. She grabbed her phone and opened a new text. There was only one way to dispel Tenley's suspicions. *Have apt 2 myself 2nite*, she texted Guinness. *Want 2 come over? Need 2 talk.*

Guinness's response came almost instantaneously. *Be there in an hr.*

Sydney moved quickly through the darkroom, cleaning up. She'd been hoping one of these shots would work for the RISD application's "unique and awe-inspiring hometown image." But that clearly wasn't happening.

She blinked as she emerged into Winslow's brightly lit hallways. She did an automatic scan of the corridor. Empty. Relieved, she made her way toward the exit. There was no one to follow her, at least for now.

Night had always been her favorite time to be at school, when there was actually space to breathe. It was the only time she could really appreciate the beauty of Winslow: the sweeping molding that lined the ceilings, preserved for more than a century; the redbrick starfish in the center of the auditorium floor; the carved wooden archway over the double-door entrance.

She ran a finger along a row of shiny green lockers. If she hadn't won a scholarship to Winslow Academy in first grade, she'd be stuck at Harbor High right now, with its dented, scratched-up lockers and a mop closet instead of a darkroom. She found herself forgetting that lately. As much as she hated most of Winslow, with its Flagpole of Shame and yacht-party gossip, she couldn't help but love this part— the elegance, the advantages. And, of course, the anonymous wealthy alumnus who'd insisted on using his donation to restore Winslow's old darkroom, despite the digital age.

Tacked up on one of the lockers was a pink sheet of paper. Abby's official Homecoming Nomination Memo. Sydney's eyes went automatically to the third name on the list. She kept expecting it to vanish, replaced by a big JUST JOKING. But there it was, in the same bold font as all the others: SYDNEY MORGAN. It made no sense. Winslow's hierarchy of popularity was written in stone, and Sydney's place had always been at the very bottom. She was pretty sure Miss Hilbrook had a better chance of being crowned queen than she did. So how had her name ended up on the ballot?

She ran a hand through her shaggy hair as she headed out to the parking lot. It didn't matter. She wasn't going to the dance and she certainly wasn't going to campaign. This might be someone's idea of a joke, but she refused to play a part in it.

She'd just turned her car onto Echo Boulevard when a loud blast of horns rang out behind her. As she glanced in her rearview mirror at the convertible that had swerved onto the street, causing the commotion, a figure next to the Crooked Cat Diner caught her eye. The person was wearing a long navy coat with the hood up, obscuring his or her face. Whoever it was seemed to be staring right at her.

Up ahead, a car slowed for a pedestrian, and Sydney slammed on her brakes, just barely avoiding collision. When she checked her rearview mirror, the person was gone. Sydney squeezed the steering wheel, turning her knuckles white. Had she just imagined it? Ever since she got that text, her imagination had been out of control. Everywhere she went, she could swear she saw shadows out of the corner of her vision, leaving her skin prickling with goose bumps. At school today, she'd actually screamed when she bumped into someone in the bathroom—positive it was the darer. But it was just Principal Howard, who proceeded to ask her if she needed to see the school counselor. Humiliating.

Trying to distract herself, Sydney turned on the radio. The sound of commercials blasted through her car. She was about to change the station when a familiar name caught her attention. "Danford Academy, a preparatory school in the heart of Boston, has made this year's ranking of top boarding schools in the country," the ad announced. Sydney turned the volume up, suddenly interested.

A few weeks ago she'd learned that Joey Bakersfield had transferred to Danford. She felt awful when she found out he was gone. She, Tenley, and Caitlin had wrongly accused him of being the darer—of stalking them. After the night out on the *Justice*, when they learned the real darer was Tricia, she and Tenley went to the police and had all charges against Joey dropped, explaining that they'd been mistaken, that it had been nothing more than a childish prank by their friends, and Joey hadn't even been involved. Sydney had hoped to talk to him and apologize in person, but he left for Danford before she could. She'd sent him two separate e-mails saying how sorry she was, but she'd never heard back.

"Students at Danford Academy choose from a myriad of electives to go along with the core curriculum," the ad continued. "Everything from architecture to sports therapy to engineering. If it's the arts you're interested in, Danford's theater is renowned for its acoustics, and its art wing is comparable to those found on college campuses."

Art *wing*? When she'd found out that Joey was switching schools, she felt so responsible. It lingered in the back of her mind for weeks: Once upon a time, she and Joey had been friends, and now something she'd done had chased him out of town. But from what she heard, Joey was at Danford on an art scholarship for his drawings. Maybe he'd actually be happier at a school with an entire art wing. It helped ease the guilt she'd been feeling, at least a little.

"Syd?" her mom called out as Sydney headed into the apartment a few minutes later. "Is that you?" Her mom walked into the living room wearing her favorite purple dress, paired with black kitten heels and gold earrings. Her dark brown hair was swept into a low ponytail, and her turquoise-blue eyes were sparkling. Between those eyes, her dark hair, and her skinny frame, Sydney felt as if she were looking into a crystal ball of her future. She could only hope that the guy in hers was nothing like her father. "Your dad said he's taking me for a surprise on our date tonight," her mom told her excitedly. "What do you think, is this outfit good?"

Sydney was tempted to tell her it was much too good; she hated the idea of her mom looking so pretty for her dad. But she swallowed her words and nodded cheerfully. When her mom broke into a wide smile, she was glad she had. She might despise her dad, but she loved seeing her mom this happy.

"Will you be okay on your own tonight?" her mom asked worriedly.

"Always am," Sydney said cheerfully. She was careful to avert her eyes as she said it. At school she was considered a loner, and she never minded. But she'd always had a secret weapon at home: her mom. Tracey Morgan had gotten pregnant with Sydney when she was only twenty, which meant she often felt as much like a friend to Sydney as a parent. Or she used to, until Sydney's dad dived back in and plucked her away.

Her mom flashed that happy smile again. "Thanks, hon. And don't worry about waiting up, okay? I could be late."

Somehow Sydney managed not to gag. She did *not* like to think about what kept her parents out that late.

Her mom gave her a quick kiss before leaving. Sydney shut the door behind her, locking and bolting it. Then she quickly moved through the apartment, switching on every light and turning on the TV to make the apartment feel less empty. She'd just popped a frozen veggie casserole into the oven when someone pounded on the apartment door.

She jumped to her feet, her pulse spiking. She hadn't buzzed anyone in, and she wasn't expecting Guinness for another half an hour. Every nerve in her body was suddenly on high alert. What if the same person who'd come for Tenley was now here for her? Her breath came fast and shallow. She was all alone. No one to help her. No one to save her. She spun around, her eyes landing on the phone. How long would it take the police to arrive if she called them? Five minutes? Ten? The pounding grew louder, more insistent. Her hand went to the phone. Maybe if she told them it was an emergency—

"Syd? You there?"

Sydney's hand slid off the phone. Relief flooded through her. "*Guinness*," she breathed, yanking the door open. "You're early. And you didn't buzz."

Guinness shrugged. "Sorry, some woman let me in with her." His wavy black hair hung in his face, and when he reached up to brush it away, Sydney caught a glimpse of the black tattoo on the inside of his wrist, the one she used to love to kiss.

As Sydney stepped aside to let him in, a familiar dart of excitement shot through her. She gritted her teeth in frustration. When would he stop making her feel like this?

"Blue." Guinness wrapped his arms around her. Her skin warmed at his touch and she quickly slipped out of his grip. "I'm really glad you texted," he said. "You haven't responded to my calls all month. I've missed you." He sighed, and it hit her just how exhausted he looked. The circles under his eyes were a bruised purple color, and he kept blinking as if he was struggling to stay awake.

"I wanted to talk to you about something," she said warily.

"Uh-oh, I know that tone." He gave her a small smile. "Are you going to try to get me to protest the senseless murder of lobsters again?"

"Fifty-six million lobsters caught each year in Maine alone?" Sydney shot back automatically. "It deserves to be protested!"

"I know, I know." Guinness held up a hand to stop her. "If that many people were killed a year, it would be considered a genocide. Okay, Blue, you've convinced me. I will protest the lobster genocide with you."

A laugh slipped out of Sydney before she could stop it. She cleared her throat. She had to be careful; she couldn't let herself fall into their old rapport. "Actually...I wanted to talk to you about Kyla Kern."

Guinness tensed. "Kyla Kern?" he repeated slowly. He stared at her, his dark eyes as unreadable as ever. It was one of the things she'd both loved and hated about him. Most of the time he was impossible to read, but when she did catch a glimpse, it was like opening up a fairy tale that had been written just for her.

"How come you never mentioned you knew her?" Sydney asked.

"I—uh, because I didn't really." He started to say something else but a huge yawn ate up his words.

"Not at all?" she pressed.

"I mean, we ran in the same group of friends, so we'd end up at the same parties when I was in town. But, you know, that wasn't that often."

Sydney nodded as she moved away from him. Guinness had grown up in Boston; his mansion in Echo Bay had just been a vacation home. It wasn't until his dad married Tenley's mom that they'd moved here full time. She found herself in her bedroom and sank down on the edge of the bed, trying to work up the courage to ask her next question. Guinness settled beside her. His ankle brushed against hers, making something flutter in her chest. *Stop*, she chided herself. She'd asked him here for a reason; she had to stay focused. "Tenley found pictures of Kyla on your bed," she said quietly. "Pictures that made it look like you knew her pretty well."

Guinness looked over sharply. "Excuse me? Tenley went in my room when I wasn't there?"

"That's the least important part of what I just told you, Guinness." Sydney could feel herself growing exasperated. "Why do you have photos of Kyla?"

Guinness shook his head angrily. "I cannot believe that girl. She has no respect for privacy. She acts like she owns the world."

"Guinness!" Sydney snapped. "Please answer my question."

Guinness flopped back on her bed and stared up at the glow-in-the-dark stars she'd put there when she was ten. "I'm telling you the truth, Syd. We went to some parties together, that's all. I took pictures of anyone I could back then. Kyla was a good subject." He twisted around to look at her, the tiniest of smiles creeping back onto his face. "Not as good as you, though."

Sydney dug her fingers into the edge of the bed, refusing to take the bait. "So the night Kyla died...you don't know anything about it?"

Guinness fell silent. His eyes drifted shut, and for a minute Sydney thought he might have fallen asleep. But finally he wrenched them open again with a sigh. "I was actually in town that night for Fall Festival," he said quietly. "I almost went out on the water, even. Some friends and I thought it would be fun to sail out to where all the Winslow seniors were partying on their boat floats...." He trailed off, letting his eyes shut again.

Sydney stiffened, thinking of Tenley's newest theory. She'd

told Tenley Guinness couldn't have had anything to do with Kyla's accident. But if he'd been there… "How come you didn't?" she asked.

Guinness's shoulders rose in a small shrug. He didn't bother to open his eyes when he spoke. "We were all trashed, and the wind was completely dead, so we ended up never making it out of the marina. Good thing, I guess, considering…"

He let out a huge yawn and rolled onto his side. "I don't want to talk about Kyla," he mumbled. "I want to talk about us, Syd. I miss you. I was so happy you texted tonight. I… I didn't want to be alone."

Sydney looked down. He sounded so exhausted, so *small*. More like a little boy than a twenty-two-year-old man. She wanted desperately to make him feel better, to rub his back and promise him he wasn't alone. But she couldn't give in; she had to ask him about that note. "There's one more thing, Guinness."

Guinness groaned into her pillow. "Fine. I need coffee, then." He let out another yawn. "Lots and lots of coffee."

She stood up reluctantly. If coffee would get him talking, then coffee it was. "I'll be right back."

She thought about Kyla as she waited in the kitchen for the coffee to brew. Before Caitlin and Tricia, Kyla had been the only Lost Girl she'd ever known. At the end of sixth grade, all Winslow students were paired up with a junior "buddy." Kyla had been assigned as hers. She was supposed to act as Sydney's mentor the next year—teach her study tricks and help her talk to boys. When Sydney met her at the introduction assembly at the end of the year, she was almost starstruck by her. Kyla was beautiful and popular and so *happy*, always smiling and laughing. She was everything Sydney wasn't, and Sydney found herself growing excited to spend the next year getting to know her. But just a few months later, before Kyla ever got to act as Sydney's buddy, she was dead.

Sydney blinked the memory away as she filled a mug with coffee and added a single cream, the way Guinness liked it. She wasn't looking forward to asking him about that note, but she had no choice. She had to make absolutely sure he wasn't involved with the dares.

But when she returned to her room, she found Guinness lying on his back, breathing the deep, even breaths of sleep. "Of course," she sighed. She frowned as she looked down at his sleeping form. He'd clearly been in a bad place tonight. She heard his words again. *I didn't want to be alone.* They reminded her of that horrible night at the Sunrise Center, the one she'd tried to forget.

She hadn't known him very long at that point, but she'd sneaked into his room after hours to show him her latest photos. When she got there, she found him draped across his bed, barely conscious, a half-empty bottle of pills in his hands. "Don't leave," he whispered, his words a slurred jumble. "I don't want to be alone."

She stayed with him all night as he threw up again and again, never leaving his side. It was the night she found out what his tattoo really stood for, the three inky lines wrapped around his wrist: not a prank with friends or a symbol of beliefs, but a mask, a cover for his last suicide attempt. She'd kept him alive that night, and he'd done the same for her a dozen other times, in a dozen other ways. He might have treated her terribly at times, but when she needed someone there, when the last thing she could be was alone, he'd always, always come through.

She went over to her desk, where she'd left the ring he'd given her. She hadn't even gotten a chance to mention it. She flipped open the box. The stone glittered in its silk bed, its facets catching slivers of light.

No one had ever given her something so beautiful, so *perfect*. It made her want to put it on and never take it off. But she'd promised herself she wouldn't be sucked back in. She wouldn't become her mom.

She carried the ring box to her bed and slipped it carefully into the pocket of Guinness's coat. She couldn't keep it. She let her hand linger on his side a moment longer than necessary. He looked so peaceful sleeping like that, his face relaxed, his chest rising and falling in rhythm with his breath. He looked like the Guinness she wanted to remember, the one she'd fallen in love with. It made her even more certain Tenley was wrong. Guinness wouldn't hurt anyone. Especially not her.

Moving quietly, she lay down on her bed and curled up beside him. She'd have to wake him and kick him out eventually, before her mom got home. But for now, she wanted to hold on to this Guinness a little longer. Her head fit right into the crook of his neck like it always had, and she felt something fiery burn under her skin. It had always been like that with Guinness, like their bodies were wired together, short-circuiting at every touch. He was trembling a little, so she wrapped her arms around him. She could feel his hair brushing her cheek and his heart beating against hers. And for the briefest of seconds she could forget it all—the breakup, the notes, the lies—let it all slide off her like water.

Despite everything, she'd loved him. A real love, the kind that stained you, the kind you could never truly wash off. She knew they could never go back to the way they'd been, but there was one last thing she could do for him. She could prove to Tenley—and herself— that Guinness had nothing to do with anyone's death. And she knew just how to do it.

Years ago she'd caught a glimpse of one of the photos of Kyla's accident when she was at the firehouse with her dad. Normally, photos like that were filed publicly and could be accessed by anyone, including reporters. But because of Kyla's young age, the Kerns had them marked as classified, the file locked away in the firehouse. Those photos could prove to Tenley that Kyla's death was purely accidental—no Guinness in sight. If she had to break into the firehouse to get them, she would.

Then she would put Guinness behind her at last.

CHAPTER SEVEN
Tuesday, 8:25 PM

"YOU'RE QUITE THE LITTLE CUTIE, AREN'T YOU?" Emerson cooed.

Holden the duckling responded by taking another peck at her leg. She was sitting cross-legged on the floor, giggling as he tried to scamper over her ankles. The whole thing felt so surreal. She'd never had a pet before. The closest she'd come was a goldfish she'd won at a state fair back in Florida—and found floating in his bowl two days later. She used to tease Caitlin about skipping parties to stay home with her dog, but for the first time, Emerson found herself understanding the impulse. She would so much rather stay home and play with Holden than go on this stupid Haunted Boat Ride.

Then again, the boat ride was no party.

She put her hand down, letting Holden waddle onto her palm. He stretched out his tiny yellow wings and gave them a hard flutter— which promptly tipped him over. He landed on his side, his webbed feet sticking into the air. Emerson laughed as he looked up at her with wide, dismayed eyes. "You'll get it soon," she promised.

She'd spent her free period at school today researching ducklings. It earned her a zero on her history homework, but she now knew more about ducks than she'd ever thought she would, including that they first flew around two months old. The research had been a good distraction. Thinking about Holden was a whole lot easier than thinking about the person who'd brought him. She watched the duckling climb clumsily back to his feet. She still couldn't believe that Josh was here in Echo Bay, and that she'd promised him an hour. The thought tangled her insides up into one big knot.

She sighed as she put Holden back into his cage. She couldn't think about Josh now, not with this dare looming. No matter how many times she'd dissected the note today, she couldn't figure out the point of the boat ride. Was the darer really trying to scare her with fake ghosts and goblins? Not that the reason really mattered; if she wanted to keep her Matt secret safe, she had to go through with it regardless. Besides, right now it was her only shot at catching the darer in action. She figured the best way for the darer to know if Emerson was on that boat was for him or her to be there, too.

She just wished she didn't have to go alone. But there was no way she was telling anyone about that note. She'd managed to keep Matt Morgan a secret this long; she wasn't about to ruin it now. Even if it meant coming face-to-face with the darer on her own.

Emerson's stomach churned uneasily as she drove to the pier. She couldn't help wondering about Sean again. He'd definitely been closest with Tricia. But did that make him the darer? And if he was...would she find him on the boat tonight? She'd tried calling him a bunch of times after cheer practice as she'd promised Tenley, but he still wasn't picking up. And so far, she hadn't gotten a call back.

No sooner had the thought crossed her mind than her phone started ringing. She reached for it, hoping to see Sean's name. Instead, she saw Josh's.

She froze up at the sight of his name. Part of her ached to answer it, hear his voice again. But another part of her wanted to throw her phone into the street and drive right over it. It reminded her of how she'd felt those first few weeks after returning from New York. After she left six days early without a good-bye—just a note taped to his apartment door—Josh called and e-mailed and texted her every day. She still remembered the last e-mail he sent her. *I've been going crazy waiting for you to call, Em. Every time my phone rings, I leap for it, hoping it will be you. But it never is, and I have to accept that it's never going to be. So I guess this is a good-bye. I hope you get every wonderful thing you want, Em, because you deserve them all.* She hadn't responded to that e-mail, just as she hadn't responded to all the others. How could she, after what had happened? There was nothing she could say that would make up for what she'd done.

Who she'd done.

Her skin flushed at the memory. She'd worked so hard to become this girl: Em, the model who inspired jealousy, whom girls emulated and guys pined for. But it was a mirage—a suit of armor. Inside she was a ticking bomb, self-destructing every chance she got.

Her phone rang out again. Before she even registered what she was doing, she pressed accept. "Hey." Her voice cracked a little, and she cleared her throat to hide it.

"It's the duckling police," Josh said solemnly. "I'm calling to make sure Holden is still alive."

Emerson made an indignant noise. "Of course he's alive!"

"Well, I know your history with goldfish, so..."

"Ha, ha," Emerson said. "Holden is thriving, thank you very much. He even attempted to fly tonight."

"Did you design any clothes for him yet?" Josh's tone was teasing, but she knew his interest was sincere. He used to get so excited in New York whenever she showed him an outfit she'd sketched.

"Oh yes," she said dryly. "A whole wardrobe of duck suits."

"I wouldn't put it past you," Josh joked. "Anyway, I did actually have a real reason for calling. I wanted to see about tonight for hanging out? I finished writing and am suddenly craving a burger. Want to show me a good spot?"

"The Crooked Cat Diner," Emerson answered automatically. "But I can't go tonight. I'm...busy."

"*Busy?* That's all you've got? The Emerson I knew could come up with a better excuse than that in her sleep. What about: I had a hair-straightening emergency? Or there's a romantic-comedy marathon on TV that I'd die if I missed?"

Emerson smiled despite herself. Josh used to love to tease her about her addiction to romantic comedies—or "troublemakers" as he called them, since, according to him, no guy in the world could live up to the inhuman perfection of a rom-com hero. She found herself answering the way she would have in the past. "What I meant to say was, I don't have a free second, what with cultivating my ant farm and all."

"Much better. Now I don't feel slighted in the least." Josh fell quiet, leaving an awkward silence hanging in the air. It surprised her; awkwardness never used to be a problem between them. Their conversations would constantly ebb and flow, like the tide going in and out. But that was when there was a *them*.

"You did promise me an hour," Josh pressed. "You sure you can't come out? Even just for a walk?"

Emerson swallowed hard. That had been their thing in New York: traipsing aimlessly around the city until they stumbled upon a hole-in-the-wall Chinese restaurant or a food truck Josh had read about in an issue of *TimeOut*. "I really can't tonight," Emerson answered honestly. *I have a date with the darer.*

"All right," Josh conceded. "Tomorrow, then? Or Thursday? Please just agree to *some* time, so I don't have to pull a John Cusack and show up at your house carrying a boom box over my head."

A laugh escaped Emerson. She'd made Josh watch *Say Anything*, her favorite classic romantic comedy, on one of their first dates in New York. He spent the rest of the summer teasing her about the best scene, where Lloyd Dobler stands under Diane Court's window, blasting "In Your Eyes" on his boom box. "Good luck finding a boom box in Echo Bay," she retorted.

"Fine, an iPod, then. I'm still showing up and blasting music loud enough to wake the whole neighborhood."

"Okay, okay," Emerson relented. "Tomorrow night. You'll get your hour."

"Good." Josh sounded pleased. "Make sure you've finished cultivating your ant farm by then." Emerson tried to keep a straight face as she hung up the phone, but her lips rebelled, twisting into a smile. Josh hadn't changed a bit. The problem, of course, was that she had.

A few minutes later she was pulling into the parking lot at the pier. The boat was impossible to miss. It was docked at the end, right next to the yacht club's large, white deck, and it had been fashioned to look like a submarine. A man in a captain's uniform stood at the entrance, waving people on. "Welcome aboard the Haunted Explorer!"

he bellowed. "Where we travel high and low—well, mostly low—to witness ghosts and ghouls and goblins galore. But beware, the journey may be treacherous." He lowered his voice to a hushed whisper. "You never know what dangers await you in the sea...."

A girl who looked to be around ten let out an excited squeal as her parents ushered her into the cabin. Emerson was about to follow them when a black cat suddenly darted past her on the pier. She froze. There was no worse luck than a black cat in your path. She was filled with a desperate urge to turn around and race straight home. But she couldn't risk the darer's wrath. Black cat or not. She gritted her teeth and hurried onto the boat.

The cabin was tiny, and it was already crowded with people. The windows had been blacked out, the only lights a few dim lanterns swinging from the ceiling. She looked up, but she saw no security cameras anywhere. It made her only more sure. The darer *must* be here somewhere.

Emerson swiveled around, nervously scanning the crowd. The boat was packed with families and a few older couples, dressed up for a date night out. She saw no one from Winslow—no one she even recognized. Then her gaze landed on a couple in the back of the boat. They stood close together, the man's arm wrapped tightly around the woman's shoulders.

Oh no. Emerson's legs went wobbly. She had to get off this boat before he saw her. She shoved her way through a pair of squabbling siblings, making a beeline for the exit. "Whoa, there." The captain stepped in front of Emerson, the door to the cabin clicking shut behind him. "Where are you off to? The frights haven't even begun yet!"

"I have to get off," Emerson mumbled, carefully angling herself so her back was to the couple. "I, uh, forgot something in my car."

"Too late for that," the captain said cheerfully. "We're already on our way!" As he spoke, Emerson could feel a telltale whirring under her feet. He wasn't lying; the boat's engine had started. A clock in the back of the boat struck nine and strains of creepy music filled the boat.

"Here we go," the captain said, taking his place up front. Somewhere up on deck there was a loud noise and the boat suddenly lurched, water splashing against its blackened windows. "We have submerged underwater," the captain announced. All around the boat, kids leaned forward, listening intently. "We are now traveling at the speed of light. Any minute we will reach the bottom of the ocean, where anything at all could await us. But while we wait, let me tell you a little story. . . ."

As the captain launched into a ridiculous tale about underwater goblins, Emerson stole a glance at the back of the boat. There he was, whispering into the woman's ear, wearing that playful little smirk she used to find so hot. Matt Morgan.

He was dressed more nicely than usual, a button-down shirt tucked into a pair of stiff jeans, but he still had his trademark stubble on his cheeks. The woman with him had long, dark hair; big blue eyes; and a pretty, purple dress hugging her slim frame. Emerson swallowed hard. It was Sydney's mom, Tracey.

She'd seen her around town before, but she'd never been in such close quarters with her. In fact, she'd done everything she could to avoid it. But that hadn't stopped her from imagining what it would be like. How Tracey would look right at her, hatred in her eyes and venom on her tongue. How she'd spew terrible, hurtful words, words that would tear Emerson apart. *Home-wrecker. Tramp. Slut.*

In those scenarios, Tracey had been cruel and heartless, a monster full of rage. But watching her here, the Tracey that Emerson had carefully constructed came crashing down around her.

It struck Emerson first how beautiful she was. Not exotic in the way people said Emerson was beautiful, but a warm, effortless kind of beauty. She looked like Sydney, but more lived-in, with a throaty laugh and eyes that lit up when she smiled. There was no venom or hatred, no rage or resentment. Her face was open and friendly, and the glow on her skin was unmistakable. She was thrilled to be there with Matt.

Emerson jerked backward, feeling as if she'd been punched in the gut. She didn't need Tracey to scream the words; they came flying at her anyway, sharp-edged and full of poison.

Home-wrecker. Tramp. Slut.

Home-wrecker. Tramp. Slut.

Once a slut, always a slut.

Tracey said something that made Matt look up. Emerson ducked, trying to melt behind an elderly couple who seemed to be enjoying the captain's tale as much as the kids. But it was too late; by the way Matt's eyes suddenly widened, she could tell he'd spotted her. The expression on his face was one of complete shock. He stepped behind his wife and wrapped his arms protectively around her waist. Only when he was safely out of Tracey's sight did he fix his gaze back on Emerson. The shock was gone, and it was replaced by something much worse. Fury. Pure, unbridled fury. His eyes blazed as they met Emerson's. *No!* he mouthed.

Emerson's face burned. She felt hot all over. She was here alone, on a ride meant for kids and cheesy dates. Matt would think she came for him—to *watch* him, or to confront him in front of Tracey. Tears pricked at her eyes as an awful realization hit her. The darer had planned this.

She wanted so badly to forget Matt, to forget the person she'd been when she was with him. But the darer wouldn't let her. She had to have it thrown in her face all over again. She'd been nothing but a toy to Matt, someone to pass the time with until he found his happily-ever-after with Tracey. The thought made her want to slip out of her own skin, molt like a snake, and step into someone else's life entirely.

A tear wound down her cheek and she angrily swiped it away. The black cat had been a warning. She should never have gotten on this boat.

"And now, passengers, I have a secret to share with you all." Emerson started at the sound of the captain's voice blasting over the loudspeaker. She hadn't realized she'd been holding her breath, but suddenly it came out in a long rush. The darer must have planned this, too! The final straw in her humiliation. The captain would tell everyone her secret and then Tracey would cry and Matt would yell and she'd be turned into a leper and—

"The goblins, who almost never come out of hiding, have chosen today to descend on the boat!" the captain continued. The boat lurched again, and the lanterns all went out in a puff of smoke. It took Emerson several seconds to process: It wasn't about her. Her secret was safe. At least for now.

For a moment the boat was blanketed in darkness. Then, one by one, the windows lit up. Outside, fake waves rolled angrily against the hull of the boat. The cabin began to rock and, outside, something flashed. A shock of white hair. Several kids screamed as the hair was swept away on the waves, replaced by the toothless grin of a plastic goblin. "It's them!" the captain bellowed. "The ghosts, ghouls, and goblins!"

Kids shrieked and parents laughed and somewhere a baby was wailing, and all Emerson wanted was to get off this boat, as far away from Matt and Tracey as possible. But the engine was still whirring away under her feet. Her eyes landed on a bathroom sign in the corner of the boat. *Thank god.* She darted around the elderly couple and slipped inside, locking the door behind her. She sank to the floor, trembling all over as she pulled her knees to her chest.

What did this darer have against her? What had she done to make someone hate her this much? She pressed her forehead against her knees. *Once a slut, always a slut.* How would she ever change that if the darer kept rubbing her nose in her mistakes?

Her phone buzzed inside her bag, vibrating against her leg. Anger simmered low and hot as she reached for it. The instant she saw the screen, it erupted, scalding through her veins. *Blocked.* She clenched her jaw as she opened the text.

You can run, Emmy, but when it comes to your past—and to me— you can never hide.

CHAPTER EIGHT
Tuesday, 11:13 PM

TENLEY WRAPPED HER BLANKET AROUND HERSELF, shivering in spite of the heat she had blasting in her bedroom. Discovering those photos of Kyla on Guinness's bed had made her feel vulnerable in her own house. It didn't help that she was home alone. Sahara had long since left for the day, her mom was out at some work party with Lanson, and who knew where Guinness was.

Guinness. The note she'd found with his photos felt branded in her mind. Had he written it? Had he written *all* the notes? The possibility that her own stepbrother was trying to hurt her sent icy fingers crawling down Tenley's spine. She thought of the photo the darer had sent her at Caitlin's memorial: her and Guinness, inside a coffin. Had that been Guinness's way of taunting her? She'd seen all those cameras in his bedroom. Who was to say one hadn't been put on automatic, set up to take surveillance photos of his room?

Or was that just crazy? Maybe Sydney was right; maybe her instincts were off about this. Sydney claimed the darer could have planted the note on his bed, setting up Tenley to believe it was Guinness. Tenley groaned. The whole thing made her head hurt. She didn't know what, or whom, to believe anymore. She needed more information—and until then, she needed a way to protect herself.

She grabbed her laptop off her desk and opened up a search engine. *Pepper spray*, she typed in. A whole slew of links popped up, and she clicked on one at random. According to the site, she could have a bottle of pepper spray—in a neon-pink bottle, no less—in her mailbox by tomorrow. *Spray your fears away!* the site declared. "Or the darer," Tenley muttered. She put a bright pink bottle in her cart. Then at last minute she added two more. Sydney and Emerson would thank her if the darer ever cornered *them* near a hot tub. She'd just pressed confirm when her phone let out a beep.

Immediately she tensed, thinking of her last text message. But it was just a Facebook alert. She had one new message on her page. She clicked open the site. If Abby was now using Facebook to campaign for Delancey, Tenley would defriend that girl faster than you could say *virgin*.

The name on the message wasn't Abby's, though. It wasn't anyone's. It was two words: *A Warning*. The user had no profile picture and zero friends. An alarm hummed deep in Tenley's bones. *Delete!* her brain screamed. But it was too late. The message was open on her screen.

A friendly word of advice: Forget about Caitlin's diary. You know what they say... Curiosity killed the cat.

Tenley's phone felt hot in her hand, the words searing themselves into her skin. The darer wanted her to stay away from Caitlin's journal? A journal all about Cait's kidnapping—about who she thought her kidnapper could be?

Tenley's jaw dropped as the full meaning of that hit her. The darer wanted to keep the identity of Caitlin's kidnapper unknown.

Which meant... the darer was connected to the kidnapper.

Excitement tingled through her. The darer might have thought that note would send her a warning, but instead it had given her a lead. She made a mental list of everything she knew about Caitlin's kidnapper. She was female, and since Cait had called her a "woman" in her journal, not a "girl," she'd probably been at least twenty at the time of Cait's kidnapping. Which would make her twenty-six now at the very youngest. It wasn't a lot to go on, but it was more than she'd had before.

Somehow this woman was connected to the darer—Guinness or Sean or whoever it was—which meant if Tenley found her, she'd find the darer, too.

Tenley jumped up, pacing through her bedroom. Sydney was investigating Guinness, and Emerson was on the Sean trail, which left Tenley holed up here alone like some sitting duck. Well, not anymore. The darer could find out if she went to the cops, but how would anyone know if she quietly followed a little clue?

She went over to her backpack and rooted around for Caitlin's journal. Thanks to the mystery hand that had pushed her under in the hot tub earlier, she'd never gotten a chance to finish reading it. Where *was* it? She was sure she'd left it in there. Annoyed, she dumped the whole thing over, its contents splaying everywhere. It took her half a second to confirm her fear. The journal wasn't there. The darer must have stolen it out of her bag, right after trapping her in the hot tub.

Adrenaline thrummed under her skin. Whatever was in that journal, this person *really* didn't want her to see it. Lucky for her, she'd already read part of it. She grabbed a spiral notebook off her desk and dropped down in the yellow chevron armchair she'd brought with her from Nevada. She planned to write down every word, before she forgot it.

Thud! She was halfway through Caitlin's hypnosis recollection when a noise from outside made her jump. She leaped to her feet, hurrying over to her window. Down below, a long, lean shadow slithered behind a tree in the front yard. A second later, another noise wafted up, a muffled thump.

Tenley sucked in a breath. Someone was definitely out there.

She looked desperately around for something to protect herself with. Her eyes landed on a hideous marble bust of a gymnast she'd won years ago and couldn't bring herself to throw out. She hoisted it off its shelf, staggering a little under its weight. If worse came to worst, she could throw it at someone to ward them off—

"Ten?"

"I'm armed!" Tenley yelled. She whirled around, shielding herself with the marble bust.

Guinness stood in the doorway, watching her. "With a girl's head?" he asked dryly. His dark, wavy hair was more messy than tousled, and his words slurred together, making it obvious he was drunk.

Tenley took a step backward, swallowing hard. She didn't know whether to feel relieved or terrified. If only she had that bottle of pepper spray.

"Aha!" Guinness said suddenly. "This is a new pageant act, isn't it? Bust balancing?"

Tenley stared at him. He was swaying as if he were being tossed on an invisible breeze. She could smell the alcohol pouring off him. His dark eyes were bleary and bloodshot and strangely flat, too, as if whatever he'd been drinking had dulled him around the edges. It hit her that he wasn't just party drunk, but *drunk* drunk. "What are you doing in my room, Guinness?" she asked shakily. Her heart was beating so loudly she was worried he could hear it.

"I wasn't ready for my night to end." A hard look crossed his face. "Though, apparently, the bar thought I was when they kicked me out. Just for having one drink too many." His fists clenched and unclenched at his sides. "So I thought I'd see what my little sis was up to." He gave her a sudden grin. It reminded her of a joker playing card: a sinister kind of happy.

A litany of options raced through Tenley's head. She could scream, run, call her mom....Or she could do some Guinness sleuthing of her own.

She put down the bust, then cocked her head, plastering on what she hoped was an annoyed-little-sister expression. "What happened to you at that bar?" she asked, wrinkling her nose. "Did you take a bath in a bottle of Scotch?"

Guinness stared at her, unblinking. "You're too young to understand," he said, but he was slurring, so it sounded more like, *youtooyoongtoundertttnd*. Tenley took a deep breath. Guinness's baby jokes usually bothered her, but she pushed her annoyance aside. "Oh look, your diary!" Guinness went on, eyeing the notebook she'd been writing in. He put a hand on the mantel, steadying himself. "Dear diary," he intoned, raising his voice several octaves. "Today I found the perfect lipstick!"

Diary. Tenley inhaled sharply. He knew—he was taunting her!

Or was it just a drunken coincidence? Her world suddenly felt upside down and inside out. It was impossible to tell which way was up.

"How about this?" she shot back. "Dear diary, today I dug up pictures of Kyla Kern!" She crossed her arms against her chest, glaring at him. "Want to tell me why that is, Guinness? Or is it yet another secret you want to keep from me?"

"Secret?" Guinness threw his arms up in the air so hard, it made him stumble backward. "What is *wrong* with you girls? You all have the same jealousy issues!"

"Jealousy?" Tenley fumed. "Are you really that vain? This has nothing to do with jealousy. It has to do with you lying, Guinness."

"Ha!" He took a jerky step toward her. His eyes narrowed and she could see a muscle twitching in his jaw. "Are you seriously calling me a liar, after everything you've done? After all your *games?*" The last word came out in an angry hiss.

Tenley's breath caught in her throat. "What the hell does that mean?"

For a second Guinness just stared at her. His nostrils were flaring and his hands were balled into fists. He looked like an animal ready to pounce. "It means you were in my room!" he said finally. "Going through my things. You have no boundaries, Tenley."

"Some things are more important than boundaries," Tenley replied tightly. She took a step back, putting space between them. "Like a dead girl. Answer me, Guinness! Why do you have photos of Kyla?"

He backed toward the door, shaking his head. "I don't need this. Not from you of all people." Spinning clumsily on his heels, he stormed out the door and pounded down the stairs.

"Wait!" Tenley yelled after him. "I'm not done asking questions!"

The only response she got was the loud clap of the front door as it slammed shut behind him. Tenley kicked at her dresser, sending a shock of pain through her foot.

Her phone let out a beep, and she went over to it warily. If the darer texted her now, *right* after Guinness left...it would seal her theory. But the text was from Marta. *Just remembered where I'd seen that train! Where did you get a drawing of Rabies-Mobile???*

"Of course," Tenley whispered. The memory came flooding back to her. In fourth grade everyone had been required to bring in a toy to share with the class for the year. Joey had brought in that train, and she and Marta had immediately coined it the Rabies-Mobile. They'd made fun of it all year, saying Joey belonged in one of the circus cars more than any elephant.

She sank down on her bed, reeling. According to Caitlin's diary, her kidnapper had been a woman, and she'd had this train—*Joey's* train—in her basement. Could that make the kidnapper related to Joey? Did he have any older sisters? Or maybe a cousin? An aunt? A *mom*? Tenley's mind raced, thinking it through. She knew Mrs. Bakersfield was a single mother with a son on scholarship at Winslow. Maybe she'd been struggling financially. . . . Maybe she'd needed ransom money. It was an awful, sick theory, but it was a plausible one.

But if Caitlin's kidnapper was connected to the darer somehow, who did that make the darer? *Joey?* She wasn't rushing to jump to that conclusion; making that mistake once was more than enough. Besides, Joey was at a boarding school in Boston now; he couldn't have anything to do with the latest messages.

Right?

CHAPTER NINE
Wednesday, 2:15 PM

"WAIT UP, PAM!" ABBY FLICKED HER WRIST, MAKING her life-size puppet chase across the stage after Delancey's. Her hair was pulled back into a tight ponytail, making her face seem even longer than usual. "I was hoping we could talk!"

"Of course, Polly," Delancey crowed, making her puppet kick its legs up in delight. With her porcelain skin, heart-shaped face, and bushy curls, Delancey could almost blend in with the dolls. "Let's sit!" The two puppets teetered on their strings, flouncing over to the single prop on the stage, a beat-up plastic tree stump.

It was the Purity Club Puppet Show, which all of Winslow was being forced to attend. The good news was, Sydney got to miss Señora Tucker's recitation of the Spanish conjugations for harvesting and tilling and seeding. The bad news was, she was stuck watching Abby and Delancey and two wide-eyed freshmen parade their creepy purity puppets for an entire period. Abby and Delancey had been talking up the show for weeks now, claiming it was "life-changing." Sydney couldn't help but wonder if it was all just a ploy to win that stupid purity contest Abby kept yammering about.

Onstage, the puppets sat down side by side on the tree stump, their strings tangling together. They were roughly the size of ten-year-olds and built out of shiny wood, with overly expressive faces painted onto them. One was wearing what looked to be a hand-knitted yarn dress and had the same wild curls as Delancey. The other was in a khaki atrocity: khaki pants and a khaki button-down, with a khaki scrunchy tying back its very Abby-like straight brown hair. Both puppets wore gold promise rings on their knobby wooden fingers that matched Abby and Delancey's own.

"What did you want to talk about, Polly?" Pam the puppet asked, as Delancey struggled to untangle several of the puppets' strings. Instead, the two puppets became even more tangled. Frustrated, Delancey gave the strings a hard yank—and Pam the puppet punched Polly the puppet smack in the face. The whole auditorium burst out laughing as Polly was flung backward off the tree stump.

"That's what you get for being pure," Sydney heard someone snicker. Calum twisted around in the row in front of her, shooting her a horrified expression.

"Only thirteen and a half more minutes," she mouthed to him.

"Eight hundred ten seconds," he mouthed back.

She rolled her eyes at him. Of course Calum could calculate that in less than a second. Ever since Monday night on the beach, when she'd mentioned she hadn't seen him around much lately, Calum had been popping up everywhere. He'd even dragged her *inside* the cafeteria during lunch today—a scenario she usually avoided at all costs.

They ended up sitting just a few tables away from Tenley and Emerson's group. But even though she'd been texting with the two of them all week about Darer Numero Dos, the quick hand-lift Tenley gave her could barely constitute a wave, and Emerson didn't even deign to look in her direction.

It wasn't until after lunch—when none of their friends were there to witness it—that Tenley dragged Sydney over to talk to them. "I got us all pepper spray," she announced. "It should be here tonight. I just think that after what happened in the hot tub yesterday..." She trailed off, the color draining from her face. "We need to be able to protect ourselves," she finished fiercely.

"With pepper spray?" Sydney asked doubtfully. She couldn't imagine tiny Tenley holding anyone off with a bottle of pepper spray, let alone the *darer*.

"With whatever we can," Tenley shot back. She went on to fill in Sydney and Emerson on the train she'd seen in Caitlin's journal, the one that had belonged to her kidnapper.

"Just promise me you'll leave Joey Bakersfield out of this," Sydney insisted. "Just because he once, *years ago*, owned a train like that does not make him the darer. So no going on a Joey warpath, okay? We've put him through enough already."

Tenley agreed, but she had a grudging look on her face as she did.

"Wow!" Polly the puppet chirped now, drawing Sydney out of her thoughts. Onstage, Abby was struggling to right her puppet amid a thicket of tangled strings. "Your passion for purity just *knocked* me out, Pam! And speaking of purity..." Abby finally yanked the puppet upright. "I wanted to talk to you about homecoming."

Pam the puppet clapped her hands together. "I hope I get voted queen!"

"I bet you will, Pam. But we have to make sure we don't forget our Three Ps to Purity in all the excitement of homecoming."

Both puppets jumped to their feet. "Pam and Polly's Three Ps to Purity!" Abby and Delancey sang out in unison.

"One," Polly the puppet announced, oblivious to the snickers peppering the auditorium. "*Pamper* yourself! Remember, girls: Pure doesn't have to mean boring. When you're feeling temptation, go get a pedicure! Fill your time up with things you enjoy."

"What I enjoy is hooking up!" Hunter Bailey hollered a few rows up, making his friends hoot with laughter. Sydney watched Tenley and Emerson laugh along with them. Was it seriously possible they found him amusing? "*A lot!*" he added.

Sydney stifled a groan. She couldn't wait to go to college.

"Silence!" Principal Howard scolded from the aisle. Up on stage, Abby tossed her long ponytail over her shoulder, narrowing her eyes in Hunter's direction. "What's number two, Pam?" she asked loudly.

"Two," Pam the puppet said, "is *pull* a friend aside." She put a hand on Polly the puppet's shoulder. "Never be scared to ask a friend for help. And, of course, three is *pride* yourself on your decisions." At that, the puppets launched into a song titled "I'm the Guard of my V-Card."

Two excruciatingly long songs later, Abby and the others finally took their bows onstage. "Thank you!" Abby called out. "This homecoming, remember the Three Ps!" Lifting their puppets, they all made a clumsy exit.

Immediately everyone began to jostle out of the auditorium. Sydney hung back, waiting for Calum to catch up with her. She had a huge favor to ask him, and she wanted to get it over with.

"I have one *P* to say about that," Calum said as they pushed their way out through the mob. His white-blond curls were especially unruly today, and his stuffed backpack looked ready to split at the seams. "Pathetic."

"Pain in the ass," she suggested.

"Phenomenally pitiable."

"Pleasure-killing."

Calum laughed. "Concisely said." He followed Sydney to her locker, waiting as she filled her backpack with books. "So, hey," he said, fiddling with the zipper of his bright orange sweatshirt. "Want to accompany me into town for a bit? I need to pick up something at the Gadget Shack, but we could swing by Galileo Gallery, too, and maybe grab some coffee?"

Sydney smiled. This was the perfect opportunity. She'd spent all day working on a way to get into the firehouse that afternoon. She'd come up with a plan, but she couldn't put it into action until four o'clock, when nosy Tammy—the unofficial firehouse "secretary"— left for the day. And when she did, she was going to need Calum's help.

"Let's do it," she agreed. "I could go for some caffeine right now."

"Gee, shocking," Calum replied. He broke into his lopsided grin. "I would venture to guess that you have caffeine and sugar in your veins instead of blood, Syd."

"Don't forget chocolate."

"How could I?" Calum deadpanned.

After a quick stop by the Gadget Shack and a longer stop at Galileo Gallery, Sydney and Calum headed to Bean Encounters. "I am ready for my cup of joe," Calum announced as he held the door open for her.

Sydney looked up at him through her bangs. "Please tell me you did not just say 'cup of joe.'"

"Oh, but I did," Calum said cheerfully. "I absolutely did."

With a smirk, Sydney headed to the counter. All day long the task of getting Kyla's file had hung over her head, like an ever-present rain cloud. But being downtown and joking around with Calum made the whole thing feel blissfully distant. "I'd like a large coffee with a double flavor shot of hazelnut," she told the barista. "And he'd like a cup of joe, whatever that is."

"A small black," Calum said, smacking her with his Gadget Shack bag.

"Ow!" Sydney yelped, rubbing at her hip. "What do you have in there? Knives?"

"Sorry." Calum looked sheepish. "The new motherboard for my computer must have sharp edges. That or someone's bones are weak because she exists solely on sugar."

"Possible," Sydney admitted, grabbing her coffee off the counter. "Ah," she said, taking a big sip. "Caffeiney-sweet goodness."

"So tell me, Sydney Morgan," Calum said as they took a seat by the window. "How does it feel to be one of the esteemed few on this year's homecoming ballot?"

"Like I'm the luckiest girl in the world," Sydney sang out, pretending to swoon.

Calum laughed. "If you're looking for a campaign manager, I have pretty impressive credentials. My dad even has this new printer that makes amazing posters. I'd consider letting you borrow it if I'm hired."

"I appreciate the offer," Sydney said. "But there's no way I'm campaigning for this charade. The whole thing is obviously someone's idea of a nasty joke. I mean, me, as homecoming queen?" She made a gagging motion. "Yeah, right."

"If you say so." Calum shrugged. "But I'm at your service if you change your mind."

"Thanks. If I ever decide to pull a Tenley Reed, you'll be the first to know." Sydney grinned at him. "I mean, I owe you, after all. You *did* just buy me a cup of Ted."

Calum shook his head, looking appalled. "You can't just substitute any guy's name in there, Syd."

Sydney leaned back in her chair, taking a long sip of coffee. "Mmmm," she said cheerfully. "A delicious cup of Mark." Outside, a familiar figure caught her eye. A dark-haired guy strolling slowly along.

Guinness. She quickly slumped down in her chair, not wanting him to see her.

"Everything okay?" Calum twisted around to look out the window. "Is the crazy lady performing one-woman Shakespeare in the street again?" He paused. "Oh," he said knowingly. "Beer boy." Over the summer Calum had witnessed plenty of her angst over Guinness.

Sydney gave him a sheepish look. "Can you tell me when he's gone?"

Calum kept his eyes on the window for a few more seconds. "You're free to sit up." He studied her as she did. "I thought things were over between you guys."

"They are," Sydney said quickly. "I just…It's hard, you know? Getting over someone." She sighed. "I'm working on it."

"Well, if you ever need reinforcements, you just let me know," Calum said. "I have a wide range of skills outside of campaign management."

Sydney paused. She wouldn't get a better opening than that. She glanced at the clock. *3:45.* It was now or never. The bubble of peace-fulness she'd been swept up in popped instantly. "Actually...there is something I was hoping you could help me with." She shifted nervously in her chair. "A favor."

Calum nodded gravely. "So you require the irrepressible genius of Calum Bauer." He tapped his finger against his chin. "What's the predicament? Is your computer broken? Do you have furniture that needs to be moved? You know I do have brawn as well as brains."

"I'm sure you do." Sydney still remembered the first time she saw Calum with his shirt off when they worked together at the Club. It had shocked her that he'd actually be kind of hot if he stopped using SPF 75 and pounding his fists against his chest like Tarzan every time he blew on his whistle. "But it's actually your phone-dialing skills I'm after." She hesitated, fiddling with her coffee cup. "I need you to call the firehouse and report a fire on Neddles Island." She said it all in a single breath, turning the words into a long rush of syllables. But by the way Calum inhaled sharply, she knew he'd understood.

"That's a pretty serious request," he said carefully. "Unless there's a fire raging outside my house that I'm not aware of?"

"Probably not," Sydney admitted. "The thing is, I need to clear the firemen out for a few minutes, so I can get into the firehouse. It...it has to do with my dad. Some family drama." It was a white lie, but Sydney was hoping it would put a crashing halt to any questions. You couldn't live in Echo Bay without knowing Calum's tragic family history. Four years after his sister, Meryl, became the first Lost Girl, his mom—still struggling with her daughter's death—killed herself in the very spot where Meryl had drowned. Calum had been just a kid. The one time Sydney had brought family stuff up with him in the past, he'd changed the subject so fast she'd practically gotten whiplash. "You can tell them something vague," she added quickly. "Like you see smoke in the cliffs by your house."

"And when they arrive?" Calum asked.

"The smoke easily could have dissipated. A false alarm."

"Just someone making s'mores," Calum said thoughtfully.

"Exactly." Sydney squeezed her hands into tight fists, her nails digging into her palms. She felt terrible bringing Calum into this, but she didn't know whom else to turn to. She was sure Guinness would have agreed, but the last thing she wanted to do was ask him, not after last night. "So will you do it?"

Calum sighed. "You are aware you'll be indebted to me after this, right? And not a minuscule, little favor, either. I'm talking gargantuan, mammoth, more colossal than the Incredible Hulk."

Sydney laughed. She bet he had a T-shirt that said that. "Big," she confirmed. "Got it." She glanced at her watch. "Wait ten minutes and then call, okay?"

"Aye, aye, Captain."

Sydney twisted her ring around her pointer finger as she climbed into her car. "I can do this," she chanted under her breath. She repeated it the whole drive over, as if saying the words enough times could make them come true. "I'm just a regular teenage girl visiting my regular loving dad."

Ha. She was going to have to dig deep into her acting reserves for this one.

She tried to calm her nerves as she parked across the street from the redbrick firehouse. An American flag waved over its entryway, and in its driveway sat a single fire truck, as immaculately waxed as always. Most days, waxing that truck was the only thing the Echo Bay firemen had to do. Not today. In fact, pretty much never, when it came to her.

An image of a fire rose in her mind: flames roaring and embers glowing, cause unknown, except to her. She shook away the memory and climbed out of the car. She could do this.

"Sydney!" Bob Hart exclaimed when she crossed through the firehouse's red double doors. Bob was her dad's closest friend at the firehouse. He weighed roughly three hundred pounds and had a beard that made him look as if he'd just returned from a year in the jungle. When her dad still lived at home, Bob used to come over for barbecues all the time. Sydney still remembered how bits of the food would get stuck in his beard, as if he were saving them for later. "Your dad told me you were growing up quickly," he continued. "He wasn't kidding. Look at you, a real woman!"

Sydney tried not to cringe. She hated when middle-aged men called her a woman. "I'm actually here to see my dad," she said. "I brought a book for him." She held up the copy of *Echo Bay's Unsolved Mysteries* that she'd thought to stick into her backpack that morning.

"Oh, that's a shame. I'm sure he would have been happy you stopped by," Bob told her, "but it's his day off."

Sydney smacked her forehead. "I forgot." She hadn't, of course. Her mom had mentioned it just that morning. But she wasn't about to tell Bob Hart that. "Do you think I can leave this on his desk for him?"

The words had just left her mouth when a shrill bell rang out through the firehouse. "Twenty-one, a dwelling!" The dispatcher's voice came through on Bob's pager. "Neddles Island, Echo Bay Township, sixteen hundred hours."

Bob, who acted as chief on her dad's day off, jumped to attention. "Everyone gear up!" he called out. Instantly the firehouse exploded in a frenzy of activity: turnout gear flying and men calling out orders and a bony, redheaded woman sliding down the fire pole, landing with a soft thud next to Bob.

"Go on back, Sydney," Bob called over his shoulder as he jogged to his locker and pulled out his gear. Sydney couldn't resist watching him for a beat. His face had hardened into a mask of concentration, the same one she'd seen her dad wear so many times. In three seconds flat he was dressed and racing toward the door, moving so fluidly he made it look like a dance. Tearing her eyes away, she slipped into her father's office.

As chief, her dad had the only office in the small firehouse. It was a cramped, crowded room, with a desk too large for the space and a line of filing cabinets jammed along the back wall. Sydney made a big show of placing the book on his desk, even though everyone was focused on getting out to the call. She stuck a Post-it Note on the cover. *Thought this seemed up your alley!* she wrote. She couldn't make herself write *love*, so she just scrawled her name across the bottom. Her dad would probably be confused beyond belief when he found that book, but at least her story to Bob would check out.

Sydney took a quick glance around the office. Everything looked the same as it had years ago, when she was a frequent visitor to the firehouse. She still remembered hearing that bell ring for the first time, how everything had changed so instantaneously. It was like watching a window shatter: one second light was streaming through it, and the next second pieces were flying everywhere, sharp-edged and blinding, and you couldn't see a thing. She'd never known something to have that kind of power—the ability to cut through everything, make only one thing matter. She'd instantly wanted it for her own.

It was during that time that she'd learned all the ins and outs of the firehouse: who read in the loft space after lunch and who was the quickest to change into his gear and, of course, where her dad hid the key to the locked files.

Sydney could hear the familiar pounding of boots in the main room as everyone jostled toward the exit, voices calling out checklists and shouting commands. Seconds later the siren began wailing, pulsing through the air. And then, just like that, it was moving: growing fainter and fainter until, finally, it was gone. An eerie silence was left in its wake. Sydney blew out a breath, hearing it amplified in her ears. It was now or never.

She hurried over to the fake hanging plant her dad kept in his office. Standing on her tiptoes, she stretched her arm up, feeling around inside the pot. Her fingers brushed up against something smooth and cold. Sydney broke into a smile as she pulled out the small metal key.

It took only a few minutes to find Kyla's file. Her dad might be a creep, but he was an organized creep, every drawer of his filing cabinets chronologically ordered and meticulously labeled. She found it in the third cabinet, second drawer down: KERN FIRE, stamped in thick red letters.

Sydney yanked the folder out and quickly skimmed over the report. According to the notes, Kyla's boat float had been named "Twinkle, Twinkle, Little Star." It had included a whole pyrotechnics display featuring a large, sparkling, golden star that was supposed to shoot from one end of the float to the other. But on the sea that night, something had gone wrong with the wiring. Instead of shooting, the star had exploded.

Sydney paused at the conclusion of the report, where the cause of the fire was identified. *Accidental*, it said. She snapped a photo of it with her phone, to show Tenley later.

She was just about to move on to the photos when her eyes landed on the signature line at the very bottom of the page. She was surprised to see it wasn't her dad's signature there, but Gerry Hackensack's, the chief before him. Sydney thought back. Her dad had been promoted to chief the summer after she finished sixth grade, which would have been the summer after eleventh for Kyla and Guinness. So the Kyla Kern case must have been one of Hackensack's last. Curious, she peeked into the next oldest file, a beach bonfire mishap that took place only a week after Kyla's death. Her dad's familiar signature was at the bottom of the report. Apparently, Kyla's case hadn't been one of Hackensack's last; it had been *the* last.

She glanced up at the clock as she returned to Kyla's file. It wouldn't be long before the firemen discovered the whole thing was a false alarm and came filing back in, grumbling loudly about the waste of time and resources. She had to get moving. Quickly, she removed the photos from Kyla's file. The first one was a fuzzy "before" shot that had probably been taken by one of Kyla's friends. The quality was terrible, but Sydney could see why their float was favored to win that year. In person, it must have been amazing. It was a midnight blue, so dark it would have blended in with the waves—if it weren't for all the stars. There must have been hundreds of them: tiny lights embedded in its surface and strung through the air, glowing and winking, like a starry night floating in the ocean. And at the back of the float, hanging high above them all, was a huge, sparkling, golden star. The one that had exploded.

Sydney flipped to the next image. It was clearly an "after." The explosion had caused a fire, and the once-beautiful float was destroyed.

Planks were scalded and torn out, holes were burned right down to the base. The large, gold star was gone, and the glass lights that had twinkled so prettily in the last photo were now shattered everywhere, fracturing the camera's flash into tiny diamonds of light. In the front of the boat, the sleeve of someone's shirt was tangled in one of the piles of broken glass, blackened and dripping with blood.

Sydney's stomach seized. She used to find fire beautiful, even its aftermath: the way it ate through everything in its path and left a blank slate behind, like a sand castle swept away by the waves. But on the *Justice*, she'd finally seen how ugly it could be, how it sucked the life out of everything, leaving behind not blankness, but *remains*—wilted, charred, dead.

She steeled herself as she went through the rest of the images, photographing each of them with her phone. She'd just finished going through the stack when she noticed it. "That's strange," she murmured. She flipped back to the second to last photo in the pile. The number stamped on the bottom was twenty-one. She turned to the next photo, the final one. Twenty-three was stamped on the bottom.

Quickly, she rifled through the whole pile again. There was no twenty-two. She leaned back against her dad's desk, staring blindly at the folder.

A photograph was missing from the records.

Out in the main room, a staticky radio burst to life. Bob's voice filtered into the firehouse. "Twenty-one was a false alarm. Returning to coop."

Coop. It was what the firemen called the firehouse: their very own chicken coop. She had to get out of there.

She quickly shoved the folder back into the filing cabinet and returned the key to its hiding spot. On her way out, she paused, taking one last look at her dad's office. She imagined his returning to work tomorrow to find that book waiting on his desk. She couldn't help but wonder if he'd smile, or if he'd just toss it aside.

It didn't matter either way. Turning on her heels, she hurried out to the parking lot. She could already see the fire truck in the distance, a red bullet, shooting toward its coop. She floored the gas, driving off just in time—away from the truck and the files and Bob, and any last thoughts of her dad.

CHAPTER TEN
Wednesday, 5:18 PM

"WE'LL GROWL! WE'LL ROAR! WE'LL BEAT YOU THEN we'll wipe the floor!" as the line of cheerleaders behind her launched into their best impersonations of lions, Emerson stepped forward with Jessie, unfurling a Winslow Lions banner.

"Ready?" Jessie asked.

Emerson nodded. They were practicing their big halftime show for the homecoming game, and Emerson and Jessie's performance was supposed to be the grand finale. "One," Jessie murmured. "Two. Three!" In unison, they tossed the banner up into the air behind them, for two juniors to catch. As Emerson launched into a series of cartwheels next to Jessie, she tried to keep her attention focused on the routine. But she just couldn't shake the thought that had been trailing her all day.

Tonight, she would see Josh again.

A rush of adrenaline shot through her as she moved on to the final combination, doing handsprings in sync with Jessie. Two handsprings and a double tuck later, they landed in perfect unison, standing side by side. "Yeah!" the squad cheered behind them.

"That rocked," sophomore Jane Rossi squealed. Emerson managed a half smile at her. There was nothing wrong with Jane, one of the squad's two new additions. She was cute and bubbly, and she did a mean basket toss. But every time Emerson looked at her, she saw the girl who should have been standing there instead. Emerson turned away, squelching the memory of Caitlin.

"You were amazing, Em!" Marta came jogging onto the field, her silky, red hair flying out behind her. "You're going to kill it on Saturday."

Emerson gave her a distracted smile, still thinking about her approaching hour with Josh. "Thanks, Marta. I have to run, but I'm glad you came to watch."

"Oh no you don't." Marta put a hand on each of Emerson's shoulders, which at her height of five foot five meant she was practically standing on her toes. "Emerson Cunningham, I'm here to cheernap you."

"You're here to *what*?" Emerson asked.

"Cheernap you," Marta repeated. "Jessie and I are going to grab dinner at Mama Mia's with some of the guys, and you're coming with us."

"Oh, Mart, I really can't," Emerson said apologetically. "I have something I have to—"

"Uh, uh," Marta interrupted. "Whatever it is, cancel it. You are coming to dinner with your friends if I have to carry you there myself." She took her hands off Emerson's shoulders and shoved them into the pockets of her brown twill coat. "I know it's been hard, Em," she said softly. "I miss her, too. So much it's like a physical pain sometimes, you know? But I've already lost two friends. Please don't make me lose another." When Marta looked up, Emerson was surprised to see that her eyes were wet. "Please. I promise it will be fun. Hunter can't make it, but Nate and Tyler will be there, and I even convinced Sean to climb out of the hole he's been hiding in and come with us."

That got Emerson's attention. She'd been trying to get in touch with Sean all day, but he'd been M.I.A. ever since lunch yesterday, even skipping another practice this afternoon. Tyler had mentioned that he'd come down with a cold, but that didn't explain why he hadn't answered any of her texts or calls. "Sean's definitely coming?" she asked.

"Yeah. Or at least he says. And now it's *your* turn to say the same. We tried to get Tenley to come, too, but, apparently, her mom's chained her to the house for a wholesome family dinner."

Emerson tugged absently at the red sweatshirt she was wearing to keep warm on the field. In less than an hour, she was supposed to meet Josh for a walk. But Marta was right; she'd been a terrible friend lately. And this could be her best chance to talk to Sean. "Okay," she told Marta. "I'm in."

"Yes!" Marta pumped her fist into the air triumphantly. "Nate doubted me, but I told him we hadn't lost you yet."

Emerson winced. "You're not going to lose me," she promised. "Okay?" She gave Marta a quick hug. "I just need to grab my stuff. Meet you in the lot?"

"Of course," Marta replied. She broke into a smile. "You're driving with me. Top down while we still can!"

Emerson laughed as Marta skipped over to Jessie. Her friend's enthusiasm really was infectious. She grabbed her stuff out of her locker, automatically touching a finger to the rabbit's foot in her bag. Then she sent a quick text to Josh saying she had to postpone for another night. A strange mix of disappointment and relief bubbled up inside her as she made her way outside. She wouldn't be seeing him tonight.

Marta was waiting in her car, the top rolled down and a red polka-dot handkerchief tied around her head to keep her hair out of her face. She tossed a matching one to Emerson. "Hair protection," she said solemnly. "The number one priority of convertible ownership."

"Obviously," Emerson agreed. The wind rushed over her as they sped down Ocean Drive, lifting goose bumps on her arms.

"I think I'm hungry enough to eat a whole Hungry Man Pizza tonight," Marta declared.

Emerson leaned back against her seat, closing her eyes. The Hungry Man Pizza was Mama Mia's specialty: a personal pan pizza piled high with every topping they had. It had been Caitlin's favorite dish at the restaurant, despite the strange smell that always accompanied it—a potent mix of veggies and meats and cheeses. "If you're going to get a pie, you might as well get *the* pie," she used to say whenever Emerson teased her about it. Emerson felt a sharp needle of sadness stab at her. If Caitlin were here, she would know exactly what Emerson should say to Josh. She always gave just the right advice.

Emerson opened her eyes and glanced over at Marta, who was humming loudly to the radio as she drove. She loved Marta, but she wasn't exactly a beacon of sage advice. Emerson and Caitlin used to joke that Marta was like a hyperactive puppy: well-meaning and loving, but too busy chasing her own tail to ever really sit still and listen. "Oh, guess what," Marta chirped. "I found a dress for homecoming!

It's this really deep green color, which my mom insists goes well with my hair, and I'm *obsessed* with the material."

Marta was still detailing her homecoming ensemble as they joined Jessie, Tyler, and Nate at one of the round tables in the back of Mama Mia's. The restaurant was pure old-school Italian, with white table-cloths and murals of Italy covering the walls. Emerson's gaze flickered longingly toward the booth that she and Caitlin always chose when-ever they came here. It sat empty and quiet now, looking lonely in the crowded, chattering restaurant.

"Don't you think, Em?" Marta asked, nudging her in the side.

Emerson forced her attention back to the group. "What did you say?"

"I'm thinking maybe we should order one of every pizza on the menu, and then we can all share."

"Like pizza tapas!" Nate chimed in.

"Exactly," Marta said, sounding pleased. "That way everyone can have a little taste of everything."

The Hungry Man Pizza already *was* a taste of everything, Emerson wanted to point out. But Marta looked so proud of her idea that she found herself saying, "Sounds great. Should we wait for Sean to order, though? Or is he not coming anymore?" She tried to keep her voice casual, but Marta gave her a strange look.

"What's with all the Sean-obsessing?" She leaned closer to Emer-son, lowering her voice. "Is there some kind of crush going on that I should know about?" She elbowed her playfully in the side, but there was a strange note in her voice: concern, maybe.

"Of course not," Emerson said quickly. "I'm just...worried about him, that's all."

Marta nodded. "We all are. But he's meeting us here soon, and then we're all going to have a *fun* dinner, okay?" Marta scrunched her face up into a funny expression, and Emerson couldn't help laughing.

"Deal," she said.

The waitress had just taken their order when Jessie suddenly let out a squeal, making a stray brown curl spring into her face. "You guys have to hear what Abby posted on Facebook a minute ago." She paused dramatically, waiting until she had everyone's attention. "'This homecoming, don't just vote for the model. Vote for the model student!'" She let out a loud groan. "Clearly, she thinks Em is Delancey's biggest competition."

Emerson rolled her eyes. She found it absurd that someone could care about homecoming—about *anything* in high school—that much.

"Since when do people campaign on Facebook for homecoming?" Marta snorted.

"Since when does anyone understand what Abby does?" Tyler offered.

"Don't worry," Jessie assured Emerson. "It doesn't matter how much Abby campaigns. Everyone knows the real race is between you and Tenley."

"And you've got me to campaign for you," Marta said. "I know I'm no Cait," she added, her face clouding over a little, "but I do make a mean poster."

"She always got gold stars back in art camp," Nate confirmed, flicking his straw wrapper at Marta.

Marta stuck her tongue out at him. "Yeah, and Nate always got red marks."

"I was ten," Nate replied. "How was I supposed to know that pee isn't allowed to be used as paint?"

As everyone laughed, Emerson caught sight of someone lingering outside the restaurant. Sean. He was standing next to the window, staring in at them with a stony expression. When he caught Emerson's eyes, he turned away and slumped against the side of the building.

"What's up with *him*?" Jessie asked, her gaze following Emerson's. "Is he coming in or what?"

"I'll go find out," Emerson said, standing up. She cut quickly through the restaurant, sidestepping two waitresses and a screaming kid who was throwing a tantrum over his spilled spaghetti. "Ah, peace and quiet," Emerson breathed as she walked outside, letting the door clap shut behind her.

Sean started at the sound of her voice. "Oh, hey, Emerson."

"You have us all worried in there," Emerson said, leaning against the building next to him. "Everything okay?"

"Eh, not really." Sean's eyes lingered on a pair of trees in the back of the restaurant's garden that leaned together until they were touching, creating a red-and-gold-leafed canopy. The Kissing Trees, they'd been coined. In the summer, people held wedding ceremonies under them. "I guess I'm just having one of those days, you know?"

"Oh, yes," she said honestly. "Lately I just call them 'every day.' "

Sean let out a short chuckle. He was wearing a checkered polo that could use a wash and a pair of beat-up jeans and untied sneakers. Normally, Emerson would have immediately mentally edited an outfit like that, but right now she was too distracted by the expression on his face. He looked deeply, truly *sad*. "Sounds familiar," he said.

Emerson watched him for another minute. It was strange how much time you could spend with someone and never really get to know them. She'd partied with Sean countless times, eaten lunch after lunch with him, watched him fall for Tricia after Hunter broke her heart—but when it came down to it, she hardly knew him. Sure, she knew what beer he drank (Yuengling) and that he ate turkey on rye for lunch, and, thanks to Tricia, that he wore tighty-whities instead of boxers, but she had no idea about the stuff that mattered: what she would find if she peeled away the shiny top coat they all wore like a varnish.

"You must really miss Tricia." It was the only thing she could think of to say.

"Sometimes it feels like it's strangling me, how much I miss her. And then sometimes..." Sean cleared his throat. "The whole thing just feels really weird, you know?"

"Weird?" Emerson stiffened. "How so?"

"All of it. That she's gone. That things can already be so normal again." He motioned toward the restaurant, where, inside, Jessie and Marta had their heads bent together in laughter. "That we never got to say good-bye."

"I know, I think about that a lot, how different it would be if we could have just had one last chance to talk." She paused. This was her opportunity. "Before the *Justice* accident, did Tricia seem...different to you at all? Like maybe she had something going on? Something she didn't want to talk about?"

Sean's head snapped up. For the first time, he looked right at her, his eyes wide and shiny. "So she told you," he said flatly. "Who was it? Hunter? Or someone new?"

Emerson wrinkled her brow. "What about Hunter?"

"The other guy," Sean said impatiently. "Who was it? You can tell me, Em. No need to keep it a secret anymore, right?"

Emerson straightened up, her heart beating fast. "You think Tricia was seeing another guy before she died?"

For a long second Sean just stared at her. "So you didn't know?"

Emerson shook her head mutely.

"Well, now you do." Sean let out a sharp laugh. "I'm not positive that she was, but when she broke up with me the night of the accident, she just kept saying, 'I don't deserve you,' which everyone knows really means, 'I'm cheating on you.'"

"Wait, Tricia broke up with you that night?" Emerson knew she was starting to sound like a parrot but she couldn't help it. Her head was spinning with this new information.

"Yup. Last conversation we ever had," Sean replied. "Nice, huh?"

"And you really think she was cheating on you?" Emerson asked.

Sean nodded. "Even before that night, she'd been acting shady for a little while. She was always preoccupied, constantly checking her phone and making excuses to leave dates early. She went from being so into me, to practically forgetting I existed. And then at dinner a few nights before the accident, I heard her talking on the phone to someone when I came in from parking the car. Something about meeting up later. When she saw me, she hung up so fast you would have thought her phone was a bomb. She claimed it was her mom, but I didn't buy it for a second. So when she went to the bathroom, I looked at her phone." He shot Emerson a sheepish look. "I know it's not cool, but I was getting desperate."

"I get it." Emerson squeezed his arm, struggling to keep her voice neutral. "So was it her mom?"

Sean shrugged. "I couldn't tell. It was a blocked number."

Emerson's heart felt as if it were about to zoom right out of her chest. The messages she, Sydney, and Tenley had been getting all came from a blocked number.

"And you really have no idea who it could be?" she pressed.

"None. Unless it's Hunter. All I know is that the articles have it wrong. I don't think Tricia took fireworks onto the *Justice* to celebrate the end of Fall Festival. I think she took them to celebrate the end of us."

Emerson looked down, guilt and relief cascading through her all at once. Tricia had been cheating on Sean. Or at the very least, meeting up with someone behind his back—someone with a blocked phone number. It screamed one thing loud and clear: *accomplice*. Sean wasn't the person they were after at all. Tricia's mystery boy was.

Emerson bit down on her lip. She wished she could tell Sean how crazy Tricia had been—how lucky he was to have escaped her clutches unscathed. But she couldn't. So instead she gave him a quick hug. "She was right, you know. She didn't deserve you. Not if she was cheating," she added quickly.

"Thanks, Em." Sean pulled back, clearing his throat. "I guess we should get in there, right?" He glanced through the window at the waitress carrying a huge platter of pizzas over to their table.

"We're having pizza tapas," Emerson informed him. The heady scent of garlic and tomato rushed at her as she followed him inside.

Emerson tried to concentrate on her friends' conversation as they took their seats at the table. But her thoughts kept zooming back to Tricia. They'd been right. Tricia *hadn't* been working alone. They'd just been wrong about Sean. There had been someone else all along.

Her eyes flickered over to Nate and Tyler. Could Tricia have been cheating on Sean with one of them? Or Hunter? Could she have plotted and planned while curled up in the arms of one of their friends? The whole thing made Emerson want to bang her head against the table. Once again, they had more questions than answers.

Emerson was midway through a slice of sausage pizza when her phone buzzed in her bag. She reached for it, halfheartedly listening to the cheerleading story Jessie was telling. When she saw the screen, Jessie's voice seemed to fall away—replaced instantly by the sharp, insistent buzzing of fear.

Blocked.

No. Her skin went clammy as she jabbed open the message.

It's not just monsters that lurk under the bed! Your fireman friend has something that belongs to you. Get it back ASAP, or your affair becomes front-page news.

CHAPTER ELEVEN
Thursday, 7:15 AM

TENLEY MOVED QUIETLY DOWN THE STAIRS, CAREFUL to avoid the creaky step near the bottom. She was hoping to make it out of the house without her morning dose of motherly love. It was bad enough facing a barrage of questions about school before 8 AM; it would only be worse when she wasn't actually *going* to school.

Last night, as the hours passed and sleep continued to evade her, she'd lain in bed obsessing over the phone call she'd had with Emerson. Sean couldn't be the darer. Before her death, Tricia had been messing with him almost as much as she'd been messing with them: cheating on him, or at the very least meeting up with someone behind his back. Someone with a blocked number. *That* was the person who knew the most about Tricia. *That* was the person they wanted.

Guinness was still an option. Sydney kept swearing it was impossible, but she'd agreed to look into it. They knew their best bet was to get into Tricia's bedroom to search for clues, but right now there was no way to. The Suttons had left town after Tricia's funeral, and they still hadn't returned. Their house was locked up tight; Emerson had checked.

That left only one other lead: the toy train Caitlin had seen in her kidnapper's basement. The darer clearly didn't want Tenley to know who Caitlin's kidnapper was. Which of course meant she *had* to know. If she could just find the kidnapper, it would lead her straight to their darer. She could feel it in her bones.

Around two in the morning Tenley had made a decision. She'd promised Sydney she'd leave Joey Bakersfield out of this, but how could she? He was the only connection she could find to that train. She had no choice; she had to go to Danford Academy to talk to him. Even if it meant skipping school to do it.

Now she padded as quietly as she could down the slate-tiled hall-way, clutching the box of bright pink pepper spray bottles against her chest. They'd arrived last night and she planned to distribute them as soon as she got back from Danford today. She squeezed the box a little tighter. Just knowing she had some kind of protection made her feel a little safer.

As she passed by the dining room, she could hear her mom's voice floating out, lecturing Lanson on the latest TV special she'd seen about the Lost Girls. "In the past ten years, there have been more teenage deaths in Echo Bay than in any other town on the North Shore!" she was saying. Tenley could just picture her: painted lips pursed, double Ds spilling out as she leaned over the table. "It's an *epidemic!*"

"You forget where breakfast room is, Miss Tenley?"

Tenley started at the sound of Sahara's voice. The maid was

balancing a tray of croissants and fruit on her hip as she glowered down at Tenley.

"Shhh." Tenley pressed a finger to her lips, fixing Sahara with her most withering stare. "I was just on my way out," she whispered. "Tell my mom I was in a rush to get to school."

Sahara didn't bother masking her disgust as she bustled into the dining room. Tenley waited a beat, smoothing down the striped maxi dress she was wearing under a black cardigan. As soon as she heard Sahara start speaking, she slipped quietly out of the house.

An hour's drive later, she was walking through the stained-glass doors of Danford's main building. The lobby was filled with dark mahogany wood and had a crystal chandelier hanging from the ceiling. The left wall was lined with floor-to-ceiling bookshelves, a rolling ladder propped up against them. Tenley skimmed over some of the leather-bound titles. There was everything from *The Great Gatsby* to *The Encyclopedia of Mosquitoes*. A framed sign sat on one of the shelves, declaring it Danford's lending library. TAKE A BOOK, LEAVE A BOOK!

"Are you a visitor?" Tenley turned around to find a skinny, pimply-faced guy watching her from behind the front desk. He was clearly a student volunteer, a freshman most likely. "Because all visitors must sign in." He said it snootily, as if he wasn't sure he deemed Tenley worthy of visiting his precious school. Normally, she would have been quick to tear into him with a retort, but she forced herself to hold back. She needed his help if she was going to find Joey.

She smiled prettily as she walked over to the desk. The boy was wearing a khaki-and-blazer uniform, and he had a name tag pinned to his lapel. "Hi, Jeffery," she said. She leaned against the desk, looking up at him through her lashes. "I was hoping you could help me." She lowered her voice conspiratorially. "I'm here to surprise this guy I have a crush on." It was the story she'd come up with on her drive into the city. "I decided it was finally time to tell him how I feel. Seize the day, you know?" She beamed up at him. "Could you just tell me his room number? His name's Joey Bakersfield."

"I'm not supposed to do that," Jeffery said. But there was a hesitancy to his voice, and by the way he was shifting from foot to foot, she could tell he wasn't used to being this close to the female of the species.

"Oh." She infused her voice with disappointment. "Are you sure you can't make an exception? Just this once?" She leaned even closer, until she was practically whispering in his ear. "I swear I won't tell anyone."

Jeffery's eyes darted uneasily around the empty lobby.

"It would really make my day," she continued. She grabbed his hand in a last-ditch effort. "Please?"

Jeffery's cheeks blushed bright red. "A-all right," he stammered. "As long as you don't tell anyone it was me."

Tenley pressed a finger to her lips for the second time that morning. "Not a soul." She waited as Jeffery made several clicks with the mouse.

"Make a left out of the exit and walk three buildings down," he whispered. "Dorm Saturn, room 3C. Use code 7777 to enter." He cleared his throat, looking relieved that that was over. "And make sure no teachers see you! It's one of the male dorms, and we have very strict dorm visiting hours here. You'll stand out, being, you know..." His eyes darted over her, making his skin turn an unflattering shade of strawberry red. "...a girl," he finished falteringly.

"I'll be invisible," Tenley promised.

Outside, the buildings were swathed in ivy, and a brick path wound between them. A sign proclaimed Danford OUT OF THIS WORLD! and she soon understood why. The plaque on the first dorm declared it Dorm Mars, the second, Dorm Jupiter. She stopped in front of Dorm Saturn. It was an old stone building layered with ivy and speckled with maroon-and-white signs in almost every window. DANFORD ROBOT-ICS! DANFORD WRESTLING! DANFORD DANCERS! DANFORD GOES GREEN! Tenley smirked. Apparently Danford accepted all types—as long as they had school spirit.

Her smirk faded as she typed the code into the keypad and stepped into the building. The nerves she'd been fighting the whole trip multiplied instantly: a flock of birds attacking her insides. It wasn't as if this was the first sketchy thing she'd ever done, she reminded herself. She'd certainly done worse, often in the name of a pageant win. But it had never involved a boy she'd falsely—strongly—accused of being a deranged stalker.

She tried to distract herself as she climbed the stairs to the third floor, admiring the carved wooden banister and oil painting portraits that lined the walls. Engraved into each step was an elaborate crest, featuring a large *D*. This place made Winslow look almost shabby.

The distractions didn't help as she arrived on Joey's floor. She remembered how desperate she'd been the last time she'd seen him. She'd accused him point-blank of being a criminal. She knew that dropping the charges couldn't make up for what they'd put him through. "Gabby Douglas, London," she murmured under her breath. "Nastia Liukin, Beijing." She was in the middle of Carly Patterson, Athens, when a noise from behind startled her.

Footsteps.

They were rounding the corner, brisk and clipping. "I expect to see your essay by the end of the day, Mr. Seabourne!" a voice rang out. An adult, *teacher's* voice.

She spun frantically around, looking for a hiding spot. Her eyes fell on a bathroom nearby. BOYS, the sign read. Of course it did; this whole dorm was one big BOYS sign. The footsteps drew closer. She had two options: possible naked boys versus definite teacher run-in. She lunged for the door. Naked boys she could handle.

She pulled the door shut behind her just in time. She sagged against it, breathing hard as she listened to the teacher's footsteps click-clack their way toward the stairwell.

"I think I just stepped into my Ultimate Bathroom Fantasy."

At the sound of a male voice, Tenley whipped around with a yelp. A short, freckly guy was standing next to the showers on the other end of the bathroom, nothing but a towel wrapped around him. He had a mop of bright red hair on his head and a thin line of red hair running down his bare chest. He also had a very pleased grin on his face.

Tenley quickly composed herself. "Here's some friendly advice," she said after a beat. She kept her voice frostily matter-of-fact. "If you go around telling girls you have a 'bathroom fantasy,' you're never going to have anything *but* fantasies."

She spun on her heels without waiting for a response and stalked out of the bathroom. Before she could get waylaid again, she hurried over to Joey's room and knocked on the door.

No answer.

She tried again, listening hard. The door stayed closed. Inside the room, nothing stirred. Either Joey was still sleeping or he wasn't there.

Slowly, she twisted the handle. It was unlocked. She glanced furtively over her shoulder, then pushed the door open before she could change her mind.

The room was empty. It was also tiny, with a single twin bed against one wall and a doll-size desk and dresser against the other. The bed was swathed in an ugly plaid blanket, and on the wall were several of Joey's drawings, which he'd clearly taped up in a weak attempt at decorating. The desk was OCD-esque clean, with just a single framed photo sitting on it. In the photo, Joey and his mom were standing with their arms around each other on Great Harbor Beach.

Tenley wandered around, unable to keep from admiring Joey's drawings. They were actually kind of amazing: intricate illustrations of everything from old, gnarled trees, to Echo Bay tourist sites. She paused by one hanging next to the window. In it, a pretty girl was walking her dog, her long blond hair stirring in the breeze. *Caitlin.* Tenley recognized the drawing immediately. It was a page from the Winslow comic book Joey had been drawing, the one that had been so eerily focused on Caitlin. She leaned in, studying the picture. In it, Caitlin had her head tilted toward her dog, a tiny smile tugging on her lips. She looked relaxed, happy. The old Caitlin, unencumbered by dares and pills.

"Having a drawing of someone is not stalking, you know."

Tenley whipped around. Joey was standing in the doorway with his arms crossed against his chest. He looked different from a month ago. His long, sandy-blond hair had been cropped close, making it impossible for him to hide his face, and he'd swapped his ever-present hoodie for Danford's khaki-and-blazer uniform. It was strange to see him like that. Without all the freak-boy trappings, he was almost cute.

"W-what are you doing here?" he stammered.

She took a deep breath, mustering up her friendliest voice. "Your door was unlocked," she said. "I saw your drawings and just couldn't resist. They're…amazing." She glanced back at the page on the wall. The image was so lifelike that she almost expected Caitlin to lift her head and smile. She tore her eyes away. "You really captured Caitlin."

Joey gave her a guarded look. "Is this a setup?" He glanced sharply over his shoulder. "Are the cops about to swoop in on me again?"

"No! I, uh, well…" Now she was the one stammering. Tenley cleared her throat. Pageant queens three times over did *not* stammer. "I wanted to see if you knew anything about this toy." She held out her phone, which had the picture of Caitlin's train drawing on the screen. She launched into her lie. "I'm trying to find it for my cousin—he drew that—but apparently they're really rare. Someone mentioned that you might have one like it that I could buy."

Joey looked down at the picture, saying nothing. She suddenly worried that he simply wouldn't answer. As it was, this was the most she'd ever heard him talk. He shifted from foot to foot. What had to be a full minute passed before he finally spoke again. "I had a train like that." He kept his gaze on her phone, avoiding eye contact. "Got it for Christmas years ago. A Steinhard Limited Edition Circus Train. It's rare, a collector's item, actually."

"Did your mom get it for you?" Tenley chose her words carefully. She knew Joey's story. Everyone at Winslow did: His dad was M.I.A., his mom was a hairstylist, and he was at Winslow—and now Danford—on scholarship. His wasn't exactly the family she'd expect to run out and buy a collector's item for Christmas.

"Kind of." Joey glanced uneasily over his shoulder. He looked ready to bolt at any minute.

"Kind of?" Tenley pressed. She struggled not to let her frustration show. "How so?"

Joey transferred his gaze from the hallway to the floor of his room. "It was from one of those Re-Gift drives, you know, that Pat-a-Pancake runs every year? Usually the gifts were pretty crappy, beat-up stuffed animals, or board games missing half their pieces, so I couldn't believe my luck when I got that train. It was barely even used." He said it all in a single breath, like he just wanted to get it out. "Now, can I please have my room back?"

"Sure, as soon as you show me that train," Tenley said hopefully.

Joey sighed. "I don't have it anymore. Haven't for a long time. I brought it to school in fourth grade, and it was stolen out of the classroom."

Tenley looked up sharply. She didn't remember that part. "Who stole it?"

Joey lifted his head, meeting her eyes at last. The anger in them made Tenley squirm. "Some sick creep. Whoever it was replaced it with a dead squirrel. Obviously in honor of its oh-so-creative Rabies-Mobile nickname." He watched Tenley with a pained expression. "You sure it wasn't you?"

This time, Tenley was the one to look away. After Joey got mauled by a dog in first grade, she'd been one of the first to start calling him Rabies Boy. She hadn't left it at that, either. She'd made bite marks in his lunch sandwiches and filled his backpack with "rabid" foam. At the time, she'd believed it was all just fun and games. But if there was one thing she'd learned from the darer, it was how little fun those games really were. "It wasn't me," she said softly. Her stomach knotted up as she rocked back on her heels. "So you never got it back?"

Joey toyed with the textbook he was holding. INTRO TO ANIMA-TION was printed across the cover. "Nope. Gone forever."

Tenley thought backward. Caitlin was kidnapped in sixth grade. Which meant that whoever had stolen Joey's train was the person whose basement Caitlin had seen it in. Joey—and his family—couldn't have been involved at all.

But whatever psycho had replaced the train with a dead squirrel could have been.

The whole thing made her want to scream. She'd gone all the way out to Danford, and all she'd learned was that the kidnapper was somehow connected to Winslow—at least enough to get inside a fourth-grade classroom. It wasn't much to go on.

Gritting her teeth, she refocused on Joey. "You're sure you don't remember anything else?" she pushed. "About the train, or who could have stolen it? *Anything?*" She knew she was starting to sound desperate, but she didn't care. If Joey knew something, she was going to get it out of him, even if she had to ask a hundred times. She took a deep breath and flashed Joey her friendliest smile, not wanting to startle him back into silence. "For my cousin, of course."

"I...Well, I did look it up online once," Joey said reluctantly. "To see how much it would cost to replace it. I found a few listed at estate sales, antique stores, places like that. But, you know, they were pricey." He fidgeted with his textbook again. "Now, if that's it..." He stepped aside, leaving an open pathway to the door. He looked strained, as if the effort of conversation had worn him out.

"Yeah, I guess so," she said, disappointed. "Thanks." She'd made it halfway to the door when she stopped. "Actually, that's not it." She turned back around to find a horrified expression on Joey's face.

She ignored it, forging ahead. "I—I also wanted to talk to you," she said haltingly. "We—I—never got to say sorry last month. What we accused you of...We were so wrong. We found those in your locker and—"

"Someone planted them there," Joey cut in.

"I know," Tenley said quickly. "Now I do. But at the time, we got really freaked out. We jumped to conclusions that we shouldn't have. And...I'm sorry." She traced a scratch on the floor with her eyes. She couldn't help thinking of the Rabies-Mobile, of all those years she'd taunted him, played games of her own. "Really sorry," she added softly. She looked back up to find Joey staring at her. She expected to see that anger in his eyes again, maybe even hatred. But instead, he just looked sad. "For everything," she finished.

Joey nodded. "Thanks," he said quietly. He paused, picking at the spine of his textbook. "Did you ever find out who it really was? Was it really just a prank like you said?"

A lie automatically sprang to her tongue, but she swallowed it back. Lies were what had sent Joey to Danford in the first place. She couldn't take back what she'd done—would never be able to change it—but maybe this was a chance to give him a little peace of mind. She couldn't ignore that.

"It wasn't a prank," she said finally. "One of our friends was angry about something we did to her as kids and...she wanted revenge." She bit nervously on her bottom lip. The darer would skewer her if it ever got out that she'd told Joey the truth about Tricia. Then again, the darer already wanted to skewer her. And then barbecue her to a crisp. "She set you up," she continued. "Made us believe it was you."

"Which you all did without batting an eye." Joey let out a harsh laugh. "Easy, right? Just blame Rabies Boy for all that creeps and crawls at Winslow."

"I'm sorry," she said again. The apology sounded useless even to her.

A shrill beep sounded in the room. "A school-wide assembly will commence in ten minutes," a voice announced over the loud-speaker.

"I guess that's my cue," Tenley said hesitantly. She waited for Joey to reply, but he just nodded again. "Thanks again for your help." She pushed past him awkwardly, hurrying into the hall. She'd made to the stairwell when her phone let out a beep. She stopped so abruptly she almost tumbled down the steps. She had no memory of reaching into her bag, but suddenly the phone was in her hand, the text message staring up at her.

Thought you could play Nancy Drew and get away with it? I warned you. . . . Now it's time to pay. T-48 hours till D-Day. And by D, I do mean death.

Tenley opened her mouth, but no sound came out. She'd been caught. The darer was everywhere, knew everything. Anger surged through her like an electric storm. And with it, a sudden sense of clarity. It didn't matter what she did. It didn't matter what rules she followed. She was prey, and the darer was predator. This wouldn't stop until the darer went in for the kill.

She squeezed her phone in her hands. She had forty-eight hours left. Forty-eight hours to stop this.

She was in her car and speeding toward the Echo Bay Police Station before she'd even consciously made the decision. If the darer planned to kill her regardless, why *not* go to the cops? She had nothing to lose anymore. Sydney and Emerson might not like it, but that was too bad. She was the one who was next on the darer's hit list.

She made it back to Echo Bay in record time. Her tires squealed as she jerked to a stop in the police station parking lot. Her mind was already racing through what she should say to the cops. Should she show them the texts? Would they know how to trace their origin? Should she tell them about Tricia? Should she—

Her thoughts were interrupted by a loud beep. Her phone.

"No," she whispered. "It can't be."

It was.

I see all. Set foot in that building and Mommy Reed will end up right where she belongs.

The darer had to be following her! She spun around in a circle, frantically scanning the lot. But other than the cop cars, it was completely empty. Echo Bay wasn't exactly a hotbed of crime. Or at least it hadn't been.

Goose bumps spread across Tenley's arms as several cars drove past on the street. This darer was like a shadow: stealthy and invisible, tailing her every move.

She was quaking all over as she turned her attention back to her phone. There was a photo attached to the message. Holding her breath, she clicked it open.

The photo showed a graveyard plot with a single tombstone on it. BENJAMIN GREER, the stone read. LOVING FATHER, HUSBAND, AND FRIEND.

A cry escaped Tenley. It was their family plot in the local cemetery. Tenley remembered how hard she'd cried when she found out that it included a spot for her mom as well. "You can't leave me, too!" she'd shrieked over and over again at the time, clinging desperately to her mom's legs.

Tenley's eyes flitted back to the message. *Set foot in that building and Mommy Reed will end up right where she belongs.*

"No," she gasped. She staggered back to her car, collapsing inside. She thought she had nothing left to lose, but she'd been wrong. She jammed her key into the ignition and slammed down on the gas. Then she tore out of the lot and away from that building, as fast as her car would take her.

CHAPTER TWELVE
Thursday, 2:35 PM

SYDNEY SAW THE CARD TACKED TO HER LOCKER FROM halfway down the hallway. it was a robin's-egg blue, with the silhouette of a ring printed on the front. It was the end of the school day and the hallways were packed with people, but Sydney suddenly felt as if she were standing in a tunnel all alone. The hallway seemed to disappear as the card pulled her toward it with a magnetic force.

She pulled off the Winslow Academy sticker—the kind cheerleaders gave out at pep rallies—that was holding the card in place. Behind her, some freshmen were whining about a killer test, but Sydney barely heard them. All she could focus on was the typewriter font on the inside of the card.

Roses are red, your ring is blue. I really
wish I could see it on you....

Sydney squeezed the card so hard it crumpled in her grip. *The ring.* It hadn't been from Guinness at all. It had been from the darer.

That, or Guinness *was* the darer.

The thought crept up on her like an attack. She'd been so insistent that Guinness wasn't involved. But that gift practically screamed his name. Not just because it was blue, or because he'd once promised her a ring, but because it was so *her*. She was not a big jewelry person, but she would have picked out that ring herself. Could someone else know her taste that well? Her stomach roiled. She could taste bile in the back of her throat. If the darer had been watching her for long enough, maybe the answer was yes.

Sydney took off blindly for her car. She'd already been planning to drive out to Chief Hackensack's house, and this only made her more determined. She knew she should shoot some photos first—it was Thursday, and she still didn't have a "unique and awe-inspiring hometown image" for her application due Monday—but she couldn't fathom focusing on photography right now. Ever since she'd managed to get into Kyla's file yesterday, those images had been skating through her mind, consuming every one of her thoughts. It was the anger in them that had gotten under her skin. The fire had seemed almost human in its fury, the way it assaulted the boat with a vengeance, eyes burning and weapons slinging. It reminded Sydney of the fire on the *Justice*: how it had felt like a punishment, a *judgment*.

And then, of course, there was the missing photo, number twenty-two. It kept taunting her: What could it be of? The whole thing was just so strange. She knew firsthand how meticulously the fire department maintained those files. A missing picture would be a huge deal, at the very least worthy of an annotation to the report. But there hadn't been a single mention of it.

She'd thought about asking her dad, but then she'd have to admit she'd sneaked into his files. Besides, he hadn't even been the chief on the case. Gerry Hackensack had. Hopefully he could clear up this whole thing—prove without a doubt that Kyla's death was an accident. Once she knew for sure that Guinness wasn't involved, she could move on, *forget* him, and concentrate on finding the real darer.

It took Sydney forty minutes and three wrong turns to drive out to Pippsy, the small, ritzy boating town where Gerry Hackensack now lived. Finally, she pulled up to a tall stone house with three white pillars out front. "Whoa," Sydney murmured. She knew how much her dad made as fire chief, and it could never buy a house like this.

There were two cars in the driveway, a Prius and an SUV. The SUV had a handicap parking tag, which made Sydney pause. She had a vague memory of Gerry and his wife, and she didn't remember either of them being handicapped. She looked back at the opulent house, with its elaborate wooden door and fancy iron flower boxes in the windows. Maybe she had the wrong place.

She took a deep breath, squaring her shoulders. There was only one way to find out.

She reached into her bag to check for the small pink bottle of pepper spray. Tenley had brought it with her when she showed up late to school that afternoon, muttering something about a stomachache. Sydney had smirked as she accepted the bottle, but she was suddenly very glad to have it.

She was jittery as she strode across the lawn. She had no idea what she was walking into. Her palms were sticky as she lifted her hand to knock on the door.

A woman who looked to be in her early thirties answered. She wore wire-rimmed glasses and had a polite smile. "Can I help you?"

Sydney swallowed hard. Her throat felt like sandpaper. "Is this Gerry Hackensack's house?" She cringed a little at the crackly sound of her voice. She had to get a hold of herself if she wanted this to work.

"Yes, I'm his daughter, Margot." A wrinkle formed between her eyebrows. "What can I do for you?"

Sydney cleared her throat. "My name's Sarah," she said, rushing into the cover story she'd come up with. She felt guilty using a fake name, but the less chance the darer—or anyone—had of tracking her here, the better. "I'm a student at Winslow Academy, and I'm doing a report on the Kyla Kern accident for school. Since Mr. Hackensack was the fire chief at the time, I was hoping I could maybe ask him some questions?" The words tumbled out fast, one after another.

Margot's polite smile widened into a real one. "You know what? I bet he'd love that." She ushered Sydney inside. "He tries to hide it," she whispered confidingly, "but I can tell how much he misses that firehouse. Sometimes I have to wonder if his early retirement somehow played a role in his stroke."

"Stroke?" Sydney asked. Something tightened in her chest. That would explain the handicap parking tag.

"Oh, yes." Margot gave her a somber look. "You didn't know? My dad had a stroke six months after retiring." She led Sydney down a long hallway with fancy molding along the ceiling. An iron chandelier cast a soft glow over a plush oriental rug. "He can still communicate," she continued. "But very slowly. And you know how it is. Some days are better than others. But hearing about the firehouse always cheers him up. You know he gave thirty-five years of service to that place?"

"Wow," Sydney said quietly. She thought about telling Margot who her dad was, but the look on Margot's face stopped her. This woman clearly idolized her father; Sydney had no interest in pretending she felt the same. An uncomfortable flush crept onto her face. Margot was being so nice to her, and all she was doing was lying in return.

"You have a visitor, Dad!" Margot called out. Sydney tried to steady her breathing as she followed her into the living room. From the sound of it, Gerry Hackensack was a nice man, one who'd loved serving his town. She could do this.

The living room walls were painted a soft gray, and a flat-screen TV hung on one of them. Sitting in a wheelchair by a large bay window was Gerry Hackensack. He looked too young to be retired, sixty or so at the oldest. At first glance, he didn't even seem to require a wheelchair. But when he smiled at Sydney, she saw that only half of his face smiled with him. He gave his daughter a crooked nod.

"She was hoping to talk to you about the Kyla Kern accident for a school project. That was your last case as chief, right?"

"I believe it was," Gerry said. His words were thick and clunky. It sounded like they took great effort.

"I know how much you like to talk about the firehouse," Margot continued. "I thought you two could chat for a few minutes."

"About Kyla Kern," Gerry Hackensack said slowly, laboring over each word.

"I was hoping I could ask you a few questions," Sydney jumped in. "I already got permission to look at the old file in the firehouse, but it would be great to hear a firsthand description as well." She rushed on before he could catch her lie about the firehouse. "You know, the kind of details that aren't in a report: what it smelled like, how the heat felt. Who you saw, and how Kyla's friends reacted. Things like that. Maybe I could even look through your old records, too?" It was a gutsy move, but Sydney had no choice; she had to go for it. She pressed on before she could lose her nerve. "I noticed photo number twenty-two

152

was missing in the official file, and I was hoping maybe you had a copy of it here?"

She was talking fast, hoping the speed would distract Gerry from all her lies, but at the mention of the missing photo, she stopped short. Something in Gerry's demeanor had changed. A stiffening. It might have been indiscernible if it weren't for the way his hands clamped down on the arms of his wheelchair. His eyes darted up toward hers. He looked as if he was about to say something when a terrible cough wracked his body. "I—" he attempted. But the coughing only grew worse, and he gave up trying to speak as he doubled over in his chair.

Margot was by his side in an instant, gently rubbing his back. "Let's get you to bed, Dad," she said soothingly. She glanced at Sydney. "It looks like you're going to have to come back, Sarah," she said apologetically. "Maybe tomorrow?" She grabbed a glass of water off the table as she spoke and pressed it gently to Gerry's lips. "Coughing fits like these come out of nowhere, and it takes my dad a while to recover."

Sydney nodded politely, but inside, she was reeling. That coughing fit hadn't come out of nowhere. It had been the mention of the missing photo; it had agitated him—she'd *seen* it. She couldn't leave now.

"Could I use your bathroom first?" The request burst right out of her. "It's a long drive back to Echo Bay."

"Sure, of course." Margot waved Sydney down the hallway as she began rolling her dad in the other direction. "Third door on the right. And sorry again about this, Sarah."

Sydney gave Margot a weak smile. She waited for her to disappear around a corner with Gerry, then took off down the hall. She moved as quietly as she could, flinging open every door she saw. A guest bedroom, a linen closet, the aforementioned bathroom. And then, finally,

153

what she was looking for: an office. She'd hoped it would be down here, since Gerry had no way of getting up to the second floor.

Guilt swelled in her as she sneaked into the room. This wasn't some file in a firehouse; this was snooping around in someone's *home*. But she had no choice. She needed answers. She took a quick glance around. There was a desk, along with a bookshelf piled high with novels and a fancy leather reading chair. Her eyes skimmed over the rest, going straight to the back corner of the room. There it was, exactly what she'd hoped for: a stack of boxes.

She glanced nervously over her shoulder as she squatted down in front of them. She could hear the faint sound of Gerry's coughing drifting down the long hallway. She still had a minute. She rifled quickly through the boxes. The first was filled with personal mementos: a certificate of honor signed by the mayor, a Rotary Club plaque memorializing Hackensack's years of service, and a whole stack of thank-you cards. She moved on to the next one. It was packed with files, all lined up in date order.

Sydney looked at their labels as she flipped through them. 118 KNOX RD. 22 WILLOW LANE. 7 ECHO BOULEVARD. She recognized that one as Pat-a-Pancake's address. A memory danced in her mind, making her pulse quicken: blue flames tearing through Pat-a-Pancake's awning, melting it to ash. It had taken the restaurant a whole year to rebuild after that fire. She flipped to the next file, banishing the tantalizing image from her mind. YACHT CLUB KITCHEN. 83 HERSHAW LANE. 4 DUNE WAY. WINSLOW SCIENCE LAB. And, finally, the very last file in the box. KYLA KERN. "Jackpot," she whispered.

She glanced over her shoulder again, listening for footsteps. Instead she heard another bout of coughing, this one louder than the last. Her heart was thudding as she turned back to the file. It looked identical to the one in the firehouse: the same report, the same "before" shot, the same stack of photos. She thumbed furiously to the second-to-last image. There, at the bottom, was a number. 22. Sydney's breath came out in a long rush. It was the missing photo.

She drew the photo close, studying it. Unlike the others, which photographed the entire boat float, this one was a close-up. It focused on a crater in the floor of the float, right in the center. It was deep, with a web of cracks spreading out of it. The crater had been easy to miss in the other photos, but zoomed in like this, there was no doubt that it was the largest hole on the ruined float. In fact, it looked as if *that* was where the explosion had taken place.

Sydney bunched up her forehead, turning back to Hackensack's report. In it, he clearly stated that the large, gold star had been hanging in the back of the float when it exploded, not the center. She shuffled through the rest of the photos. Now that she was looking for it, it seemed glaringly obvious in every one: the worst damage was in the center of the float. Something had definitely landed there.

Sydney leaned against the box, thinking. The wind must have turned the star into a giant fireball after it exploded, propelling it to the middle of the float. Her stomach lurched at the thought of Kyla caught beneath it. She knew from experience what wind could do, how it could take a gentle flame and turn it into a ruthless hunter. It must have been horrible to be out there that night, with sparks tossing wildly on the wind, hounding their victims.

Except—*there was no wind that night.*

That was what Guinness had said. He and his friends never left the marina because the wind was dead. She'd looked it up later that night, too, curious to see if his story matched up. It had. She'd seen it in several news articles: how still a night it had been, windless and dry.

With no wind, the star should have landed right where it had exploded—in the back of the float. She stared down at the image in her hand. The crater in the center stared back at her, splintering outward. She'd seen many fires before. They ate through whole structures and turned wood to ash, but they didn't make craters like that. No, something had definitely *landed* there. But if not the star...then what?

She could only think of one possible explanation. Something else had caused the fire—something that had been *thrown* at the boat. The weight of what that meant thudded through her.

Tenley was right; the Kyla accident hadn't been an accident at all.

And someone had hidden the only photo that proved that.

Sydney's head was swimming as she slipped the photo into her purse and hurried out of the Hackensacks' house. Facts danced through her head, falling into place one after another. Gerry Hackensack had retired right after Kyla's case closed. A photo was now missing from Kyla's file—the only photo that seemed to prove that her death wasn't an accident. And here Hackensack was, living in a house you could never in a million years buy on a fireman's salary. If it didn't sound so crazy, she might just think that someone had paid Hackensack to take that photo and run.

It was a chilling thought, but she couldn't shake it. What if someone had bribed him to retire and stay quiet—the same someone who had caused the explosion? It might help explain the stroke Hackensack had six months after retiring; the stress of deceit could have sent his health spiraling downward.

That would make this a lot more than just a boat float gone wrong, another Lost Girls tragedy. That would make this a homicide...and a cover-up.

Sydney felt sick as she jogged to her car. She kept envisioning Kyla's bright smile. She'd been so friendly, so full of life. Who would have wanted to take that away? Now that she'd seen the missing photo, Sydney couldn't just let it drop. She had to do *something*. But what?

She couldn't go to the cops. Not with the darer breathing down their necks. Maybe she could go back to the firehouse instead. Tell them there was another photo that should be included in the case file—an important one. Let *them* go to the cops. But even as she was planning out her course of action, she couldn't help thinking about whom that might implicate.

Who had not only known Kyla but was now *hiding* the fact that he'd known her? Who had the obvious means—and family influence—to pull off a bribery scam like this? The answer slammed into her like a concrete block: Guinness.

She'd gone to the Hackensacks' hoping to prove Guinness's innocence, but even she couldn't ignore the facts. Every finger pointed directly at him. The ring. The note on his bed. And now this.

She wobbled on her feet. What if Tenley was right? What if Guinness *was* the darer?

The question reared wildly in her head, but when she saw what was on the windshield of her car, it fled instantly, stamped out by fear. A square of paper was tucked under one of her wipers: too white to be a ticket, too small to be a takeout menu.

She looked around the quiet street. A ways down, a little girl was riding her bicycle as her babysitter watched. Next door, the smell of lasagna wafted through an open window, along with the theme song for *Friends*. There was no one suspicious, nothing amiss. *It's probably just a coupon*, she told herself. Still, panic slithered its way up her throat as she unfolded it. There it was: the typewriter font.

She let out a choked cry. First her locker at Winslow, now her car forty minutes away in Pippsy. It didn't matter where she went, or what name she used. The darer would find her.

Sydney was quaking all over as she began to read.

```
I spy with my little eye...a Curious
George. Go to the Vault Friday at 10 pm if
you want to dig deeper. But careful: When
you play with fire, there's always a chance
you'll get burned.
```

CHAPTER THIRTEEN
Thursday, 4:45 PM

EMERSON TURNED THE SILVER KEY OVER IN HER PALM. Matt had lent it to her once, and she'd never gotten around to giving it back. When she'd searched through the junk drawer in her desk this morning, there it had been, as if it were waiting for her. At the time, she'd been flooded with relief. But now, as she stood outside the weathered beach house where Matt rented the top floor, her relief was replaced by a cold sense of dread. She'd tried so hard to forget the whole Matt Morgan part of her life. Now, she was walking right back into it.

She could turn back. But the darer's threat remained inked in her mind, like the worst kind of tattoo. *It's not just monsters that lurk under the bed! Your fireman friend has something that belongs to you. Get it back ASAP, or your affair becomes front-page news.* She'd faked a headache to get out of cheer practice early for this. It was time to go through with it.

She slid the key into the lock. A second later she was inside.

The house was empty, just as she'd known it would be. The owner technically occupied the bottom floor, but, according to Matt, he'd spent the last two years living in France. She jogged up to the second-floor apartment. She knew Matt wouldn't be home. As much as she hated it, she still knew his weekly work schedule by heart. How could she not? She'd planned her whole summer around it. The thought made her sick to her stomach.

Inside, she turned on the lamp that sat next to Matt's worn leather couch. The apartment was a true bachelor pad, not a woman's touch in sight. This summer, she'd loved that about it. She was taken back to the last time she'd been here. She and Matt had been tangled together on the couch, and he'd been telling her about his plans for after her graduation. They would take the whole summer together, travel somewhere far and exotic, somewhere where they'd be seen as equals, where no one would judge them. At the time, she'd looked around his apartment—at the makeshift kitchen and the undecorated walls, all so temporary feeling—and she'd believed him. Once Sydney graduated, there would be nothing tying Matt to Echo Bay. Certainly not this home. Maybe they'd even make it permanent. Never come back. *Hawaii*, she'd told him. *That's where I want to go.*

Now, as her eyes landed on a new framed photo on the TV stand, a shot of Matt and Tracey by Motif No. 1, a famous fishing shack in Rockport, it hit her all over again just how ridiculous she'd been. The whole thing had been nothing but a fantasy; she'd seen what she'd wanted to see.

She went into the bedroom, wincing when she saw the woman's robe discarded on the edge of his bed. She'd only spent one night in that bed, and it wasn't one she liked to think about. Matt had spent the night making it very clear that *sleeping* was not on his agenda. Emerson had managed to resist that night, and for many nights after. She could never explain to him what was holding her back; it wasn't as if it would be her first time. But for some reason it seemed different with Matt, as if she'd be stepping over some kind of invisible barrier. In the end, they'd only really been together once, during that night at the Seagull Inn.

She'd felt strange afterward—not bad, but not good, either, as if she'd let some essential part of herself go. Sometimes she wished she could just turn back the clock to *before*. But that was just a fantasy, too. Emerson braced herself as she pulled open Matt's closet, scanning for something that belonged to her. Nothing. She'd just moved onto the dresser when it hit her: *It's not just monsters that lurk under the bed!* She dropped down at the foot of the bed, pushing the half-strewn blanket aside. There it was. Sitting amid dust bunnies and a stray shoe: a small plastic storage box, with one of her pom-poms sticking out of it. She'd left that pom-pom in Matt's truck the night he ended things with her. She'd chosen to buy a new one rather than face him again.

She pulled the box out. It was filled to the brim with her belongings: one of her T-shirts, a note she'd written Matt that morning in the Seagull Inn, a perfume sample she liked to carry in her purse. She pulled out a pair of panties. They were neon yellow, with a bright pink bow on the butt. Emerson gasped. The underwear slipped from her grip, tumbling back into the box. That was *not* hers.

She dug deeper. There were other things, too, that weren't hers. A thin volume of love poems. A Winslow homecoming queen sash. A C-cup bra that would hang on her slender frame. "Oh my god," Emerson whispered. The burger she'd eaten for dinner rose in her throat. This wasn't some sweet Emerson Memory Box. This was Matt's trophy collection. These were mementos from his conquests.

Thud!

The faint sound drifted up from downstairs, making Emerson

freeze. Someone was here. Her eyes flew to the clock. Matt should still be at work! Footsteps began making their way steadily up the stairs. Emerson jumped up, still clutching the box.

Ba-bum. Ba-bum. Ba-bum.

The footsteps climbed upward. Her heart beat wildly in time to them. The only way out was past whoever was on the way up. What if it was the darer? What if she'd been set up? Her free hand went automatically to her purse, where the bottle of pepper spray from Tenley was nestled.

The footsteps drew closer, punctuated by the ringing of a cell phone. The person paused. A second later she heard a man's voice. "Hey, Trace. I'm just stopping by my place."

Matt. She expected relief, but she just felt queasy. If Matt found her here after seeing her on that horrible boat ride...he would be convinced she was stalking him. She had to hide.

She took a hasty look around the room. If she curled up under the bed, there was a chance Matt wouldn't notice her. As long as he didn't look down. She was just about to make a dive for it when her gaze landed on the fire escape in the back of the bedroom. *Perfect!*

The apartment door creaked as it swung open. Matt's laughter spilled in. "I said no such thing!" she heard him tease.

Emerson raced over to the fire escape and shoved the window up. She was outside, box still in hand, in under thirty seconds. She glanced back at the window, which now sat widely askew. She could hear Matt in the living room. She had to leave it.

She bolted down the metal stairs, clutching the box to her chest. She'd parked her car half a block down, and she refused to look over her shoulder as she sprinted toward it. Only when she'd driven to the end of the street did she allow herself a glance in the rearview mirror.

She could just make out Matt's outline through the window. His back was to her, but his head was thrown back, as if he was still laughing.

Tears welled in Emerson's eyes. Matt's box seemed to scream at her from the passenger seat: *Naive!* She pressed down harder on the gas, making the car jolt forward. The whole time she'd been with Matt, there had been one thing she'd been confident of: He'd chosen her. He was older, and experienced, and a hero in town, and he wanted *her.* Even after he ended things, even after the illusion had been shattered, that one tiny bit of knowledge had stayed with her. But it was a lie; it had never been just her.

Was that what the darer wanted? To make sure she knew she'd never been special? The humiliation came flooding back—a whirlpool of it, sucking her right in. It was New York all over again. She wasn't special. She wasn't wanted. She was just easy.

Pain knifed through her chest. She squeezed her hands around the wheel, fighting against it. She couldn't fall apart. She refused to give the darer that satisfaction. She was *Em Cunningham.* She was beautiful, she was a model, she was the girl every other girl at Winslow strived to be. She was *better* than this darer—whoever it was.

By the time she got home, Emerson had managed to push Matt's box-o'-creepy to the back of her mind. She was above it; she had to remember that. She shoved the box under her bed, where she would never have to see it again.

On the floor, Holden let out a long string of peeps. She crouched down in front of his cage. "You're right, he *is* scum," she said, smiling as he chirped even louder. She flipped open the door, and Holden waddled out, pecking eagerly at her hand. She scooped up the duckling and gave him a kiss on his fuzzy head. "What do you say to a little fresh air, buddy?"

She carried Holden to the front porch and sank into one of the overstuffed lounge chairs. The porch had always been her favorite thing about her family's house in Echo Bay. It wrapped all the way around, like a moat shielding them from the outside world. She and Caitlin had spent half their freshman year on that porch, dissecting every detail of school. They were like hyenas, her mom used to joke, picking apart their days until only bone and carcass were left.

Emerson leaned back in the chair, smiling down at Holden as he scampered across her lap. After all this time, Josh still knew just how to get to her. A *duckling*. No one else would ever fathom giving Emerson an animal. But Josh had always known her best.

She remembered how excited Caitlin had been when Emerson met Josh. "A real live New York City boy," she'd joked when Emerson called her at two in the morning after their first date. "I'm so jealous!" She'd missed Caitlin so much that summer, living in the cramped modeling dorms, sharing bathrooms with catty girls who thought iceberg lettuce was a meal. She felt so out of place there, so alone. But then she met Josh.

It was on the subway. He was smirking as he watched her struggle with the ancient map she'd found in her dorm room, until finally she turned to him and snapped, "Didn't your mom teach you it's rude to stare?" He went all courtly on her after that, offering to walk her where she needed to go. Two subway stops and eight blocks later, they had a date set up for that night.

Before long they were inseparable. She'd never connected with a guy like that before, never dated someone who actually made the *friend* in *boyfriend* make sense. He'd been the best part of her summer in New York. Until she had to go and ruin it. She closed her eyes as the memory rushed back to her.

It had been one of those sticky, hot New York City days. The blast of AC in the modeling studio was a welcome relief. They were shooting a group ad that day, and she instantly disliked the other two models. She could tell they were the kind of girls who'd always been pretty, who'd never been teased a day in their lives. As she worked alongside them, all of Emerson's old insecurities came railing back at her, like an assault. She wasn't Em, the Neutrogena model, anymore. She was Emmy, the girl who would never deserve any of this.

But then the photographer, Remsen, a young, hot up-and-comer, started focusing on her. He put her in the center of the shots and had her inch in front of the other girls. He told her she was beautiful, perfect, the star of the ad; and the way he said it, she believed every word. She *was* this girl. By the end of the shoot, she was riding high. She could feel the other girls' jealous glares, could feel their looking at her the way she'd looked at them only hours before. When Remsen asked her to the back room to comb through some shots, she was eager to accompany him.

But when they got there, there was no computer, no photos. Remsen closed the door. Before she could ask him what was going on, he pulled her to him and kissed her. It took her completely by surprise. It was different from kissing Josh: fiercer, more intense. For a second she found herself kissing him back. Then she heard it: the voice in her head, hissing like an angry cat. *Josh.*

She pulled away. "I can't," she whispered.

"No problem," Remsen said easily. He smiled, his hands working their way through her hair, sliding down her arms. "I probably shouldn't have anyway. But there's something about you, Emerson." He leaned in close, whispering into her ear. "You're that girl, you know?" His breath was warm against her neck. "The one you always hope to find. You're irresistible."

He kept talking, about her beauty and her career, about her *specialness*; and she wanted so badly for it all to be true. For him to be right. Then he was kissing her again, and she *felt* it, as if she really was that girl: Emmy erased forever. The voice in her head tried once more—*Josh*—but Remsen was already pulling her onto the table. His hands slid under her shirt and unbuttoned her pants, and she was powerful, beautiful, the girl she was meant to be. Soon, the voice faded into nothing.

Afterward, he gave her a quick kiss on the cheek. "Thanks, beautiful," he said. Then he pulled his clothes on and strolled back into the studio, as if it had meant nothing, been nothing. Standing there, alone and half dressed, the weight of what she'd done slammed into her. She'd never felt so awful in her life. She spent the next two days crying and avoiding Josh's phone calls. She thought of a thousand ways to tell him, but in the end she knew it wouldn't matter. What she'd done couldn't be forgiven. So she'd tacked a note to his door, and she'd left.

"Nap time?"

Emerson's eyes flew open. There he was, on her porch, watching her with those green-brown eyes. She couldn't help but smile at his sweater with a retro walrus on it. He'd been obsessed with walruses when they'd dated.

"Josh." She quickly extracted herself from the chair, balancing Holden in her palms. "What are you doing here?"

She was standing closer to him than she'd meant to, and a familiar warmth spread through her. It was the way he'd always made her feel: As if beneath all the excitement and nerves, there was something burning deep inside her, warming her from the inside out. Around other guys, she was so meticulous, careful—say the right thing, do the right thing, look the right way—but around Josh, she could just breathe.

"I came to check on my gift," Josh informed her. He gave Holden a stroke on the back, and the duckling nipped at his wrist in response. "And I have to say, he actually looks healthy."

Emerson narrowed her eyes. "I will have you know that he is on a very regimented eating schedule. And exercise routine. Last night we held some Olympics-worthy races across my bedroom floor."

"Did you win?" Josh asked with a laugh.

"Well, it's not really about *winning*," she said, as Holden lifted his wings and made an awkward fly-leap into Josh's hands.

Josh lifted Holden up until they were nose to beak. "I'll take that as a no."

"He's one fast little duckling," Emerson admitted. She held out her hands and made a soft clucking noise. Immediately Holden turned around and began waddling back down Josh's arm. He let out a soft chirp as he clumsily jump-flew back into her outstretched hands. "I taught him that."

Josh raised his eyebrows, looking impressed. "Emerson Cunningham, duck whisperer."

"I've been called worse," Emerson joked. As soon as the words were out of her mouth, she regretted them. The darer's notes sprang to her mind. *Slut.* She turned away, not wanting Josh to see the flush spreading across her cheeks.

"So I was hoping I could finally cash in my hour of your time," Josh said. "Want to go for a walk? And before you say anything, let me provide you with your three acceptable responses. Response A: *Okay.* Response B: *Fine.* Response C—my personal favorite: *Great!*"

Emerson tried to conceal the grin tugging at her lips. "Sure," she said smugly, drawing out the word.

Josh groaned. "You just have to be a rebel, don't you?"

Emerson eyed Josh's half Mohawk and patched-up leather coat. "That's me," she said wryly. "Rebel with a capital *R*."

She left Josh laughing on the porch as she went to put Holden back in his cage. She took her time returning down the stairs, giving herself a pep talk on the way. It was just a walk. She would be friendly but platonic. Nice but hands-off. It didn't matter what feelings Josh stirred up; she had no room in her life for a guy right now. Not with the darer throwing the Monstrous Matt Morgan Mistake in her face at every turn. She'd say what she needed to so Josh would let her be. As long as it didn't involve the truth.

She paused at the door, smoothing down the vintage polka-dot shirt she was wearing under her favorite black blazer. She could do this.

"The duck's all settled," she announced, stepping back onto the porch. She beckoned for Josh to follow as she started down the stairs. "I still can't believe you're here," she said. "All the way from the Big Apple." She kept her tone light. The longer she could keep them on small talk, the less time Josh would have to ask her that dreaded question, the one she'd managed to avoid for over a year.

"Boston, actually," Josh said as they strolled down the street. "I've been living there for the past year."

"Mr. Manhattan himself abandoned the island?" she asked, feigning disbelief. Josh was a born-and-raised New Yorker. When she'd met him, he'd been entering his eighteenth consecutive year in the city that never slept. "What happened to starting at NYU?" As she spoke, she pointed him in the direction of downtown, and their steps fell into sync as they always used to on their walks in New York.

"Remember that manuscript I was working on that summer?" Josh asked.

"The one you would never let me read?"

Josh smiled sheepishly. "That's the one."

That whole summer Emerson had tried to get Josh to show her the novel he was writing, claiming she knew all about the writing process from her dad—even though her dad's historical-fiction tomes usually put her to sleep by page three. It was strange how long ago that felt, like another, happier, Technicolor life. "I remember," Emerson said.

"Well, I sold it to a publisher." He stole a glance at her, his eyes flashing green-brown-green-brown in the sunlight. "So I deferred NYU and moved to Boston to work on my revisions. I felt like I needed a fresh start if I wanted to see the book in a fresh way, you know?"

"Oh my god, congratulations, Josh! That's huge." Simply finishing that book had been his dream. She couldn't believe he'd surpassed that and actually sold it. "I mean really huge. You're what, nineteen? And you've sold a *book*? Do you know what a big freaking deal that is?"

"I'm aware," Josh said with a laugh. "It's also, as I'm learning, a big freaking amount of pressure."

"So are you just in Echo Bay for a vacation from it all?" she asked.

"Not exactly." Josh paused, stealing another look at her. "After you told me so much about Echo Bay that summer, I just couldn't get it out of my head. I ended up setting the second half of my book in a North Shore town. My editor wants me to rework the ending, so I thought I'd come up here and see if I could soak up some inspiration."

They turned a corner and Echo Bay's downtown came into view, with its brick buildings and colorful awnings. Trees dipped over the road, stretching toward one another like open arms. The packed streets of summer were gone, but the town was far from quiet, people spilling out of Pat-a-Pancake and crowding the arched windows at Bean Encounters. "Plus," Josh went on, his voice softening, "I wanted to see you."

She kept her gaze focused on town. Down the block, Abby Wilkins and Delancey Crane were coming out of Downtown Books, their heads bent together in laughter. They looked so easy together, so natural, their arms looped through each other's in a way that told you right away: best friends. A sharp pain wrenched through Emerson, shredding its way through her insides.

Grabbing Josh's elbow, she took a sudden left, steering them away from town. "I thought we could go to the water," she explained when Josh gave her a curious look.

They walked quietly for a while, neither saying anything. The sun was setting above, the sky glowing red behind a scattering of gray clouds. Before long they reached Dove Cove, a tiny inlet lined with rental homes and inns, mostly empty now that summer was over. Josh looked over at her as they started down the concrete walkway that bordered the beach. "I called you so many times after that summer, Em. But it was like, poof"—he snapped his fingers—"you had just vanished into thin air."

Emerson watched the waves licking at the thin strip of sand down below, pearly white shells glinting underneath the froth. Next to her, an errant strand of hair fell into Josh's eyes, and she was surprised by a sudden urge to push it back. With Matt—and with her previous boyfriend, Scott Ratner—things had never been what you could call tender. But she'd wanted it that way: as different from Josh as she could get. Anything to forget him. "I guess I didn't know where to begin," she said.

"How about why you left?" Josh offered. "Why you didn't even say good-bye?"

"It's not that easy," Emerson began, but she stopped short as something wet splashed against her hand. "Was that rain?" She looked up.

The sky had turned stormier, and a pregnant cloud hung right above them. As she stared up, several fat raindrops pelted from the sky, landing on her cheeks.

"Talk about standing under a dark cloud," Josh commented, and it was such a *him* thing to say that she couldn't help but smile.

"Echo Bay has some serious freak storms," she told him. "You should put that in your novel."

Even as she spoke, the rain was starting to thicken, drops landing in all those hard-to-reach places: in her ears and behind her neck. "We should probably get—"

The rest of her sentence was drowned out by a massive, ground-quaking clap of thunder.

"Uh-oh," she said slowly.

Josh looked down at her, his lashes shiny with water. "Don't tell me you're scared of a little rain."

Emerson shook her head. "Believe me, there is no such thing as 'a little rain' in Echo Bay." No sooner had the words left her lips than thunder clapped again, booming like a bass drum. Lightning followed, slicing fast and bright through the air. And then, in a blink of an eye, it was happening.

The sky exploded, a wall of water rushing toward the ground, soaking their clothes and pooling at their feet. "Armageddon!" Josh yelled. He grabbed her hand, pulling her toward the street. "Come on, my place is only a block away, we can wait it out there!"

Josh kept her hand firmly in his as they broke into a sprint, racing blindly through the rain. Her hair whipped into her face and rain slashed at her back, the world a swirl of leaves and wind and sand and water. "Two minutes until the end of the world," Josh called out. He squeezed her hand and she could see him laughing through the rain.

"I'm not sure we're going to make it!" she joked back.

"Oh no, you're not going down on my watch." He dropped her hand, wrapping an arm around her instead. "Hold on!" He picked up his pace, half carrying her as they tore down the street. "We're flying," he yelled with a laugh, and for a second she really felt as if she were lifting into the air, the rain gliding off her like silk. It was one of the things she'd always loved about Josh, how he could make the world seem like an adventure, a storybook—every page filled with magic.

"This one!" he said, pulling her up the steps of a tiny beach cottage. Rain pounded down on them as Josh jammed the key into the door, throwing it open. They tumbled inside at the same time, arms scraping together. Josh kicked the door closed as they collapsed on the floor, breathing hard. "That is definitely going in my book," Josh choked out.

Emerson pushed her soggy hair out of her eyes. Across the room, she caught a glimpse of her reflection in the mirror. Her hair was kinking and plastered to her face, and most of her makeup had washed off. "Oh god! Just make sure I'm not in it. I look like a survivor of the *Titanic*."

Josh laughed. "A beautiful survivor," he assured her. He sounded so sincere. He was looking at her as if she were wearing a ball gown and tiara instead of a drenched blazer and clingy bits of sand. It gave her a sharp pang for the way she'd felt that summer, knowing that someone had seen every bit of her—every Emmy, ugly-duckling bit—and liked her anyway.

"Ha," Emerson scoffed. She looked down, hoping he couldn't see her blushing. "I take it back. I look like one of the ones who *didn't* survive."

Josh laughed even harder, sagging against the wall. "In that case, I must look like a wild thing from *Where the Wild Things Are*."

A giggle escaped her. "If he'd been dunked in a wild-thing-size toilet."

"And plastered with sand," Josh added.

"And buried in a pile of leaves." She reached over, plucking two crumpled, orange leaves out of Josh's hair.

"We really should model," Josh said thoughtfully. "Oh, wait, you did!"

Emerson couldn't help it; she lost it at that. She collapsed in a heap, laughing so hard she snorted.

"Aw, I missed that little Miss Piggy laugh," Josh said, which just made Emerson snort again.

"It's like Kermit's dream sound," Josh went on.

"Stop it," Emerson wheezed, snorting twice in a row as she bent over with laughter. There were very few people she ever truly laughed in front of: her real, convulsing, snorting laugh. Other than her dad, Josh was the only guy who had ever heard it.

Josh leaned over, pushing a wet strand of hair behind her ear. "Man, I missed you, Em."

Her laughter caught in her throat. His breath was warm on her cheek, and she felt herself leaning toward him involuntarily, as if an invisible string were pulling her. She could smell his familiar woodsy, clean scent, and it made her feel seventeen again, as if the past year had never happened. They were so close, his leg grazing hers, his eyes on her lips, his arm wrapping around her back. One more inch, and they'd be kissing. She could hear every one of her cells screaming for it, could feel the string tugging her closer and closer—

She yanked away, breathing hard. His hand dropped from her back, his forehead scrunching up. "What's wrong?"

She stood up abruptly, shivering a little. "I just realized how cold I am," she said, rubbing her hands up and down her arms. "We should probably dry off a little, right? Before Armageddon becomes Flumageddon." She let out a shaky laugh as she went over to what looked like a linen closet. She kept seeing Matt's box of trophies in her head. If Josh knew about any of it, about him, about the photographer... kissing her would be the last thing he'd want to do. There were only so many times you could ruin something great. With Josh, once was enough.

"Are there towels in here?" she asked, trying to keep her voice from quaking. Without waiting for an answer, she yanked open the door and grabbed one. She'd just started to dry off when her phone dinged across the room.

Josh reached for her purse. "Do you want me to—?"

"No!" Emerson flung herself at him before he could get to her phone. She wrenched the purse out of his grip. "I—I can get it."

Josh gave her a curious look, but she barely registered it. Because on her phone, the word she feared most was flashing at the top of her text messages. *Blocked.*

Her towel tumbled to the floor.

A is for Adultery, E is for Em! Be at Sunset Point in half an hour to capture a couple's Kodak moment—or I'll make sure the whole town knows about your scarlet letter.

Emerson staggered backward, the words dancing in her vision. Something wet ran down her cheek, rain or tears, she couldn't tell. It didn't matter what she did now, what choices she made. Her past had already marked her. And so had the darer.

"Is everything okay, Em?" The concern in Josh's voice drew Emerson out of her stupor.

"I—yeah, it's just my, uh, parents," she stammered. She swallowed hard, trying to steady her voice. "They're worried about the storm and want me to come home." She glanced at the time on her phone. *Twenty-eight minutes and counting.* "Looks like we're going to have to cut our hour a little short." She gave him an apologetic shrug and started toward the door. But before she could leave, he grabbed her arm, stopping her.

"Hey, hold on. If I freaked you out, Em, I'm sorry. It was just so nice being around you again. Maybe I got carried away."

She forced a smile. "It's fine, really. Just my parents. I'm telling you, people in Echo Bay *really* don't like their storms." She pointed a finger at him. "Put it in your book." Before he could protest any more, she slipped out into the rain.

She had to go home first to get her car, which meant she made it to Sunset Point with barely three minutes to spare. The sudden downpour had ended just as quickly, leaving only a light drizzle behind. Despite her racing pulse, she couldn't help but admire the view. Sunset Point was one of the few flat areas of Dead Man's Falls, Echo Bay's rocky, jagged expanse of cliffs. The ocean surged down below, spraying foam into the air. Along the horizon the sun had finished setting, and spirals of yellow moonlight swept across the dark sky. The recent rain gave everything a glossy quality, as if she'd just stumbled into a photo shoot.

She pulled her car up behind a tall stretch of rock and quickly killed the lights. She twisted around, craning her neck, but she couldn't see a thing. The area where cars usually parked was on the other side of the rocks. If she wanted to get close enough without being seen, she was going to have to do this on foot. She grabbed her phone and the old umbrella she kept in her car and climbed out as quietly as possible. The drizzle had slowed even more, but she opened her umbrella anyway, wanting to keep her phone dry.

Crouching low, she rounded the rocks until the cliffs' parking area came into view. There was only one car there, a small, beat-up Honda with the lights on inside. Emerson crept a little closer, careful to stay out of sight. Two people sat in the front seat of the car, their heads bent close together as if they were deep in discussion. The guy's back was to her, but she could vaguely make out the girl. She was short, with a pixie haircut. Every few seconds, she took a nervous scan of the parking area before returning her attention to the car. Emerson crouched even lower as she glanced at the time on her phone. In less than a minute, a half hour would have passed, and there wasn't another person in sight. This pair had to be her mystery subjects.

She aimed her phone's camera at them, but there was no way she was getting any kind of usable shot from this angle. Pushing a wet strand of hair out of her eyes, she inched toward the car. She was careful to keep her back pressed against the rocks, staying safely in the shadows.

When she got close enough, she could see that the girl was around her age, and the guy—balding and broad-shouldered—was definitely older. She didn't recognize either of them. The guy put his hand on the girl's shoulder and slowly trailed it down her arm. When the girl gazed up at him, her eyes were wide and innocent.

Emerson's stomach lurched. She knew it was going to happen before it did. She could barely stand to watch as the older guy leaned in and kissed the girl hungrily. Tears sprang to Emerson's eyes. Whatever that was...it was definitely illicit. Maybe even adulterous. The darer's words blasted through her head. *A is for Adultery, E is for Em!* She'd been chosen for this job for a reason.

Quickly, she snapped several photos with her phone. Then she hurried back to her car and booked it out of there. Her car fishtailed a little, and she turned desperately at the wheel, trying to regain traction. Only when she'd made it safely back onto the main road could she breathe again. She wanted to get away from that scene—from that *reminder*—as fast as possible.

Was that all this was? A slap in the face from the darer—a reminder of who she was and what she'd done?

She'd just turned onto Ocean Drive when her phone dinged with another text. The sound sent a tremor shuddering through her. She pulled over to the side of the road and grabbed her phone.

One more thing: E-mail your best shot to Admin@anaswan.com. Do it tonight . . . or YOUR indiscretion goes public tomorrow.

Emerson threw her phone across the car, squeezing her eyes shut as it bounced against the passenger seat. *Who the hell is Admin@anaswan .com?* If it was that man, or someone he knew . . . she'd probably ruin his life forever.

But if she didn't do it, the darer would ruin hers.

Emerson let out a frustrated scream. The sound echoed around her, ringing in her ears. She had no choice. No options.

She had to go through with the dare.

CHAPTER FOURTEEN
Friday, 7:18 AM

TENLEY TOOK A LONG GUZZLE OF COFFEE BEFORE pulling out of her driveway. She needed it; she'd barely slept the night before. Every time she drifted off she'd dream of that family grave-yard plot—with Tenley and Trudy headstones to match her dad's. The darer's latest threats were like a noose around her neck. The instant she started to relax, it would tighten: a constant, gasping reminder. *T-48 hours till D-Day.* And if she told anyone, her mom would go first. She wondered if this was how Caitlin had felt those last few weeks. Like no place was safe, not even her mind.

Tenley gulped down more coffee as she slowed to a stop at a red light on Ocean Drive. Down by the water, a surfer was trudging across the sand. She watched, grateful for the distraction. She couldn't even imagine going in the ocean right now. Echo Bay's water barely reached manageable temperatures during the summer. You had to be completely nuts to subject yourself to it in early-morning autumn. The surfer moved closer, his features sharpening into focus. For the first time in what felt like days, a laugh bubbled up in Tenley. Apparently, Tim Holland was that nuts.

She pulled her car over to the side of the road and popped open the passenger door. "Going for hypothermia?" she called out.

Tim broke into a smile when he saw her. Up close, she saw it was a boogie board he was holding, not a surfboard. "Oh, this is nothing. December is when my parents start locking me in my room. I thought I'd get a little boogie boarding in before then." He nodded toward the open passenger door. "Does this mean you're offering me a ride to school?"

"School?" Tenley eyed the wet suit he was wearing, shimmering with beads of water. She could feel her eyes dipping from his broad shoulders down to his flat abs, and she quickly tore them away. "I'm pretty sure that's not on Winslow's dress code." *Though*, she thought, stealing one more glance at the black material stretched tightly across his chest, *it probably should be.*

"Give me one minute, and I'll be in school-appropriate attire," Tim promised, waving his sandy backpack at her. "I was going to walk home to get my car, but this would mean I would actually get to school on *time*." He pressed his hand to his chest in shock.

Tenley glanced at the clock. "You have literally one minute or we're going to be late for homeroom." She gave him a stern look, but it was just for show. The truth was, she'd happily be late if it meant one less car ride alone with her thoughts.

"Time me," Tim called over his shoulder as he sprinted to the shed that housed the beach's bathrooms.

Fifty-three seconds later he was wearing jeans and a shirt and depositing his boogie board, wet suit, and backpack into her trunk. His shaggy blond hair and hemp necklace were still wet, but other than that he looked fully school-appropriate. "Impressive," Tenley admitted.

"Just one of my many hidden talents," Tim told her with a grin. "The others include sick foosball skills and an uncanny ability to spot caterpillars."

"No way. Where were you when I was doing my caterpillar project in fourth grade?"

"Surfing, most likely."

"Really?" Tenley glanced at him out of the corner of her eye. "Even in fourth grade?"

"Oh yeah, fourth grade was a big year for me. I won the prestigious Surf Babe competition. *Babe* as in *kid*," he added quickly. "Not as in, well…"

"Hunk?" Tenley supplied. "Hot stuff? Dreamboat?"

"Exactly. Though I do one day hope to win the Surfing Dreamboat award."

Tenley laughed. "Fourth grade was a big year for me, too. You're looking at the Massachusetts State Gymnastics Champion, Under Ten Division."

"Gymnastics? Really? I have to say, I wouldn't peg you as a tumbler, Tenley Reed."

Tenley made a sour face. "Why does everyone always say that? Okay, fine, what would you peg me as, then?"

"Let's see…" Tim paused, tapping out a beat on the dashboard. Suddenly he snapped his fingers. "Spelling bee champ! Yes, you have spelling master written all over you."

"*Seriously?* You think I look like someone who studied the *dictionary?*" Tenley glanced over to find Tim smirking at her, his eyes wrinkling up at the corners.

"Just kidding," he said sweetly.

"Jerk!" She grabbed a crumpled-up napkin and tossed it at him.

Tim held up his hands in mock surrender. "Peace for surfers!"

"I wonder if that would make a good motto for a homecoming campaign," Tenley mused. She was surprised by how good it felt to joke around with someone. It made the dares and the darer feel like what they should be: a bad dream.

"Sure, if you want me, Tray, and Sam to vote for you," Tim replied.

"The three surfketeers," Tenley declared as she turned into Winslow's crowded parking lot.

"Uh, the what now?"

"That's what Cait used to call you," Tenley explained. The second the words were out of her mouth, she regretted them. At the very mention of Cait, the mood in the car darkened.

"I never knew that," Tim said quietly. He leaned back in his seat as Tenley pulled into a parking spot. "Man, I *hate* that. There's so many things we never got to talk about."

Tenley looked down. Memories were suddenly winging at her from every direction. It took all her strength to beat them back.

"Hey, sorry." Tim reached out, touching her hand. "I didn't mean to get you down."

Tenley stared at his hand, resting on top of hers. The strangest feeling was zipping through her, hot and sharp, like a surge of electricity. She yanked her hand away, busying herself with reaching for her purse. "I'm fine," she said. The distant sound of the warning bell rang out from inside Winslow, making her look up. A few final stragglers were rushing into school, leaving the parking lot empty.

"We should probably hurry," Tim said. "If I get one more detention for being late, I think Mr. Sims might start calling me 'son.'"

Tenley laughed weakly as she climbed out of the car. She couldn't shake the sensation she'd had when he touched her hand. She hadn't felt a connection like that since Guinness. And before that…she couldn't even remember how long.

It doesn't matter, she chided herself silently. Caitlin had been her best friend. Which meant Tim was squarely in the no-go zone. Besides, she was Tenley Mae Reed. She dated football players and bad boys. Not hemp-necklace-adorned surfers.

Overnight, the hallways of Winslow had been transformed into homecoming central. Voting took place at the game on Saturday, which meant it was the nominees' final day to campaign. Everyone had gone all out. Marta had made glittery posters for Emerson, featuring her washing her face in a Neutrogena ad. LET EMERSON MAKE A SPLASH! the posters declared. Jessie had brought cookies with Tyler's face on them, and Abby had set up an advice booth in the hallway, with the advice centering on "voting Delancey."

There was a surprisingly large number of girls gathered around the booth. They were all talking frenziedly, one person calling out over another. Tenley stopped short. There was no way anyone could get that excited over advice—especially Abby's. She inched closer, listening in on their conversation.

"Did you know she was hooking up with her gym teacher?" Sadie Miller asked breathlessly.

"Is Anaswan going to expel her?" Hope Chang chimed in.

"What about the contest?" one of Abby's freshman Purity Club crones—Nina, something-or-other, the one who always wore her hair in braids—squealed. "Does this mean they're disqualified?"

"How did this even happen?" a beak-nosed girl asked hungrily.

Tenley wrinkled her brow. What were they talking about?

"Hold on." Abby held up a hand for silence. "If you all give me a second, I'll tell you everything I know." She looked around the group, clearly soaking up the moment. "Last night someone sent an anonymous e-mail to Anaswan's entire Listserv—students *and* teachers—with a picture of Hannah Baker, Anaswan's own Purity Club president, kissing the school's gym teacher. It's a horrible situation, and I wouldn't wish it on anyone."

She smiled primly, looking anything but horrified. "At this point it is still unknown who sent the e-mail. However, I e-mailed the vice president of the Massachusetts Purity Project as soon as I heard, and it does appear that, in light of Hannah's behavior, Anaswan's Purity Club *will* be disqualified from their annual competition."

"Which means we're a total shoo-in for winner!" Nina-braids shrieked. "Spa trip, here we come!"

Abby tossed her long brown hair, looking like a peacock ruffling her feathers. "It does seem that way, doesn't it?" She kept her tone neutral, but she couldn't disguise the joy in her eyes. She was eating this up.

Tenley took off for her locker. She couldn't care less about Winslow's Purity Club drama—let alone Anaswan's. She had enough drama of her own.

After homeroom, she pulled the flyers she'd made last night out of her backpack, admiring her handiwork. They included side-by-side pictures of her and Hunter. Hers was from the last pageant she'd won. She was standing on the stage in her crown and sash, waving at the camera. Hunter's had a similar feel. He was out on the lacrosse field, and he had last year's MVP trophy hoisted above his head. She'd included a slogan on the bottom: VOTE FOR THE COUPLE WHO ALREADY KNOW HOW TO REIGN! She knew it was corny, but she also knew from experience that corny won votes.

Winning homecoming king and queen together would be the best way to help Hunter keep his secret under wraps. She'd hated seeing him so wrecked the other day. Tricia had clearly gotten to him, and if anyone knew how that felt, it was Tenley. But even as she hung up the posters, homecoming was the last thing on her mind. Instead, she kept thinking about her latest text messages. At least her mom was safe; she'd assured that when she'd bolted away from the police station yesterday. But that still left her own safety to worry about. She had less than forty-eight hours to catch this darer...or she might not live to see hour forty-nine.

Caitlin's kidnapper *had* to be the answer. Sydney was still looking into Guinness, but deep in Tenley's gut, she was sure: Find the kidnapper and it would lead her straight to the darer—Guinness or not.

She ticked off a mental list of facts in her head as she moved down the hallway. The kidnapper was a woman, probably twenty-six or older. Eight years ago, she'd had enough access to Winslow to steal Joey's train out of their classroom. That narrowed her down to a few likely options. She either worked at Winslow, was a Winslow alum, or was related to a Winslow student.

It wasn't a major lead, but it was all she had. She blindly tacked a poster to the first-floor bulletin board. It all led back to that toy train. It felt like some kind of crazy crossword puzzle: If she could solve that one mystery, everything else would fall into place. Which was why she planned to spend her free last period in the computer lab, doing some serious sleuthing.

But first she had a full day of school to get through. She sighed, staring at the display she'd absently arranged on the wall. Thanks to these posters, the whole school would think she and Hunter were a couple now. Last night that hadn't bothered her at all. But out of nowhere a tiny worm of apprehension wiggled its way through her.

"Finally!" Marta let out a squeal as she approached Tenley. "It's about time you and Hunter became official." She grabbed a flyer out of Tenley's hand, posting it for her. "Tell me how it happened!"

Tenley considered telling Marta it was just a campaign ruse, but an image of Hunter from Tuesday night flashed through her mind. He'd seemed so fragile, pleading with her to keep his secret. She couldn't break his trust. "He asked me this week," she lied. "With a dozen roses. Said he'd been trying to work up the courage forever."

Marta tacked up several more posters. "I didn't think Hunter had a romantic bone in his body," she said with a laugh. "But it just goes to show, all it takes is the right girl."

More like the right lie, Tenley thought. But she gave Marta her best girly swoon. "Guess so."

The rest of the day passed in a blur. Tenley suffered through a math quiz and fake-smiled during a lunch-period debate over who would win king and queen the next night. But her thoughts were like a one-way road: All signs pointed to the darer. When would the psycho come for her next? Would it be at school? In her car? Another at-home attempt? The uncertainty was driving her crazy. By the time her free last period rolled around, she was one big ball of nerves.

She hurried over to the computer lab and took a seat in the back of the room. There was a girl she didn't recognize a few rows up, a freshman or sophomore probably, but otherwise the room was empty. She opened a search engine. *Steinhard limited edition circus train,* she typed into the search field.

Several links popped up, including a Wikipedia entry and Steinhard's company website. She went through them both, skimming over the content. Apparently, the train wasn't just a collector's item; it was part of an extremely limited run, 250 trains in all. Each of the trains from the run was marked with a number on its back wheel: 1 to 250.

"A number..." Tenley murmured. She grabbed her phone and opened up the photo she'd taken of Caitlin's drawing. There it was—just as she'd remembered. Caitlin had written a number on its back wheel. *111.*

Tenley drummed her fingers against the desk. She was suddenly bursting with energy. If she was able to find some of these trains online... maybe she could pinpoint the exact one that had been in the basement of Caitlin's kidnapper: number 111. If there were only 250 to start out with... A dart of hope shot through her. It wasn't likely, but it also wasn't impossible.

She launched a new search, adding *111* and *for sale* this time. She knew it was a long shot, but maybe the person who stole Joey's train had sold it at some point after Caitlin's kidnapping. If she could find a record of a sale, she might be able to trace it back to its seller....

Links to several pawnshops popped up on the screen, as well as a few eBay stores. She opened one at random. *Perfect replica of a Steinhard Limited Edition Circus Train*, the sale touted. The others were more of the same: newer models, near-perfect reproductions. No originals, and no number 111. She went back to the search field, switching *for sale* to *estate sale*, as Joey had suggested.

This time, something interesting popped up. It was a site featuring Massachusetts Estate Sales. *Sale 3241*, the link read. Tenley clicked on the site excitedly. *Your valuables, sold with care*, the page read at the top. Some of the sales had family names or addresses attached to them, but Sale 3241 was marked as anonymous. The seller's list of items was impressive, everything from a Persian rug to an extensive collection of Fabergé eggs. There had been some jewelry, too. It had all been taken off the market, but the pictures were still up, and Tenley couldn't help ogling them. There was one seriously glittery emerald bracelet, along with a pair of sapphire earrings, a matching ring, and the largest diamond pendant Tenley had ever seen. Whomever these had belonged to had some serious money.

Tenley tore her eyes away from the jewelry and kept skimming. Halfway down the page, she spotted it. *Steinhard Circus Train, part of a limited edition run. This collector's item is in moderately good shape, with just one scratch along the back. It comes with its original papers, certifying that it was the 111th train produced in the 250 train run, as corroborated by the number on its back wheel.*

Tenley bolted forward so hard her nose almost hit the screen. *111th train!* Her eyes flew from the photo on her phone back to the computer screen. The number on the back wheel was the same on both.

She'd actually found it. The very train Caitlin had seen in her kidnapper's basement was now part of an estate sale online. An *active* estate sale.

Tenley leaned back, her head spinning. The question was: Why *now?* The dares start and suddenly the kidnapper is trying to get rid of the one item that Caitlin had remembered from her kidnapping? There were other items in the sale of course, but still...It *couldn't* just be a coincidence.

Tenley let out a frustrated groan. It was definitely a connection, but it didn't bring her any closer to uncovering the darer's identity. All it told her for sure was that the kidnapper definitely wasn't related to Joey. Not only had Joey's train been stolen long before sixth grade, but there was no way anyone in the Bakersfield family had ever owned a massive diamond pendant or Fabergé eggs.

She gazed unseeing at the screen. The estate sale was listed anonymously, but maybe there was a way to dig up some more information...She clicked on the CONTACT US tab. Beneath an e-mail address and fax number was a single line. *For questions on listings or how to bid, give us a call!* Listed next to it was a phone number. Tenley grabbed her phone and dialed before she could change her mind.

"Massachusetts Estate Sales!" a peppy voice answered.

"Hello." Tenley lowered her voice in an attempt to sound older. "This is Lady Marie Cornwall." Inwardly, she blanched. *Lady?* Where had *that* come from? She cleared her throat, trying to recover. "I'm very interested in estate"—she quickly clicked back to the page featuring the train—"number 3241."

"Well, that's wonderful to hear!" the woman trilled on the other end of the line. "It's certainly one of our most impressive estates."

"Certainly," Tenley agreed. "I would love to place a bid, but first I just need to know a little more about the origin of the estate."

"Unfortunately, this estate has requested that all background information remain confidential," the woman said apologetically.

"Of course, of course," Tenley replied. "It's just..." She thought quickly. "Being a lady, as I am, it's essential I be confident that I'm not bringing anything...well, *unseemly* into my home. In these days of bedbugs and hidden germs, you can never be too careful!"

"I can assure you that with Massachusetts Estate Sales, no such issues will arise." The woman's voice had become markedly less peppy. "We take the utmost care in vetting the items on our site."

"I'm sure you do, but if you could just—"

"I'm sorry, Lady Cornwall," the woman interrupted. "I really can't help you any further with this."

"You can't even tell me the seller's town?" Tenley pressed.

Her response came in the form of a resounding *click*. The woman had hung up. Tenley threw her phone onto the desk and glared down at it. Another dead end.

"Hey, Ten." Tenley gave a start as Emerson dropped down at the computer next to her. Emerson raised her eyebrows when she noticed the website open on Tenley's computer. "In the market for some antiques?"

Tenley clicked out of the estate sale and took a quick glance around the room. The freshman girl was gone; they were all alone. "I'm following that train lead," she said quietly. "I'm not sure if it's going anywhere, though." She was about to say more when Emerson suddenly leaned in close.

"I need to talk to you, Ten," she cut in. Her voice was tight, and there was a cautious look on her face.

Tenley tensed. "About you-know-who?"

"Kind of." Emerson wrung her hands together. "You know that photo everyone's been talking about today, of Anaswan's Purity Club president kissing her gym teacher? Well...I'm the one who e-mailed it." She picked nervously at her nails. "The darer made me. I—I created an anonymous e-mail address and everything."

"You sent an e-mail to the entire Anaswan Listserv?" Tenley burst out. Emerson looked alarmed, and she quickly lowered her voice. "Why didn't you tell me?"

"I thought the e-mail address was just a single person," Emerson said miserably. "I didn't know it was a Listserv! I didn't think anyone else would find out." Emerson buried her head in her hands. "But now two entire schools know and the gym teacher is being fired and the girl is probably being tormented and it's *all my fault.*"

"No way," Tenley said fiercely. "It's not your fault." She squirmed angrily in her chair. "This is the darer's fault. Just like everything else. Seriously, Em." She grabbed Emerson's shoulder and tried to shake her out of it. "You can't let yourself spiral. It's what the darer wants.

Besides, is what you did even that bad? The girl was hooking up with her gym teacher, for god's sake. She was kind of asking for it. And so was he."

Emerson jerked her head up sharply. She blinked several times, looking as if she'd just been slapped. "Really," Tenley promised. "Don't look so guilty. This is not your fault. Besides, you did make one person's day."

"Abby," Emerson groaned. "I know. She's been telling anyone who'll listen that the Purity Club is definitely winning that stupid competition now." Emerson ran a hand over her glossy black hair. "Just the person I wanted to do a favor for." She blew out a long breath. "This darer is out of control, Ten. Whoever it is...we have to stop them."

"You're preaching to the choir." Tenley sighed. "I'm just trying to work out the whole *how* issue."

Emerson leaned forward in her chair. "I've been thinking a lot about who Tricia might have been cheating on Sean with. And I think Sean could be right. Hunter really does make the most sense."

"Impossible." It slipped right out, and Tenley's eyes widened at her mistake.

Emerson gave her a strange look. "Why?"

"It's just..." Tenley thought quickly. "I don't know if you saw the posters, but Hunter and I are finally official." She was lying through her teeth, but she had no choice. She'd promised Hunter she'd keep his secret. "The other night he, well, he told me he's felt this way about me since I moved back. He said he hasn't been able to even think about another girl, let alone hook up with anyone. So there's no way he was seeing Tricia secretly. It's got to be someone else."

Tenley chewed her lower lip, thinking. "What we need is proof of whoever Tricia was seeing behind Sean's back," she said. "And I know where we can look for it." She pulled up Tricia's Facebook profile on the computer. Emerson leaned in, looking over her shoulder.

The first few pages were filled with messages and photos and quotes, tributes to a lost friend and a Lost Girl. Tenley ignored them, scrolling further back, to before her death. Tricia had posted a whole album of photos from Tenley's housewarming party, and Tenley skimmed them quickly, refusing to focus on the ones of Caitlin. Nothing in the album stood out; they were just typical high school pictures from a typical high school party.

Her other posts were just as boring: photos of Sean and the cheer squad and a day trip she'd taken to the beach with her parents. *Love ya!* she'd written to Sean only days before her death, including a stock photo of a kitten sitting on top of a Saint Bernard. "Nothing," Emerson groaned.

Tenley gritted her teeth, scrolling further back. They looked at page after page, but eventually she had to accept it: They weren't going to find anything useful. At least not here. In fact, there was only one place she could think of where they might be able to get a glimpse into the *real* Tricia. "We need to get into Tricia's bedroom," she said.

"I think we might finally be able to," Emerson said. "I heard from Sean that the Suttons got back into town last night. But"—Emerson glanced at her watch with a sigh—"you're going to have to handle it. I have cheer practice now."

"Seriously?" Tenley balked. "You're going to go to cheer practice when there's a murderous psychopath after us? We *have* to get into that room, Em. It's our best bet at finding out who Tricia was working with. There's got to be a secret stash of crazy hidden away in there somewhere." She crossed her arms against her chest, fixing Emerson with her most withering stare.

Emerson reached up to rub her temples. "It's the day before the homecoming game, and I left practice early yesterday. If I skip today, Coach will have my head!"

"Better than the darer," Tenley shot back. "You were friends with Tricia, Em," she pressed. "Her parents know you; they trust you. You're our best shot at getting into her room."

"All right, all right," Emerson gave in. "Let me go break Coach's heart. I'll meet you at your car in five."

A few minutes later Emerson emerged into the parking lot. "What did you tell Coach?" Tenley asked as she climbed into the passenger seat.

"That a relative died." Emerson shook her head. "I'm so going to hell. But I didn't know what else would get me out of practice, short of death."

Tenley blew a few strands of hair out of her face as she started the car. "Someone could die if we don't do this," she said bluntly. "And it's not going to be some distant relative. It's going to be one of us." She squeezed the steering wheel. What she didn't say was that, most likely, it was going to be *her*. *She* was the one the darer had attacked twice. *She* was receiving blatant death threats. Which was why this trip to Tricia's house was so important.

She filled Emerson in on her plan on the drive over. "Ready?" she asked as they pulled up to Tricia's Cape Cod–style house.

"Ready to get this over with," Emerson replied.

There was a large framed photo of Tricia sitting on the porch, the last remains of the memorial that had popped up after her death. Tenley gave it a kick as they walked by, and Emerson shot her a warning look. According to the plan, they were heartbroken, mourning friends, starting now. Tenley twisted her face into an appropriately sad expression. This might be her toughest performance yet.

"Emerson!" Mrs. Sutton lit up when she opened the door to find Emerson and Tenley waiting on the porch. She was a large woman, with pale blond hair and puffy cheeks that reminded Tenley of a chipmunk's. Tenley remembered her from the pageant she and Tricia had participated in—the one Tricia had won after getting Tenley kicked out. Unlike Tricia, her mom had never shed the old Fatty Patty family trait. "And it's Tenley, right?" Mrs. Sutton asked.

Remembering the pageant sent a fresh bout of anger searing through Tenley. She kept her lips pressed firmly together as she nodded. "We wanted to come say hi, Mrs. Sutton," Emerson said. Her voice was sugary sweet, and there was a sympathetic smile on her lips. "See how you're doing after your trip."

"Oh, that is so nice of you, girls. Tricia had such wonderful friends." There was a glimmer of tears in her eyes as she waved Tenley and Emerson in.

The inside of the house was sparkling clean. The counters gleamed, the rugs looked freshly vacuumed, and every pillow on the overstuffed yellow couch was perfectly fluffed. An oil painting of Tricia hung above the mantelpiece, a small, knowing smile on her lips. "Tricia liked to call that her *Mona Lisa*," Mrs. Sutton said, following Tenley's gaze. "I keep wondering if I should take it down, but..." Her voice grew choked up. "I can't bring myself to."

Tenley's eyes lingered on Tricia's smile. It *was* like the Mona Lisa: a little, mysterious smirk. She wondered what she'd been thinking as she posed, if she'd already been plotting their demise. "It's a beautiful painting," she managed.

Mrs. Sutton led them over to the couch. "Would you like something to drink, girls? Tea? Water?"

"We're fine," Emerson assured her. "We wanted to give you this." She took a rolled-up paper out of her backpack. It was a poster-size photo of Tricia in her cheerleading uniform. Someone had hung it up in Winslow's Hall of Fame a few weeks ago, and it had turned into an impromptu memorial. Now it was covered in messages and notes, all honoring Tricia. Tenley had taken it down while Emerson talked to her coach, knowing it would give them the perfect excuse for visiting Mrs. Sutton. "We thought you might like to have it," Emerson continued. Tenley tried not to blanch as she caught sight of Sadie Miller's message: *Beautiful AND sweet. You'll be missed, Trish!*

"Thank you, honey." More tears welled in Mrs. Sutton's eyes, threatening to spill over. Tenley had a feeling that if they didn't act soon, they'd be trapped listening to her blubber for the next hour.

"We also have a favor to ask you," Tenley said. As Mrs. Sutton cleared her throat, trying to pull herself together, Tenley gave Emerson a sharp jab in the side.

"Right," Emerson said quickly. "I, uh, left a pretty special necklace in Tricia's room a while back. I'm so sorry to bother you, but would you mind if I take a look to try to find it?"

"Unless you already cleaned her room out?" Tenley added, in her best heartbroken tone.

"No." Mrs. Sutton's gaze flickered sadly to Tricia's portrait. "We left so soon after the funeral, and I just haven't been able to make myself go in there...." She trailed off, the waterworks starting all over again.

"Of course," Emerson said. "I'm so sorry to even bring it up." Tenley was surprised by how choked up she sounded. When she looked over, she saw there were tears in Emerson's eyes, too. "We don't have to—" she began.

But Mrs. Sutton waved her off. "No, no. Of course, go look for your necklace. I'll stay here and read this lovely memorial you brought me."

"What a performance," Tenley whispered as she followed Emerson to Tricia's bedroom. "I didn't know you had it in you, Cunningham."

"I wasn't acting," Emerson said with a shrug. She paused outside the last door in the hall. "Sometimes it's easy to remember who Tricia used to be. Back before all of this, when we were actually a close group...she was one of my friends."

Tenley reached in front of her, pushing open the door. "No, she wasn't," she said. "She was only pretending to be." She looked up. Emerson was so much taller than her, but in that moment, she seemed so much younger. "We can't forget that."

Emerson nodded. She took a deep breath before following Tenley into the room. "Whoa," Tenley murmured.

"Whoa," Emerson repeated. Her jaw dropped as she looked around.

Clothes were flung everywhere, as if Tricia had emptied the entire contents of her closet onto the floor. Books, too, were piled haphazardly around the room, half with spines cracked and pages bent. A row of used coffee mugs sat on the desk, several stained with lipstick. "Was she always this messy?" Tenley asked.

Emerson shook her head, looking stunned. "Not even close. You saw downstairs. The Suttons are neat freaks. I remember one dinner where her mom vacuumed up crumbs before we were even done eating. Tricia was like that, too."

"*Was* being the operative word," Tenley said. "Clearly, something changed."

"Or," Emerson said slowly, "someone got into her room while the Suttons were gone."

"Someone like the darer." With a grimace, Tenley dropped down on the ground and began sorting through the mess.

They worked quickly, moving steadily through the piles. Tenley kept her eyes peeled for anything that could connect Tricia to someone other than Sean.

"Look at this," Emerson whispered a few minutes later. It was a book, one Tenley had seen in the window of every local bookstore lately. *The Lore (and Lure) of the Lost Girls*. Tricia had flagged half of its pages with Post-its. Emerson flipped to one at random. A passage about Fall Festival was underlined. *MUST BE MONDAY!!!* Tricia had written in the margin. Tenley shivered. The Monday of Fall Festival was when Tricia had taken them out on the *Justice* to kill them.

"So freaking creepy," Tenley muttered. "But not really news." She moved on to another pile. Tricia's assignment book was buried under a wrinkled mound of bathing suits. Tenley's fingers tingled with excitement. Maybe there would be some kind of meet-up with her mystery friend written in her calendar! But a quick flip through told her it belonged to the same fake Tricia as the Facebook page. With a sigh, she moved on to another stack of books. She was halfway through them when a box of photos over by the bed caught her eye. "Yes," she whispered. If Tricia had taught her anything, it was just how much the right photo could reveal. *Especially* if Guinness was involved.

She could hear Emerson rifling through Tricia's desk as she scooted over to the box. She thumbed quickly through the photos. Most of them she'd already seen online. But at the bottom of the box was a stack of shots she'd never seen before. "Look at these," she said.

Emerson put a binder on Tricia's desk and crossed the room. She'd just dropped down next to Tenley when both their phones lit up. Tenley's pulse quickened. What if the darer knew they were here?

Slowly, Tenley reached for her phone. Next to her, Emerson did the same. "A Facebook blast," Emerson murmured.

Tenley's shoulders sagged with relief. It wasn't the darer.

The blast came from Sydney. *GOT THE NIGHT-BEFORE-HOMECOMING BLUES? THEN COME TO THE VAULT TONIGHT AT 9 PM FOR A PICK-ME-UP! ALL DRINKS ON ME...HAPPY HOMECOMING!*

Tenley cocked an eyebrow as she read it. "Sydney is throwing a *party*? I would not have pegged her as the homecoming campaigning type."

"I wouldn't have pegged her as the *fun* type," Emerson added.

Tenley stifled a laugh. "I guess we don't really know her." She fell quiet as she returned to Tricia's photos. They were all of a yacht, mostly close-ups of the interior: everything from the engine to the video monitor. Almost as if they'd been taken so Tricia could study the features.

"Oh my god," Tenley blurted out. All thoughts of Sydney and the party flew out of her head as she gaped down at the photos. "These must be from Tricia's boating lessons! She told us about them on the *Justice* that night. How she'd studied yachting so she would know how to sail us out to the Phantom Rock."

"That's sick," Emerson murmured as Tenley passed her several photos. "But also not really news, right?"

Tenley froze as she reached the very last photo in the pile. "No, it's not," she whispered. "But this is." She held the photo out to Emerson. In it, Tricia stood on the deck of the same boat. The wind was whipping her hair into her face, and the ocean unspooled behind her, a deep, glistening blue. Standing next to her, her arm wrapped firmly around Tricia's shoulders, was a smiling Abby Wilkins. "I thought Tricia stopped being friends with Abby after she ditched the Purity Club," Tenley said shakily.

Emerson looked from Tenley to the photo and back again. "So did I."

"Looks like we were both wrong. Abby must have been taking those boating lessons with Tricia." Tenley flipped the photo over. A handwritten message was scrawled across the back. *Us laughing at Captain Louis and his senior-citizen pickup lines! xoxo, Ab*

Tenley sank back against the bed as she realized what this meant. It wasn't Hunter or Nate or Guinness who Tricia had been spending time with behind Sean's back. It wasn't a guy at all.

It was Abby.

Tenley stared openmouthed at Emerson as she connected the dots. Tricia wasn't trying to hide who she was with from Sean; she was hiding what they were *doing*. Tricia and Abby had been working together.

CHAPTER FIFTEEN
Friday, 9:56 PM

SYDNEY SAT IN HER CAR, CLUTCHING THE DARER'S latest note. *Go to the vault friday at 10 PM if you want to dig deeper.* Across the street the white limestone building of the Vault loomed, its parking lot already filled to capacity. She looked from its moldings of cherubs to the golden clock face above its doorway. The Vault had once been Echo Bay's oldest and most opulent bank, until two years ago, when it became the North Shore's flashiest club. Winslow students loved to party there, mainly because of their lax ID policy. Technically, you had to be eighteen to enter, twenty-one to drink, but from what Sydney had heard, the club rarely ID'd at the bar, and never at the door. Not that she would know firsthand. The only time she'd been inside was for a fund-raiser thrown by her mom's hospital.

She crumpled up the note and stuffed it into the car's glove compartment. She didn't need it anymore; she'd read it so many times she could recite the whole thing by heart. She'd spent hours last night obsessing over its meaning. Was she supposed to learn something about Kyla's death at the Vault? And if so, why would the darer *want* that—especially if it was Guinness? Squaring her shoulders, she climbed out of the car. There was only one way to find out.

She had to put all her weight into opening the Vault's heavy limestone door. Immediately the music accosted her. It vibrated under her feet and thrummed through her body, pounding in her ears like a heartbeat. The smell of beer and sweat and perfume wafted out at her as strobe lights flashed behind a thick velvet curtain. A burly bouncer gave her a brusque nod, saying nothing as she walked past. Apparently, the ID'ing rumors were true. Screwing up her courage, Sydney pushed aside the velvet curtain and stepped into the club.

The first thing she saw was the crowd. The room was jam-packed, people spilling off the dance floor and lined up by the bar, and all of them, every single one, went to Winslow. Before Sydney could even *begin* to process that, she noticed the posters. They were plastered on every surface, the strobe lights painting them highlighter colors: yellow, green, pink. Her eyes bounced from one to another, the same photograph staring back at her from every one. It was a photo Guinness had taken of her during a winter day in Boston. Snowflakes coated her hair, and her eyes looked impossibly blue against the pink of her cheeks. At the top of each poster was a bold headline. VOTE THE PARTY QUEEN 4 HOMECOMING QUEEN! "What. The. Hell?" Sydney murmured.

"There she is!" Sadie Miller's voice grabbed Sydney's attention. "This party's amazing," she yelled over the music. "You've got my vote tomorrow, Sydney!"

"Mine, too!" Lauren Allon raised a glass in the air, making its amber-colored contents slosh over the sides. Above her, the lights flashed and winked, sending spirals of color skittering across the marble floors.

"It's the party queen!" Sean Hale came up behind her and clapped her on the shoulder. He smelled strongly of liquor, and there was a slight slur to his words. Sydney tensed. She knew Emerson and Tenley had written Sean off as a suspect, but she wasn't as sure. "Your Facebook blast was genius, Sydney," Sean continued. "And the open bar was even more genius. Exactly what I needed tonight."

"Facebook blast?" Sydney whispered. Her limbs were suddenly paralyzed.

"Genius," Sean repeated. He opened up Facebook on his phone and passed it to her. A message had been posted on his wall in all caps. *GOT THE NIGHT-BEFORE-HOMECOMING BLUES? THEN COME TO THE VAULT TONIGHT AT 9 PM FOR A PICK-ME-UP! ALL DRINKS ON ME...HAPPY HOMECOMING!* Next to it was Sydney's name, along with the same snow-laced photo from the posters. "I can't believe you got this out to every single person in our grade," Sean went on. "I didn't even know you were on Facebook."

Because I'm not, Sydney thought. She took a step backward, her heart pumping so loud she could hear it over the music. Whoever had created that profile, whoever had sent out those messages...it hadn't been her. Which left only one person: the darer.

"Are you all right?" Sean asked. "You look a little green."

She wasn't in the vicinity of *all right*. She wasn't even in same *world* as *all right*. "Just the lights," she croaked.

"Sean!" Marta Lazarus approached and threaded an arm through Sean's. She was wearing a bright pink top that showed off her curves, and huge dangly earrings. "Come on, let's go dance—oh, hey, Sydney."

Sydney started at the sound of her actual name coming out of Marta's mouth. She'd gone to school with Marta for twelve years now, and up until that moment, she'd called her Cindy or Celia every time they spoke. "Nice party!" Marta continued. She shouted out each word, making it sound like a drunken cheer. "Especially the cocktail waitresses! They don't care at *all* about IDs."

Sydney glanced around the room. For the first time, she noticed the waitresses weaving through the crowd in silver-sequined dresses. They were all model-tall and carrying trays of test tubes filled with pink liquid. "Fun," Sydney said weakly.

"It is! I haven't had this much fun since..." Marta trailed off as, next to her, Sean's face clouded over. "A long time," she finished hastily. She cleared her throat, giving Sean's arm a quick squeeze.

Madalyn Hershey and Alana Cohen walked past, lifting their glasses in Sydney's direction. Ayden Doyle was with them, his curly brown hair bobbing as he nodded along to the music. "This party rocks!" Madalyn called out.

Sydney managed a half smile in return. Behind them, several members of Winslow's audiovisual club swarmed one of the waitresses, snatching all the test tubes off her tray. Test tubes they thought *she* was paying for. Was that what the darer wanted? To *bankrupt* her? Sydney swallowed hard. "Where's Tenley?" she asked Marta.

"She and Emerson are on their way. I don't know what's taking them so long." Marta pouted. "They're going to run out of test tubes soon!"

Sydney's mouth went dry as she took another scan of the room. Marta was right. The test tubes were flying off the waitresses' trays faster than candy on Halloween. She had to do something to stop this.

"Excuse me," she mumbled, pushing past Marta and Sean. Sean said something in response, but she was too busy fighting her way through the crowd to catch it. She lowered her head like a bull, ignoring the voices swirling around her. She didn't stop until she reached the long marble bar.

There was just one bartender serving drinks. She had strawberry-blond hair, barely-there eyebrows, and a smattering of freckles on her pale cheeks. Her name tag said LACEY. Sydney leaned over the bar, waving to get her attention. Lacey looked right past her, her hands flying over the counter as she poured several drinks at once. "Hello?" Sydney yelled over the music. "Can I talk to you? I'm Sydney Morgan!"

That got her attention. "The girl of the hour," Lacey said. She deposited several drinks onto the counter before walking over to Sydney.

"Actually, I wanted to talk to you about that." Sydney twisted her ring. "You have to stop serving drinks!" she blurted out. "I...I didn't plan this. And there's no way I can pay for it."

"Pay for it?" Lacey wrinkled up her forehead. "What are you talking about? It's all prepaid. Wait—you didn't know?"

Sydney shook her head mutely.

Lacey laughed. "Well, that's quite a surprise gift. Exclusive use of our club, open bar, the cocktail waitresses—the whole thing's been covered." She wiggled her eyebrows at Sydney. "Someone must *really* like you."

Sydney's head felt as if it were about to explode. The darer had thrown her a *party*?

A chill snaked down her spine. The last time a darer had lured her somewhere, it had been to the *Justice*, and she'd walked right into a death trap. What if this party was another attempt?

"Oh, I should give you this." Lacey grabbed a glossy four-by-six photograph off the bar. It was the same image that graced all the posters: Sydney in the snow. "Someone left it here this afternoon, along with the stack of posters." As she held it out, a flash of black ink on the back caught Sydney's eye.

A message. Fear zipped through her, turning her insides to ice. She wanted to turn away, run, but her hands ignored the impulse, reaching for the photo instead. The note on the back was short.

I always knew you were Royal material, Blue. Better enjoy it...

Blue. Details crystallized in Sydney's mind, one after the other. The photo taken by Guinness. The use of "Blue" in the Facebook blast. The spending of thousands of dollars as if it were nothing but spare change. And, of course, the Kyla connection. The world seemed to blacken around her despite the bright, flashing lights. It all seemed to confirm her worst fear: Tenley was right. Guinness was the darer. He must have written that note just to get her to the Vault.

She held tightly to the bar, suddenly light-headed. "Do you know who paid for all this?" she asked breathlessly. "Was it someone named Guinness Reed?"

Lacey burst out laughing. Sydney could smell alcohol on her breath. Apparently, serving didn't stop her from indulging. "Oh, honey, Guinness Reed might be a charmer, but he would never do something this nice for a girl. Believe me, I would know."

Sydney's head snapped up. "What does that mean?"

Lacey rested her elbows on the shiny wooden bar. "He and I had a thing in high school. Maybe have one now, too, I don't even know."

She rolled her eyes to the ceiling. From the way her elbows slipped a little, making her stumble forward, Sydney could tell it wasn't just one drink she'd had. It looked as if Sydney was the only one *not* enjoying her own party. "He's so impossible to read," Lacey continued. "I don't know what I was thinking hooking up with him again when he came in on Tuesday night." She gave Sydney a sheepish grin. "We girls never know what's best for us, right?"

Sydney couldn't find it in herself to smile back. All she could think was: *Tuesday.* That was the night Guinness came over to her apartment. The night she'd lain in bed with him, kept him warm. It had taken all her strength to finally send him home in a cab. Or at least she'd *thought* he'd gone home. Apparently, he'd gone to Lacey instead. The realization felt like a hammer, cracking against her heart. It was one more black mark in the Guinness column. "I guess we don't," she whispered. The pounding music ate up her words, but Lacey must have been able to read her expression, because she shook her head ruefully.

"He got to you, too, huh? How does he *do* that?" On the other end of the bar Hunter Bailey yelled something about drinks, and Lacey gestured for one of the cocktail waitresses to handle it.

A seed of an idea began to take root in Sydney's mind. Lacey had known Guinness in high school ... which meant she'd probably known Kyla, too. The note might have been a false lead, but that didn't mean she couldn't get what she'd come for. If Guinness really was the darer, the more she could find out about Kyla the better.

Sydney cleared her throat. Here went nothing. She leaned on the bar, assuming her best gossipy-girlfriends pose. It wasn't one she used often. Or ever. "You know," she said confidingly. "Guinness has been talking about Kyla Kern a lot lately. You know, the Lost Girl?" She was about to ask Lacey if she'd been friends with Kyla, when Lacey suddenly burst out laughing.

"Hi," Lacey said dryly, offering out her hand for Sydney to shake. "I'm Lacey Kern. Better known in this town as Kyla's older sister."

Sydney gaped openly as she shook Lacey's hand. The music seemed to silence, and all she could hear was that name. "Kyla was your sister?" she choked out.

"Miss Lost Girl herself." Lacey's tone was detached, but the sudden pain flooding her eyes was unmistakable. Sydney averted her gaze. The worst part was, Lacey didn't even know the truth. Her sister's death wasn't some tragic Lost Girl accident as everyone said; someone had *done* this to her. And then it had been covered up. The thought made Sydney more determined than ever. Guinness or not, she had to find this darer—figure out how it was all connected. For everyone's sake.

"So you were both close with Guinness?" she pressed.

"I guess you could say that," Lacey replied. "I hooked up with him, and he pined for her. As cliché a triangle as they come. Tuesday night I really thought he was finally here for *me*. Then he had to slip and call me Kyla. Five years later and I'm still just her replacement." Her lips twisted into a sad smile. "Don't worry, I kicked him out after that."

Sydney stood immobilized, her thoughts racing. After evading every one of her questions, why would Guinness send her to the Vault knowing that Lacey—his old flame and Kyla's *sister*—worked there? It made no sense.

Down the bar, people were starting to get restless. "Are you going to serve us drinks or what?" someone yelled.

"I need to get back to work," Lacey told her. "But try to enjoy your party. Don't let Guinness get you down. He's not worth it." She started to turn away, but Sydney shot her hand out, latching onto her wrist.

"Wait. How do you know for sure that Guinness didn't pay for this party?"

"This isn't a little townie bar," Lacey said with a smirk. "We don't just take a check when it comes to this much money. We need a credit card, an ID, the whole works, even if the party-thrower plans to pay cash. My manager said the girl was actually pretty pissed off about it. She kept saying she wanted it to be a surprise."

"A *girl?*" A powerful rush of relief flooded through Sydney. If a girl had paid for this, then the darer couldn't be Guinness! All the signs had been wrong. "Do you know her name?" she asked eagerly.

Lacey shook her head. "I'd have to check the record book in the basement."

"Could you go do that? I just...really want to thank her," she added quickly.

"It will have to be at the end of the night." Lacey nodded toward the crowd at the bar, which was growing larger by the minute. "For now, can I have my wrist back?" She glanced pointedly down at her arm, which Sydney was still latched onto.

"Sorry," Sydney mumbled. She had just released her grip on Lacey's arm when someone suddenly grabbed onto hers. Sydney's heart leaped into her throat as she whirled around.

"Pretty jumpy for someone throwing a massive party," Tenley said. She yanked Sydney to a quiet corner in the back of the bar. Emerson was waiting there, her arms crossed against her chest. She caught Sydney's eye, then looked guiltily away. Sydney gritted her teeth. The last thing she needed right now was a rendezvous with Daddy's Girl.

Just being around Emerson made her old yearning to light a match return with a vengeance. "I didn't realize you were such a party girl, Syd," Tenley said. A waitress wandered by, and Tenley reached up and snagged a test tube off her tray.

"That's because I'm not." Sydney kept her gaze on Tenley, doing her best to ignore Emerson. "I didn't throw this party."

Tenley froze, the test tube halting halfway to her lips. Slowly, she lowered it back down. "Then who did?"

Sydney glanced nervously around the room, at face after familiar face. "That's the question of the week."

"You mean it was the darer?" Emerson hissed. Sydney forced herself to look up at her. She seemed unusually frazzled, her eye makeup smudged and wrinkles marring her brightly patterned silk dress. Even still, she was beautiful. It wasn't hard to see why Sydney's dad had fallen for her. The thought made Sydney even angrier, and she quickly averted her gaze, focusing back on Tenley.

"Who else?" She handed Tenley the photo Lacey had given her, with the note facing up.

"Blue..." Tenley read. She looked up sharply. "Isn't that what Guinness calls you?"

Sydney nodded. "But before you go all crazy on me, it can't be Guinness. I was starting to think it was, too, but the bartender told me a *girl* paid for everything."

Tenley and Emerson exchanged a startled look. "Oh my god," Emerson whispered.

Sydney glanced back and forth between them. "What is it?"

"We went to Tricia's house after school...and we found something," Tenley said. "We've been trying to call you all night to tell you about it—and ask you about this weird party—but your phone's been off."

Sydney's forehead furrowed. "No, it hasn't." She reached into her purse and felt around for her phone. "I just used it earlier, when I was shooting photos...." She trailed off. Her fingers hit up against her wallet, a roll of film, a memory card, a tube of hand lotion, and a smushed package of gummy bears. But there was no phone.

She yanked her bag up and looked inside. Her phone was gone.

"The darer stole it," she whispered. "To keep me from hearing about the party."

"Honestly, we have bigger things to worry about than a missing phone right now." Tenley pulled a photo out of her pocket. "Take a look at this."

Sydney lapsed into a stunned silence as she stared down at the image of Tricia and Abby, standing together on the deck of a yacht. She flipped it over, her eyes widening as she read Abby's friendly little message.

"Remember on the *Justice*, how Tricia said she'd been taking boating lessons?" Tenley asked. "Well, apparently, Abby was taking them with her."

Sydney's heart skipped a beat. "Does that mean it's *her*?"

"It would make sense, wouldn't it?" Tenley pushed a strand of chestnut-brown hair behind her ear. "Abby *was* the one who planned the whole Tricia memorial."

"And she benefited more than anyone from Caitlin's death," Emerson added. Her fists clenched at her side. "She finally got her wish to be student-body president."

"And the darer's latest ploy exposing that girl and her gym

teacher was the best news of the *year* for Abby and her beloved Purity Club," Tenley finished. "Almost as if she'd arranged the whole thing herself."

Sydney leaned against a white limestone table to steady herself. High above her, colorful beams of light danced off a stained-glass window. "So what do we do?"

"I'm not sure what we can do," Tenley replied. "We spent the past few hours driving around trying to find Abby, but we had no luck. Her house was dark, she wasn't at school, we didn't see her in town—"

"Did you ask Delancey?" Sydney interrupted. "I think she's here."

"I just did," Emerson said. "She hasn't heard from Abby all night. Said she's been M.I.A. since the end of the school day."

Panic raced through Sydney. She suddenly felt freezing cold, as if the temperature had just dropped twenty degrees. "It's because she's planning something. She's got to be. We have to find a way to stop her!"

"I agree, but first we need to make *sure* it's her," Tenley said. "The last thing we need is Joey Bakersfield 2.0."

Emerson nodded. "We need some kind of tangible proof, more than just a photo of her with Tricia."

"The record book!" Sydney clasped her hands together in excitement. "The bartender said there's a record book downstairs that should show who paid for the party. If we can find that—"

"Then we get our proof," Emerson finished. "That's brilliant!"

"Thanks." Sydney gave her a small smile before she even realized what she was doing.

"Sydney Morgan!" Sydney jolted at the sound of Calum's voice. She looked over to see him walking toward her, a test tube in hand and his trademark lopsided grin on his face. He was wearing a sweater vest with a bow tie, in what must have been his attempt to dress up. "I've been looking all over for you! Why didn't you tell me you were throwing such a delightful party?"

"Because I didn—" Sydney began. Tenley interrupted her with a swift kick to the ankle. "—didn't know I was going to until the last minute," Sydney finished lamely. "It was kind of a spur-of-the-moment thing."

"Well, I, for one, am glad." Calum held out the test tube shot. "Anyone want? I've heard these are scrumptious. Not that I personally have imbibed. I want to keep my wits about me. You know"—he looked at Tenley, his grin widening—"in case anyone here is dared to kiss me."

Tenley cocked an eyebrow at him. "If that's what you're waiting for, you should probably down that drink yourself. Now, if you don't mind, we're in the middle of some girl talk...." She made a shooing gesture with her hand.

Calum exchanged a look with Sydney. *Dictator*, he mouthed. Sydney managed a halfhearted smile in return. "I'll come find you in a bit," she promised.

Calum gave her a strange look. "Is everything okay?"

"Girl talk, Calum!" Tenley snapped.

"Well, then. Looks like I'll leave you ladies to it." With an awkward bow, he backed away.

Tenley shook her head, watching him go. "Geniuses," she muttered. "They have no social graces."

"Neither does half our grade, apparently," Emerson pointed out. She glanced around the room. Almost every square inch was filled with people spilling drinks and bumping into one another and grinding much too closely on the marble-tiled dance floor. It was clear the test tube shots had done their job.

"Which," Tenley said thoughtfully, "makes it the perfect time to find that record book. Everyone's too drunk to notice we're gone." The words were barely out of her mouth when Mason Willis, the star of last year's musical, stumbled past them, singing the lyrics to "Ice Ice Baby" at the top of his lungs. "Point proven," Tenley said.

"You're right." Sydney swallowed hard, trying to ignore the sharp nerves prickling their way through her. "It's time we nail this darer."

CHAPTER SIXTEEN
Friday, 10:32 PM

EMERSON BOUNCED NERVOUSLY ON HER TOES AS she peered across the Vault at the crowded bar area. "Sydney's talking to Calum," she told Tenley. It was part of the plan they'd constructed to get their hands on the record book: Sydney, the girl of the moment, would keep up appearances in the club while Emerson and Tenley sneaked down to the office. Emerson frowned as she watched Sydney lift her arms in the air and wave them furiously around. "What is she *doing?*"

"I can't see a thing," Tenley grumbled. The room was alive with movement, and even standing on her toes, Tenley was still a head shorter than everyone else.

"Good thing you're with a giraffe," Emerson muttered. It was what Tenley had called her in the past, before the darer had forced them into being semifriendly. She gave Tenley a small smile to show she was joking. By the bar, Sydney lifted her voice. Emerson caught a few snippets of what she was saying—something about homecoming. A group began to gather around her. Sydney swiveled as she spoke, her eyes sweeping the crowd. It looked as if she was making some kind of speech.

"Winslow forever!" Marta cheered, joining the crowd with Sean. Nate, Hunter, and Jessie were close behind. It was more Winslow students than Sydney had probably ever spoken to in her *life*. There was an uncomfortable expression on her face as she raised a test tube shot in the air. Everyone followed suit in some kind of toast. But Emerson knew it was more than that. It was a distraction.

"Now!" Emerson exclaimed. She grabbed Tenley's arm, pulling her toward the stairwell in the back of the room. "If anyone spots us, we'll say we're looking for the bathroom," she whispered as they jogged down the stairs.

"I do a very convincing I-have-to-pee dance," Tenley whispered back.

It was musty and dimly lit downstairs. They were in a wide hallway, with low ceilings and several large silver doors lining each side. Each door had an intricate, round lock system displayed on the front. The bank's old vaults, Emerson realized. She reached for a light switch, but Tenley grabbed her wrist, shaking her head sharply. Emerson dropped her hand. Tenley was right; the less attention they drew, the better. "Which one do you think is the office?" she whispered.

Tenley shrugged. "Guess we start opening doors." She pulled at the first one in the hallway. It opened into a small, windowless room. Every inch of wall space was covered in metal lockboxes. Shelves lined the center of the room, stuffed with supplies for the bar. The next few vaults were more of the same: lockboxes around the sides and shelves in the center; napkins, straws, and coasters crowded among cases of alcohol and mixers.

Emerson crossed the hall, opening door after door. They were all the same: stacked with bar supplies. At the second-to-last vault in the row, she paused. Instead of metal lockboxes, the walls were covered in a purple velvet fabric. There was a row of silver filing cabinets along one side and in the back sat a rolltop desk, stacked high with papers. Emerson's eyes went instantly to the leather ledger lying open in the center.

She reached the desk in three strides. "Tenley!" she called out. The ledger was opened to the first page. A date was marked at the top, a receipt stapled beneath it. Emerson thumbed through more pages. Each one had reservations written out on the top, and the corresponding receipts stapled below. Her heart gave a patter as she found the page for today's date. A pre-Halloween drink special had originally been penciled in, but it had been X'd out with a red marker. Underneath was a new note: *Winslow party, 9 pm–1 am.* A receipt was stapled on the page. Emerson didn't even see the price on it. All she could focus on was the name, signed neatly along the bottom. *Abby Wilkins.* "Holy. Shit," she said.

"Did you find something?" Tenley asked excitedly, coming up behind her. Silently, Emerson pointed at the book. Tenley's mouth rounded into an O as she took in Abby's signature. "It's really her," she whispered.

Emerson grabbed the ledger off the desk. It was heavy, but she drew it close, studying the receipt. She'd seen Abby's signature just the other day, at the bottom of the Homecoming Nomination Memo. It had looked exactly like this: painstakingly neat, each letter rounded to perfection.

"Uh, Em," Tenley said slowly.

Emerson looked up to see Tenley staring at the desk. The color had drained from her face. Emerson followed her gaze. There, lying innocently on the desk, was a single sheet of paper.

"It was hidden under the book," Tenley said shakily.

Emerson stepped closer. On the paper were five school pictures, the kind taken at Winslow every year. The first was of Meryl Bauer, the second of Nicole Mayor, the third of Kyla Kern, the fourth of Tricia Sutton. The last one was of Caitlin. They were photos of the Lost Girls.

At the bottom was a note.

You're next—cross my heart and hope to die. Correction: hope YOU die.

"She knew we'd come down here," Emerson breathed. "She left this for us."

No sooner had the words left her lips than the door to the office slammed shut with a resounding *bang*. Tenley leaped backward with a scream, bumping up against the desk.

Emerson sprinted to the door, pushing at it with all her might. It didn't budge. She tried again and again, but it was futile. "We're locked in," she whispered. At that moment, someone cut the lights.

Total darkness washed over the room. Emerson yelped, holding tightly to the door. She couldn't see even an inch in front of her. "Don't move," Tenley ordered. Emerson could hear her rummaging around. A minute later a beam of light broke through the darkness.

"Meet my new friend," Tenley said darkly, "the flashlight app." She jabbed at the phone's screen several times. "I don't have any service."

"Of course you don't!" Emerson cried. "We're in a *vault*. Underground." She couldn't stop the fear from creeping into her voice. Already, the air seemed to be growing thinner, staler. "How are we going to get out of here?"

Tenley shined the flashlight around the room. There were no vents visible, no heating ducts, nothing. The beam passed over Emerson, making bright spots dance before her eyes. "We scream," she declared.

They both dove for the door at once. "Help!" Emerson yelled, pounding her fists against it.

"Let us out!" Tenley joined in. Their voices looped around the tiny room, echoing in Emerson's ears.

"Abby!" she howled. Her knees felt weak, as if she might collapse at any minute. "Come back! Let us out!"

"Emerson?" The familiar voice cut through their screams.

"Josh?" She banged wildly against the door. "We're in here!"

Tenley raised her eyebrows at her. "Who's Josh?" she mouthed.

Emerson ignored her. "Get us out!" she begged.

Emerson could hear a clicking sound as Josh fiddled with the lock. "Hold on," he said. "This thing is complicated.... I don't know if you need a code." There were several more clicks, and the sound of something spinning. "Got it!" he said. "No code." With a loud creak, the door opened. Emerson threw herself into the dimly lit hallway. A wrinkle formed between Josh's eyebrows as he peered into the dark vault behind them. They all spoke at once.

"What happened?" Josh asked.

"Who are you?" Tenley asked.

"What are you doing here?" Emerson blurted out. She was trembling all over, and she took several deep breaths, trying to calm herself.

"Why don't we get you upstairs," Josh said gently. "Then we can—"

"Forget upstairs," Tenley snapped. She marched over to him. She barely reached his chest, but the glower on her face made her look scary nonetheless. "I want to know exactly what just happened," Tenley demanded. "How did you find us in there?"

Josh held his hands up in surrender. "I'd just gotten to the club when I saw you and Emerson go downstairs," he explained. "I grabbed a drink and checked out the place for a bit, but when you guys didn't come back, I thought maybe there was a second party room down here or something. I was on my way down when I heard a bang."

"Was there anyone else down here?" Tenley asked eagerly.

"No one. Though the door to the fire exit is open." Josh gestured to a door in the back, which stood slightly ajar. A red EXIT sign dangled above it. "I think I might have heard footsteps out there, but I stopped paying attention when I heard you screaming."

Emerson's heart plummeted. No matter how close they got, the darer—*Abby*—was always a step ahead of them. "You sure you didn't see anyone at all?" she pressed.

Josh shook his head. "Sorry, Em." He put a hand on her arm, looking concerned. "Do you want to tell me what's going on?"

Emerson shifted uneasily. "I...we..."

"It was a prank," Tenley jumped in. "Just this stupid thing seniors do at our school. Emerson got a little freaked out." She glared warningly at Emerson. "Right, Em?"

Emerson managed a weak smile. "Right."

"Well, you still look shaken up." Josh said. "Let's go upstairs. I'll get you some water, okay?"

Nodding mutely, Emerson let Josh guide her up the stairs. Out of the corner of her eye, she could see Tenley making faces at her, trying to catch her attention, but she ignored her. She was still trembling, and it was taking all her effort not to burst into tears. Tenley had told her all about the hot tub and the bottles, but this was the first time Emerson had experienced it for herself—just how far this darer was willing to go.

She squinted as they reentered the club, readjusting to the flashing lights. The music rushed at her, pulsing under her skin. "I'll get you both water," Josh said, gesturing toward the bar. "Unless you want something stronger?"

"What I want is to get out of here," Tenley snapped. "I've had enough *pranks* for one night. You coming, Emerson?"

Emerson bit down on her lip. If she left, she'd end up alone in her room, jumping at every sound. "I think I'm going to stay for a bit," she said.

Tenley shook her head. "It's your grave. I'll find Sydney before I go. Tell her about the prank," she added pointedly.

Emerson made no move to follow her. "Your grave?" Josh asked, watching Tenley walk away. "What did she mean by that? And is she *always* that scary?"

"It's just an expression," Emerson said. They took a seat in the back of the club. "And, yes. If there's one thing Tenley is, it's intense." Across the room, Emerson could see her friends on the dance floor, laughing, having fun. It seemed strangely faraway, as if she were watching it on a TV screen.

"What really happened down there, Em?" Josh asked. He touched her arm and, despite everything, she felt a rush of warmth jolt through her. "Are you covering something up for Tenley?"

"No," Emerson said quickly. "The whole thing was a stupid prank, just like she said." She did her best to feign annoyance. "High school crap. I bet you don't miss it. Speaking of which"—she crossed her arms against her chest—"what exactly are you doing at a high school party?"

"I came to see you," Josh admitted. "I overheard some guys in town talking about the party, and I thought you might be here." He gave her a sheepish look. "First you bolt from my cottage, and now you're avoiding my calls? I didn't know what else to do. It feels like last summer all over again, Em. I came to Echo Bay to get closure, not to repeat history."

Emerson looked up. Under the flashing strobe lights, his eyes seemed to flicker colors. "Is that the real reason you came to Echo Bay? To get closure on us?"

Josh toyed with the silver napkin holder on the table. "Yeah," he said softly. "Everything about the book is true, but I guess I kind of used it as an excuse to see you. I've tried so hard to move on, Emerson, but it's just not the same with anyone else. I think about you constantly. Wonder what you're doing, what you'd say about things. I had to come here. I had to see you."

Something kicked deep inside Emerson's chest. When she left New York, she'd thought there was no other option. They could never be together again after what happened. But maybe she was wrong. Maybe she could finally forget it, move on. She looked up at Josh. There were so many emotions flitting across his face: hope and desire and fear and affection. She felt them, too, every single one. They sparked inside her like flames, lighting her skin on fire.

"I just want—" Josh began.

She didn't let him finish. The impulse stole through her, and before she could change her mind, she acted on it. Leaning across the table, she kissed him.

Josh made a sound of surprise. Then he wrapped a hand around her neck and kissed her back. His lips were soft and his skin was warm against hers, and in that moment, the rest of the world seemed to evaporate: no music, no light, no people. Nothing but them.

Ding! Ding!

The shrill sound of her phone snapped Emerson back to the present. Her heart was soaring as she pulled away from Josh. "I've just, uh, got to get my, uh, phone…" That kiss had turned her into a blathering pile of jelly barely able to string two words together. She smiled up at Josh as she plucked her phone out of her purse.

"You sure are attached to that thing," Josh said, looking amused.

Under any other circumstance, she would have shot back a cute response, made Josh's smile widen even more. But the words caught in her throat. Because on the screen of her phone was a text.

The table seemed to sway beneath her as she read it.

Thanks for doing my dirty work for me, Em!

Attached was a photo. It was of Matt's trophy box. Underneath Emerson's bed. Inside Emerson's room.

No!

Emerson leaped to her feet, her chest constricting dangerously. Abby was inside her house.

"What is it, Em? What's wrong?"

Josh's voice seemed tinny and distant. She had to get home. She had to try to catch Abby. "I—I have to go," she choked out.

Josh threw his hands in the air. "Seriously? *Again?*"

She didn't have time to explain. Without another word, she turned and sprinted toward the exit. She heard someone else call her name as she left—Marta, maybe—but she didn't stop. She didn't stop until she was in her car, speeding home. And then she didn't stop again until she was racing up the stairs of her house and stumbling into her bedroom.

The room was empty. There was only Holden, chirping away in his cage. She was too late. She groaned loudly as she crouched down to let Holden out.

That's when she saw it. Her bedspread, which she'd made up carefully that morning, was now askew, the corner tossed behind one of her bedposts. Her eyes went automatically to where Matt's creepy box sat.

Lying on top of it was a handheld mirror—shattered right down the center. A sheet of paper was propped up behind it.

Emerson dropped onto the floor, barely noticing as Holden waddled onto her lap. The walls felt like watching eyes as she began to read.

```
Seven years of bad luck is nothing
compared with my wrath. Rest up, Emmy...
          tomorrow's a big day.
```

Emerson crumpled the note up with a scream. Abby was taunting her—using her own fears against her! Enough was enough. Abby was right; tomorrow was a big day. Tomorrow they ended this.

CHAPTER SEVENTEEN
Friday, 11:37 PM

SILENCE. TENLEY RESTED HER FOREHEAD AGAINST the steering wheel, savoring it. Her ears were still ringing from the music blasting in the Vault. At least she'd parked on a side street a block away from the club. It had allowed her to sneak out the side exit without any of her friends noticing. Not that they would have anyway. They'd all looked very entranced by the chugging contest taking place between Blake Hamilton and Tommy Wayland.

Her phone rang inside the cup holder, where she'd tossed it. *Emerson*, the screen flashed. Tenley didn't bother with a hello. "Please tell me you've caught Abby and delivered her to jail in a nice little gift box."

"Not yet," Emerson barked. "But that's exactly what I intend to do."

Tenley straightened up. She'd never heard Emerson sound so mad before. "What do you mean?" she asked slowly.

"I mean I have a plan," Emerson announced. "And it involves sending Abby straight into the arms of the sheriff."

"Hold it," Tenley interjected. "You know what she threatened to do if we went to the cops!"

"If she's in jail, she won't be able to do *anything*."

"And you think some *party* receipt is really enough to get her locked up?" Tenley squirmed in her seat. She kept seeing that photo in her head: her family graveyard plot, with plenty of room for another tombstone.

"Of course not," Emerson said. "We'll need some real proof. Something that implicates Abby in an actual crime. In other words, her phone."

Tenley froze. "All the darer texts," she whispered.

"Exactly. There's no denying those text messages. It's stalking and harassment just for starters. *And* proof that she assaulted you."

"That just might work...if we could miraculously get our hands on it."

"That's where my plan comes in," Emerson said excitedly. "What we need to do is get Abby somewhere we can trap her. Then we can force her to give her phone up to us. I'm thinking the dance is the perfect place to do it. She's student-body president. She has to be there."

"We would need some kind of bait to get her alone," Tenley said slowly, thinking it through.

"Delancey," Emerson shot back. "If there's anything that will get Abby worked up, it's hearing that her BFF might lose her precious *purity*." Tenley could hear the sneer in Emerson's voice. "I say we pull a darer and send her a message of our own."

"Tell her you overheard Blake Hamilton bragging at the club tonight," Tenley jumped in. "About how he can't *wait* to bang Delancey at the dance." On the other end of the line, she could hear Emerson typing furiously.

"I made a fake e-mail address," Emerson said tightly. "Abby's going to receive a very concerned message from one Nina Stein."

Tenley burst out laughing. "The braids-wearing purity crone?"

"Yup," Emerson replied. "She's *very* worried about Delancey's pending 'deflowering.'"

"Tell Abby it's happening in the bio lab right before the dance tomorrow," Tenley suggested. "And she really, really hopes Abby can be there to lend a helping hand."

Emerson made a soft clucking noise with her tongue. "Done," she announced a minute later.

Tenley squeezed her hands around the steering wheel. "This is good, Em. We'll meet Abby there and we'll finish this once and for—"

Emerson interrupted with a loud squeal. "She responded already! Abby will be there." She let out a snort of disgust. "She'll make sure Delancey stays 'true to her values.'"

"And we'll make sure we destroy hers," Tenley replied.

Excitement wormed its way through her as she hung up the phone. Finally, they were the ones calling the shots. Once they had their proof, they'd go straight to the cops. And this time, there would be nothing to stop them. A smile spread across Tenley's face. *Let's see Abby try to kill me from prison.*

A sharp rapping on the window made her jump.

A person loomed over her car. For a second, all she could see was a striped beanie, drawn low over the face.

The world turned. Tomorrow would be too late. Abby was here for her now.

She heard the piercing scream before she realized it was coming from her.

She was reaching for her pepper spray when Tim pulled his hat off, revealing a staticky mess of blond hair.

"Whoa." His voice was muffled by the window. "Is my outfit really that unfashionable?"

Tenley tried to catch her breath as she rolled down the window. Cool air rushed in, lifting goose bumps on her arms. "Sorry..." Her voice came out in a squeak. She paused to clear her throat. "I thought you were someone else."

"Well, judging by the horror on your face, I'm glad I'm not." Tim leaned over, resting his arms on the windowsill. "Are you leaving the party already? I haven't even gone in yet!"

"I'm not feeling great," Tenley lied. "I want to rest up for tomorrow."

"For the big crowning," Tim said knowingly. "I can hardly wait to see it."

Tenley managed a small smile. "You don't strike me as the homecoming type, Tim Holland."

"I'm a recovering homecoming hater," Tim admitted. "But people can change, right? Especially if they have the future homecoming queen as their date..." He smiled almost shyly at Tenley. "Know where I could find one of those?"

Tenley blinked. It sounded very much as if Tim Holland—*Cait's* Tim—was asking her to homecoming. She thought of the spark she'd felt when he touched her hand the other day. It made her wonder what it would be like to dance with him, to have his arms around her, drawing her close....

"I—I can't," she choked out.

Tim's smile faltered. "I know it could be weird," he said softly. "Because of Cait. But I guess I thought that's why it *wouldn't* be weird, too. Like if we were there together, it would almost be for her." He looked down. Tenley couldn't help noticing how long his eyelashes were. They brushed against the tops of his cheekbones. "The only time I've felt even seminormal this past month is when I'm talking to you. I don't know what it means, but...I have to think it means something." A tiny smile crept back onto his face. "Plus, I think we'd have fun."

"Oh, I know we'd have fun," Tenley retorted. *Especially once Abby is locked away,* she added silently. "And I really wish I could." For the briefest of seconds she thought about just saying yes. But Hunter was counting on her; she couldn't do that to him. "Unfortunately, I already have a date. You didn't see the posters at school today?"

"I didn't see much of anything at school today," Tim admitted. "After first period, Tray talked me into furthering my surf education instead."

Tenley laughed. "Of course he did. Well, Hunter and I are...well, we're...uh..."

Tim's face fell. "Oh. I get it. You're dating."

"It's just for show!" she blurted out. She hadn't planned on saying it, but the smile that crept back onto Tim's face made her glad she had. "We're both on the court, so we decided a relationship would up our chances of winning. But," she added playfully, "I didn't promise my faux-beau every dance."

Tim sighed dramatically. "Unfortunately, my homecoming rule of thumb is, I only go if I have a future queen on my arm." He ducked farther into her car, until his face was only inches from hers. "Guess we'll just have to wait till next time."

A tingly feeling was spreading through Tenley. "Too bad," she said. "I've been told I'm a pretty good dancer."

"Not as good as me, I bet. I do what I like to call the 'surfer shuffle.'"

Tenley laughed. "I can't believe I'm going to miss that."

She was still thinking about Tim when she got home a few minutes later. It was probably a good thing she couldn't go to the dance with him. It could have been strange, and people would have talked.... She was in the middle of convincing herself that it was for the best when something on her bed caught her eye. It was a blue silk scarf, resting casually on a mound of pillows. She picked it up. The silk was buttery soft against her skin. HERMÈS, the label read.

"What...?" she murmured. She'd seen this scarf before. She'd *made fun* of this scarf before. It belonged to the one and only Abby Wilkins.

Which meant Abby had been here. In her bedroom.

She staggered backward into the hallway. The room seemed dirty all of a sudden, tainted.

"Watch, Miss Tenley!"

Tenley whirled around to find Sahara standing barely an inch behind her. She made a big show of glaring at Tenley as she stepped out of her way. "You're the one who should watch it," Tenley snapped. "What are you doing here at midnight anyway?"

"I work late," Sahara said indignantly. "I heard a noise up here and came to check."

"A noise?" That got Tenley's attention. "Did you see anyone?"

Sahara shook her head. "Just you, who almost trampled me."

"So you have no idea how this scarf got on my bed?" Tenley dangled the blue scarf in front of her, holding it gingerly between two fingers as if it were poison.

"Of course I do," Sahara replied. "I put it there. Landscaper was here today and he say he found it in the woods." She gave Tenley a strange look. "It's not yours?"

Tenley didn't reply. *The woods.* Abby hadn't been in her bedroom at all; she'd been in the woods. She took off running down the stairs, ignoring Sahara's calls behind her. The rear floodlights switched on as she flew out the back door. They turned the grass around her a vibrant rain-forest green. But down by the woods, the grass was so dark it was almost black. The light didn't reach that far.

Tenley hesitated. Warning flags waved in her mind: scenes from every horror movie she'd ever seen. *Don't go in the woods alone.*

She turned back. Whatever nasty surprise Abby had planned for her in the woods, it could wait until tomorrow.

Her hand was on the door handle when she heard it: Abby's voice, in her head. *I never pegged you for a wimp, Tenley.* Tenley froze. Abby had said it as a joke the night of the beach party—the night the darer's new round of messages first started.

Tenley bristled. She might be a lot of things, but a wimp was never one of them. She was Tenley Mae, the girl her dad used to say could move mountains. She looked down at the scarf. Abby had left it here, *knowing* she would find it. She let her hand slide off the handle. She refused to let Abby scare her. Grabbing her pepper spray out of her purse, she marched across the lawn.

The air smelled sweeter in the woods. A faint trickle of moonlight leaked through the trees as she walked farther in. A breeze wrapped around her, soft and cool, and somewhere in the distance an owl hooted. She'd forgotten how nice it could be back here, so serene.

Then she saw the body.

The scarf and pepper spray slipped right out of her grip, falling to the ground. *"No."* It was supposed to be a scream, but it came out barely a whisper. She ran over to the body, falling to her knees. "Guinness. Guinness!" His eyes were closed, black waves falling across his forehead. *"Guinness!"* She shook him, slapped his face, but he didn't move.

Time slowed as she fumbled through her purse for her phone. Her cheeks were wet, but she couldn't feel herself crying. She couldn't feel the phone against her ear, either, or Guinness's jacket under her hand as she tried again and again to wake him. She kept looking for some kind of wound, but she found nothing.

"Hello, nine-one-one." The voice was calm, professional. "What's your emergency?"

"It's my stepbrother," Tenley sobbed. "He's unconscious.... I can't tell if he's breathing!" The words tumbled out of her, not her own.

"What's your address, ma'am?" the calm voice asked.

"One Dune Way. Hurry! I think...I don't know..."

"Ma'am, I'm going to need you to calm down and check for a pulse." The woman spoke slowly, as if talking to a child. "Can you do that?"

Tenley's hand was shaking like crazy as she slid it down to Guinness's wrist. She pressed her fingers against his tattoo. "I feel something!" she gasped. "It's faint, but I feel it."

"Good. Now I need you to stay with him. The ambulance should be there in an estimated two minutes."

Tenley didn't remember the rest of the conversation, but soon she could hear the sirens roaring into the driveway. "Back here!" she screamed. In the distance, she could hear her mom yelling for Lanson. "We're back here!"

The EMTs were halfway across the lawn when her phone let out a sharp beep. A new text flashed on the screen, the number blocked. The first EMT reached them, kneeling next to Guinness. "He's breathing," he yelled to the others. Tenley could see her mom and Lanson racing outside, their screams muffled by the sirens. She tried to push delete on the text. Whatever the darer had to say, it didn't matter right now. But her shaking thumb accidentally hit the read button instead.

Dropping like flies! Make sure the right girl wins queen tomorrow, or who knows who you'll lose next. . . .

CHAPTER EIGHTEEN
Saturday, 7:22 AM

SYDNEY HUGGED HER OLD STUFFED TEDDY BEAR TO her chest. Ever since freshman year, Teddy had resided on the top shelf of her closet. But last night, after Tenley called her about Guinness, she'd gotten him back down. She'd needed all the comfort she could get.

"Syd?" Her mom came into her bedroom. Clearly, she'd felt the same way, because she was wearing Syd's dad's ancient Red Sox sweatshirt—the one Sydney had used as a blankie when she was younger. "I just got off the phone with Marie at the hospital."

Sydney pulled herself up, bringing Teddy with her. Her cheeks felt raw from the hours she'd spent crying, and Teddy's fur was stiff where her many tears had landed. "What did she say? Is he okay?" Her throat was raw, too, her voice hoarse.

Her mom sat down on the edge of her bed. "He's stable, hon." She took Sydney's hands in hers. "He's going to be okay."

Sydney closed her eyes, a shudder of relief running through her.

Last night, Sydney had come home to find her missing cell phone lying on her bed with one of the darer's notes:

```
Had to borrow it--couldn't ruin the
surprise!
```

Sydney had freaked. How had Abby gotten *inside* her locked apartment? But then Tenley called, and nothing else was important after that.

Tenley was in hysterics. All Sydney was able to glean from their conversation was that Guinness was in the hospital from what looked to be some kind of drug overdose. "Abby texted me," Tenley hissed. "She knew about it. She was *gloating*!" Then Tenley had to get off the phone, and Sydney hadn't been able to reach her since. She stayed awake half the night, alternating between crying and willing her phone to ring. When she still hadn't heard from Tenley by 7 AM, she woke up her mom. Her mom's friend Marie worked the morning shift in the ER on weekends, so she'd asked her to call to see what she could find out.

Sydney faced her mom. "Did you learn anything else?"

"They found heroin in Guinness's blood," her mom told her gently. "They're calling it an accidental overdose. He's feeling a lot better today, but they're restricting all visitors, by his father's orders. Marie said he's supposed to be transferred to a rehab center tomorrow."

"Heroin?" Sydney whispered. She leaned back against the wall, reeling. "That can't be right. Guinness had problems with pain-killers and alcohol in the past, but he would *never* do heroin. Hard drugs terrify him."

"He's an addict, hon," her mom said. "There are no boundaries when it comes to a relapse." She squeezed Sydney's hands. "Something must have been really haunting him to drive him to this point. But he's going to get the help he needs in rehab."

Sydney blinked. Her mom was right. For Guinness to spiral this badly, something *must* have been haunting him. She thought of the note Tenley had found on his bed.

Had he believed the note was meant for him and not Tenley? Guinness had already been in a bad place because of their breakup; what if finding that note had driven him over the edge? Sydney gulped as she remembered what Tenley had said about her text. Abby had been *gloating*. Somehow, she must have known what Guinness had done.

If only Sydney had just *talked* to Guinness! But she'd been too busy obsessing over whether he could be the darer. She'd let her fears consume her, blind her, when instead she could have been helping him. And now it was too late. Tears burned in her eyes again. She didn't have the energy to blink them away.

"You look exhausted, Syd." Her mom bent down, kissing her on the forehead. "Why don't you try to go back to sleep for a bit?"

Sydney agreed, but when her mom left the room, she reached for her phone. A tiny part of her was hoping that she'd missed a message from Guinness since she'd last checked—even though his phone had been off every time she'd tried to call. She had no new texts, though, and no new calls.

She was about to put her phone down when a message popped up. It was from Tenley. *Sorry, hospital made me turn off phone last nite. G's ok. Lanson is sending him 2 rehab tmrw. I'll keep u updated . . . but in the meantime, I forgot 2 tell u what ELSE Abby said last night.*

Another text came through, this one forwarded from a blocked number.

Dropping like flies! Make sure the right girl wins queen tomorrow, or who knows who you'll lose next....

Before Sydney could digest that, Tenley sent a third text. *Em got a similar 1. Abby CLEARLY wants Delancey 2 win. I say we all drop out of the race 2nite. Make her think we're caving. Then at the dance we STOP her. Meet us @ school @ 6:30. We have a plan!!!*

Sydney tried to make herself feel something: fear, anger, remorse. But she just felt numb. Her head was a sticky maze of webs. *U can take my name out of the running,* she texted back. *But count me out of ur plan. I'm not coming 2night.*

Tenley sent three texts in rapid succession.

WHAT?!?

You can't just ditch us!

All THREE of us need 2 be there!!! We need u!

Sydney twisted her ring. Thanks to Abby's sick little game, she'd abandoned someone she truly cared about. She was done playing. *Sorry,* she wrote back. *I'm out.*

Ten's response was curt. *I thought we were in this 2gether.*

Not anymore, she replied. *I'm not in this at all.* Before Tenley could make an attempt to change her mind, Sydney turned off her phone.

A long shower and two iced teas later, Sydney was starting to feel slightly less like a zombie. "I'm so sorry I can't stay home with you today," her mom said for the fourteenth time that morning. She pulled a bagged lunch out of the fridge and stuffed it into her purse. "I can't believe my boss is out with the flu."

"It's fine," Sydney assured her. "I'm a big girl."

Her mom wrapped her arms around her, giving her a tight hug. "You're all grown-up, aren't you? I don't think I say it enough, but I'm so proud of you, hon. For handling this so well and…everything. You've come a long way these past few years."

Sydney gave her a small smile. After her relapse with a kitchen fire last month, she wasn't sure she'd ever hear her mom say that again. "How about a mother-daughter dinner one night soon?" her mom continued. "We can go anywhere you want."

"What about tonight?" Sydney suggested. "Unless you're busy with Dad again." She couldn't keep the edge from creeping into her voice.

"No…" Her mom brushed Sydney's shaggy bangs off her forehead. "But you're not going to homecoming? I know you're not into football, but not even the dance? Aren't you nominated, hon?"

Sydney shrugged. "Who cares? I'm going to college next year. I'm ready to be done with Winslow. I'd rather have a nice night with my mom. *Alone*," she added pointedly. "And…at Vegetarian Kingdom!"

Her mom groaned loudly. "The things I do for my daughter."

Sydney felt the tiniest bit better as she made herself breakfast. Her favorite restaurant and alone time with her mom was exactly the combo she needed right now. Maybe it would help her focus on something *other* than Guinness or the darer for five minutes. Namely, her scholarship application, which had to go out Monday, no matter how uninspiring her hometown photos were.

She'd just finished her cereal when the apartment's buzzer rang. With a yawn, she dragged herself over to the video monitor their building had installed in every apartment last year. It was a bulky plastic box with a grainy video feed, but it was better than the ancient sound system that had been there before it.

She steeled herself as she turned the monitor on. If her dad had chosen this moment for a surprise visit, she wasn't sure she could be held accountable for her reaction. "Hello?" she said grudgingly.

No answer.

Something white filled the video feed. "Is it broken already?" She clicked it off and on again. "Hello?" she repeated.

Silence. The screen was still awash in white. Sydney looked closer. There was something in the center. Several fuzzy black lines. She squinted. It almost looked like...

"No," she gasped.

She was downstairs and outside as fast as her legs could carry her. There it was, taped over the building's video screen: a note. Adrenaline shot through her, chasing away her exhaustion. She whirled around, scouring the parking lot. Over by the trash cans a squirrel gnawed on an acorn. In the street a young couple jogged past. Abby was nowhere in sight.

Her insides did somersaults as she tore the paper off the monitor. Her head was so fuzzy that at first glance, she couldn't make sense of the jumble of letters. She collapsed on the building's front stoop. Slowly, the letters untangled themselves. A sentence emerged.

Guess your love wasn't his drug. Good
thing my laced weed was. Congrats--you're
Guinness-free!

The world turned black. Fury burned through her veins. Abby had *done* this. Not her notes: *her*. She'd laced Guinness's weed—poisoned him.

Sydney could barely see straight as she stood up. Abby was everywhere, tearing through every part of her life. And Guinness had gotten caught in the crossfire. It was Sydney's fault he was in the hospital, Sydney's fault he was going to rehab. He'd been nothing but an innocent bystander.

Unless...

Sydney stopped breathing as a wild thought struck her. Unless, all along, he'd been a target, too.

Her thoughts sped into overdrive. They'd assumed the note on his bed had been meant for Tenley, but what if it *hadn't* been? What if it had actually been for Guinness? She couldn't believe she hadn't thought of it sooner. She closed her eyes, trying to remember what the note had said. *Like a powerful photo, past mistakes can haunt us until death. Good thing yours will come soon. That's what happens when you know too much.* It would fit. Guinness had taken a sudden interest in Kyla lately, looking through her pictures, seeing her sister. What if *that* was what he'd known too much about? What if that was why he'd ended up nearly dead?

Sydney's brain felt as if it were splintering into a thousand pieces, fragments crashing and colliding. Abby and Kyla, Kyla and Abby... how did it *connect*?

A sudden ache consumed her. A fire would make everything feel better. It was the only thing that could chase the demons—Abby—out of her head. She could keep it under control this time. Just the note in a trash can, small and contained. The compulsion rolled through her in waves. She wanted so badly to forget, just for a moment.

No! She dug her nails into her palm. She'd come too far to let Abby send her spiraling backward. She refused to let her win like that. She hurried back inside and grabbed a recently finished roll of film off her dresser. She knew only one other way to escape.

She didn't take a full breath again until she was inside the dark-room. Out in Winslow's parking lot she'd heard the faint sounds of the field being set up for the homecoming game, but in here everything was still. She breathed in the familiar mix of chemicals and paper. The scent always reminded her of Guinness. Not the drunken mess he'd become lately, but the real Guinness. The one who'd shown her the magic in photography, who'd taught her about shutter speed and light-ing, who'd chased her off a bridge and led her to the darkroom instead. He would become that Guinness again one day; he had to. Maybe rehab would be good for him in the end. At least he would be safe from Abby's clutches in rehab.

She took her phone out of her bag and turned it back on in case her mom called about Guinness. She'd missed six angry texts from Tenley, and two more from Emerson. She deleted them all in quick succes-sion. Then she got to work, letting the familiar process lull her. She still needed a hometown photo for her application, something that would blow the judges away. This roll she'd taken on Art Walk was one of her last chances.

Soon she was in the zone, the rest of the world fading into a soft blur. Her thoughts meandered back to her trip to Gerry Hackensack's house. The craziness of last night had pushed the questions she'd been obsessing over since Thursday out of her mind. But in the quiet peace-fulness of the darkroom, they were resurrected, coming at her from every side.

What did the image prove? Was Kyla's death really not an accident? And if so...what could have made that crater? Sydney had spent hours Thursday night researching explosives online, but it hadn't gotten her any closer to an answer. And now it seemed as if the only person with some insight was on his way to rehab.

She was so focused on her thoughts that it took her a minute to register the sound of her phone beeping.

She froze, wrist-deep in a bin of developer. If it was Abby, if she was texting to taunt Sydney about Guinness...Sydney shuddered. She wasn't sure what she'd do.

But she couldn't just ignore it. It could be news about Guinness. She cleaned off her hands and grabbed her phone. She was both disappointed and relieved when she saw the name on the screen. Calum.

What are you up to? Football = Barbaric. Want to boycott the game with me?

Sydney's lips twisted up as she stared down at her phone. The prospect of doing something away from Winslow and homecoming and the darer actually sounded amazing. *Def,* she wrote back. *What r u thinking?*

Why don't you come over? Got house to myself today. Can hang out in the yard!

Sydney laughed as she shot him back a yes. By *yard,* she knew he meant *private island.* She quickly packed up her stuff. She suddenly couldn't wait to get to Calum's. Neddles Island was so isolated, it almost felt as if she'd be leaving Echo Bay.

Before long Sydney pulled up to the bridge to Neddles Island. It was tiny, one of those narrow wooden bridges that could fit only one car at a time. The ocean stretched out on either side, silvery blue and rippling, catching ribbons of sunlight like stained glass. Behind a tall iron fence sat the Bauers' property. The house stood in the center, lifted on stilts and checkered with more windows than walls. A broad yard wrapped around it, sloping down to the ocean on every side. Sydney paused in front of the fence, taking it all in. She'd been to Neddles before to drop off Calum, but the pure grandness of it took her breath away every time.

There were a steel keypad and video screen attached to the locked gate. According to the text Calum sent her on her way over, the video system was down, so he'd texted her the password. *Cassandra*, she typed in. She was pretty sure it was his mom's name, which surprised her. Considering how little Calum liked to talk about his family history, she had to imagine it was his dad who'd chosen it. Sydney's eyes flitted to the cliffs in the distance as she drove down the long, winding driveway. Echo Bay's Dead Man's Falls bordered the left half of the island, cutting tall and rocky across the sky.

Calum stepped onto the porch as Sydney parked her car. He was in jeans and his favorite Superman T-shirt. He must have gotten out of the shower recently, because his usually wild curls were damp and flattened against his head. "Welcome to my humble abode," he called out.

"There is nothing humble about this place," she retorted. She followed him inside. "Unless, of course, you're comparing it to Buckingham Palace." She looked around the soaring entryway. Between the marble floors, the three-tiered chandelier, and the gilded oil paintings, she might as well have been in a palace.

"Personally, I like to think of it as the antifootball headquarters," Calum said.

"Where computers are the real sport," Sydney quipped.

"I do have thirteen hundred different video games, if you're interested," Calum offered.

Sydney raised her eyebrows. "What did you do? Rob a Best Buy?"

"Just wait until you see my dad's office. *Then* you can ask that.

Speaking of which, before we head outside, would you like the official tour?"

"Yes!" Sydney clasped her hands together in exaggerated excitement. "I've never been in a real, live palace before!"

"Ha. Ha. Ha." Calum stuck his tongue out at her.

Sydney's sarcasm quickly faded as Calum led her from a gorgeous living room to a formal dining room to an even more formal second dining room to a state-of-the-art kitchen that could have held her entire apartment. "I think I might lose count of the rooms soon," she said. Her voice sounded as awed as she felt.

Calum grinned. "Then on to the second floor, m'lady." He started toward the spiral staircase, gesturing for her to follow.

"There's *more*? I don't think I'm in good enough shape for this house tour." She admired the large watercolors of beaches adorning the walls as she followed Calum upstairs. Above them, a huge skylight let in a blast of sunshine, warming her shoulders. "I love how open this place is," Sydney said. "It's almost like you're still outside."

"You'll be a fan of my room, then." Calum embarked onto the second floor. "It has the best view in the house. But first, the rest of the living quarters." He led her down the hallway. "On your left you will find the Bauers' linen closet," he announced, "filled with a thrilling variety of sheets and pillowcases, none with a thread count lower than five thousand, of course."

"Of course," Sydney said solemnly.

"And to your right is a guest bedroom," Calum continued, waving Vanna White–style at a half-open door. Sydney could see a flowery, pastel-colored room behind it. "One of twelve in the house, in case you're curious. Or if you and your eleven closest family members ever need a place to bunk."

Sydney laughed. "I don't think I even have eleven family members."

He pushed open a door at the end of the hall. "And this is the office," he announced with a flourish.

"Whoa. That's a lot of computer equipment." A flock of computer screens lined the room. Seven in all, Sydney counted, each one larger than the last. Their screen savers flashed photographs of Echo Bay. A printer the size of a small car stood in the middle of the room, flanked by two smaller ones.

"No theft involved," Calum swore. "My dad's in the tech business." Sydney knew that was an understatement. From what she'd heard, Sam Bauer *was* the tech business. He'd built Bauer Industries when he was just twenty-one and had done work for everyone from Target to the president's Secret Service.

"I think you might actually have more computer equipment than I have photography equipment," she joked. "Though it's probably a close race. I do have about a thousand memory cards."

She blinked as the joke brought a memory back to her. "Actually, that reminds me. I completely trashed one of my cards at the beach the other night. Clobbered it with wet sand." She fished around in her purse until she found it at the bottom, right where she'd abandoned it Monday night. "Any chance you could use some of your genius-enhanced computer magic to salvage it?" She smiled prettily and batted her eyelashes in her best damsel-in-distress imitation.

"How could I say no to such a fetching look? Besides"—Calum rubbed his hands together eagerly—"I never turn down a computer challenge."

Snatching the memory card out of her hands, he took a seat in front of the largest computer screen in the room. "This is going to be fuuun," he sang out.

"I think we have different definitions of *fun*," Sydney said dryly as she sat down next to him.

"I don't know," he countered. "That party you threw last night seemed plenty fun to me. I bet you have homecoming queen in the bag now."

"Ha." Sydney snorted. "I doubt that."

"Seriously," Calum said as he turned the computer on. "That party was crazier than the theory of quantum entanglement." Sydney didn't bother asking what that was; she could only imagine it would involve a mind-numbingly boring scientific explanation. "Though, I've got to ask you." Calum pressed several buttons on a keyboard before turning to look at her. "Wasn't it...kind of expensive?"

Sydney looked down, pretending to be fascinated by the green shoelaces on her Keds. "It was an early birthday gift from my grandfather." It was a terrible lie—her mom's dad was in a nursing home in Florida and barely coherent, and her dad's dad was dead—but it just came right out. "He worries I don't have enough fun," she continued. The lie kept on building, as if it had a life of its own. "So I guess he thought what better gift than a party the night before homecoming? He set it all up before I could tell him I'm not exactly a party girl." She snapped her mouth shut before she could ramble her way any deeper into the lie. She was sure the whole thing was completely transparent, but Calum just nodded.

"He knows you well. The only way to get Sydney Morgan to go to a party is to make her throw one. Or," he added, tapping his chin thoughtfully, "to lead her there with a trail of candy and coffee."

"Don't get any ideas," Sydney warned, pointing a finger at him.

"I make no promises," Calum replied. His expression grew serious as he inserted the memory card into the computer. He began clicking and typing away, grunting in concentration under his breath.

Sydney suppressed a smirk. "Do you always sound like a gremlin when you work?"

"Unnn," Calum grunted in response.

Sydney leaned back in her chair, watching him. There was something compelling about his focus. His lips were set in concentration, his fingers were tight around the mouse, and there was a light in his eyes she'd never seen before. He looked as if he fit there, as if the computer was exactly where he was supposed to be. It made her itch for her camera. Maybe *Genius at Work* could have served as her hometown photo.

On the computer screen, an image of Great Harbor Beach suddenly popped up. Then another, and another. Sydney shot forward in her chair. "Oh my god. You actually did it."

Calum dusted his palms off on his jeans. "All in a day's work, *ma chérie.*"

Sydney scooted in, propping her elbows up on the desk. More photos were filling the screen by the second. She felt a stir of excitement as she began to click through them. There was one in particular she was looking for. That night, she'd seen five lights flash over the ocean: five ghostly flickers.

She knew it was probably just some freaky reflection. She knew there was very little chance her camera had caught it even if it wasn't. But still...she had to see for herself. She couldn't imagine a more "awe-inspiring" photo than Echo Bay's ghost lights.

She clicked through boring shot after boring shot. Next to her, Calum stood up and began fiddling with another computer, grunting under his breath again. Sydney's vision was just starting to blur over when she saw it. She let out a soft exhale.

It was an incredible shot. The tip of the Phantom Rock jutted out of the ocean, sharp and jagged and gray. And shooting into the sky above it, like a hand reaching for the moon, were five wispy beams of light.

She could barely stay in her seat as she clicked on the photo and watched it fill the massive screen. Magnified like that, the image was even more unbelievable. It was both crisp and luminescent, every shadow just right. It was one of the best photos she'd ever taken. And there was no doubt what it captured: the ghost lights.

Sydney's skin sizzled. It was the perfect shot for her application. But how was it even possible? The ghost lights *couldn't* be real. Could they?

She bent in, studying the lights. They arched from the Phantom Rock all the way up to the cliffs. In the smaller version, the cliffs had been barely a blip in the corner. But blown up this large, she could make out their rough curves and craggy peaks and—what was *that*?

She leaned even closer, until her nose was skimming the screen. There was a black shadow on the edge of the cliffs. It was strange.... Up close like this, the shadow looked as if it belonged to a person. A person who was standing *right* where the lights originated. She e-mailed the photo to herself, only half paying attention to what she was doing. Her thoughts were too scrambled to focus on anything else.

If this photo was really of the ghost lights ... and that shadow at the origin of the lights really belonged to a person ... then there was one very logical conclusion. Someone was *creating* the ghost lights.

She closed her eyes, feeling dazed. She'd wondered a million times over the years if the lights were a trick of the moonlight or some fluke of nature or just the result of one too many overactive imaginations. Never once had she considered the possibility that they might be faked.

"Holy cow!"

Calum's voice made Sydney's eyes pop back open. He was standing over her, staring wide-eyed at the computer. "That looks like..." he began.

"I know," she said shakily. She was about to point out the shadow on the cliffs when Calum suddenly let out a laugh.

"Forgive me," he said, looking aghast. "For a microsecond there I almost became one of them!"

"One of the ghost lights?" Sydney asked, confused.

He shook his head, making his wet curls fly from side to side. "No, one of the charlatans with an IQ of negative three who actually believes in all that nonsense." He peered closely at the image. "It's clearly just an illusion. Probably the oxidation of phosphine, diphosphane, and methane. We learned about that at science camp one year. The combination can cause photon emissions."

Sydney stared at the shadow on the cliffs. Her heart was beating so loudly she was sure Calum could hear it. "Photon emissions," she repeated. "Obviously."

Calum reached over her shoulder and pulled out the memory card. The computer screen went blank. "Come on," he said, tossing the card to her. "Your photos have been saved by Super-Calum. Let's bring this tour to completion."

Sydney tried to stay calm as Calum led her up another flight of stairs. He was probably right. She could still use the photo for her application, but in reality it was probably photo—whatever he said— a phenomenon fully explained by modern science. If anyone would know, it was Calum.

"This is it," Calum announced. They came to a stop in front of the only door on the third floor. "The place where the magic happens, where the genius is born, where—"

Sydney nudged him aside and opened the door. "To borrow a phrase from you, *holy cow*," she said as she stepped into the room. Calum's bedroom took up the entire third floor of the house. There was a seating area on one side, a king-size bed on the other, and a huge work space in the middle, featuring a massive flat-screen computer. It was surprisingly well decorated for a teenage boy's room, with striped green pillows on the couch; a soft green rug on the floor; and actual paintings hanging on the walls. But Sydney paid little attention to any of it. Her eyes went directly to the floor-to-ceiling windows that ran along the entire back wall.

Outside, Echo Bay unspooled before them, perfect and miniature, like a page out of a pop-up storybook. She could make out the line of mansions on Dune Way, the colorful awnings on Main Street, and even part of Great Harbor Beach, where white-tipped waves crashed steadily against the sand. "This is amazing."

Looking down on Echo Bay like that, it made her whole life seem far away—like Abby and the Kyla mystery and even Guinness were nothing more than tiny pieces on a checkerboard. "I don't think I'd ever leave the house if I had a view like this," she said, only half joking. She walked up to the window and pressed her nose to the glass, imagining the lives unfolding beneath her: people arriving at the homecoming game, or putting out pumpkins on Echo Boulevard. "I'd just stay up here all the time, feeling like I was queen of the town."

"You might very well be queen soon," Calum pointed out. He went over to stand next to her. "Just a few hours until the moment of truth, right?"

Sydney shrugged. "I guess. Who cares? I'm not even going to the dance."

"*What?*" Calum turned to her with a stern expression. "You're nominated for homecoming queen, Syd. It's essentially your duty to go."

"This coming from the guy who's boycotting the homecoming game?"

"That's the game, not the *dance*. Besides, I'm not nominated to the court." Calum put his hands on her shoulders, forcing her to face him. "I know you're a high school cynic, Sydney Morgan, but I refuse to let you skip your senior year homecoming dance. You're going tonight, and I will escort you."

"That's nice, Calum," Sydney began, "but—"

"No buts. Remember that colossal favor you promised me in return for the whole fake-fire thing?" Calum smiled triumphantly at her. "Well, I'm calling it in. Which means you can't refuse. We're going, and we *will* have fun."

Sydney groaned loudly. "You're the worst."

"I believe you've got your adjectives confused." Calum's smile widened. "I'm sure what you meant to say is, I'm the best."

Sydney narrowed her eyes at him. "Okay, Mr. Conniving, answer me this: What am I supposed to wear tonight? I don't exactly have a closet full of dresses at home."

"You?" Calum feigned surprise. "Shocking." He cocked his head to the side, looking thoughtful. "I think I might actually be able to help you with that."

Sydney put her hands on her hips. "I am not wearing a tux from your closet, if that's what you're suggesting."

"Never. I'll be back in a minute. If I don't return with a dress that meets your approval, then you're excused from your favor. Deal?"

"Sure," Sydney replied. Her phone beeped inside her purse, and she dug around for it as she talked. "But, for the record, I'm very picky about my dresses."

Sydney sighed as Calum disappeared from the room, pounding

loudly down the stairs. Normally, she'd be almost touched by his concern for her high school experience. But after everything that had happened this week—this *day*—a dance was the last thing she could handle. She would just have to be honest with Calum, tell him about Guinness and that she wasn't up for being around a lot of people tonight. Besides, she already had plans with her mom.

She found her phone and scrolled to her new text message. She couldn't help wishing it would be from Guinness, reaching out to her at last. But more likely it was from Tenley or Emerson, giving their harass-Sydney-into-joining-us ploy another go.

It was neither. *Blocked.* Her heart rate spiked. She glanced over her shoulder to make sure Calum wasn't on his way back. Holding her breath, she clicked open the text.

Tonight's the night, Syd! It's do or die... and I expect you to be there to hear the results.

Sydney's breath came out in a long rush. She stared blindly at the text, unable to tear her eyes away. Only the sound of Calum's footsteps finally pulled her out of her trance. She deleted the message just as he returned, carrying a turquoise dress on a hanger. Sydney's eyes popped at the sight of it. It was gorgeous: one shouldered and floor-length, and crisscrossed with filmy layers of turquoise tulle. "What do you think?" Calum asked. He sounded almost shy as he held it out to her.

"It's...beautiful," Sydney said honestly. Her heart was still racing from the text as she took the dress from him. The material was silky in her hands. She whistled when she saw the label on the tag. VERA WANG. "Why do you have this?"

"It was my sister's," Calum said. "She bought it for her prom, but..." He hesitated. "She never got to wear it."

Sydney gingerly turned the dress over, admiring its back. The tulle dipped low, and beneath it was a line of tiny turquoise buttons. "You kept it all these years?"

"My dad doesn't get rid of anything of theirs," Calum said quietly. It was the first time Sydney had ever heard him talk about his family's past. It made him sound different, like he'd aged ten years. "He left everything exactly how it was. My sister's bedroom, my mom's art studio in the basement. Personally, I think it keeps him from moving on, but he refuses to hear it. Which is why I've contemplated signing him up for that reality show *The Life of Hoarders*." Calum smiled, and just like that, he was his old, goofy self again. "He's like their dream case. But until then, I figure we might as well make use of his compulsive behavior, right?" He gave the dress a loving pat. "Besides, someone should get a chance to wear it. And who better than a girl with turquoise eyes?"

Sydney's stomach lurched. The idea of wearing Meryl Bauer's dress—a *Lost Girl's* dress—gave her a horrible, sinking feeling, as if she'd be climbing into the skin of a ghost. "I—I don't think it's a good idea, Calum."

"Uh, uh." Calum crossed his arms against his chest. A curl slipped into his face. He reminded her of a little boy about to throw a tantrum. "A deal's a deal. We're going to that dance, and unless you have something better than this at home, you're wearing the dress."

Sydney nervously twisted her ring, picturing the contents of her closet. She was pretty sure jeans and a flannel shirt didn't constitute *better*.

"That's what I thought," Calum said smugly. "Besides . . . it really would be nice to see someone wear it." He looked at her with such sad eyes that Sydney's heart wrenched.

"All right," she relented. She didn't seem to have another choice.

"Score!" Calum cheered. He broke back into his lopsided grin. "It looks like you're going to homecoming, Syd."

In her head, Sydney saw Abby's text again. *It's do or die.* The words slammed into her with the weight of a speeding train.

"Looks like I am," she said. She pulled her phone back out and opened a text to Tenley and Emerson. *Change of plans: I'm in. Let's end this tonight.*

CHAPTER NINETEEN
Saturday, 1:35 PM

EMERSON TWISTED THROUGH THE AIR, BARELY recognizing the cheer she was chanting. It was the big intermission finale at the homecoming game and all she could think about was Abby. And Josh.

She'd kissed Josh at the club. She'd fooled Abby with her e-mail.

Abby-Josh-Josh-Abby-Kissed-Fooled. She was a human yo-yo.

She landed unsteadily on the grass, just managing to catch her balance. The sidelines loomed ahead of her, a haze of green. By her side, the other cheerleaders pumped their pom-poms and shouted their cheers, their voices circling the air.

"Go," Jessie murmured next to her. It was time for their final combination. "Now!" They both took off running down the sidelines.

Abby-Josh-Josh-Abby.

Kissed. Fooled. Fooled. Kissed.

The field was fuzzy, the crowd an assault of voices. Next to Emerson, Jessie picked up speed, sprinting full force.

Emerson's head was on overload. Was takeoff on her right leg or her left?

Abby-Josh-Josh-Abby.

She *had* to focus! If she didn't clear her mind, she'd never land this combo. She ran faster, matching Jessie's pace.

Right leg or left?

Panic seized her. She couldn't remember. Abby's smug smile flashed through her mind. This was what she wanted, wasn't it? To destroy everything—until they had nothing left.

Well, they weren't going to let her. Not anymore. They had a plan.

Voices thundered, roaring in her ears. Jessie pounded next to her. "Now!" she hissed.

They threw themselves into their side-by-side double-handspring-double-tuck combo.

Emerson wrenched her way through one handspring, then another. She was a beat off, but she kept going. She wouldn't let Abby ruin this. Time seemed to slow as she threw herself into the double tuck, the hardest move attempted by the cheer squad. She cycled once. Wind sliced at her from every side. One and a half. Her hair whipped into her face. Twice.

She hit the ground a second after Jessie, just barely sticking her landing. The impact stole her breath away as she forced her arms into the air. She'd done it. Sloppily, but she'd done it.

She was in charge now. Abby wasn't going to win.

In the stands the crowd went wild. Next to her, Jessie jumped up and down like a squawking monkey. Normally, Emerson would have been right there with her, but her mind was already swan-diving back to their plan for Abby. Tonight they were going to beat her at her own game.

As the football team jogged back onto the field, Emerson scanned the bleachers, searching for Miss Purity herself. Instead, her gaze landed on Tenley. Tenley had been a wreck when she called Emerson that morning to fill her in on Guinness's overdose and finding Abby's scarf. The memory made Emerson feel more determined than ever. She scanned harder, searching for Abby's head of mousy brown hair. She wanted to see her for herself: one last time before they squashed her like a bug tonight.

She had to be there somewhere. Abby Wilkins never missed a school function. She was always front and center, cheering on the basketball team/debate squad/academic decathlon team. She'd even shown up at last year's regional cheerleading competition. Emerson's friends used to joke that it would go on her tombstone one day: PER-FECT ATTENDANCE TO EVERYTHING! "The next thing she'll be attend-ing is her own trial," Emerson muttered under her breath. But as hard as she looked, Emerson didn't see Abby anywhere. She twisted around, locking eyes with Tenley. "Where is she?" she mouthed.

Tenley was holding her phone in her lap, clutched tightly in her fist. She shook her head and shrugged.

A cold shiver ran through Emerson as she turned back to the foot-ball field. Her body went automatically through the motion of the cheers, but her mind was far away. Abby would never miss a homecom-ing game—not unless she had a *really* good reason. Like being too busy plotting their demise.

It didn't matter, Emerson reminded herself. Whatever Abby had up her sleeve, she would never get to act on it. By the time she tried, it would be too late.

For the thousandth time since they'd found Abby's name on the Vault receipt, Emerson wondered what she'd done to make Abby hate her *this* much. Was it just because she'd been close with Caitlin? She planned on asking Abby that very question soon. Once she was safely locked away.

Before Emerson knew it Jessie was leading the squad into the final countdown cheer. The familiar words, chanted by the cheerleaders at the end of every game, shook Emerson back to the present. She'd barely even noticed the second half of the game passing. Her eyes went to the scoreboard as she helped lift Jane Rossi into a basket toss. Seventeen to twenty and forty-eight seconds on the clock. At this point, Echo Bay's only shot at winning was a touchdown.

Emerson shook her pom-poms, launching into the final refrains of the cheer. "We're the Lions, see our claws! We'll bare our fangs and snap our jaws! When we roar, our team will soar! And when it's all done, we'll have won!"

On the field, the ball was snapped to Hunter, who was in shotgun position. The defense started to swarm, but Hunter quickly dodged a tackle and took off running full speed for the end zone. All around Emerson, people applauded and cheered. She tried to get amped up as she screamed along with the rest of the squad, urging Hunter on. It was her favorite part of a game: how energy seemed to spark in the air as the squad's voices rose together—no longer a patchwork, but a crescendo, a roar. It usually made her feel so alive. But this time, as Hunter scored the winning touchdown and the crowd went ballistic and she jumped into a flawless toe touch, her thoughts stayed on one thing and one thing only. Getting Abby tonight.

The field exploded into a frenzy of excitement as the Anaswan players sulked off to their buses. "Come on, Em!" Jessie grabbed her hand to pull her onto the field, but Emerson shook her off. She could see Tenley over by the bleachers, waving at her.

"I'll be there in a minute," she said.

Jessie gave her a strange look, but it quickly vanished as she bounced onto the field, throwing her arms around Tyler.

"Behind the bleachers," Tenley murmured when Emerson reached her. She'd clearly scouted out a spot already, because she led Emerson to an empty area a ways down, where they were shielded by a tall line of trash cans. In the distance, the voices of the crowd melted into a wall of white noise. "If you haven't checked your phone yet, Sydney's in for tonight," Tenley informed her.

Emerson tensed a little. It was a good thing, she reminded herself. The more people to face off against Abby, the better chance they stood. "What changed her mind?"

"She got a text, too. 'It's do or die,'" Tenley recited grimly. "'And I expect you to be there to hear the results.'" She scowled. "Clearly, Abby is obsessed with making sure Delancey wins tonight."

"Her purity partner in crime," Emerson spat out. "Well, we'll play along. Then when Abby's defenses are down: *Wham!*" She slapped her hands together. "We'll make sure Delancey winning queen is the last thing on her mind." Suddenly Emerson cocked her head. "Oh my god, Tenley. That's it! Maybe that's what this was about all along. Think about it: Abby was the one who sent out that Homecoming Nomination Memo, right? So she probably knew days ahead of time who was nominated. This could be why she continued with Tricia's charade in the first place—and why she added me to the game. To make sure Delancey won queen."

Tenley adjusted the sheer blue blouse she was wearing over a white tank top, looking disgusted. "Who cares *that* much about homecoming?"

Emerson looked away, fixing her gaze on a patch of trampled grass. "Someone truly insane."

"I told Sydney to meet us at six thirty tonight so we can take our names out of the running before we deal with Abby," Tenley told her. "That way, we're taking no chances."

Emerson nodded, but before she could say anything, the phone Tenley was clutching in her hand let out a beep. They both went still. Their eyes darted toward the phone.

All Emerson could think was: *It's her.* "Look at it," she said tightly.

Slowly, Tenley wrenched her fingers off the screen. "It's just my mom," she breathed. "It looks like Lanson is shipping Guinness off to rehab tonight instead of tomorrow, and he wants us to visit him as a family first." Tenley pressed her lips into a straight line. "I have to go, but I'll see you tonight."

"I'll be the one dressed all pretty for our darer," Emerson replied. She leaned back against the bleachers as she watched Tenley go. If she listened hard, she could just make out Jessie's voice lifting through the air, still shouting out cheers. That girl never stopped. Emerson knew she should go join them; Marta was probably looking for her at this very moment. But she wasn't sure she could fake even one more minute of *rah-rah-rah*. She headed to the parking lot instead.

She gave herself a pep talk as she drove home. Tonight they'd put an end to this. And then her life could finally, finally move on. As she climbed up the porch of her house, she tried to imagine what it would feel like to have a bad-hair day be the worst of her problems. *Heaven,* she decided.

"Emerson?"

At the sound of Josh's voice, she jumped a solid two feet into the air. She whipped around to find him standing in her yard. His half Mohawk flopped messily over to one side, and he was carrying an ancient-looking boom box.

"Whoa, I come in peace!" He gave her one of his heart-melting, you-amuse-me smiles. "*And* offering music." He hit play on the boom box. Peter Gabriel's "In Your Eyes" blasted through the yard at top volume, making the porch vibrate.

"My eardrums!" Emerson sprinted down the stairs and spun the volume dial. The song lowered to a whisper. "Are you trying to get half the neighborhood out here?"

"If it makes you talk to me, then sure." Josh turned the music up again, just a little. Peter Gabriel's voice wound around them like a warm breeze.

Emerson fought the smile tugging at her lips. It was the scene from her favorite movie: Lloyd Dobler holding the Peter Gabriel–blasting boom box up under Diane Court's window. Emerson had watched *Say Anything* for the first time when she was ten years old, and still she remembered how wonderingly she'd stared at the TV during that scene. *I want that one day*, she'd thought. *Someone who loves me enough to tell the whole world.*

She looked up at Josh. His expression was serious, intent. Her stomach did a flip.

"You've got to talk to me, Em," Josh said. "I'm going crazy here. One minute you're hot, the next you're cold..." He sighed. "I don't know what to think anymore."

Emerson dug the toe of her shoe into the grass. She wished so badly she could just tell him everything: every single sordid detail of her life since New York. Wipe her slate clean. But how could she? She felt like one of those vaults in the club: piled high with secrets and locked up tight.

"I need to know why you left that summer, Emerson." Josh took her hand. Heat pulsed through her body. "The truth." He nodded down at the boom box. "I mean, come on: I'm reenacting a *romantic comedy* here. An *eighties* romantic comedy. You owe me that much."

Emerson took a deep breath. "The truth," she repeated. That day flashed through her mind: the photographer, the back room, her clothes discarded on the floor. She'd held the secret inside for so long. "I—I made a mistake that summer," she said slowly.

Josh smiled encouragingly at her. The gesture sent another wave of heat pulsing through her. She opened her mouth again, but this time no words came out.

After tonight, Abby would be gone—the game would finally be over. She could go back to living her own life, making her own choices. She looked down at Josh's hand, still holding hers. Their hands had always fit together perfectly, like conjoining pieces of a puzzle.

Never in her life had a choice been so shimmeringly crystal clear.

Josh. She wanted Josh. She wanted to hear his laugh and feel his touch and make him smile. She wanted to take walks with him and read his writing. She wanted to love him enough to tell the whole world.

She wanted it so badly, she was willing to lie to get it. Lie not to hurt him.

"My mistake...was getting scared," she continued. "Things got so serious with us so fast that summer and...I just freaked. I was immature. I should have told you. But instead I ran." She paused. The lie felt heavy on her tongue, but the relief written across Josh's face was clear.

"That's it?" he breathed. He put the boom box down at his feet. "That's really it?"

She nodded soundlessly, not trusting herself to speak.

A smile took over Josh's face. He wrapped his arms around her waist and pulled her to him. He smelled like beach and leather, like Echo Bay and New York. Like a memory come to life. Her whole body sang, every fiber shot through with happiness.

For so long she'd tried to evade her feelings, to bury and fool them, mask and hide them. But they'd always been there, simmering beneath the surface. You could kick love away and you could trample it down, but you couldn't erase it. "I missed you so much," she whispered.

She looked up, meeting his eyes. They were more green than brown in the afternoon sunlight, and they had a glossy sheen to them. Emerson's jaw came unhinged. "Is Josh Wright, the antihero, rom-com cynic himself, actually *crying*?"

"Of course not!" Josh's cheeks flushed. "More like...watering." He leaned down until his lips brushed her ear. There was only a sliver of space between them. "I'm glad you're back," he whispered. Then he turned his head and he kissed her. Her heart lifted and her stomach flip-flopped and she pulled him even closer, never wanting this feeling to end.

When they finally broke apart, she felt a thousand pounds lighter, as if all her fears and worries had been vacuumed right up. She was filled with a sudden urge to ask Josh. *Next time*, she promised herself. Once Abby was just a distant memory. For now, she settled for kissing him again.

Emerson felt happier than she had in weeks when she finally made it into her house a little while later. She jogged up to her room, already thinking about what makeup to wear tonight. Gold hues, she decided. Gold was always festive. And the end of Abby deserved nothing less. Plus it looked good against her black hair. In fact, maybe she'd ask her mom if she could borrow her gold neck—

:

She never got to finish that thought.

Her foot collided with something in the doorway of her bedroom, sending her careening forward. She landed with a thud on her side. Lying tipped over next to her was Holden's cage.

Holden lay inside it, his body tilted at a strange angle. "Holden?" she whispered.

The duckling didn't move.

Emerson gently lifted the cage. Holden flopped limply inside, his feathers stained with blood. "No!" Tears sprang to Emerson's eyes, darkening her vision. Again and again she shook the cage, but still Holden didn't move. There were no chirps or pecks or clumsy flaps of his wings. A sob wracked her, tears streaming down her cheeks. "Holden," she whimpered.

It was through a thick veil of tears that she finally saw it: a note taped to the bottom of the cage. She let out a cry as she tore it off.

Bad things happen when you're a bad girl.

Better behave tonight, Em! Or next, it will

be you.

"WE WANT TO WITHDRAW FROM THE HOMECOMING race." Tenley put her hands on her hips, glaring up at Harris Newsby. The dance was to begin in under half an hour, and she, Emerson, and Sydney were in Winslow's study lounge, where Harris and the rest of the Pricewaterhouse-Winslow Club—the club responsible for tallying any votes at Winslow events—had set up their ballot-counting booth.

Tenley glanced over at her friends. Well, at least Sydney was there with her. Emerson was physically present, but her eyes were glazed over and it was clear her mind was elsewhere. Probably with her duckling. The thought made Tenley's blood boil. What Abby had done to a defenseless little animal...It was sick. Her threats weren't going to work on them this time. They just made it even more important to end this once and for all.

"Excuse me?" Harris burst out laughing, making his wire-rimmed glasses bounce on his nose. "Is this some kind of joke?" He eyed

Tenley's magenta dress, which she'd picked out weeks ago. It was made of raw silk and had a high neckline that made the low dip in the back the perfect surprise. "Because you look dressed for the occasion to me."

"I might actually take that as a compliment," Tenley snapped, "if you weren't dressed like a Smurf." She eyed his bright blue suit disdainfully. "I'm serious, Harris. We want our names taken out of the running. None of us wants to win queen."

"B-but, we've already tallied the votes," Harris stuttered. He lifted up a large manila envelope. "The results are finalized."

"Then refinalize them," Tenley demanded. "Unless, of course, none of us is the winner."

"I...uh..." Harris looked bewildered. He tugged at the bright blue vest he was wearing under his bright blue suit jacket. "Miss Hilbrook? Can you come here for a minute?"

"Everything okay, Harris?" Miss Hilbrook pushed a strand of dark blond hair off her forehead as she approached the booth. In her red sheath dress, she could almost pass for one of the students. Tenley had never understood how one of the dorkiest clubs in school had ended up with Winslow's hottest teacher as its academic sponsor.

"Everything's not okay," Tenley informed her. "I was just telling Harris that Sydney, Emerson, and I would like to remove our names from the homecoming race."

"And I was just telling Tenley that the results have already been tallied," Harris replied.

"Retallying won't exactly be hard, Harris," Sydney cut in, sounding exasperated. Tenley glanced over at her. She still couldn't get over how different Sydney looked tonight. Gone was her usual uniform of torn jeans and a flannel, and in its place was a gorgeous turquoise dress that made her blue eyes pop. Her hair was pulled into a loose bun, and she was wearing makeup for what Tenley suspected was the first time in her life. "Considering there will only be one candidate left."

"I don't understand, girls." A concerned wrinkle formed between Miss Hilbrook's eyebrows. "You should be excited about this! I shouldn't be saying this, but..." She paused, lowering her voice confidingly. "One of you has already been confirmed the winner. Whoever it is deserves to get her crown. If this is about nerves—"

"It's not," Tenley interrupted. "We just don't want to be queen," she said firmly. "Any of us."

"It's a protest!" Sydney blurted out. "We're protesting the, um, rise of materialism in high schools."

"Yes!" Tenley slammed her palms down on the booth. "That's right. By not winning homecoming queen, we're telling all students it's okay to be a dork"—Sydney kicked her in the ankle and she quickly cleared her throat—"it's okay not to conform to society's impossibly high standards," she finished. She tossed her meticulously curled hair over her shoulder. "Right, Emerson?"

Emerson blinked, looking startled. "Um, right," she said quickly.

"*Emerson Cunningham* is taking a stand against *materialism?*" Harris shook his head, sounding flabbergasted. "You're a model, for god's sake. That's like the living embodiment of materialism—"

"That's enough, Harris," Miss Hilbrook interjected. "I think it's wonderful what they're doing." She gave Tenley a penetrating look. "Just as long as you guys are sure..."

"We are," Tenley promised her. She smiled as sincerely as she could. "It's a cause that means a lot to us."

Miss Hilbrook furrowed her brow. "I hope you're not planning to make any sort of scene as part of this stand you're taking."

"Not at all," Tenley assured her.

"We just aren't interested," Sydney added. She glanced at Emerson, who nodded. "Any of us."

Miss Hilbrook smiled and patted Tenley on the shoulder. "Well, then I think that's very noble. Harris, please prepare an envelope for the new winner."

Harris groaned under his breath as he returned to the booth. "Girls," he muttered.

Tenley breathed in deeply as she stepped into the hallway. The faint scent of punch and cookies drifted over from the cafeteria, where the dance was being set up. "Part One down," she said.

Emerson adjusted her dress. It was black and ruched and accentuated her model-tall figure. A gold drop necklace hung around her neck, and her hair was pulled back in a sleek ponytail. Apparently, even heartbroken she could look flawless. "Time for Part Two," she said.

Tenley looked from Emerson to Sydney. Abby should be arriving in the bio lab any second. It was now or never. "Everyone remember the plan?" she asked.

"Scream," Sydney recited.

"Grab," Emerson added.

"Lock," Tenley finished. She tossed a key to Emerson. It was large and beat-up, marked on the top with masking tape.

"Supply closet?" Emerson confirmed.

Tenley nodded. Earlier in the evening, before Emerson and Sydney arrived, she'd managed to sweet-talk Bob, the ancient Winslow janitor, into lending her the spare key to the third-floor supply closet. She told him that she was on the decorating committee for the dance and that she would need access to supplies throughout the night. She'd thrown in her sweetest smile, and he'd eaten it right up. "And if anyone needs it, I've got my pepper spray." She popped open her beaded purse to reveal the small pink bottle tucked inside.

"So do I." Emerson opened up her gold-sequined purse. A matching bottle lay next to several tubes of makeup.

Grimly, Sydney opened her purse as well. The same bottle was jammed between her phone and a pack of mints.

"Let's do this," Tenley said.

Fear stampeded through her as they headed silently to the bio lab. *Channel it.* That's what her dad used to tell her before gymnastics meets. *Channel your fear and you'll be unstoppable.*

Tenley straightened up to her full five feet two inches. She could do this. She looked over at Sydney and Emerson, walking tall by her side. *They* could do this, she corrected herself. *Together.*

A few rooms down from the bio lab, they slowed to a stop. Tenley gestured for the others to wait. She crept quietly over to the lab. Careful to stay behind the door frame, she peeked inside. Abby was sitting on top of a desk in a navy dress, drumming her fingers against her lap. Her purse lay discarded on the chair behind her. Perfect.

Tenley gave Emerson and Sydney a thumbs-up. Emerson swiveled around and took a quick scan of the hallway before giving a thumbs-up in return. That was their cue. In the span of a minute, three things happened. Tenley ducked into an empty classroom next to the bio lab. Emerson dashed into the hallway bathroom. And Sydney pushed play on a tape recorder and shoved it to the very back of the third-floor supply closet. As a single, ear-piercing shriek trumpeted out of the recorder and filled the air, Sydney darted into the bathroom to meet Emerson.

Tenley held her breath. *Three,* she counted silently. *Two—*

"Delancey?" Abby's yell exploded from inside the bio lab before

Tenley could count to one. Footsteps pounded out of the lab and down the hall.

Bingo.

Tenley flew into the bio lab. There, lying innocently on a chair, was Abby's silk, cream purse. The purse she'd left behind in her rush to reach Delancey—exactly what they'd counted on. Tenley grabbed it, her fingers wrapping greedily around its chain strap. She popped open the clasp. Inside was Abby's phone: the darer's phone. A smile spread triumphantly across her face.

Down the hall, she heard a door slam shut. She bolted out of the room, clutching the purse to her chest. Emerson and Sydney were standing outside the supply closet with the key jammed into the door's keyhole. Sydney yanked it out and tested the handle. Locked.

"Hey!" Abby's scream ricocheted through the closet. "What's going on? Who screamed? Delancey?" She pounded angrily against the door. "Let me out!"

Tenley pressed a finger to her lips. The less Darer Abby knew about their involvement with this, the better. At least until she was locked up behind bars. Then Tenley planned to rub it right in her face. No one messed with Tenley Reed and got away with it.

They padded quietly down the hallway, Abby's screams growing fainter behind them. Tenley's smile widened. The supply closet was as far from the cafeteria as you could get: two floors up and at the other end of the school. Abby could scream and bang the door all she wanted. No one was going to hear her.

They remained silent until they were back on the first floor. Tenley led the way into an empty classroom. Finally, she let out a cheer. "We did it!" She hoisted Abby's purse excitedly into the air. "We really did it!"

"Let's not get ahead of ourselves." Sydney snatched the purse out of Tenley's hand and extracted Abby's phone. "First, we need to find our proof." They huddled together as Sydney turned on Abby's phone. "No password," she said, sounding surprised. They'd come prepared with a list of numbers to try if she had one: birthdays, addresses, her parents' anniversary. "Well, that makes this easier." Sydney opened up Abby's texts. "Here we go...." she murmured.

Tenley leaned in over her shoulder. There was message after message to Delancey, along with the usual check-in messages to Abby's parents, a few messages about homework, and a whole slew announcing Purity Club meetings, and...that was it.

"No." Tenley took a staggering step backward. "It's not possible. There have to be dares!"

Sydney shook her head as she scrolled through Abby's e-mails. "Nothing," she said miserably. "She hasn't permanently deleted her trash mail in forever, and there's nothing even in there." She pushed her bangs off her forehead. "Either she was meticulous about *just* permanently deleting her dare messages, or she has a whole other phone hidden somewhere else."

"A darer phone," Tenley breathed. "Of course. This one must be her cover! That would explain the no password."

Emerson let out a choked cry. "This isn't happening. This is supposed to be over. We're supposed to have proof!"

"Don't panic," Tenley told her quickly. "We can fix this." She snapped her fingers as an idea struck her. "Delancey! She's our answer. If Abby has another phone, I bet you anything her best purity pal has seen it at some point. We just have to keep up a normal homecoming act until we find her. Then we can get her to tell us where it is."

269

Emerson collapsed into a desk chair, looking stunned. "Normal?" she mumbled.

Tenley's heart squeezed. She thought of Emerson's duckling, lying lifeless in his cage. "You can do this, Em." She crouched down in front of her. "We're going to help you through it." She glanced pleadingly at Sydney. "Right, Syd?"

Sydney cleared her throat as she joined them. "Right," she said slowly. "You're not alone in this, Emerson."

Emerson looked up. There were tears in her eyes and frown lines around her mouth. But ever so slowly, she pushed herself out of the chair. "Okay," she said. "Let's end this." Emerson took Abby's phone and opened up a text to Molly Berg, the student-body vice president. *Running late!! Hold down court for me?* She smiled weakly. "That will buy us some time."

Tenley nodded in satisfaction as Emerson pressed send. Turning on her heels, she led the way into the cafeteria. The room was almost unrecognizable, turned into a "Pirate's Ship" for the dance's theme. The tables had been removed, replaced by a silver dance floor. On the raised platform where Tenley and her friends usually sat, a band was set up, playing a cover of a classic Rolling Stones song. The cafeteria walls had been covered in a wraparound mural of the ocean, which was peppered with brightly painted fish. Scattered around the outskirts of the dance floor were antique wooden trunks with fake jewelry and coins spilling out of them. Even the hot-food line had been transformed: covered in a filmy silver cloth and lined with glittery bowls of punch and gilded platters of cookies.

Tenley's eyes darted around the room. "I don't see Delancey."

Sydney tugged at her dress. "She has to show up eventually. If she wants to get her hard-earned crown." She shot an almost-sympathetic look at Emerson. "We just have to hold on a little longer until she does."

Up on stage, Molly Berg took the mic. She was a mousy-looking girl with frizzy hair and a barely audible voice. "Hello?" she squeaked into the mic. "Welcome to the dance?" Her voice went up at the end of each sentence, making everything she said sound like a question.

"What?" someone yelled from the dance floor.

"A little louder, Molly," Miss Hilbrook called out.

Molly cleared her throat, making a loud burst of static ring through the room. "Abby Wilkins seems to be running late?" she squeaked, her voice only slightly louder this time. "So as student-body vice president, I want to welcome you all to the dance?" She squeezed the mic between her palms, looking anything but thrilled to be up on stage. "Have fun tonight? And if there are any problems, find me or one of the chaperones?" As she went on to profusely thank the chaperones, Tenley turned to the others.

"Sydney's right," she said quietly. "Until we find Delancey, we're just three happy-go-lucky girls, hoping to be crowned homecoming queen. If we act like nothing's wrong, no one will suspect what we did to Abby."

Sydney nodded in agreement. After a beat, Emerson followed suit.

"Here goes nothing," Tenley murmured. Plastering on her happiest smile, she waved to their friends on the other side of the room. They were clearly having a blast. Marta had several strands of gemstones from one of the trunks wrapped around her neck, and Nate was swatting at them like a cat. Tyler had his arm around Jessie, who looked peppier than ever in a bubblegum-pink dress. Next to them, Hunter and Sean were grinning as they watched several members of Winslow's hip-hop club shake it on the dance floor as the music started up again onstage. When Hunter noticed Tenley, he lifted his hand in a return wave.

271

"There's my elusive date," he yelled. Tenley forced a laugh. When she'd told Hunter she wanted to meet him at the dance instead of arriving together, he'd joked that she better not stand him up.

"All gussied up just for you," she quipped when he joined them. She did a little spin to show off her dress's low-cut back. It allowed her to take another quick scan of the room. It was continuing to fill up with familiar Winslow faces, but she still didn't see Delancey anywhere. She caught Sydney's eye. She was clearly thinking the same thing.

"I see my date," Sydney said. She gave Tenley and Emerson a meaningful look. "Find me if you see you-know-who," she added under her breath. Then she took off, looking relieved to be away from Tenley's friends. Over by the food bar, Calum Bauer broke into a huge grin, waving her over.

"So the loner and the loser are an item now?" Hunter commented.

Tenley was surprised to feel a stab of anger at hearing Sydney called a loser. "They're friends," she said sharply. She couldn't imagine it was anything more than that. She was pretty sure Sydney wasn't over Guinness, and she doubted computer-geek Calum would be her rebound of choice if she was. Though she did have to admit... with his blond curls actually semitamed and his perfectly fitted gray suit, he might almost look hot tonight. If he weren't Calum.

"Ahoy, mateys!" Marta teetered over to them in sky-high heels, her jungle-green dress flouncing behind her. "Em, I'm in need of some serious ER in the BR. My hair's coming out of its bun!" She gestured to the elaborate updo that swept her red waves off her face. A single rebellious strand had slipped out of its hold. "I need your magic hair skills, pronto." Before Emerson could respond, Marta grabbed her hand and dragged her off to the bathroom.

As Marta and Emerson disappeared from the cafeteria, the music abruptly cut out. Up on stage, the band's lead singer tapped the microphone. "Attention!" he called out. Slowly, the chatter died down, and everyone swiveled around to face the stage.

"Happy Homecoming, Winslow Academy!" the singer announced. He was in his twenties and had a swagger to him that made Tenley think he liked playing high school dances a little more than he should. "I'm Avery, and this is gonna be a fun night. We're going to start it off right with a song written by one of your very own. The writer wanted to remain anonymous, but their requirement was that every single one of you—and I mean *everyone*—gets out on the dance floor for it. We don't think you'll regret it. It's a pretty rad song."

The music to Billy Joel's "We Didn't Start the Fire" filled the room. When Avery began singing, the lyrics weren't the usual ones. *"Miss Hilbrook, Pajama Day, Hunter Bailey, Mr. Ray, Pledge of Winslow, South Field, Flagpole of Shame . . ."*

"Oh my god!" Tenley heard Jessie squeal. "This is amazing!"

"Did I just hear my name?" Hunter said, pretending to preen. Up on the stage, the band launched into the chorus.

"We didn't lose the ga-ame. We were always winning, since the school's been playing . . ."

Hunter grabbed Tenley's hand. "You heard the band. Everyone out there."

Jessie was already on the dance floor, dragging Tyler with her. *"We didn't lose the ga-ame,"* she sang along with the band. *"No, we didn't give up. But we did high-five them."*

"Let's do it," Tenley agreed. The dance floor was the perfect vantage spot to keep an eye out for Delancey. Winslow hadn't lost the game—and she wasn't going to, either. "I want to take this dress for a whirl." She was about to follow Hunter when a beep rose from her beaded purse.

Her phone was in her hands within seconds. Maybe Emerson or Sydney had spotted Delancey! But the number on her screen was blocked. The floor seemed to dip under her feet as she hastily clicked open the message.

Want to know how to end this? You'll find the gift of knowledge in the auditorium.

Tenley took a step backward, looking wildly around. Abby was locked in the supply closet without a phone. So who had sent that text?

Out on the dance floor, Emerson and Marta had joined Jessie and Tyler. In the back of the room, Sydney had left Calum and was now talking to Mr. Lozano, the art teacher. Tenley dug her nails into her palm as she looked back down at the message. Maybe Abby had pre-programmed it to send before they locked her in the closet. It would make sense; she would have thought she'd be too busy running the homecoming dance to be doling out dares. Which meant there could be some kind of real proof waiting for her in the auditorium—and no Abby there to stop her from taking it.

She thought about grabbing Emerson and Sydney to go with her, but one look at them made her stop. Emerson seemed as if she was almost, nearly having *fun* on the dance floor. And in the back of the room, Sydney was laughing heartily at whatever Mr. Lozano was saying. They'd all been through so much already. And there was no Abby to worry about right now. She could handle this. She'd promised Sydney and Emerson this would end tonight, and it would.

"Crap, it's... my mom," Tenley lied to Hunter. "I've got to go call her. You go ahead without me." She flashed him an apologetic smile before hurrying into the hallway.

She arrived at the auditorium to find it completely empty. The lights were off, except for a single spotlight above the catwalk. "Hello?" she called out, just to be safe. "Anyone here?" Her voice echoed through the empty room. Down the hall, she could hear strains of music drifting out from the cafeteria. Just a few yards away her friends were dancing and laughing, having a blast. Standing alone in the auditorium, it all seemed so distant.

Tenley's gaze landed on the catwalk. There was something sitting on it, directly under the spotlight. She turned on the lights and moved closer to get a better look. It was a small, elaborately gift-wrapped box, displayed on a swath of fancy brocade fabric. A mass of gold ribbons and bows was stuck to the top.

She remembered the words from her text: *You'll find the gift of knowledge in the auditorium.* She hadn't thought it would be *literal.* Tenley took a step closer. That box had to be bait. Abby had probably planned to use it to lure her up to the catwalk—so she could jump out of the shadows and shove her right off. But Abby wasn't here. She was locked up where she couldn't hurt anyone. Which meant there was no reason for Tenley not to see what was in that box.

She tossed her purse onto the stage. She was bristling with excitement as she climbed the rickety metal staircase that led up to the catwalk. If there was something in that box that tied Abby to the dares... something that she probably planned to snatch back as soon as she sent Tenley tumbling to her death...well, maybe they wouldn't need Abby's phone after all.

The stairwell shuddered a little under her weight, and she gripped tightly to the banister as she hurried up the last few stairs. Gingerly, she stepped onto the smooth metal catwalk, making it give it a small swing. Her fingers had just closed around the gift box when a terrible grinding noise made her eyes fly upward.

The one spotlight that was lit up had torn off the ceiling and was now dangling precariously above her. *Directly* above her.

Her gaze landed on a thin, wire rope tied around the spotlight. She followed it down with her eyes. It was tied to the catwalk! She let out a wail as it hit her: She'd been set up. The light had been rigged to fall the instant the catwalk swung under anyone's weight—the instant someone went for that gift box.

Slowly, slowly, Tenley backed toward the stairs. But it was too late. As soon as she moved just an inch, there was a loud *crack*, and the spotlight came hurtling down.

"No!" Tenley flung herself forward just in time. She landed hard on her stomach, the catwalk swaying dangerously as the spotlight crashed down where she'd been standing only seconds before. With a loud boom, it shattered into pieces, glass spraying everywhere. She cried out as fragments pricked at her bare legs. In all the chaos, the top tumbled off the gift box. Her eyes widened as she caught a glimpse of what was inside. *Nothing.*

Behind her, the broken light burned against the fancy fabric that had been spread out beneath the gift box. She struggled to pull herself to her feet. She nearly had when the fabric suddenly burst into flames.

Fire surged into the air, sending burning hot fingers nipping at her heels. A flame leaped up, searing her calf. Tenley screamed and yanked her dress away, desperately smothering the flames with her hem. She put it out, but the frantic movement caused her to lose her balance. She tipped heavily to the side.

Time seemed to slow as she went sliding off the catwalk.

"Aah!" She grabbed desperately at the edge, catching herself just in time. The top half of her body clung to the hot metal catwalk, while the bottom half dangled in thin air. The floor loomed beneath her, seeming miles away.

"Help! Someone! Please!" Tenley yelled. But the music pounded on in the cafeteria, drowning out her voice. Tears slid down her cheeks as one of her hands began to slip off the catwalk. She kicked with all her might, trying to claw her way back up. Knives sliced through her injured calf, the pain blinding. She was going to fall.

She heard something down below. Tenley's heart leaped with hope. "Help! Please!" She craned her neck, straining to see. It was a person, dressed in a floor-length black coat, a thick ski mask obscuring everything but two eyes and a mouth. The person paused next to Tenley's purse and dropped a single sheet of paper on top of it.

Any hope burning inside Tenley was extinguished with a single blow. It was the darer! Somehow, Abby had gotten out.

"Stop!" Tenley yelled. "Please don't do this, Abby. Help me! I'll—I'll do whatever you want."

But the person was already gone.

"No!" Tenley howled. Adrenaline pumped through her. She couldn't let Abby win like this.

Mustering every ounce of strength she had, every muscle she'd ever built from years of gymnastics, she hoisted herself up an inch at a time. Her muscles ached with the effort, and pain was searing through her left leg, but she ignored it all, throwing everything she had into getting back onto that catwalk. She landed in a crumpled ball on the hard metal, agony reverberating through her. A flame tore by, and she barely managed to snuff it out with her shoe. She took a deep breath. She had to keep going.

She crawled toward the staircase. Flames flickered around her, singing her dress. Shards of glass pressed into her palms and knees, making her cry out in pain. Sweat and tears coated her cheeks by the time she made it to the stairs. She half limped, half tumbled down. She was breathing hard as she collapsed in a heap at the bottom.

Every inch of her body hurt, but she'd done it. She'd made it.

As she lay there, she heard the muffled sound of her phone ringing in her purse. The sound got her moving again. With labored breaths, she pushed herself toward her purse. But before she could reach her phone, her gaze fell on the note Abby had left behind. There, in the familiar typewriter font, was a poem.

Ding-dong, the witch is dead!

Which old witch? The bitchy witch!

And the killer--that's me--is free.

You really thought I was Abby?

Well, wasn't that guess shabby....

Tenley squeezed her eyes shut. Realizations were slamming into her one after another, like punches to the gut.

Abby wasn't the darer.

The real darer was out there somewhere, roaming the halls.

And whomever it was had assumed Tenley would die here. This note had been left for Emerson and Sydney to find next to her lifeless body.

She forced open one eye, then the other. It looked as if the fire had mostly burned itself out on the catwalk. She crumpled the note into a ball and shoved it into her purse. She had to find the others. She had to warn them.

"Tenley? Are you in here?" The familiar voice drifted in from the hallway, followed by a quick patter of footsteps. "Tenley? Oh my god,

Ten!" Tim raced across the auditorium, pounding up the stairs to the stage. "What happened? Are you okay?"

"I—I—" Tenley took a deep breath. She had to pull herself together. She couldn't tell Tim the truth. Not with the real darer out there. "I came in here for a breather from the dance," she lied. "And the spotlight just fell! I burned my leg. I have to go. I have to—"

"Hey." Tim grabbed her, running his hands softly down her arms. Despite the heat in her leg, she felt a tiny shiver. "Calm down, Ten. It's okay." He tilted her chin up until she had no choice but to look at him. His eyes were filled with concern, and something else, too. Something that reminded Tenley of the feeling she'd gotten the first time he'd touched her: a connection. "We'll get your leg taken care of," Tim said soothingly. "But first there's something I want to do."

"I—" she tried to protest.

He didn't let her finish. He leaned down and kissed her.

For a split second she felt a dozen things at once: safe and terrified, peaceful and exhilarated. It was unlike any other kiss she'd experienced. Then the thought: *Caitlin.*

She pulled back, trembling all over. Reality crashed over her like a tidal wave. "I—I really have to get back to my friends," she stammered desperately.

"Oh no you don't." Tim took her in his arms. "I came all the way to this dance to surprise you. I even wore a suit, which my mom will tell you has happened about twice in my life." Tenley blinked. For the first time she noticed the pinstripe suit and yellow tie he was wearing. "I've been looking all over for you," he continued. "I was actually calling you from outside the bathroom—I figured that's where you had to be— when I heard your phone's crazy Madonna ring in here." He smiled, pushing a sweaty strand of hair off her face. "I'm not letting you out of my sight after a wild-goose chase like that. You're finding the nurse and I'm coming with you. Then we're having that dance you promised me."

Tenley wanted so badly to agree, to melt into him and let him take her to the nurse and make everything better. But she couldn't. Not with the darer running loose.

"We'll dance," she promised him. "Believe me, I want nothing more." She squeezed his arm. "But, it's going to have to be later. Listen—can you go find someone and tell them that the light fell? I don't want anyone else getting hurt."

"All right," Tim relented. "But you're going to get some first aid, right?"

Tenley gave him a weak smile. "Right," she lied.

She hurried out of the auditorium before he could stop her. She was limping, but she refused to let it slow her down. She had to find Emerson and Sydney. If she didn't . . . If the darer got to them first . . .

Tenley shuddered. That wouldn't happen.

No one was going to die tonight.

CHAPTER TWENTY-ONE
Saturday, 7:36 PM

"I CAN'T BELIEVE THEY'RE PLAYING THE BIEBS FOR the first slow dance of the night." Calum tightened his arms around Sydney's waist as they swayed to the song blasting through the cafeteria.

"I can't believe you just called him the Biebs," Sydney said. The dance floor had thinned out a little, leaving plenty of room for them to dance. She found herself leaning into Calum, relaxing for the first time all week. Abby was locked up where she couldn't hurt them. As soon as Delancey showed, they'd get what they needed to finally go to the cops. Then life could go back to normal at last.

"My dad and I were at a dinner in DC with him once," Calum replied. He did a side step, moving Sydney smoothly across the dance floor. "If the secretary of state calls him the Biebs, I figure I should, too."

"You were at a dinner with the secretary of state and Justin Bieber?" Sydney gaped up at him. "How come I never knew that?" She wrinkled her brow as Calum guided her through a graceful spin. "And while we're at it, since when do you know how to dance like this?"

Calum grinned down at her. "There's multitudes you don't know about me, Syd." He pushed a loose strand of hair off her face, and she was surprised to feel her stomach do a tiny leap.

"I know a lot," she retorted. "I know that you use SPF seventy-five sunscreen every day and that you hate chocolate but love vanilla and that you think every single James Bond movie is Oscar-worthy and your dream is to make computer games for a living." She smirked at Calum. "Should I keep going?"

"Please, no," Calum said with a laugh. His hands pressed against the small of her back. He did another side step, leaving barely an inch between them. "I promise there *are* things you don't know." He paused, and she could hear his breath quickening. "But I would really like you to, Syd. I want you to know it all." His eyes searched hers and suddenly she knew: He was going kiss her.

Her breath snagged in her throat. For so long, Guinness had wielded such power over her, left her with tunnel vision: him, him, only him. But as she looked up at Calum, she saw a whole world outside that tunnel, wide and sprawling, a thousand different paths. Calum's face lowered toward hers. Her stomach leaped again, impossible to ignore. She could smell his citrusy shampoo, could feel the pressure of his hands sliding down her back. His lips moved closer.

"I can't." It burst out in a single breath. She pulled away, putting space between them. Conflicting emotions were dueling inside her: regret, relief, regret, relief. "I'm sorry, Calum." She looked down. They were standing on the edge of the dance floor, where the silver platform bled into gray linoleum. "I just..."

"It's Guinness, isn't it?" Calum asked tightly.

"No," Sydney said quickly. "Well, yes, but not like you think. I'm done with him. It's over. But for so long he was everything to me, you know?" She paused, thinking of all the roles he'd played: mentor, friend, more than friend. "I guess I just need some time to myself. A chance to see what things look like without him." She lifted her head. "I really am sorry. I didn't mean to give you the wrong impression."

Calum's face flushed red. A muscle twitched in his jaw. "I guess I misread the situation." His voice was tense, but there was a wounded undercurrent to it that tugged at Sydney's heart.

"I'm sorry," she said again.

"Sydney!"

The sound of Tenley's voice made Sydney turn around. Tenley was limping toward her. Her dress was torn and singed, a line of blood was caked on her arm, and there was a nasty red burn running down her left calf.

"I need to talk to you." Tenley stopped in front of Sydney. There was a fierce, determined look on her face. "Now."

"W-what happened?" Sydney stuttered. Her eyes jumped between Tenley's injuries. "Are you okay?"

Tenley swung her head toward Calum. For a second Sydney had almost forgotten he was there. "I'm fine," Tenley said, her tone sounding anything but. "I, uh, just tripped and fell." She gave Calum the fakest smile Sydney had ever seen. "Clumsy old me!" She grabbed Sydney's hand. "Now, can I talk to you?" she hissed. "In private?"

Sydney turned shakily back to Calum. "I, uh..." She gestured toward Tenley, the words getting twisted in her mouth. "We'll talk more later," she managed finally.

Questions swarmed her as she followed Tenley to the corner of the cafeteria. Emerson was there waiting for them. "Keep your backs to the room," Tenley ordered. "I have something for you to read."

She handed Sydney a crumpled ball of paper. Even before Sydney smoothed it out, she knew what it was. "How?" she whispered. A moment later she had her answer. She looked up from the note. "It's not Abby," she said dully.

"That's not possible," Emerson wailed. "How could we have been wrong?"

Tenley shook her head. "I don't know. But what's important is the real darer is *here*. Whoever it is just tried to kill me."

A loud burst of static cut into their conversation. It was the microphone, being lifted out of its holder on stage. "Ladies and gentlemen, the moment you've all been waiting for has arrived," Avery announced. "It's time to crown this year's homecoming king and queen! To do the honors, I welcome to the stage your student-body vice president, Molly Berg."

"Hi?" Molly squeaked into the mic. "Since Abby still seems to be, uh, unavailable, I will take over the honor of crowning this year's homecoming king and queen?" Applause filled the room as Avery handed Molly a manila envelope. "Congratulations to..." Molly was in the middle of tearing open the envelope when a chorus of sounds filled the air.

Beep!

Buzz!

Ding!

Their phones.

Sydney had hers out in the span of a single breath.

Who will win... and who will die? Welcome to Judgment Day, girls!

Sydney held her breath as she looked up at the stage. Molly was waving the homecoming results through the air. "...Hunter Bailey and Delancey Crane!" she finished. Sydney let her breath come out in a long rush. At least that part of their plan had worked.

The noise in the cafeteria lifted to a roar as Hunter strutted to the stage, people hooting and cheering in his wake. "Just call me Your Highness," he yelled out.

"Where's the queen?" Up on stage, Molly scanned the room. "Delancey? Are you here? Oh, there you are?"

Sydney, Emerson, and Tenley all swiveled around to follow Molly's gaze. Delancey was cowering in the doorway to the cafeteria, looking as if she'd just arrived at the dance.

"Of course, *now* we find her," Sydney muttered. "When it doesn't matter anymore."

"Delancey?" Molly repeated.

Delancey stood frozen in the doorway, her hands clenched around her purse. By the look of horror on her face, you would think it was a guillotine waiting for her up on stage instead of a crown.

Avery grabbed the mic out of Molly's hands. "Don't be shy, beautiful!" he crowed. He waved Delancey over to the stage. "Come get your rightful crown!"

For several long seconds, Delancey stood there wide-eyed, like a deer in headlights. Finally, she started across the floor. The band launched into a drumroll as she climbed up on stage and Avery handed Molly back the microphone.

"As Winslow's student-body vice president," Molly squeaked, "I officially crown Hunter and Delancey king and queen?" She returned the mic to its stand, then placed a gold sparkly crown on each of their heads. "Now, in the age-old tradition of Winslow coronations, the king and queen shall share a dance?"

Hunter leaned into the microphone. "Don't forget to bow to us," he announced. "Curtsying is fine, too." He offered Delancey his hand, helping her off the stage. But as they stepped onto the dance floor, she pulled out of his grip.

"I—I can't do this," she said. She ducked her head, letting her curls fall across her face. "I shouldn't have won." She grabbed her purse and raced out of the room, leaving Hunter standing on the dance floor alone.

"What was that?" Emerson asked slowly.

Before anyone could answer, all three of their phones rang out at once. Sydney was overcome by déjà vu as she pulled her phone out once again.

Second-floor bathroom. Now.

They were out of the room and running up the stairs without a word. Sydney reached the bathroom door first. "Wait!" Tenley yelled. But Sydney had already flung it open.

Inside, leaning against the back wall, was Delancey Crane.

"What are you doing here?" Tenley howled. She pushed in front of Sydney. "You need to get out, Delancey. We're waiting for—"

"Me," Delancey finished. "You're waiting for me."

Sydney's jaw dropped. Tenley and Emerson emitted frightened squeaks.

"*You?*" Sydney gulped. "It was really never Abby?"

Delancey shook her head forcefully. "I set her up. It was me." She wrung her hands as she kept her gaze on something above their heads, refusing to make eye contact.

"But the receipt at the club," Emerson began.

"I forged it," Delancey cut in. "Abby's my best friend. I know her signature almost as well as I know my own. I did it all: the signature, the scarf, the dare that exposed Hannah Baker and her gym teacher. Even Abby's little disappearance." She clenched her fists at her sides. "I arranged for a surprise early-admissions interview for her at Princeton."

"But the picture," Emerson protested. "Abby was taking boating lessons with Tricia!"

"Because I convinced her to," Delancey said impatiently. "We took them together."

The bathroom swam around Sydney. Innocent, doll-faced Delancey, Abby's obedient little sidekick, was the *darer*? And Abby was innocent? Just thinking of what they'd put Abby through today made Sydney sick to her stomach. They were just as bad as Delancey. "*Why?*" she whispered. "What did we ever do to you?"

"And why would you frame your best *friend*?" Emerson spat out.

"Were you working with Tricia all along?" Tenley added furiously.

"I . . ." Delancey hesitated. She had the strangest expression on her face, as if she'd just bit into something rotten and was trying desperately to swallow it down. "I can't tell you any of that," she said at last. "Y-you all ruined everything. I wasn't supposed to win tonight! Sydney was! The party at the Vault was supposed to help her!"

"*What?*" Tenley exploded. "Why? What are you *talking* about?"

Delancey finally looked right at them. Sydney blinked in surprise. She'd expected to see fury in her eyes, or hatred, like there had been in Tricia's. But all she saw was fear. "That's up to you to figure out." Delancey pushed past them. "I have to go."

"No!" Sydney grabbed her arm, holding on tight. "You at least have to tell us if it's over!"

Delancey looked back at her. Up close, her eyes were red and glossy. "It's never over," she said. Then she wrenched her arm away from Sydney and raced out of the room.

"Wait!" There was a scraping noise outside as Tenley hurtled toward the door. When she pulled at it, it didn't budge. Something was blocking the way. "She trapped us in here!" she howled.

"That's karma if I ever saw it," Emerson grunted. She and Tenley grabbed the door handle, trying to wedge it open. Sydney was about to go help them when she noticed Delancey's silver purse lying abandoned against the back wall.

"She left her purse!" She crouched down to grab it. As she lifted it up, the clasp jostled open. Sydney sucked in a breath. There, sitting right on top, was Delancey's cell phone. And on its screen was a text.

Blocked, read the name at the top.

You might have won homecoming, D, but you lost the game. It's time: Confess to the girls. Or the next announcement you hear will be your BFF's eulogy.

The message stared up at Sydney, mocking her. Her hands went slack and the phone slid out of her palm, clattering to the floor.

Delancey wasn't the darer at all. Delancey was being dared.

CHAPTER TWENTY-TWO
Saturday, 9:40 PM

"NOT HERE." EMERSON POUNDED HER FISTS AGAINST
the dashboard of Tenley's car. They were at Reed Park, the last place
they could think of to look for Delancey. After they'd finally shoved
their way out of the bathroom and past the chair Delancey had used
to jam the door, they'd spent an hour and a half searching for her.
First, they'd looked in every room at Winslow. When they hadn't
found her there, they'd sent a quick text to Molly Berg from Abby's
phone, instructing her to bring Janitor Bob up to the third-floor supply
closet—then they'd booked it out of the building.

They'd been scouring the town ever since. They'd gone to Delancey's house, Abby's house, Echo Boulevard, the pier, and Great Harbor
Beach. Finally, they'd just started driving through the streets, hoping
to find her walking. But so far: nothing.

"I can't believe Delancey would drop a bomb on us like that and
then bolt," Emerson said angrily. "She didn't even explain why she was
doing *nice* things for Sydney!"

"Nice?" Sydney snorted. "Parties, homecoming queen... That's like the very embodiment of everything I hate! No offense," she added quickly.

Emerson shook her head, too frustrated to muster up a response.

Tenley let out an exhausted groan. "Well, clearly, we're not going to find her this way. We need a new game plan."

Emerson eyed Tenley's calf. It was red and blistering and coated in dried blood. "That looks terrible, Ten. Honestly, before we do anything else, I think we should take care of it."

Tenley shook her head stubbornly. "What we should do is find Delancey."

"I'm with Emerson on this one," Sydney jumped in. "We should really get you to a hospital."

"No!" Tenley exploded. "The only way we're going to figure out who this darer is once and for all is if we find Delancey. We can't go to the cops if we don't even have a *name*. The darer will kill all of us before the cops have time to open a new file! Delancey has to be priority number one. Everything else comes after."

"Including infection," Sydney shot back. "Gangrene. Leg amputation—"

Emerson held up a hand to stop her. "How about this? We're close to Tenley's house. We'll skip the hospital, but we'll make a quick pit stop to clean up her leg and the cuts on her hands. Then we'll get back to searching."

Sydney nodded her agreement in the backseat. "Fine," Tenley grumbled. She slammed down on the gas. "A *quick* pit stop."

They were all quiet as Tenley whipped through the streets, the only sound the faint thumping of the car's wheels against the ground. Back at school, the dance was still going on. The punch bowl had probably been spiked and someone had undoubtedly fallen into one of the trunks of "jewels." Harris Newsby would already be handing out flyers to recruit new members to the Pricewaterhouse-Winslow Club.

Emerson should be there. She should be laughing with her friends and turning down Ben Wiley's five thousandth request to dance. She closed her eyes, trying not to scream. The darer had taken everything from her. Caitlin, Holden, her privacy, and now any semblance of *normal*. A steely resolve settled over her as she opened her eyes. Tenley was right. As soon as they took care of her leg, they had to find Delancey. They had to get answers once and for all.

Most of the lights were on in Tenley's house when they pulled into the driveway, making the whole place glimmer in the night. Sydney let out a low whistle. "I always forget you live in fairy-tale land," she said.

Emerson stared out at the mansion, with its turrets and columns, its windows that seemed to stack up to the sky. "That's my life," Tenley replied. "A real fairy tale."

The lawn was a blanket of leaves. They crunched under Emerson's heels as she crossed it. A breeze blew in from the ocean, and she pulled her coat tighter around her.

"In and out," Tenley declared. The ocean clapped behind them, punctuating her words. It made Emerson think of Caitlin, how she used to sleep with her window open so she could fall asleep to the sound, her own personal lullaby. The memory made her feel even worse, and she picked up her pace, hurrying toward Tenley's front porch.

They were nearly there when Tenley grabbed Emerson's hand, her fingers cold against her skin. "Hold on." Tenley reached for Sydney on the other side, making them all stop short. "Do you see that?" She nodded to the woods behind her house. Tiny pinpricks of light shone through the trees, casting patterns across the grass.

"Lights?" Emerson shifted from foot to foot, trying to stay warm. "So?"

"We don't have lights back there," Tenley said. Her nails dug into Emerson's hand. "Lanson is obsessed with keeping the woods all pristine. He didn't even have lights on the lawn until my mom and I moved in and she put her foot down."

"Maybe your mom put her foot down about the woods, too," Sydney offered.

"If she did, it happened today, because there were no lights out there last night." Tenley paused. She was watching the trees sway in the breeze, momentarily eclipsing the lights. "Maybe someone's back there with a flashlight or something. What if it's Delancey? Maybe she came to hide from the darer, and wait for us!"

Emerson tensed. She'd heard that voice from Tenley before. A plan almost always followed.

"We're going back there." It was a statement, not a question. Tenley started forward, pulling them with her.

"Ow." Emerson wriggled her hand out of Tenley's grip. "You are freakishly strong for someone so tiny," she grumbled.

Tenley laughed, but it was so choked it sounded more like a cough. "You try swinging on uneven bars for ten years."

The ground crunched and rustled beneath them as they neared the woods. "I don't know about this...." Sydney murmured. "We should really take care of your leg, Tenley."

Tenley ignored her. She paused at the edge of the yard and reached into her purse. Out came her small pink bottle of pepper spray. Wielding it in front of her, she limped into the woods.

Emerson looked at Sydney. Sydney looked at Emerson. "I guess we're going with her," Sydney said.

Emerson dug her own pepper spray out of her purse. With a sigh, Sydney did the same. Holding tightly to their pink bottles, they followed Tenley into the woods.

The world seemed to still inside the thicket. Trees draped over them like a tent, making the house and road feel miles away. "This way," Tenley whispered. She pushed aside some brush and stepped over a fallen log, following the thin stream of light.

"I bet your mom is just having lights installed," Emerson insisted. A bush snagged at her ankle as she struggled to keep up with Tenley.

"I vote we turn back and get a bandage," Sydney chimed in. She sounded impatient as she kicked several sticks out of the way.

"I'm on Sydney's side," Emerson said. She raised her voice as Tenley powered ahead, ducking under a low-hanging branch. "We need to concentrate on—"

An earth-shattering scream drowned out the rest of her sentence.

For a split second Emerson and Sydney just stared at each other. Then they surged forward at the same time, racing after Tenley. A branch slapped against Emerson's back but she barely felt it. She emerged into a small clearing. In the middle of it stood an old, worn gazebo. It had clearly been unused for a long time, but someone had strung white Christmas lights along its beams and rafters. With the lights twinkling prettily and the gold-hued trees sweeping overhead, it might almost look like a Christmas card. If it weren't for what was inside.

Hanging from the beams, strung up by their own marionette strings, were the Purity Club's life-size puppets. They'd been slashed open down the middle, leaving their insides gaping and exposed. Across two of their faces, names had been scrawled in red marker. DELANCEY. TRICIA.

Hanging in the center of them, looking like a doll herself with her long curls and porcelain skin, was Delancey Crane.

"No." Emerson tripped away from the horrifying sight. Her eyes rebelled, clamping shut, but it didn't matter. The image had been stamped behind her eyelids: Delancey, a rope snug around her neck, her feet dangling over a stool, her head twisted into an unnatural position. And her eyes: wide open, as if something had shocked her in her very last breath.

Distantly, Emerson could hear Sydney crying, Tenley gagging. Someone kept whimpering: *oh my god oh my god oh my god*. It took Emerson a second to realize it was her. "You guys..." It was Sydney's voice. "Look at this."

Emerson wrenched open her eyes. The world seemed to cycle around her, ground-sky-ground-sky. She clutched a twinkling beam to steady herself. Sydney was standing in front of one of the purity puppets, the one marked Delancey. Pinned to it was a small note. Silently, Sydney pulled it down. Her face went ghostly white as she read it. She passed it to Tenley, who made a small moan before handing it to Emerson. Emerson's stomach heaved as her eyes landed on the typewriter font.

```
It's easy to find the puppets--and even
easier to silence them. Utter a word to the
     cops and you'll be the next to hang.
```

Tenley staggered backward. "Delancey was just a pawn."

"And so was Tricia," Sydney whispered. Tears were streaming down her face. "Someone else was controlling them all along."

Emerson looked frantically from puppet to puppet. Her gaze landed on Delancey's hanging form. She buckled over, unable to breathe. The game wasn't over. Delancey had been right: It never would be. People would keep dying, one after another, until finally it was her turn. She would never be free. She would never escape.

She forced herself to look up. The same naked terror was inscribed on her friends' faces. "Then the question is," she choked out, "who's the one holding the strings?"

CHAPTER TWENTY-THREE
Sunday, 9:30 AM

"BREAKFAST IS READY." SAHARA BUSTLED INTO THE dining room, carrying a tray stacked high with blueberry pancakes. Tenley pounced on it the instant it hit the table. The promise of food was the only thing keeping her from crawling back into bed and never coming out again.

Last night was already a black web in her mind. The ambulance coming for Delancey. The EMTs pronouncing her dead. The cops sweeping in, wrapping the gazebo in yellow tape. And through it all, the sharp, stinging undercurrent of fear. *The darer had done this.*

By the time it was all over, it was midnight. Emerson and Sydney had decided to sleep at Tenley's house rather than go home alone. Which, of course, meant they'd stayed up for hours more, obsessing over who the master darer could be.

On the other side of the table, Sydney pulled something out of her pocket. It was the darer's note, crumpled and worn from being passed among them so many times. She slapped it down on the table, typewriter font up. "I say we shred this," she declared.

Emerson pushed her food around on her plate. "We could still bring it to the cops," she said halfheartedly.

"We could also dig our own graves," Tenley offered. She shoveled a bite of pancake into her mouth and chewed furiously. She wondered if they were all thinking what she was: that she already had.

When the pair of cops had shown up last night, chock-full of suicide theories, Tenley had snapped. Delancey hadn't killed herself. She'd been *murdered*. She'd been taunted, tortured, tied in strings, and made to dance. And when her performance grew old, she'd been strung up and left to hang. And the cops were blaming *her*.

Fury had roared inside of Tenley, impossible to control. "It wasn't suicide!" she yelled. "She was *killed*! Someone *did* this to her. We have the text messages on her phone to prove it!"

Immediately she shrank back, regretting it. *Utter a word to the cops and you'll be the next to hang.* She'd gone against the darer's wishes, and now the words were out in the world, impossible to erase. Emerson recoiled and Sydney's face turned green and they all stood immobilized, time hanging in suspension as they waited for the cops to react.

But they completely dismissed it.

"I doubt that, hon," the taller cop informed her, "since we have a suicide note."

"A note?" Tenley exclaimed.

"It's true," the other one chimed in. His voice was gentler, and he patted Tenley on the shoulder, as if she were a little kid in need of comforting. "Her parents called it in just a few minutes before you did. They wanted to file a missing-child report because they'd found a suicide note in her bedroom. A pretty explicit one, from what they told us. Even said that this was how we'd find her." The cop sighed, shaking his head. "It's these overachiever suicides. Dotting all their *i*'s, even in death. We see it a lot more than we'd like."

The cops ushered them away from the scene after that. But they made it only halfway to Tenley's house when her phone let out a sharp beep. The screen glowed in the night as she clicked opened the text.

Tsk, tsk, Ten. Looks like I have another girl to silence. Delancey might have failed to end you, but I ALWAYS succeed.

Instantly, Tenley broke into a cold sweat. The darer had *heard* her tell the cops. Which could mean only one thing.

The darer had been there. The darer had been watching.

"Hey, Ten." Emerson gave Tenley's arm a soft shake, drawing her out of the memory. "It's going to be okay. I promise. We're going to make sure nothing happens to you."

Sydney stabbed at her pancakes with her fork. "Emerson's right. We're smarter now. We know more. We're going to find a way to stop this."

"*How?*" Tenley dropped her head onto the table, banging her forehead against its smooth wood surface. "We're no closer to figuring out who the darer is than we were a week ago. I've managed to escape death traps three times now! What if the fourth time's the charm?"

The doorbell rang, making her jump. "Tenley, door for you!" Sahara called out. Tenley exchanged a nervous look with Sydney and Emerson. Tenley's mom and Lanson were at the rehab center with Guinness and weren't able to get back until later in the afternoon. "Are either of you expecting anyone?" she asked tensely. Sydney and Emerson shook their heads.

"Wonderful," she grumbled. She rose unsteadily from the table. To her surprise, Sydney stood, too.

"We're coming with you," she said. She glanced at Emerson, who nodded and stood up.

"Thanks," Tenley croaked, tears stinging at her eyes. Together they headed for the front door.

Waiting on the porch was a short, balding man Tenley didn't recognize. Her first thought was: *cop*. But then she noticed the Echo Bay Hospital badge clipped to his white polo. He was holding a clipboard and a blue plastic pouch stamped with EBH on the front. He looked from one girl to the next. "Lanson Reed's daughter?" he asked.

Tenley thought about correcting him—*step*daughter—but she didn't have the energy. "That's me."

"Mr. Reed asked the hospital to drop off his son's belongings." The man held up the blue pouch. "It's what was in his pockets when he was admitted. Can you sign for it?"

Tenley blew out a relieved sigh as she took the clipboard. This had nothing to do with the darer, nothing to do with her at all. "Thank you, Miss Reed," the man chirped when she returned the clipboard to him. He handed her the pouch. "And please give your father the hospital's best."

Tenley rolled her eyes as she shut the door on the hospital brownnoser. She doubted just anyone got personal deliveries from hospital staff. But she'd learned that when you donated an entire wing to the hospital, they'd cook you dinner if you requested it.

"I hate being so paranoid," Tenley complained as she stomped back into the dining room with Emerson and Sydney. "And all over some stupid crap Guinness had at the hospital."

The comment just slipped out, and she glanced nervously at Sydney as she tossed the pouch onto the table. With all the darer craziness yesterday, they hadn't had a chance to discuss Guinness and his hospitalization. She was worried Sydney might jump down her throat for calling his possessions *crap*, but Sydney looked too tired to react.

"Don't let me stop you from opening it," Sydney said, dropping back onto her chair with a yawn. She rested her chin on her hands, letting her eyes drift shut.

Tenley unzipped the pouch and dumped its contents onto the table. A packet of Listerine strips tumbled out, followed by a crumpled receipt, a thumb drive labeled PHOTOS, and a small blue box.

"What's in the box?" Emerson asked curiously.

Tenley picked it up with a shrug. Inside on a bed of white silk was a sapphire ring. She rubbed her thumb against its faceted surface. It was gorgeous. And it looked familiar, too. Had she seen it in a store recently? She wondered if Guinness had bought it for Sydney. The thought left a sour taste in her mouth. "Have you seen this before, Syd?"

Sydney groggily opened her eyes. But when she saw the box, she bolted upright, looking wide-awake. "Was Guinness wearing his green jacket when you found him?" she asked.

Tenley nodded. "Why? Did he give this to you?"

"I thought he did." Sydney twisted at the gold band on her pointer finger. "I found it in my mailbox late Monday night. I figured it was from Guinness, because he always called me Blue. . . ." Her voice broke and she paused to clear her throat. "So I stuck it in the pocket of his coat the last time I saw him. But then I got a note. The ring was from the darer. At the time I thought that could mean Guinness *was* the darer, but now . . . well, he's obviously not."

Tenley pulled the ring out of the box. It caught the light as she turned it left and right, making its facets glitter. It was simple, but elegant, too, and the stone was stunning. It was clearly a valuable piece of jewelry. As she slid it absently onto her finger, something shifted in her mind.

"Oh my god," she whispered. She remembered exactly where she'd seen that ring before. It wasn't in a store; it was in that online estate sale.

Tenley yanked the ring off. "I've seen this before," she said breathlessly. "Remember that drawing of a train I saw in Cait's dream journal, the one that belonged to her kidnapper? Well, it was number one eleven in this really limited train run, and I found that *exact* train in an estate sale online. There was a ring just like this, too, but then all the jewelry was taken down. Just in time for the darer to give the ring to Syd."

"So you're saying Caitlin's kidnapper also owned this ring?" Emerson asked.

Tenley nodded. "I think so."

Sydney bunched up her forehead. "But if that's true, it would make the puppet master—"

"—connected to Caitlin's kidnapper," Tenley finished. "Exactly." She squeezed the ring. The metal was cool against her skin. "I called the estate sale company, but I couldn't get them to tell me anything about the seller. And then we found that photo of Tricia and Abby, and I thought it didn't matter anymore. But now every suspect we ever had was wrong. Sean, Guinness, Abby..." She trailed off, shaking her head. "The kidnapper is the only clue we have left."

"Well, not the only one," Sydney said.

Tenley snapped her head up. "What does that mean?"

"It means I found out something about Kyla Kern." Tenley's pulse began to race as Sydney filled them in on her suspicion that Kyla's death wasn't accidental. "I think it's possible Guinness knew something about it, and that's why he was targeted," Sydney finished. "I think the darer hoped he'd carry the secret—whatever it is—to his grave." Sydney paused. "And I found something else, too."

She passed her phone to Tenley. Emerson scooted in, peering over her shoulder. On the screen was a photograph of five lights, wavering over a coal-black ocean. "That looks like..." Emerson began.

"I know," Sydney said. "If you look closely, there's a shadow on the cliffs. It's hard to see this small, but...it looks a lot like a human shadow. Right where the lights originate."

"You think someone's been *creating* the ghost lights?" Tenley burst out. She looked up to see Sydney nodding gravely.

"I think it's possible. Calum claims there's got to be a scientific explanation for the lights, but the more I look at that photo...I don't know. They look a lot like real lights to me. And that shadow—it looks a lot like a real person." Sydney tapped a finger against the table. "It makes me wonder: What if all this is connected somehow? What if the same person who's been tormenting us is not only the person who kidnapped Caitlin, but also the person who killed Kyla? And all along, they've been manufacturing these lights to make everyone believe in the whole Lost Girls lore?"

"An entire myth to cover up murders," Emerson said wonderingly. "If it weren't so sick, it would be brilliant."

Tenley massaged her temples. "If that were true...if this has all been one person...it would mean the puppet master isn't just connected to Caitlin's kidnapper. It would mean the puppet master *is* Caitlin's kidnapper." She looked from Sydney to Emerson as that realization sank in. It sent a chill straight to her bones. One person could have been haunting Echo Bay for all these years.

Emerson leaned forward in her seat, looking stunned. "So what do we do? If the same person is connected to all these crimes, if this has really been going on for that long…whoever it is isn't going to stop now!"

"Miss Tenley?" Sahara stuck her head into the room, making them all jump. "I need you to come see something."

"Can it wait?" Tenley snapped. "I'm kind of busy right now."

Sahara frowned, a thin web of wrinkles creasing her skin. "It's important."

"Fine, make it quick." Dragging herself out of her chair, Tenley followed Sahara out to the driveway, with Sydney and Emerson close behind.

"I was just cleaning your windshield, like Mr. Reed ask," Sahara told her. "And I move rearview mirror, like I always do. It's best way not to get streaks, you know—"

"I don't need a cleaning play-by-play, Sahara," Tenley cut in.

"Fine." Sahara stopped in front of Tenley's car with an annoyed sniff. She pointed silently at the windshield. "That fell loose."

Inside the car, a wire was dangling from the rearview mirror. From the end of it hung a small black box.

"What's *that*?" Sydney murmured.

Tenley climbed into her car. Up close, she saw a green light glowing on the bottom of the box. There was small label above it. "Look up Tracker XY 3000," she called out.

Emerson pulled her phone out. A few seconds later, she drew in a sharp breath. "It's a GPS tracker. Super high-tech. Transmits the car's location every three seconds."

"Mr. Reed track your car?" Sahara asked.

"No," Tenley whispered. She looked from Sydney to Emerson. She could tell they were thinking the same thing she was. *The puppet master had.*

303

This was how Tricia and Delancey always knew her location. This was why it felt like she was always being followed, being watched. It was because she was.

She looked up, doing her best to arrange her features into a mask of calm. "Thank you, Sahara," she said briskly. "I can take it from here." Only when Sahara had retreated into the house did she let her face crumple. "We're being surveilled," she choked out.

"*Of course* we are." Sydney slumped against the side of Tenley's car. "It makes sense. No one could be in that many places in one day!" Panic crept into her voice. "There are probably trackers in our cars, too. And who knows what else this puppet master could have gotten to—"

"Our phones," Emerson said suddenly. Her face took on a green tinge. "Think about what you would know if you had access to our phones."

Fear thickened in Tenley like black smog. "Not just GPS, but our phone calls, our texts, our Web browsing..."

"Everything," Sydney said dully. She held her phone up, staring at it in dismay. "Our phones would give the darer—the puppet master—everything."

"Then we stop letting them." Tenley tore the GPS tracker off its wire. Fury pulsed through her as she climbed out of the car. She snatched Sydney's phone out of her hands, then went for Emerson's. "Try to find us now," she said through gritted teeth. Her limbs felt like steel as she added her own phone to the pile and dropped the whole thing in the driveway.

"What are you doing?" Sydney cried. "That phone cost me fifteen shifts at the club!"

Tenley climbed into her car and started the ignition. "It's going to cost you a lot more than that if it's been bugged. I don't know about you guys, but I'm *done* being prey. It's time we show this puppet master that we have some moves of our own." She squeezed her hands tightly around the wheel. "Any objections?"

"None," Emerson growled.

Tenley looked over at Sydney.

"Floor it," she said with a sigh.

Tenley slammed her foot on the gas. She heard the sickening crunch of metal as her car sped over the pile. She jerked to a stop at the edge of the driveway. Behind her, Sydney and Emerson were staring wide-eyed down at the remains. She went over to join them. What had once been three phones and a tracker was now nothing more than a mangled, flattened heap. "Well," she said slowly, "no one's following us now."

"If only we had some way to tell the puppet master," Sydney said. "Let whoever it is know that we're on to them."

Tenley bit down on her lip. An idea was taking root in her mind. "Maybe we do." She broke into a run, racing toward her house. "Keep up!" she called over her shoulder.

A minute later, they were all in her bedroom, gathered around her laptop. "Our puppet master might know how to block phone numbers, but there's another way to make contact." Tenley opened Facebook on her computer. There, sitting innocently at the top of her messages, was the threat labeled *A Warning*. The user might have made a fake name, but there was still a reply option. "It's time we turn the tables," Tenley said.

Emerson and Sydney leaned in close as she typed out a message.

It's over. There's no more tracker, no more phones. If you want us, you're going to have to come get us. The pier, tonight at midnight. It's show and tell, remember? And it's finally time you show.

ACKNOWLEDGMENTS

I'm grateful to so many people for helping usher this book into the world....

The amazing Paper Lantern Lit team of Lexa Hillyer, Lauren Oliver, Rhoda Belleza, Angela Velez, Hayley Wagreich, and Adam Silvera: I'm a better writer, and author, for having worked with you all. Thank you for believing in me, and for being my teachers, my editors, my cheerleaders, and so much more. You've made me feel like part of your team, and I've loved every moment of it.

Stephen Barbara and Rachel Hecht: Thank you for finding such a perfect home for this series, both here and abroad. I've always known these books were in good hands with you and Foundry behind them!

Elizabeth Bewley, Farrin Jacobs, Pam Gruber, Pam Garfinkel, and Eloise Flood: I've been so lucky to work with an editorial team—and a publishing house—as wonderful as yours. From plot kinks all the way to line edits, you've made these books better every step of the way. I've been so grateful for your insight, your support, and, above all, your enthusiasm.

Lisa Moraleda, Stephanie O'Cain, and Julia Costa: Every time I see these books online or at an event, I know it's because of you. Thanks for working so tirelessly to get this series out into the world!

Sasha Illingworth: These covers! I want to frame them and hang them on my wall. Thank you for giving the books such an amazing first impression.

And, of course, my family:

Nate Resnick: Thank you for being my steady ground in a rocky world, my gourmet chef when I'd otherwise be eating cereal, my constant pep-talker and first-reader and biggest fan, and, above all, my very best friend. I don't know what I'd do without you here to keep me sane.

Mom, Dad, and Lauren: Thank you for coming to every event and reading every word and being behind me from the beginning. You talk me through the bad days and cheer me on during the good ones, and you'll never know just how much that means.

The Resnick-Wachtel clan: You've put up with my crazy schedule and been there to celebrate every step of the way. Thank you for surpassing everything I dreamed in-laws could be.

To the rest of my family and friends: I'm so lucky to have people who support me so wholeheartedly. Thank you for coming out to book events and listening to the ups and downs and being there with your encouragement whenever I needed it.

Finally, thank you to all the fans of this series who have e-mailed, Goodreads-messaged, Facebooked, and tweeted over this past year. Your messages kept me going through long hours of writing!

FIND OUT WHO'S REALLY PULLING THE STRINGS.

It wasn't Tricia. It wasn't Abby.

Will the girls find the real darer before they

become Echo Bay's newest Lost Girls?

KISS

AND

TELL

Turn the page for a sneak peek at *KISS AND TELL*,
the final book in the Truth or Dare trilogy.

Available February 2015

PROLOGUE

THE CLIFFS WERE SLICK WITH SNOW, AND SHE SLIPPED as she climbed higher, slamming hard onto her knees. Pain reeled through her, but she refused to stop. In the distance, a round beam of light broke through the snow. *A flashlight.* The killer was here.

She pushed herself further. One foot, then the next, then—*ice.*

Her foot slid out from under her. Suddenly she was careening forward, the edge of the cliff much too close. She cried out as she caught herself on a jagged rock. She stretched a toe out, searching for a safe pathway, but at every angle she was met with ice. This high up, it coated everything.

Behind her, the flashlight burned brighter. She was trapped.

She looked out over the cliff. The storm was colorless: stark white brushstrokes against a black sky. Down below she could hear the ocean roaring and crashing. She wrenched the sapphire ring off her finger. She was breathing hard as she threw it over the cliff.

She was nearly at the edge now. Just a few more inches and, like the ring, she, too, would fall into nothingness.

The icy crunch of footsteps rang out through the night.

There was nowhere left to run. Nowhere left to hide.

CHAPTER ONE
Sunday, 11:37 PM

SYDNEY WAS DRIVING MUCH TOO FAST. THE SCENERY blurred outside her window, but it didn't matter; she could dredge up every inch of it from memory. The sprawling Cape Cod–style homes. The paved walking path that wound alongside the ocean. The taut stretches of golden sand, dotted with seagulls. On the surface, Echo Bay looked like a picture-perfect beach town. But things weren't always what they seemed. Sydney had learned that the hard way.

Her phone buzzed from inside the car's cup holder. Instantly, her muscles tensed, but she forced herself to relax. *It can't be from the darer,* she reminded herself. Earlier that morning, she, Tenley, and Emerson had destroyed their cells, running over them with Tenley's car. Sydney was now using an ancient, beat-up phone that had once belonged to her mom—probably back when smartphones were first invented. The upside was that no one but her parents, Emerson, and Tenley had her new number.

She grabbed for her cell at a red light. *23 minutes till MOT*, Tenley had texted.

MOT: Moment of Truth. It was what Tenley had taken to calling tonight ever since they'd sent a threat to the darer on Facebook that morning: *It's over. There's no more tracker, no more phones. If you want us, you're going to have to come get us. The pier, tonight at midnight. It's show and tell, remember? And it's finally time you show.*

Sydney slammed on the gas as soon as the light changed, making her car lurch forward. She was sick of being played and tortured, taunted and teased. She was ready to catch whoever was sending the dares.

Dares. The word made rage boil under her skin. Every time her focus slipped, the memory would assault her: Delancey's lifeless body dangling from the beam last night. She'd looked so young up there in her homecoming dress, and so scared, her eyes frozen wide with horror. Bile rose in Sydney's throat. Delancey would never be in school again. She'd never run another Purity Club meeting or choose another photo for the yearbook or spend another lunch period whispering with Abby Wilkins. She would never graduate from high school or go to college, leave Echo Bay or get married. She would be a high school senior forever, just like Caitlin and Tricia—and it was all because of one person's sick, twisted game.

For over a month now, someone had been after them: sending them threatening notes and punishing them when they disobeyed.

Caitlin had paid the ultimate price, dying out on the ocean, and now Sydney, Emerson, and Tenley had been promised a similar fate. They'd blamed Tricia, then Delancey. But it turned out that those two were just puppets. There was a mastermind behind them both, pulling their strings.

Sydney screeched to a stop on Hillworth Drive. Tenley was already there. She wore black jeans and a black sweater under her dark coat, her long chestnut waves swept back in a ponytail. With Sydney's own all-black ensemble and ponytail, they almost matched: a spying uniform. "You drove?" Sydney asked. Tenley lived a short walk away, in one of the oceanfront mansions that lined Dune Way.

"Leg's sore." Tenley gestured to her left leg. Her pants covered the injury, but Sydney had seen it before it was bandaged: an angry red burn slicing across Tenley's calf. Last night at the homecoming dance, the darer had lured Tenley onto the auditorium's catwalk, where a spotlight had been rigged to fall on her. Tenley had been lucky to walk away with just that burn.

Tenley lifted up a long-lens camera. Sydney recognized it as one of Guinness's, but she quickly pushed the thought away. She couldn't let anything distract her right now. "You have yours?" Tenley asked.

Sydney responded by crawling into the backseat of her car. Her hand brushed against her RISD scholarship application, making her jaw clench up. It was due tomorrow. "My two best," she said as she climbed out with the cameras she'd brought. Their lenses glinted under the beam of her car's headlights.

"You should probably…" Tenley nodded toward the lights.

Their plan was contingent on the darer's never seeing them. It was why they'd parked five blocks from the pier. Sydney switched off the headlights, and darkness spilled in, making the hair on Sydney's arms stand on end. "Do you really think this will work?"

"It has to," Tenley said softly, and again Sydney saw it: Delancey's crooked neck, her feet swinging in her high heels. "If we can get a photo of the darer—actual, hard evidence of who this person is—then we'll finally have something we can lord over him or her."

Sydney nodded. Earlier that day, they'd taken a small step in figuring out more about the darer. So many crimes had plagued Echo Bay over the past ten years—the deaths of the Lost Girls, Caitlin's kidnapping in sixth grade, and now their own stalker—and each incident seemed tied to one another. It had made them wonder: What if the same person had been tormenting Echo Bay residents for all these years?

But how could they go to the cops? Last night, when the police came for Delancey's body, Tenley had blurted out that it was murder, even though they'd been warned against it. The cops had explained that wasn't possible: Delancey had left behind a suicide note. Immediately after, the darer had texted Tenley. *Tsk, tsk, Ten. Looks like I have another girl to silence.*

Even if they could convince the police, it would take the cops weeks to hunt down the culprit—plenty of time for the darer to exact retribution. But if the girls took in a photo of their stalker, then the police would have a real lead, which meant they wouldn't have to waste time searching.

A pair of headlights flashed in the distance. The car flew toward them without slowing, its lights blinding. Sydney shielded her eyes, her brain frozen on a single thought: *Darer.* Next to her, Tenley grabbed Sydney's arm, her hand cold and clammy.

The car skidded to a stop a few feet away. The headlights switched off, and Emerson Cunningham climbed out. She, too, wore all black, but in her leather jacket and black scarf, she still managed to look photo-shoot ready.

Sydney sagged with relief as she handed Emerson a camera. "Phones on vibrate?" Emerson asked. Sydney nodded. So did Tenley. "Okay, then." There was a tremor in Emerson's voice. "Let's do this."

They were silent as they walked the five blocks to the pier. Sydney's pulse raced faster with each step. "I guess it's time to split up," she said hesitantly. None of them moved. Sydney felt for Tenley's hand in the dim light of the pier. "*M-O-T,*" she said.

They all turned away at once. They'd chosen their individual stakeout spots during a run-through earlier that day; they were each to cover one section of the pier. Soon the darkness swallowed up the others, leaving Sydney all alone. It was cold by the water, and she wrapped her coat tighter around her as she located the boat she'd chosen earlier in the day. Small and tethered close to the pier. A perfect hiding spot.

She clutched her camera to her chest as she climbed into the boat. It rocked under her feet, making her stomach flip as she knelt beneath its rim and dropped her purse next to her. Minutes crept past, the only sound the shriek of a seagull overhead. The ocean slapped against the docks, punctuating the silence.

A clock on the boat glowed. *11:56.* What if no one showed?

Sydney's chest hitched. Or what if someone did—and her hiding spot wasn't good enough?

Her grip tightened on the camera as time ticked by.

11:59.

There was a sound.

Sydney froze, every nerve suddenly on high alert. There it was again—a footstep! It came from above. Sydney lifted her camera, her gaze landing on the country club's pool deck, which jutted out over the ocean at the end of the pier. Her hands shook as she trained her camera on the deck. But the darkness formed a barricade; she couldn't see past it.

Her finger rested on the camera's shutter button. She could press it—set off a flash and clear the cobweb of darkness. But what if it wasn't the darer? Or what if it was and the flash scared him or her away before she could get a clear shot?

A loud scuffle up on the pool deck gave her a start. Her finger slammed against the button before she could catch her balance.

Flash.

For a single instant, the sky lit up. The light caught something tumbling over the railing of the pool deck. Arms and legs and— *oh god.*

Her camera slipped from her hands. The world seemed to stop as Sydney watched the body plummet through the air. She heard it hit the water with a sickening splash. She was moving before she could fully process what had happened, grabbing her flashlight and sprinting off the boat and down the pier.

Was it the darer?

No. The darer didn't lose, didn't make mistakes. Which could mean only one thing: It was another victim.

Panic clutched at Sydney's chest. If this was retribution...If someone else had died because of something they'd done...

Tenley and Emerson must have seen the fall, too, because Sydney heard them running behind her, their footsteps breaking open the silence. It didn't matter. None of it mattered anymore, not their plan, not the photo. All that mattered was getting to the victim. Could someone survive that fall?

Sydney reached the shore at the end of the pier first. She scrambled to turn on her flashlight, shining its thin beam over the ocean. Body parts caught the light as they tossed on the waves. A leg. An arm. A flash of long blond hair. It was a girl. "We need to get her out!" she heard Tenley scream.

Instinct took over as Sydney dropped the flashlight and launched herself into the ocean. She gasped as the cold water stabbed at her. Her limbs screamed in resistance, but she ordered them to move, kicking and paddling toward the body. *Please don't be dead.* The thought crashed into her with each wave, again and again.

Two splashes sounded behind her. She could hear Tenley and Emerson in the water now, but she kept her eyes locked on the body. The girl was bobbing facedown, her hair floating in a halo around her.

Paddle. Kick. *Please don't be dead.* Paddle. Kick. *Please don't be dead.*

"Who is it?" Tenley screamed. Sydney shook her head soundlessly. It was too dark to tell. The darkness made everything seem mercurial, as if at any moment she could blink and this would all disappear.

Another stroke and Sydney was at the girl's side. She hooked her arm around the body, but the girl was slippery and heavy—soaked with water—and when a wave hit, she couldn't hold on. Sydney paddled desperately, trying to stay afloat. "I need help!" She tried again, but a fresh wave hit, pulling her under instead.

She came up gasping for air. Emerson was there, wrapping her arms around the body. "Let's get her to shore." Tenley reached them, too, and together they towed the body to the sandy beach at the end of the pier.

"On three!" Tenley said. "One, two—"

Together, they crawled onto shore, dragging the girl's body with them. Sydney's teeth were chattering violently, but all she could focus on was the girl. "Is she—?" Tenley began.

She stopped short.

The girl was on her back, blond hair splayed around her. Except she wasn't a girl at all.

Sydney collapsed onto her knees next to the body. A red clown nose and black beady eyes stared up at her. "A doll," she choked out. "It's a clown doll." Scrawled across the clown's face in thick red marker was a message.

This is no joke.

Sydney couldn't breathe. Once again their tormentor had bested them. He or she had been there—had fooled them—and then had vanished again without a trace.

Unless...

Her camera. She raced down to the pier, panting as she snatched her camera off the boat. She jabbed at the screen. There it was: the photo that had lit up the night. The pool deck was too tiny to make out any details. She zoomed in, and then zoomed in again. A doll came into focus, hoisted on top of the deck's railing. Behind it, a shadowy figure ducked low.

She zoomed in again and again, as close as the camera would let her. But the figure on the deck remained nothing more than a dark outline, impossible even to tell if it was male or female.

Buzz!

The noise made Sydney jump. It was coming from the boat. From inside her purse.

Buzz!

There it was again, this time from behind her. Emerson joined her on the pier, then Tenley. They were both holding their phones.

Buzz! Buzz!

"How?" Emerson whispered. "We have new cells, new numbers!"

No one replied. Terror became a noose as, with a single click, the text message popped up on Sydney's phone.

Mutiny leads to war—and I fight dirty.

CHAPTER TWO
Monday, 7:50 Am

TENLEY IGNORED THE ACHE IN HER LEG AS SHE sprinted toward Winslow's red double doors. She'd overslept, and now she was ten minutes late to school. Which would look just great alongside the math test she'd recently bombed and the classes she'd recently skipped. For a while the "my best friend died" excuse had allowed these things to slide, but she could tell it was starting to wear thin. What was she supposed to tell the attendance office today? *Sorry I'm late, but I was awake half the night thanks to a clown doll haunting my dreams.*

Tenley felt sick at the memory of what had happened last night. At first, she'd been sure it was a person—another casualty in this cruel game. As she'd watched the body fall, the possibilities of who it could be had curled around her like smog, until she was choking on them. *Mom. Marta. Tim.* But the whole thing was just a sick joke, the darer's way of showing them that they weren't in control.

Mutiny leads to war—and I fight dirty.

The darer had already tried to kill Tenley twice—in her hot tub and on the catwalk in the auditorium. What was dirtier than that?

She was halfway to her locker when two large hands grabbed her from behind. The scream that slipped out of her was so high-pitched it sounded like it belonged to a little girl.

"Whoa there." The voice was low and lazy. And familiar. Tenley spun around to find Tim Holland staring down at her, an amused look in his dark blue eyes. "You being chased?"

Tenley tried to speak, but her voice was trapped somewhere beneath her still-pounding heart. She forced herself to focus on Tim: his messy, damp blond waves; his beat-up hemp necklace that he never took off; his calm, easy smile. "I overslept," she managed, finally.

"I oversurfed. It happens." Tim pushed a strand of hair off her cheek, and Tenley had to fight the urge to bury her head in his chest and not lift it again until Christmas. "Did you get my messages, Tenley? I've called you, like, ten times since you disappeared on me Saturday night."

Tenley tried not to wince. Tim had shown up at the homecoming dance Saturday night just for her. They'd kissed, and it had been amazing. But then everything had spiraled out of control and she hadn't spoken to him for the rest of the weekend. "I got a new phone number yesterday. I'm sorry. I meant to call and tell you, but it was a pretty rough day."

"Delancey, I know. The whole town's been talking about it." Tim entwined his fingers through hers. "How are you doing?"

Tenley sighed. "Honestly, I'm just trying really hard not to think about it."

"Maybe I can help with that." Tim pulled her into a hug. She closed her eyes, letting herself melt against him. His arms were strong and warm, and he smelled faintly of the ocean. She could feel the muscles in her neck unclenching, just a little.

"Miss Reed and Mr. Holland!"

Tenley drew away from Tim with a start. Mr. Lozano, the art teacher, crossed his arms against his chest as he strode toward them. "May I ask why you two are not at the assembly?"

Tim fiddled with the tangled mess of string bracelets tied around his wrist. "Assembly?"

"The suicide-prevention assembly that was announced just before homeroom?" Mr. Lozano arched an eyebrow. "It's mandatory."

"Oh *that* assembly," Tenley backtracked. "We're on our way right now. Tim was just helping me out." She gestured down to her left leg, which was thicker than her right thanks to the bandage underneath her jeans. "I hurt my leg, so I'm moving more slowly."

"Oh." Mr. Lozano nodded, looking placated. "Take your time, then."

Tenley gave the art teacher her sweetest smile before limping off toward the auditorium. "Impressive," Tim murmured as he made a big show of assisting her. "I should keep you around to get me out of detentions."

Normally, Tenley would have been quick with a retort. *You*

should keep me around for more than that. But her thoughts were stuck at a standstill on the assembly. *Suicide prevention.*

Everyone in town, cops included, believed Delancey's death was a suicide. Besides the darer, only Tenley, Sydney, and Emerson knew the truth. Their tormentor had hunted Delancey, torturing and toying with her before going in for the kill.

Tenley's eyes went immediately to the front of the room as she and Tim entered the auditorium. The same person had tried to kill her on that very stage. In the two days since, the stage had been mended and scrubbed clean. If it weren't for a few cracked planks on the catwalk above, you'd never know anything had happened.

"Looks like your fan club saved you a seat." Tim nodded toward the back of the auditorium, where Emerson and Sydney were waving her over. Between Sydney's rat nest of a ponytail and Emerson's unusually drab outfit, they looked as terrible as Tenley felt.

"I should probably—"

"Go," Tim agreed. "Find me later." He gave her a quick smile before sauntering over to the exit row, where his best friends, Tray Macintyre and Sam Spencer, were seated.

"Did you show up with Tim Holland?" Emerson whispered as Tenley dropped into the empty seat next to her. Emerson's brown sweater dress might have been unusually plain for her, but her cocoa-latte skin glowed as always. "What were you talking to him about?"

Tenley hesitated. She hadn't told anyone she'd kissed Tim at the homecoming dance. Caitlin had dated Tim before she died, and Tenley knew how touchy that made this situation. But Tenley and Tim had bonded over missing Cait, and she'd been surprised by how much she liked him.

"I bumped into him in the hall," Tenley answered vaguely. Her gaze fell on the thick manila envelope Sydney was clutching. "What's that?" she asked, hoping to change the subject.

"My scholarship application for RISD." Sydney tugged at the red flannel shirt she was wearing, looking nervous. "It has to be postmarked by today, so I'm taking it to the office."

"I can't believe you're already doing applications," Tenley murmured. "I can't even *think* about applying to college until all this is over."

"I don't have a choice." Sydney gripped the folder more tightly. "Scholarship applications are due earlier in the year." She didn't say it accusingly, but, still, Tenley felt her face flush. She busied herself by pulling out her new phone. She'd splurged on the nicest case in the store: matte gold, with white polka dots.

Emerson pulled her own phone out with a smirk. It was identical to Tenley's. "Nice case."

"Better than mine." Sydney held up her phone, which had a hideous orange case on it, imprinted with the letter *S*. She gave them a wry smile. "It was the only one I could find that was old enough to fit."

"No phones, girls," Miss Hilbrook called out sternly. Her lips were pursed as she patrolled the aisles of the auditorium. "Eyes up front."

Tenley turned obediently to the stage, where Mrs. Shuman, the school counselor, was standing with Principal Howard. "Delancey Crane was a beloved student at Winslow," Mrs. Shuman said, her voice trembling as it poured through the auditorium's speakers. "She was cofounder of the Purity Club, head of the yearbook committee, and enrolled in all honors classes. She was a kind person and a dedicated student, and now, because of a tough time, she's gone."

Mrs. Shuman teetered on her heels. Her eyes flitted across the auditorium, wide and dismayed, and suddenly Tenley got the feeling that she knew something—knew the truth. But then she cleared her throat, and her lips curled down at the corners, and she was just naive Mrs. Shuman again, the counselor who passed out lollipops to high school students.

"Delancey was just like the rest of you," Mrs. Shuman continued. "And I think she'd want us to take a lesson away from this. Depression and suicidal thoughts can happen to anyone. If you notice a friend who's down or acting strange, it's your responsibility to talk to them, to ask a question." A motto flashed across the screen behind her as she spoke: ASK A QUESTION, SAVE A LIFE. "We'll be passing out information packets on suicide prevention at the end of the assembly, but first, Abby Wilkins has put together a touching slide show to help us honor Delancey's life. I hope it reminds you all what's at stake here. We're at this school together, and that makes us responsible for one another's well-being."

As classical music played, photographs faded in and out on the screen. Delancey running into the ocean, curls flying in the wind. Delancey volunteering with the Red Cross, her porcelain skin reddened by the sun. Delancey posing with her parents, her arms draped around their shoulders. As a photo of Delancey wearing this year's homecoming crown filled the screen, someone began to cry nearby. Soon the auditorium was filled with muffled sobs and sniffles.

On the screen, a photo of Delancey playing with her cat faded out, replaced by an image of Delancey and Abby. Delancey was smiling widely as she leaned against her best friend, and suddenly it wasn't Delancey that Tenley saw, but Caitlin. Caitlin squinting as she hung on to Tenley's every word. Caitlin brushing Tenley's hair after Tenley sprained her wrist in gymnastics. Caitlin yelling, "Race you!" and sprinting down the beach, her blond hair whipping in her face as she looked back at Tenley, laughing.

Tenley bit down on her lip so hard she drew blood. Caitlin was gone, and Delancey was gone, and Tenley had no idea who would be next. The darer had swept through their lives like a tornado, leaving only wreckage behind. Tenley looked over at Emerson and Sydney. She saw her own fierce expression reflected back at her.

"We're going to end this," Sydney whispered grimly.

"We're going to make this person pay," Emerson added.

Tenley nodded. She wanted to agree, to *insist*, but, for the second time that morning, her words were trapped inside her, just out of reach.

A burst of static drew Tenley's attention back to the stage. The screen showing the slide show had gone black. "What's going on?" a voice called out. There was another burst of static as a video flickered onto the screen. In it, a girl stood inside Winslow's empty locker room. Tenley sucked in a breath. The girl in the video wasn't Delancey. It was Tenley.

"What is this?" someone screeched from several rows up. Tenley recognized the high-pitched voice immediately. Only Abby Wilkins could sound that whiny and indignant at the same time. "What happened to my slide show?"

On the screen, Tenley walked over to a locker and looked around furtively before opening it. Tenley watched in horror as the video showed her pulling a water bottle out of the locker. Two large red initials were inked on its side. *JM.* Video-Tenley glanced hastily over her shoulder again. When she saw that no one was coming, she took a small pink pill out of her pocket and dropped it into the water bottle. Then she shoved the bottle back into the locker and slammed the door shut.

Scandalized gasps filled the auditorium. People were twisting around, gaping at Tenley. She ignored them, her eyes glued to the screen. The footage skipped ahead. The locker room door swung open, and the cheerleading squad jogged in. Jessie Morrow, the captain of the squad, was at the front of the group. "This routine is going to kick ass," she said with a grin over her shoulder. She stopped in front of her locker and pulled out her water bottle. Two red initials—*JM*—winked in the fluorescent light of the locker room. "I'm talking epic pep rally." She lifted the bottle to her lips, taking a long swig of water.

A time stamp flashed on the screen. It was the day Jessie had a seizure during the pep rally—just minutes before the rally started.

"Oh my god!" someone shrieked in the auditorium.

"Did she drug her?" someone else cried.

The world darkened around Tenley. Voices lifted, swirling around her in a tunnel. *Insane...Criminal...Evil...* And then Principal Howard, screaming, "Quiet, everyone! Order!"

In her own head, the words from their text: *I fight dirty.*

"Ten—" Emerson began.

Tenley didn't stick around to hear the rest. Faces spun around her as she raced out of the auditorium. She flew down the hallway, searching for a place to be alone. She could still hear the voices behind her, in an uproar. There was a bathroom, but that was too public. An unmarked door caught her eye at the end of the hallway. *The janitor's closet.* She squeezed inside it. Tears clogged her vision as she slid to the ground on top of a mop head.

Everyone knew.

Everyone knew.

How could she ever leave this closet?

Beep!

The sound reached down through her thoughts, shaking her into awareness.

Beep!

Her hand clamped around her phone. The number was blocked, just as she'd expected.

Like I said: I fight dirty.